THE COLONEL AND THE EUNUCH

(人生海海)

MAI JIA

(麥家)

English translation by

DYLAN LEVI KING

An Apollo Book

First published as 《人生海海》 *Rensheng hai hai* in China in 2019
by Thinkingdom Media Group Ltd

This translated edition first published in the UK in 2024 by Head of Zeus Ltd,
part of Bloomsbury Publishing Plc

This edition published by arrangement with Thinkingdom Media Group Ltd
and Georgina Capel Associates, Ltd

9 7 5 3 1 2 4 6 8

A catalogue record for this book is available from the British Library.

ISBN (HB): 9781804540268
ISBN (XTPB): 9781804540275
ISBN (E): 9781804540244

Cover Design: Matt Bray | Head of Zeus
Cover Illustration: Zhang Jiahan / Alamy Stock Photo

Typeset by Siliconchips Services Ltd UK

MIX
Paper | Supporting
responsible forestry
FSC
www.fsc.org   FSC® C013604

Printed and bound in Great Britain by
CPI Group (UK) Ltd, Croydon CR0 4YY

Head of Zeus Ltd
First Floor East
5–8 Hardwick Street
London EC1R 4RG

WWW.HEADOFZEUS.COM

PART ONE

One

I

Grandpa used to tell me that Head Mountain used to be a dragon. There's a saying that if you can see the head of a dragon, you can't see the tail. The mountain is just as mysterious. Head Mountain looks like the ocean. Some people called it Sea Dragon Mountain. Grandpa used to say that Tail Mountain was a tiger that escaped from Head Mountain. That's why some people called it Tiger Mountain. It looked like a tiger sleeping on its side: you could see the head, the neck, the back, the rear end, the tail, and the front left paw. Head Mountain seemed to stretch as wide as the sea. There was no central summit, but a field of peaks. It looked like a choppy ocean with its waves frozen in stone.

Tiger Mountain had spent generations fleeing from Sea Dragon Mountain. For generations, the tiger had dragged itself away, carving a stream as it went. Finally, fatigue got the better of the tiger, and it slumped over and rolled onto its side. The tiger's head rested on the ground. It looked like it was fast asleep. Only its rear end was held aloft. The tiger's tail drooped. Three of its feet were curled underneath itself. The village sat between the front paw and the tiger's tail.

If you went to the top of the mountain – the tiger's

ass – and looked down, the village seemed to be gathered up by the hands of the sky, or called together by some secret command. There seemed to be some precision to the way it was laid out. In actual fact, although the houses were grouped close together, they were more spread out than they appeared from above. It was the average Jiangnan mountain village: a densely populated hamlet, stuck between hill and river. Most of the houses were two stories, made from earth and timber, with whitewashed walls and tile roofs. The hills were green. They were covered in bamboo and brush. The water in the creek was clear. The water was so clear that the rocky bottom of the broad stream was visible. The water ran fast, coursing down from mountain lakes. The cobblestones on the village streets had been smoothed down by the rushing waters, then polished by the soles of feet and the wheels of wheelbarrows, bicycles, and tractors. The lanes twisted and turned through the village. The alleys that branched off the lanes always seemed as if they would dead-end somewhere, but they all eventually led to the ancestral hall.

The ancestral hall was the most majestic building in the village, and, like a cruel landlord, it occupied the best slice of land. A tree stood in the yard of the hall. It was a massive ginkgo tree, with a trunk so wide that nobody in the village could get their arms around it. The crown of the tree extended even higher than the roof of the hall. Generations of magpies had built nests and raised fledglings in the branches of the ginkgo. When warm spring breezes blew, tender green shoots burrowed out of the stippled bark of the tree. They were like a guerrilla army, scrambling towards the sky. It didn't take long for those shoots to grow out into fanlike leaves, giving the magpie shade for their nests, and protecting from the rain and sun anybody that sought shelter below the tree. When autumn changed into winter, the cool wind painted the tree in more sombre shades: the dark-green leaves were transformed to a pale copper. Finally, when the chill of winter arrived, the leaves fell. The dead leaves covered the front steps of the ancestral hall, spread like a carpet over the green slabstone, then out into the lanes, sticking to the soles of shoes.

The lanes wound their way through the village without any rhyme or reason. They were like an intestinal tract, going from large to small. The large lanes were wide enough to run a tractor down, and the narrowest alleys were not wide enough for two men to walk side by side.

The end of spring and the start of fall were both summer in the same way that five in the morning and seven in the evening during high summer were both basically daytime.

In the summer, the village itself seemed to be an illness, infecting each resident. The villagers hovered between life and death. Everyone was put to work: labouring in the fields, looking after animals, fixing leaky roofs, bailing out from floods, clearing out the gutters, draining the latrine pits, repairing the cattle pens, patching up the pigsties, building sheds for chicken and ducks and rabbits. The work was infectious, like a case of measles. The days were long but there was never enough time to get everything done. The heat was unbearable. The village was trapped in the mountains, so that no breeze was strong enough to dissipate the miasma. The draft that blew up the alley in the evening held the stench of village life: gurgling stinking sewers, full of dead mice, mud, dog shit, chicken shit, and kids' shit.

Every summer was like peeling the reed leaves off a rotten *zongzi*: sticky and foul-smelling. The lanes were full of vermin: flies, mosquitoes, crickets, fireflies, geckos, leeches, ants, dragonflies, locusts, centipedes, snakes, lizards, caterpillars. They seemed to be everywhere, constantly and suicidally marching into the homes of the villagers. The vermin spent the summer spreading annoyance and illness. They knew that winter was coming and their time on earth would come to an ignominious close.

When winter came, it felt as if the village was sealed

up. It felt deserted. After the first snow, the desolation was even more complete. The snow-filled alleys went silent. The chickens and dogs that usually sound-tracked village life went quiet. Snow muffled footsteps. Everyone's footsteps sounded the same: *cha.*

Cha.

Cha.

Cha.

It was a stiff, monotonous sound. It was less like a footfall than a cobblestone bouncing very slowly down the lane.

It was like a cold, dead cobblestone – or maybe a pair of cold, dead cobblestones – coming to life, burrowing up out of the snow like lithic zombies, and thudding down the lane.

Only one person's footsteps sounded different. They were no longer a *cha* but a *ka*. Each step was more solid. It was sharper, and shorter: *ka.*

Ka.

Ka.

Ka.

It was a harsh noise. It sounded like the snow was being crushed underfoot. It came most often in the early morning or late at night. It always came abruptly, echoing down the alley. The sound jumped to the rooftop, and floated up into the sky, seeming to reach all the way to the dark clouds or to the moon.

When he heard it, Grandpa would say: "You hear that? The Eunuch's back" or "The Eunuch's headed out."

Upon hearing the same sound, my father would sneer: "Hey, must be the Colonel coming back" or "The Colonel must be on his way somewhere."

II

The Colonel and the Eunuch were different names for the same person. Some people referred to him as the Eunuch, and some preferred to call him the Colonel. Grandpa and a few others called him the Colonel to his face, but used the other appellation when he wasn't around; most people, and that included my father, only ever called him the Colonel, whether to his face or behind his back. To refer to someone as a eunuch was rather nasty, after all. Out of the thousands of people in the village, the only people with the nerve to say it to his face were a few kids, and they usually only did it when they were in sufficient numbers. They would gang up on the Colonel and call out:

"Eu-nuch, pa-pa-pa! Eu-nuch, pa-pa-pa!"

They clapped along with the rhythm of their chant.

Most of the time, the Colonel would put his head down and ignore them. There were usually too many for him to handle. Occasionally, though, he would pretend to be about to give chase, and the kids would scurry off like rats. One time, Blindboy caught him when he was up on the roof of his house, cleaning out the chimney. Blindboy was alone, but he didn't expect the Colonel to come down after him. Blindboy had barely got the chant out when the Colonel dropped to all fours, scampered down the side of the roof like an ape, and swung down to give chase. The pursuit didn't last long, and when the Colonel caught Blindboy down the second alley, he held him down on the ground and put a handful of chimney dust down his throat.

Blindboy went to school with my older cousin. They shared a desk in class and they were virtually inseparable. Blindboy wasn't blind, but his nickname was inherited from his father, whom everyone called the Blind Man. His father was in fact blind – I mean, he was really blind: you'd know it as soon as you saw the milky pupils of his eyes. In the village, and at my school, too, everyone worth knowing had a nickname, so there was the Colonel, or the Eunuch, if you preferred, and the Tigress, and the Sorcerer, the Blind Man and Blindboy, the Living Bodhisattva, In Jesus' Name, the Old Perv, the

7

Fox-Spirit, the Bastard, Boot Licker, Clubfoot, Meathook, Poached Chicken, Chilli Pepper, Pork Belly, and so on... Tigress was my father's nickname, Grandpa was the Sorcerer, my older cousin was Giraffe, my best friend in school was nicknamed Stumpy Tiger, his grandpa was Clubfoot, and the Old Constable was also called the Old Perv. What they had in common was that they stood out from the crowd, for one reason or another. They had earned a reputation. If you earned a nickname, it meant you were the type of person that set tongues wagging.

Grandpa once told me: "A nickname is like a scar on your cheek. It doesn't look nice, but it was earned. Without a nickname, you're like a private in the army. No matter how outstanding you are, nobody's waiting for your orders. Your words don't carry any weight."

At our school, Blindboy's words carried plenty of weight. He grew up without a mother, and he only had his blind father to look after him. There wasn't much the old blind man could do to keep the boy in line, and he never put much effort into keeping him on the straight and narrow. Blindboy was a wild child, always getting mixed up in something... Our teachers were divided between those that hated his guts and those that were scared of him. There wasn't a drop of fear in Blindboy, though – or so I thought, until I saw the Colonel get a hold of him. Blindboy was so scared he pissed his pants. My cousin and I saw it all go down. The Colonel smeared soot all over Blindboy's face and crammed his mouth full of ashes. He looked like a body that had stumbled out of a grave. The sound he was making was even worse – squealing like a stuck pig. It was the kind of sound that makes your blood run cold. All the birds took off and flew for the hills. It was scary stuff.

Blindboy was only thirteen, after all, but it was clear at that moment that he was made of weaker stuff than his reputation suggested. There were still some things that he couldn't handle. Sure, he went around acting tough, but, when faced with a real challenge, he had turned out to be a coward. When I got home that night and told my father, his face lit up with a type of joy I rarely saw from him. He tore into Blindboy, saying he deserved what he got. My father looked like a kid my age, celebrating Blindboy's comeuppance as if they had been schoolyard rivals.

Grandpa scolded him: "It's immoral talking about a child like that. If you want to call yourself an adult, try setting an example."

"What do you mean, a child?" my father retorted. "He's a wild animal. I mean, sure, you can call him human, but he might as well have been raised by wolves." My father turned to me and said, "Watch out for that little monster."

I was only ten and I hadn't learned when to keep my mouth shut. "I never play with him. Cousin and him hang out together. All the time."

My father glared, then started cursing out my cousin: "That cousin of yours, I hope he's ready for what he's going to get himself into, hanging out with that little monster."

Grandpa grunted and turned away from my father, but he kept lecturing him. "You ought to take your own advice," he said. "You should watch who you're spending all your time with, too." I knew he meant the Colonel – or the Eunuch, whatever you want to call him. "I've said it before and I'll say it again: I've had enough, enough for a whole lifetime. Don't add to my troubles. I'm an old man. I ought to be able to spend my final years in peace."

I'd heard Grandpa say the same thing many times. He always turned his back on my father when he said it. I couldn't tell if it was because he was embarrassed to say it, or if he was simply too disgusted to look at his own son. My father had no shame, though. The lecture always went in one ear and out the other. The advice never stuck. It seemed nothing would come between my father and the Colonel. Every chance he got, my father was over at the Colonel's house. When Grandpa caught them hanging around the village, he would look up at the sky, as if addressing the Heavens, and say: "Goddammit, Tigress, you'll be the death of me."

I knew it had to be serious if Grandpa called him by that nickname. It was just as nasty as the Colonel's other moniker, and it carried the same connotation – what is a tigress but a tiger without balls? If someone from outside our family had called my father that in anger, he would have swung at him. The Old Constable used to say, a woman's breasts and a man's balls are the same: depending on who you are, you can give them a tickle or a pinch, but see what happens if the wrong person tries to take liberties! The Old Constable said my father had two sets of balls: one hanging between his legs and the other in his heart. I knew he'd got the nickname because of an occasional lapse in the fortitude of the second set. It was just a nickname, and there was nothing wrong with tossing it out if you were just joking around, but you had to know the right time and place – if you weren't careful, he might just live up to the epithet and bite your head off.

III

My father was a cipher. He never spoke at the production brigade meetings. He would just sit there, dragging on a cigarette. He didn't speak much at home, either. He farted more than he talked. But that didn't mean he was completely dormant. He had a short fuse. Maybe a landmine would be a better comparison. You could be just walking along and then – *kaboom*! Why did they call him Tigress? That was one of the reasons. A tigress looks after her cubs, right? They pounce at the first sign of trouble. Who would want to be friends with somebody like that? Nobody! Of course. My father's only friend in the village was the Colonel.

Grandpa said: "Nothing could've torn them apart."

My father and the Colonel had been born in the same month of the same year. They spent their childhoods together, catching cicadas, raiding nests for eggs, hunting for snails, raising crickets, running their little scams, and generally getting up to no good. When they were thirteen, both of them went to apprentice under the same master carpenter. In just a few years, Master Wang in Dongyang taught them everything they needed to know to open their own shop. They slept and ate together in the shop. They might as well have been actual brothers.

Grandpa said: "They split everything down the middle. When one took out a cigarette, he'd break it in half so they could both share it."

Given that fraternal closeness, my father did everything he could to protect the Colonel's reputation. He wouldn't stand for anybody calling him the Eunuch. There wasn't much he could do about the rest of the village, but the nickname was forbidden at home. The only one that could get away with it was Grandpa. If I said it, I knew I would get a slap upside the head. That's what happened the one time my cousin did it within earshot of my father. He said his ears were ringing like they were full of mosquitoes. If my father had hit him just a bit harder, he probably would've gone deaf. Grandpa knew how close my father was to the Colonel, but he hated when the Colonel came over. Can you guess why?

Obviously, it was because he was a eunuch. His family line would die with him. The way the old folks in the village thought, if someone wasn't able to produce heirs, then they must have done something horrible in a past life. To Grandpa, the Colonel was bad luck. Of course, Grandpa didn't just order him out. He would come up with some other reason to get rid of him. He might start scolding the dog, or he might break a dish, or he might start yelling at me... Whenever the Colonel came over, nobody got any rest. Grandpa and my father had argued over it many times.

My father said: "Why do you think he's bad luck? He's doing just fine for himself, I'll have you know."

"Who cares?" Grandpa said. "He's still got nothing between his legs."

"You don't know a damn thing," my father said.

"'Filial piety is the most important of all virtues,'" Grandpa recited. "And you go running around with a goddamn eunuch! You're just looking for trouble, aren't you?"

"So what?" my father said. "It's not like it's contagious."

"How do you know?"

"I already have three sons. How could it be contagious?"

"So what?" Grandpa said. "He never expected his future, either. He was the luckiest guy in the whole village. Nobody thought he would turn out like this. You have to be prepared for anything. When the rain comes, you don't want to be up on the roof patching the holes."

When Grandpa and my father argued, I was always on Grandpa's side. And Grandpa always won. Grandpa had studied at a traditional Confucian academy, and he had even taught classes at the ancestral hall. He was full of old maxims. He threw everything together into his arguments, including the Colonel's last life.

Grandpa told me that the Colonel was highly intelligent. His eyes were like gleaming marbles. He was a quick study. He picked things up far faster than the average person. When my father and the Colonel were apprentice carpenters, the Colonel quickly surpassed him. After a year, my father was still comfortably only an assistant to the master. My father could saw boards and plane down sheets of lumber, but the Colonel could already wield all the tools of the trade and build a credible cabinet by himself. By the second year, the Colonel had already learned to make staved barrels and washbasins. His work was nearly perfect. The vessels were watertight. He was close to surpassing the master. In the third year of their apprenticeship, Chiang Kai-shek sent troops to the capital of our county. Eventually, soldiers were sent into the mountains, too. They were trying to stop the Communists from retreating to Jiangxi. Master Wang decided to head home. Grandpa figured that my father's career as a carpenter was over. He called in a favour and sent my father to the county town to work. The Colonel decided to open up his own woodworking shop, though. He served as both master and apprentice. Business was good. When my father found out, he came back immediately to help out.

Grandpa said: "That's just the way your father is. He couldn't bear to part with his friend, and he couldn't handle it when his friend parted with him. The Eunuch went to join the army and your father couldn't run the shop himself. Even after all those years as an apprentice, he wasn't ready to go out on his own. He tried his best, but his washbasins always sprang a leak."

IV

The Colonel joined the army in the twenty-fourth year of the Republic of China – that is, 1935 – when he was seventeen years old. One fall day, he and my father went to the market. They sold washbasins, rice barrels, buckets, furniture, and stools. They bought lumber, nails, kerosene, tung oil, angle iron, and sandpaper. It just so happened that some Kuomintang military recruiters were in the market that day. A bearded battalion commander took a shine to the Colonel. He called for some of his men to carry the Colonel's things back to the shop for him. The commander knew exactly what he wanted when he saw it. He was looking for men like him – young, intelligent, tall, and strong. He wasn't interested in my father. Even though my father was more than willing to sign up, the commander turned him down. My father would grow into a sturdy man eventually, but he was a late bloomer. He was like a lump of dough set down on the board; the dough had not yet risen.

The Colonel and my father separated for the first time.

Grandpa said: "Your father was like a sick pig after that day. He spent a week in bed. He stayed there, doing nothing, until a parcel came from the Eunuch. There was a shirt, a pair of socks, and a letter inside. After reading the letter, your father jumped out of bed as if the Eunuch's words had immediately cured whatever was ailing him."

The Colonel's letter said that he had spent the previous week training in the mountains, and he was about to go to the front line in Jiangxi. He told my father to look after the woodworking shop and the stall at the market. The Colonel promised my father that when he returned from the war that they would go into business together. Unfortunately, the shop closed before the new year. While my father was failing in business, the Colonel was thriving in the military, and he quickly rose to the rank of battalion commander.

Four years after leaving with the army, the Colonel returned home. The villagers all went out to look at him in his uniform as if he were a foreign general. He looked quite dignified with his Soviet pistol on his hip, a silver Seiko watch on his wrist, and a gold-rimmed pith helmet. He stood ramrod straight, and his chest was always puffed up. He had come back for his father's funeral. The Colonel's father had been in the prime of his life, in his late forties, and strong as an ox. One afternoon, he found an artillery shell in his garden. It was about half as big around as a man's waist. He wrenched it from the mud and slung it over his shoulder. He tossed it in the pigpen and planned to sell it to the blacksmith. It was high summer and the blacksmith wouldn't return until the winter, so the shell sat idle for months.

Where I come from, the carpenters were all from Dongyang and the blacksmiths were from Yongkang. They spent most of the year tilling their own crops, and they picked up their other work in the winter. Most villages had a carpenter and a blacksmith that came and went with the seasons like migratory birds. The carpenter was Master Wang. The blacksmith's name was Master Zhang. He had a long scar across his face. It went diagonally from one corner of his forehead to the base of his ear. Everyone in the village called him Scar behind his back. Every winter when he returned to the village, he first went door to door buying up all the scrap metal that the villagers had collected during the months he had been gone, then he got to work turning it into kitchen knives. His knives were thick and sharp. They could cut through just about anything. They looked like the type of blade a military man would carry.

The shell that the Colonel's father had pulled out of the mud rested in a heap of straw in the pigsty. It looked like a miniature corpse. It came up to waist height, and it weighed about seventy or eighty jin. The Colonel's father knew that he could trade it to the blacksmith for a year's worth of implements and knives. The shell didn't make it to winter. It blew up that autumn, killing the Colonel's father, as well as two pigs, a sheep, and a few chickens. A constable came from the county capital with someone that knew about artillery shells. They concluded that the shell had some biological agent on it. The meat from the dead animals could not be salvaged before it melted away. The Colonel's father wasn't killed instantly, but his flesh seemed to melt as well. Before he died, he rotted from the inside. By the time the Colonel got there, his father's body looked like it had been hacked apart.

As the head of a company, the Colonel buried his father and got ready to leave. There were hundreds of troops awaiting his commands. There was no time for him to linger, but the matchmakers quickly got their claws on him. He was twenty-one that year and still single. Every woman in the village wanted him. My aunt was three years younger than him, and she wanted to marry him, too, so she stayed up every night to work on knitting a pair of socks for him. He met a few women, but none took his fancy.

Grandpa said it was the right decision. A son should be in mourning for seven days. That wasn't the right time to find a wife. It was probably also the case that none of the women were a match for him. There was no offence given and none was taken.

The Eunuch was not called the Eunuch at the time. Nobody called him the Colonel, either. And the Old Constable was still a fairly young man.

The night before the Eunuch was supposed to head back to the front line, the Old Constable put on a feast for him. In fact, the Old Constable was working for the Japanese. He was supposed to be delivering the Eunuch to the enemy. But the Old Constable never went through with the plan. The Old Constable might have sold out, but whoever had paid for his loyalty was not getting their money's worth, since he was helping both the KMT and the Communists. When the whole thing ended, the Old Constable was never tarred with the title of traitor, but was given medals for his distinguished service in the War of Resistance against Japan. The Old Constable had heard of the Eunuch's brave deeds on the battlefield, and he admired him. He knew that he had to be discreet, to avoid arousing anyone's attention, but he wanted to put on the feast to honour him.

The feast was organised at the home of one of the men that worked for the Old Constable. The Old Constable had a mistress that he wanted to be at the feast, so there was no way he could hold it at his own house. The Eunuch was placed at his own table, with a few good old boys and the Old Constable's mistress to accompany him while he drank. After everyone had eaten, a game of mah-jong was set up.

That was the way these feasts always went. But the Eunuch was in no mood to play. He had to return to the front line the next day. He said his goodbyes and went out. Everyone expected him to go home, where his mother was waiting anxiously. But after a while, the Eunuch's mother showed up at the home of the Old Constable's man, looking for her son. The Old Constable looked up from his mah-jong game and told her that he'd left a while ago. It wasn't long before the Old Constable put two and two together: his mistress had clearly taken an interest in the Eunuch, and she had disappeared at around the same time.

V

The Old Constable had many mistresses in his lifetime. The one he had then was an actress. Her name was Chun – or something like that. But nobody really knew, since she was just called the Fox-Spirit.[1] Everyone knew her story, roughly: two years before the Eunuch's father got blown up, when the Old Constable had only recently assumed his post, she had come to the village with a troupe of actors. She had a very minor role in the troupe's show, and she was mostly engaged with serving tea and sweeping up during the performance. When the Old Constable stopped by during the afternoon intermission, the Fox-Spirit was there to serve him tea. He got a good look at her. When the Old Constable gave her hand a squeeze, she smiled. The Old Constable decided to make a move, and when she bent down to get his cup, he ran his hand up the back of her leg and patted her ass. The Fox-Spirit giggled and told him to save it that night. And that's exactly what he did. They met and she stripped naked

---

[1] This is a literal translation of a poetic colloquial term for a malicious and sexually promiscuous woman.

for the Old Constable. That was just the beginning. When the Fox-Spirit ran off from the troupe, she found refuge with the Old Constable. He set her up with a little shop, and she became almost like a concubine. Their relationship lasted for many years, until the Old Constable finally lost everything playing cards in Shanghai.

Grandpa said: "That's the nature of an actress. They're frivolous. They can't control themselves."

That night, after the Eunuch disappeared, the Old Constable went to the Fox-Spirit's shop. Just as he suspected, the Eunuch and the Fox-Spirit were in bed together. The Eunuch had discarded the Soviet pistol for another weapon. The Old Constable busted into the room and yelled at the Eunuch that he was going to kill him for sleeping with his girl. He pointed his Mauser at the pair. The Eunuch was battle-hardened and fast – he had his Tokarev cocked and pointed at the Old Constable. The two jet-black barrels of the pistols stared each other down. Even the moonlight seemed to tremble with fright.

It was the reflected moonlight quivering on the barrel of the Mauser that broke the Eunuch's resolve. He begged for forgiveness. He said he was just too drunk. The Old Constable wasn't ready to back down, though. He started cursing out the Eunuch, still pointing the pistol at his chest.

The scene looked almost like the typical banquet scene of a man standing to make a toast, trying to force a reluctant comrade to drink. The Eunuch was ready to give in, though. "I'm going to count to three," the Eunuch said, "then I want you to put that gun down. I'm leaving in the morning. If you want to put up a fight for her, I'll shoot you dead. I'll be taking her with me tomorrow, either way."

"You son of a bitch," the Old Constable swore.

The Eunuch smiled, showing his big white teeth. He looked the Old Constable over and chuckled. "I don't like your attitude," he said. "How many times have you fired that gun of yours? I'll tell you, I've killed more men than you've fired rounds through that barrel. I'm the best shot in my company. I'd hit you at a hundred paces, dead between the eyes. I'm happy to show you." The Eunuch started counting: "One, two…"

Before the Eunuch counted to three, the Old Constable had dropped his Mauser. The next day, the Eunuch returned to the front line. The Fox-Spirit opened her shop as usual. It was as if nothing had happened. Grandpa said: "His father's body wasn't even cold, and he was jumping into bed with another man's woman. He was just looking for trouble. That's what all the old folks in the village said." At the time, Grandpa wasn't even old enough to be included as one of the "old folks". "But I'm old now," he said, "and I see it the same way. The Heavens couldn't forgive behaviour like that."

The old folks always assumed that the Heavens were on their side, and they were usually right. That winter, word began to spread through the village that the Eunuch was in fact a eunuch. There were two explanations for how he was gelded. The first was given by the Old Constable and it was that the Eunuch, sex-crazed, had slept with his commanding officer's woman. The Commander gave him a choice: you can either take that Tokarev and blow your brains out, or take a knife and cut your balls off. The Eunuch took the second option. The other explanation was completely different. The Eunuch was fighting hand to hand with a Japanese soldier, who swung a katana and ended up chopping off his dick. Legend had it that even with the Japanese soldier in his grasp, he was still reluctant to take his life. One story had the Eunuch as a hero, and the other had him as a coward.

There was some debate about how it had happened, but it was clear that the Eunuch's manhood had been horribly injured.

Grandpa said: "It was retribution. His father had just been buried. There was a distinct lack of filial piety. He was thinking with his crotch instead of his heart. It was unprincipled. God could never forgive him."

Grandpa said: "Upright behaviour is not only morally sound but also timely. He chose the wrong woman and he chose the wrong time. He was punished for that by never being able to be with a woman again. That's retribution."

Grandpa said: "The world is large, but God sees everything. It's like being held in the palm of the Buddha: you can run, if you want, but there's no escaping. Kind deeds pay rich dividends, and wicked deeds are punished." That rule went for everyone. On long nights in the summer, sitting out in the lane or in the courtyard, with fireflies buzzing around, Grandpa would tell me and my cousins about those sorts of things while dragging on a cigarette and fanning himself. To us, Grandpa was the same as the gods he was so fond of telling us about. He seemed familiar with all of the immortals of the mountains, each ghoul that had ever crawled up from the depths of hell, and all the goings-on in our village and beyond. He never ran out of stories to tell, and as he told them, we watched the moon soar overhead. The village got quiet, and the crickets crawled out of the rocks to accompany Grandpa with their song. It was quiet enough to hear the water buffalo snuffling in their pen, the geckos creeping up the wall, the mice chittering in the pantry, and the owls hooting in the bamboo forest at the base of Tail Mountain – Grandpa said that all of them had been human in their last lives, but they had been born as animals and insects to repent for their sins.

Two

VI

In the winter, Grandpa liked sitting out front of the ancestral hall to soak up the sun, while chatting to whoever came by. It was the old folks' favourite spot, including the Old Constable's. Grandpa and the Old Constable both loved to sit around and chew the fat, but they always ended up arguing. The Old Constable was dirty. His stories invariably involved immoral behaviour, sex, and crime. The ancestral hall faced south, looking out on a gravel highway. On market day, the road was full of cars and people, making noise and dust. Looking out from the front of the hall, it was like watching the entire world parade by. The Old Constable loved sizing up the women that went by. He would point out a woman, describe her so that everyone knew who he meant, then explain what he'd do with her, if he ever got her in the sack. The Old Constable was a dreamer. In his dreams, he could have any woman he wanted. He described his favourites as "braised pork belly". If he got his pork belly, he'd be so happy that he'd be willing to die right then and there.

Sticky mahogany braised pork belly, dripping with grease, with an aroma so enchanting it seems to cast a spell on everyone... Everyone needs food to survive, and braised pork is what they dream of eating. But the Old Constable wasn't talking about actual braised pork! He was speaking figuratively. He was talking about his ideal type: fair and plump. He liked girls that were as pale as a peeled water chestnut, and as voluptuous as a perfectly ripe peach. When he saw a woman like that go by, the Old Constable would stare. His mouth would water.

"What the hell are you looking at?" Grandpa would say, waving his hand in front of the Old Constable's face. "You're stuffing your eyes and starving your dick. Just give it up!"

The Old Constable knocked Grandpa's hand away and went back to watching. "Your dick might be starving," the Old Constable said, "but mine ain't. My dick gets nothing but the best – braised pork belly. Your dick is sniffing around for a bone to gnaw on. Hoo boy, would you look at that one? That's a thick slice of pork belly right there. You get a girl like that in bed... There's nothing like it."

"You goddamn pervert," Grandpa said. "You must've been a tortoise in your last life."

"You must have been an old crow in your last life – and you'll be one in your next life, too," the Old Constable said. "Sorcerer," he swore, invoking Grandpa's nickname.

A sorcerer was about the same thing as a witch, but a woman was much more likely to be called a witch than a man a sorcerer. Grandpa had got the nickname because he loved that way of talking – telling people what they had been in a past life, or telling them how divine retribution was coming. Grandpa loved his superstitious maxims, and he loved pulling out quotes from old books, or reciting ancient fables. He loved his unfathomable revelations as much as the Old Constable loved talking about the girls going by.

One day, I saw Grandpa talking to a tabby cat. He said: "Our human world is like a deep pond, full of fish... There are big fish and small fish, catfish, turtles, crabs, and shrimp.

Some of them swim in freshwater and some of them burrow in the mud. They come in all colours."

I chased the cat off and asked Grandpa, "What are you talking about?"

Grandpa stroked his beard and said: "A village is like a pond. It's big and it's full of fish. A village is big, too, and it's full of all sorts of people. It's all the same."

"What kind of person is the Colonel?" I asked.

"You mean the Eunuch?"

"What kind of person is the Eunuch?"

"He's a freak," Grandpa said. "He's like the forest behind Head Mountain – creepy, dark…"

VII

Our village was called Shuangjiacun – Twin Village. Most people had the surname Jiang, and the rest had the surname Lu. Around five thousand people lived there. It was the largest village in the county, which meant that it had its fair share of freaks. The Old Constable was one of those freaks, and you had to include In Jesus' Name on the list, as well as Phoenix Blossom. The Old Constable claimed a supernatural ability: he said he could "spot a slut a mile away". If a willing woman was nearby, he could sniff her out. From what I saw, he was telling the truth. Even though he wasn't a man of means, he always had company between the sheets, even when he was in his seventies. In Jesus' Name was considered a freak because he worshipped a naked foreigner. He had a statue of the nude idol at home, affixed to the wall, and he'd bow down in front of him and wail about how his life wasn't fair. Phoenix Blossom was considered a freak, too. She had slept with a hundred men, but they might as well have been screwing her with a piece of wood, since she was seemingly incapable of getting pregnant.

The Eunuch was universally acknowledged as the biggest freak of them all. All of the other village freaks together could not compete with him for that title.

First, he had fought for the KMT. That meant that he was a counterrevolutionary. After Liberation, there were some villagers that followed the official line and struggled against him, but there were others that wanted to curry his favour. They would go to the Eunuch for advice, even. Grandpa's views on the Eunuch were well known, but he would still seek him out sometimes, too. Grandpa was nicknamed the Sorcerer, but the Eunuch was treated as if he actually could tell the future.

Second, even though he had slept with the Old Constable's mistress, the two men seemed to get on quite well. After the People's Liberation Army had rounded the Eunuch up on the front lines and sent him back, rumours started to spread. There were some who said that the Eunuch had contracted leprosy. Even my father kept his distance for a while. The Old Constable was the only one that reached out to him. He called the Eunuch "nephew" and helped him rebuild his reputation in the village.

Third, even though everyone claimed to know that he was a eunuch, he didn't look like one. Like all the kids in the village, I had stolen a peek up his shorts in the summer, and it looked like there was something there. I had even seen him taking a piss – he did it like any other man, feet planted, hand at his crotch. I had always been given to understand that actual eunuchs had to squat down to piss.

Fourth, even though he didn't pick up carpentry again after the war, didn't work on his land, and appeared to have no job or source of funds, he seemed to live a life of leisure. He was usually found at home, reading the newspaper or cracking sunflower seeds. He smoked Daqian Men–brand cigarettes and went everywhere in a three-piece gabardine Zhongshan suit and a pair of leather shoes. There was always the smell of grilled fish and roasted meat in his kitchen.

Fifth, the way he treated his cats was better than the way most people treated their kids. He cared for them deeply, and spared no expense in looking after them. That was one of the surest signs of mental instability.

VIII

Everyone knew that the Eunuch kept a pair of cats, one black and one white. They looked like a pair of leopards, with long, lean bodies and bright eyes. They were the most elegant cats anyone had seen. I often saw him bathing the cats. He lathered them up with soap, then combed out their fur with a wood comb, and cut their nails with a pair of tiny gold scissors. I hated to see the way he doted on them. I never ate as good as those cats! I would rather have been a cat raised by the Eunuch – and all the other kids felt the same way.

My cousin told me that the Eunuch used to sleep with the cats in his bed. He admitted that he'd never seen it himself, but that's what he had heard. I had personally seen the Eunuch chatting to the cats, though. The cats seemed to understand him, too. I was only five the first time I saw it. My father had given me three fen and sent me out to buy a pack of cigarettes at Clubfoot's shop. Three fen would buy eight and a half cigarettes, so if Clubfoot handed me nine, I was supposed to bow to him. If he just gave me the usual eight, I didn't have to do anything – and I was even allowed to call him "Old Clubfoot". There was no way he could chase after me, since he could only walk on the tips of his toes.

Clubfoot's shop was across from the front gate of the ancestral hall, and the Eunuch's house was across from the back gate. Unlike most other people in the village, the Eunuch's house had a wall encircling it, with a small yard inside. Grandpa said that the yard used to be the pigsty, which had been contaminated by the Japanese shell when it exploded. The Eunuch usually kept his gate shut because he wanted to keep his cats safe from any wandering dogs, but it was open that day, when I passed by on my way to buy cigarettes. I could see that the Eunuch had a vegetable patch with spring onions and greens growing. His elderly mother was watering the garden with an old tin pail. The Eunuch, drowsily dragging on a cigarette and flipping through a newspaper, soaking up the sun on the steps up to the main house might as well have been her husband, rather than her son. His two cats rested at either side of him.

The white cat noticed me watching and yowled to his master. The Eunuch put down his newspaper to take a closer look at me. "You must be the Sorcerer's grandson," he said. It was the first time I had heard Grandpa's nickname.

"He must be," the Eunuch's mother said. "He looks just like his father."

The Eunuch chuckled. Imitating Grandpa's accent and tone perfectly, he said, "Come here, son. Be a good boy."

My eyes were fixed on the two cats, who were still watching me warily. "Get inside," the Eunuch said to the cats. They rose simultaneously, flashed their teeth, and went into the house. The sunshine was so bright that the entire world looked like an overexposed photograph, but the inside of the Eunuch's house was as black as a bottomless pit. It might have all been the product of an overactive five-year-old's imagination, but I was terrified. I felt like the cats were waiting inside to ambush me. I turned and ran away.

When I told Grandpa about it later, he gave me a big hug. "My boy," he said, "you made the right decision. I don't want you to ever set foot in that house. It's haunted – haunted by the Eunuch!"

"He talks to cats," I said. "They sleep in the same bed as him!"

"He's not human," Grandpa said. "He's a ghoul. He was a ghoul in his last life!"

For years after that, whenever I went to the shop or the ancestral hall, I avoided his house.

It was a longer walk, but I didn't want to walk by the Eunuch's creepy house. My cousin said that the cats were actually ghosts in feline form, too. It was the same story with the Eunuch's father, according to my cousin. That's what my cousin and I used to do to entertain each other. It was one of the reasons our friendship was so strong. We were united against the Eunuch.

One time while we were telling ghost stories about the Eunuch, my father overheard us. We were standing outside the outhouse, where my father happened to be taking a piss. He stormed out, jerking up his pants with one hand and reaching for us with the other hand. It was like we had insulted a member of his family – but we were actually members of his family! It was like the Eunuch was his actual father and we were no better than the maggots in the latrine pit.

When we were a safe distance away, my cousin asked me: "Why does he care so much about the Eunuch?"

"Because he's possessed by a ghost." The answer came quickly. I had heard Grandpa say the same thing.

Grandpa used to always say that my father was possessed. He said that good luck was yang energy and ghosts had yin energy. Yin and yang are mostly in balance, but most people had too much yin energy and not enough yang energy, which is one of the reasons there was so much suffering. My father used to be an obedient son, and everyone was envious of Grandpa. But after the Eunuch returned from the war, my father and Grandpa had drifted apart, and the house never seemed to be at peace. That bad luck was from the Eunuch and his yin energy.

IX

I don't know if bad luck can kill people, but pesticide definitely can. I think I was around five the first time I saw a person die from drinking pesticide. I was probably seven when I saw my next one. One was an old woman and one was a girl. Suicide wasn't uncommon in the village. Some people hanged themselves, some jumped into wells, some drowned themselves in reservoirs, or they took a knife to their wrist or their neck – pesticide was the most common, though. It was the most convenient method, too. All you had to do to end your life was pop open the cap and drink. That was it. Once you swallowed, you were dead – most of the time!

One night, while Grandpa and I were fast asleep, we were awoken by the sound of In Jesus' Name. He was one of the few that survived the experience of chugging pesticide.

Living beside a freak was just our bad luck, I guess. In Jesus' Name was more than a neighbour, too: he was second cousins with Grandpa. That didn't exactly make him family, since it was a fairly distant relation, but I still called him Second Grandpa.

Second Grandpa pulled a rickshaw in Shanghai for three years when he was younger. There was a foreigner that he took around sometimes that always told him to keep the change. Second Grandpa thought the foreigner was as virtuous as a Bodhisattva, and he treated him with immense respect. When he realised the foreigner was a Christian, Second Grandpa became a Christian, too. He went around saying "Amen this" and "in Jesus' name that", which is how he got his nickname.

The afternoon before he drank pesticide, he went into town and spent a bit of money, which had upset his daughter-in-law. His daughter-in-law was from north of the Yangtze, and her temper had earned her the nickname Chilli Pepper. Her tantrums were legendary. When she found out that her father-in-law had spent two yuan, she tore his Jesus statue off the wall and threw it into the cooking fire. Jesus was his entire life, so, without Him, there was no point in living. All he wanted to do was die.

The pesticide burned in his belly and if not for the Colonel – because it wasn't right to call him the Eunuch in this situation – saving his life, it would have done its work. The Colonel knew he had to extinguish the fire in Second Grandpa's belly. I was there to see all of this myself: the Colonel took a piece of soap, crammed it into Second Grandpa's mouth, and made him swallow. The Colonel jerked down Second Grandpa's pants, put his face on the floor, crammed the nozzle of a handheld crop sprayer into his ass. The tank of the sprayer was full of water, and the Colonel started pumping the handle, violently irrigating Second Grandpa's guts. The sprayer had enough water pressure to send liquid up to the tops of trees, so it must have been excruciating for Second Grandpa to have it shot directly up his ass. Second Grandpa cried out in pain between rounds of vomiting. The liquid coming from his mouth smelled even worse than what was coming out of his ass. The Colonel could barely stand the stench, but he kept working.

The Colonel opened his eyes wide and said to Second Grandpa: "You're going to live. Now, go get me a bowl of noodles." That was the Colonel's rule: if he saved someone's life, their family had to make him a bowl of noodles with shredded pork. The fact that such a rule existed testified to the Colonel's history of saving the lives of people in the village. Even though it was the first time I had seen him do something like that, it clearly happened quite often. I was eleven that year, and I could already get around faster than Grandpa. That was why he had sent me to get the Colonel. If not, I would have missed the whole scene.

It wasn't long before Second Grandpa stopped throwing up and could speak again. But instead of thanking the

Colonel, he started cursing him. "Sinner!" he roared. His curses came between his sobs. "I wanted to die!" he said. "Why didn't you just let me do it? My sins are so heavy I can barely stand."

"Who do you think sent me to save you?" the Colonel asked. "Jesus sent me to save you."

"She burned my statue," Second Grandpa moaned. "I can't go on."

"Just buy another one," the Colonel said. He didn't realise that Second Grandpa didn't have any money to buy another statue. The entire incident had been caused by Second Grandpa spending two yuan in town.

When the Colonel found out what had happened, he gave Second Grandpa a ten yuan note. He passed it to him as casually as most people would pass out a cigarette. "Here," he said. "This should be enough, right? Keep going. Look at me, right? Everyone calls me a eunuch but you don't see me drinking pesticide, do you?" Second Grandpa couldn't believe what he was seeing. His hands were shaking too much to take the bill. The Colonel pressed the bill into Second Grandpa's hands. "Take it," he said. "Don't tell my mother I gave it to you. She's a Buddhist, so all the Christian stuff doesn't sit right with her. If she knew you were using this money to buy a Jesus statue, she'd be pissed off."

After he said it, the Colonel laughed. His laugh floated up into the night sky. It was the first time I had realised how bright his eyes were. They were brighter than the moonlight. There was nothing wicked in that glint, either. He looked more like a hero than a ghoul. From that moment on, my impression of the Colonel changed. He saved Second Grandpa's life, but he also saved my image of him. I followed him out of Second Grandpa's house and watched him as he walked up the lane. He didn't walk like a eunuch, but like a courageous general. His back was straight, his shoulders were square, and his chin was in the air. Even if his manhood had been physically diminished, the Colonel was spiritually intact. I finally realised why he stood up to piss.

X

Before that night, I had always taken Grandpa's words with deadly seriousness. Whatever he said about the Colonel was what I came to believe, too. I was like a slave to Grandpa, in a way. I treated his words like a hungry dog treats a chunk of meat – I chewed up the meat, gnawed the bones clean, then crunched them up and swallowed them. So, to me, the Colonel was always frightening and disgusting and unclean. I was afraid of him and I avoided him. I spread stories about him. I looked down on him. He was like a haunted house, in fact: you might be scared to go inside, but you can't help but be curious. Grandpa had successfully dissuaded me from cracking open the door on that haunted house. But when the Colonel turned from ghoul to hero in my mind, I didn't want to be Grandpa's good boy anymore. I decided it might be worth finding out what the Colonel's real story was.

The autumn after In Jesus' Name drank pesticide, I watched the leaves of the persimmon tree turn yellow and then fall to the ground. The persimmons that had once been round and dark green turned pink, then red, then a blazing crimson, and they fell to the ground plump and heavy. The bare trees full of ripe persimmons appeared to be hung with lanterns. At a distance, the trees looked like they were on fire. The harvest began and the persimmons were picked, along with the chestnuts and kiwis. In the fields, people went to work digging up yams and sweet potatoes, and picking peanuts. In the ponds, lotus roots and clams were being dug up. It was the best time of year. There was food to eat, and the weather was beautiful. The limpid skies and cool temperatures called for us to come outside.

Second Grandpa finally received a replacement statue of Christ, brought to him by somebody that had taken a trip to Hangzhou. It was brand new and the paint on it was still glossy. It was just a bit bigger than the statue that Chilli Pepper had burned in the cooking fire. Second Grandpa carefully hung the Jesus on the wall and sat under it all night, praying and weeping. He was still there at dawn. He arrived at our house that day to tell Grandpa the good news. All he wanted to talk about was the Colonel.

Grandpa let him talk for a while, but eventually it got to be too much. "You're ridiculous," Grandpa said. "The way you're talking about him, you might as well take down the Jesus and put up a statue of him."

"He's a good man," Second Grandpa said patiently. "He does his good in Jesus' name. I know the way you talk about him and it has to change. When you insult him, you're only making yourself look bad."

"What's so good about him? Ask your Jesus for me. If your life is like this, isn't it better to die?"

"Don't tell me about death," Second Grandpa said. "I came back from the dead. What you're saying is a sin." Second Grandpa looked up at the sky. "Everything we do is under the watchful eye of the Lord. What you say about that man is going to come back at you."

"You think I'm scared of your Jesus?" Grandpa said. He rolled his eyes back in his head, mimicking In Jesus' Name after he drank the pesticide. "He couldn't save you, then. You think I'm scared of him?" Grandpa jerked his head back and scowled down at In Jesus' Name. "I've been around longer than you, I know more about the world than you ever will, and I'm not going to be lectured by you about anything." There was no chance that Grandpa was going to listen to the admonitions of In Jesus' Name.

Grandpa was like an old banyan tree, with deep roots, and broad, luxuriant foliage that could blot out the sun. He was unmovable. Even a lightning strike wouldn't have taken down a tree like that. Second Grandpa's vague warnings of a thunderstorm. But I was nothing like that. I was like a peach tree in March, capable of turning into a painting or a poem overnight. I decided I had to stand up to Grandpa.

I pulled Grandpa's hand and said, "You're wrong. The Colonel is a good man. You can't treat him like that anymore."

Grandpa stood up, shook off my grip, and ripped a loud fart. "That's what I think of him." He laughed loudly.

It was a strange moment. It seemed like he was turning me down, but he was still laughing.

Did that mean he was going to change how he treated the Colonel? He never said it, but I could tell things had changed slightly.

Grandpa still didn't like the Colonel coming over to his house, but he stopped intentionally causing trouble. That was his way of changing. He eventually took an even bigger step: he let me go with my father to the Colonel's house!

Three

XI

Although the Colonel's kitchen was over a wall and deep inside the house, anyone with a good nose would know that he ate well. There was always a rich aroma wafting into the lane, like flakes of gold on the breeze. One time, when the Old Constable went by, I heard him say, "He's making braised pork hock again! Fuck me. Smells better than sticking your nose between a pair of tits."

One night I was woken up by the smell of something delicious and discovered the bone from a pork hock beside the bed. My father had brought it back from the Colonel's place. There were still two hunks of meat on them. I ate one hunk and knew I couldn't leave the second hunk to go uneaten overnight. I had dreams that night about the pork hock. I was only nine at the time, but I'll never forget it.

The Old Constable told me that the Colonel cooked pork hocks once a month. They were reserved for two people. I knew the Colonel loved his braised pork, but I first assumed it was his mother eating with him. But she was a Buddhist, and she never ate meat. My father was the other person eating the pork hock. My father would come home on those nights smelling of the aroma of the Colonel's kitchen and sometimes a bit of liquor. They were drinking *shaojiu*. My father had offered to bring me along, too, but it was forbidden.

Grandpa said: "It won't kill the boy not to eat some pork hock. If you want to hang out with that ghoul, go ahead, but don't drag him down to hell with you." Grandpa kept telling me the house was haunted. Even though I wanted to eat with them, I listened to Grandpa. After the night that the Colonel saved Second Grandpa's life, the temptation returned to tag along.

One night, I took the opportunity and went over to the Colonel's house with my father. I expected Grandpa to scold me when he found out, but he said he felt bad that I didn't get to eat any pork hock. It was an unexpected turn of events. It was starting to sound like Grandpa was on my father's side.

Grandpa said: "A hundred blades of grass is not as good as one tree. Hearing something described a hundred times is not as good as a single glimpse."

I went back many times, but the Colonel didn't cook pork hock very often. Most of the time, he steamed pork with dried vegetables. And as for all the talk about the house being haunted and the Colonel being a ghoul – none of that was true.

Grandpa had never been there before, so he had no idea. You can't imagine how clean it was, too. The cement floor at his place was cleaner than the dining table at our house. In the summer, I could slide across it in my bare feet. When the cats came back in from outside, the Colonel's mother would be right there to wipe up after them. If you wanted to spit, you had to use a spittoon. If you wanted to smoke, you had to use an ashtray. Ants and mosquitoes weren't scared of ghosts, but they stayed out of there because it was too clean – they could starve to death looking for something to eat on those clean floors. The only visitors were those that didn't fear ghosts, like my father and I, and the Bodhisattva Guanyin.

Grandpa told me that the Colonel's birth had helped to mark him as a freak. It had been his mother's first pregnancy. The fetus was in a strange position, and there was a lot of blood. The Colonel's mother moaned and cried for two days, but he still didn't come out. Finally, it was a small piece of ginseng sent by a monk from Guande Temple that gave her the energy to make the final push. When the child had been safely born, she went to the temple to thank the monk. The monk told her that it was Guanyin that had looked after her son. From then on, she was a believer. She put a statue of the Bodhisattva Guanyin in her house and burned incense in front of it every day. She begged Guanyin to bring her another child. When that didn't work, she went back to the temple to ask the monk to intercede. The monk told her not to worry and that Guanyin would be watching over her, but she had to be content with what she had already received. She went back to burning incense in front of her statue. When her husband was blown up by the artillery shell, she went to the temple again. She wanted to know why Guanyin had watched over her husband's unfortunate death. The monk patiently explained that if not for Guanyin, she would not have had a son. Guanyin had been forced to trade in her husband's life as payment. The great fortune of her son's birth had been mortgaged on her husband's life. When rumours started to swirl – circulated first by the Old Constable, who was still angry at him – that the Colonel had received some injury to his manhood, she went to the temple again. The monk advised her that her son had escaped even greater catastrophe and that the rest of his life would be fortunate. She believed what the monk told her. She believed every word, right until the end of her life.

Grandpa said: "That old lady got her life saved by a monk. She dedicated herself to Bodhisattva Guanyin. She's an honest person. That's why they call her the Living Bodhisattva."

The Living Bodhisattva burned incense every day in

front of her Guanyin statue, went to Guande Temple on Tail Mountain, and then she walked over to Mount Putuo Temple. She prayed for Guanyin to look after her son. She wanted her son to share each other's fortunes.

Grandpa said: "Since he's a eunuch, he'd be the ideal Buddhist. He should be purified of the illusions of desire."

But the Colonel couldn't give up earthly pleasures. Until he stopped smoking, drinking, and eating meat, there was nothing Guanyin could do for him. She wasn't interested in the Colonel, no matter how much incense his mother burned for Guanyin. Whenever I went to visit, the old woman would always heap my bowl with meat, thinking that anything I ate would be one less scrap for the Colonel. He couldn't give up meat, but he tried not to drink at home, and he only smoked when he had to. That was no fun for me, since I preferred him when he was drinking. After a couple shots, the Colonel would start telling stories. I always looked forward to that. After going over there a few times, I looked forward to the stories more than the meal. The Colonel's stories were not guaranteed, though. They were sort of like the pork hock – just an occasional treat.

XII

If his mother was gone up to Mount Putuo Temple, and if he'd had just enough to drink, and if he was in the right mood, the stories would start to flow out of him. His eyes would gleam when he told his tales, the air full of smoke from the lit cigarette held between his fingers. The two cats at his feet would stir. When he started talking, the world seemed to fade away.

I loved hearing his stories. He had been around the world, and he had seen everything, Beijing and Shanghai and plenty of other places, riding by tank and train and plane... The stories were always full of the unfamiliar and the exotic. They often started "it was such-and-such year of the Republic". He knew how to set the scene, and how to tell a story with a beginning, middle, and end. There were always colourful characters, too. Even the crickets would hush to listen. I was there to pour tea and sometimes even light cigarettes, rushing between the Colonel and my father like a good private serving a pair of generals.

The first story I ever heard the Colonel tell was about his time in Northern Jiangsu and Anhui in the twenty-ninth year of the Republic. His troops were stationed in the hills outside Ma'anshan. One night, shortly after he had finished training as a medic, he was suddenly put in a jeep and driven several hours into the countryside. He was led into a ruined temple, where a wounded woman from Nanjing was sprawled. The woman was one of Dai Li's spies. She had been working in Nanjing to root out collaborators. Wang Jingwei had set up his Reorganised National Government of China with the backing of the Japanese, and they were doing their best to root out any opposition. She was a beautiful young woman, but her face was grim. It was dangerous work, and eventually her time was up: she was shot three times. There were bullet holes in her thigh, belly, and shoulder. She was lucky to have survived. What the Colonel didn't expect when he started poking around her abdominal wound was that he would find a seven-month-old baby growing in her belly. Due to the mother's chronic malnutrition, the child was only about the size of a fist or a tiny kitten. The Colonel delivered the baby and it survived. A year later, when the Colonel was in Shanghai, he saw the child again – he was already walking.

The Colonel guffawed, and said, "She didn't even know she was pregnant. I just pulled it right out. I didn't expect to be called up for midwife duty when I joined the army. That's a strange one, huh? And that was just the beginning. I saw some strange things as a medic, until they sent me to the front line."

At first, the Colonel and his men had been fighting the Communists, but they eventually went up against the Japanese. He told us once about when the Japanese had attacked Wuhan and he'd been in charge of evacuating the division headquarters. They had to get up a winding road, pursued by eighty men, a pair of tanks, with mortar rounds raining down. He had a hundred and eighty men with him when he left, and half of them went down in the first fight. The next assault, half of the survivors died, and in the next fight the same... Soldiers were being cut down like autumn wheat by a sharp scythe. Finally, the Japanese managed to break through on their flank, with a tank leading a crowd of infantry. The Colonel only had nineteen men left. They were running out of ammunition and there was no way to retreat. They made ready to fight hand to hand. They knew it would probably be their last battle. But just as the assault was about to commence, they saw the Japanese soldiers were being beaten back.

It turned out that the tank had rolled through some brush that had been occupied by hundreds of wasps' nests. The sky was suddenly full of hundreds of thousands of insects, all stinging the Japanese fighters. These were no ordinary wasps, either – they were as big as locusts, and they attacked like they were possessed. It was as if the wasps knew what the Japanese were up to and they were out for revenge. All of the firepower and armour of the Japanese military were no match for the cloud of wasps. After the wasps swarmed, there wasn't a single Japanese soldier left alive. Dead bodies littered the hills. The corpses were red and swollen and they looked more like the scalded carcasses of pigs than humans.

After that battle, the Colonel was raised to the rank that became his nickname, given his Tokarev pistol, and his silvery watch. This was right around the time the Colonel's father was dragging an artillery shell back to his pig pen. It was sort of a trade-off, in the end: he was saved from the Japanese assault by the poisonous swarm of wasps, and his father was taken by a contaminated Japanese shell. It was an eye for an eye and a tooth for a tooth.

Grandpa said: "It was fate. You can never see it before it comes, but it's so obvious after."

After hearing the story, I was forever afraid of wasps. When I went up the mountain and came across a hive, I always gave them a wide berth. Another one of his stories made me vow to myself that I would see Shanghai someday. I wanted to see for myself those tall buildings, the steamships, the neon lights, the gardens, the French Concession full of foreigners, that magnificent world where the streets were paved with gold...

XIII

The story that made me want to go to Shanghai was the one where the Colonel arrived in the city to work for the female spy that he had saved in the ruined temple. She had been impressed by his talents and wanted him under her command. He refused at first. He decided he was done killing people. If he had his wish, he would have gone back to being a medic, but she pulled some strings, and eventually an official order came down. The Colonel couldn't disobey a direct order. The Colonel arrived in Shanghai under an alias and opened a clinic. With his cover in place, he began working cases for the KMT intelligence bureau, assassinating collaborators and Japanese officials. He lived a strange double life in Shanghai. When not living the lifestyle of a Shanghai doctor, he was creeping around in the shadows, looking for enemies of the state. The female spy saw to his needs, providing him with two pistols, a wireless transmitter, a box of gold bars, and five agents. Each of the Colonel's five agents had a special skill: some were skilled at infiltration or stealing equipment and documents, some were hardened assassins that could kill without batting an eye, some were experts in explosives, and some could speak the birdlike language of the Japanese. One of the agents was a tall woman from Sichuan with a dignified nose and magnificent breasts; when she went out on the street, she would always attract the catcalls of the young Communist agitators. The Sichuanese agent became nocturnal. There was nothing unusual about that, especially for a spy. Among the Colonel's agents, she stood out mostly for this reason: she was a deaf mute. She communicated with gestures and by writing. Even when she was only wielding a pen, there was no disguising her incredible strength. She could break the grip of the strongest man with the twist of her wrist. Without much effort, her punch could crush a brick. She could lift someone clean off their feet with one hand. The Sichuanese spy had trained in martial arts and meditation for many years, and had once lived in a nunnery on Mount Emei.

The Colonel paused to take a drag of a cigarette or take a shot of *shaojiu*, then started again. Sometimes the story would go off the rails there, or he might start it again right where he had left off. He was fond of a question-and-answer format. He would sometimes slip into the accent of the characters in the story, too.

"People from Sichuan have their own language, but when they speak Mandarin, they always throw in a couple phrases. Like, they might say, 'Yuh tell me, what was a pretty girl doing up on Mount Emei?' It was always that kind of thing. 'Yuh tell me, if you told me she was a whore, I would've believed you, right?' That's how they talk. But what do you make of that? She couldn't have been a mute her whole life, right? She knew how to write, so someone must have taught her, don't you think? Do you figure something happened to

41

her voice, or it was some kind of mental thing? What the hell was going on with her?"

By the end of it, you couldn't help but picture the Sichuanese spy dotted with question marks.

He took a sip of tea and a drag of his cigarette and kept going: "There's no such thing in the world as an impenetrable wall, and exposed beams will always rot. One time, there was an emergency, and I had to go to her place in the middle of the night. She was in charge of running a radio transmitter, so secrecy was important. The best place to hide is in plain sight, of course, so rather than finding some out-of-the-way building to rent a room, she got something in the busiest part of the city, right in the middle of a commercial district, where all her neighbours were little shops selling oil or soy sauce or whatever. There were people coming and going at all hours. She made like she was running a fabric store, and filled it up with bolts of material. The transmitter was hidden among the material in the shop. Even if someone had known where to search, it would have been like looking for a needle in a haystack. She made a bed for herself in the loft. There was a window up there, so she could make a quick escape if anyone busted through the front door."

As the Colonel approached her place, the streets were empty. All he could hear were his footsteps and his pounding heart. Her room was all the way at the end of a narrow lane. Just as he was about to knock at the door, he heard a faint moan inside. It was a thin door, so it was easy to hear what was going on inside. He stood outside for a while and listened. It sounded a bit like someone crying, or maybe a cat meowing.

It was an emergency, so he didn't have much time, but he still paused for a moment.

"I figured she was just having a bad dream or something," the Colonel said. "So, I knocked, and then I went in. She looked flustered. I wondered if she had already heard about the reason I was there. Maybe she already knew about the emergency. Suddenly, I heard some rustling up in the loft. How could she be so careless, letting civilians into her hideout? It was undisciplined. I was about to start interrogating her, when a blond head appeared above me. It was a foreign woman! The foreigner came downstairs, putting her skirt back on, and gave her a hard slap across the face. I couldn't figure out what was going on at the time, but I realised later that she must have figured I was her boyfriend or something. It makes sense, since who else would be showing up at her place in the middle of the night?" The Colonel laughed and I smelled the liquor on his breath.

I only understood about half of the story, and I was particularly unclear on the ending. The Colonel continued, "She hadn't intended me to find out about her secret life. But once I stumbled on that scene, I put two and two together. She was born with that predilection. That must have been the reason she spent those years in the nunnery. Maybe that was the reason she was a mute, too. She might've stuck her tongue in the wrong hole! Whatever happened, she ended up in the big city. Birds of a feather flock together, and there were plenty of that kind of bird in Shanghai."

I definitely didn't understand that part of the story. I asked my cousin what the Colonel had meant about birds of a feather, but he was no help. Our knowledge of the outside world was limited. It was all very hazy. I didn't even know what questions to ask to get to the bottom of the story. In my imagination, there was a vast black ocean, and the truth was somewhere deep on the seabed. It was almost unimaginably deep. At the time, the deepest water I had ever seen was over at the reservoir.

XIV

There was another story he told about that time... It was in the thirty-second year of the Republic. He had an agent under him that could speak Japanese, but the agent ended up having his cover blown. Wang Jingwei's men bought him off with enough money that he was willing to give them information to start hunting down the Colonel and his men. Two of them ended up dead, two escaped, and one was caught. The one that was caught was the Colonel. He was grabbed off a tram and sent to a prisoner-of-war camp in Changxing County in Huzhou.

The five hundred or so prisoners of the Huzhou camp were put to work digging coal. One time there was a collapse in the mine and a hundred men were buried. A rescue was mounted, but by the tenth day, it was called off. Even with hundreds of men digging, they had not succeeded in reaching the trapped miners. It wasn't worth wasting more effort. It didn't make sense wasting so much effort just to pull out some prisoners, who probably hadn't survived the initial cave-in.

"There was one person that didn't give up, though," the Colonel said. "This guy was from Changshu, Jiangsu. He was in his forties and he'd been working on the docks at Shiliupu Wharf in Shanghai, so he was as strong as a bull. He had two sons. The older one was twenty-one and worked down at the docks with him, and the younger boy was seventeen. The seventeen-year-old stayed back in their hometown to help their mother run a little grocery store. Their shop was in Shajiabang, where the New Fourth Army was launching guerrilla attacks against the Japanese. Of course, the New Fourth Army needed to eat, too, so the troops stopped by the grocery store every now and then. Eventually, they got to know the seventeen-year-old and put him to work, carrying messages, ammunition, and equipment between Shajiabang and Shanghai. He decided to get his older brother involved, too, and both of them were working in one form or another for the New Fourth Army."

Going to see a movie was a fashionable thing in Shanghai

at the time. One night, the two brothers went out to see a movie. On their way out, the elder brother stepped on the heel of a woman he was walking too closely behind. She started cursing him, but he ignored her. It was the younger boy that couldn't take it. He went right back at her. Suddenly, someone from the crowd reached over and slapped the younger brother. Being cursed out by the woman had been bad enough, but there was no way he was going to take a slap. And he was at the age where nobody thinks before they act. He figured out who had slapped him, and he dived for the guy. He had no way of knowing that he was fighting a police officer. The cop drew his gun and told both of the brothers to kneel on the sidewalk and apologise to the woman. The older brother was ready to comply. But the younger brother refused, and he leapt on the cop and grabbed for his gun. In the struggle, the pistol fired. The round discharged harmlessly into the sky, and it only managed to attract even more police. The two brothers got hauled off to the nearest police station. To make matters worse, they were also carrying some documents from the New Fourth Army. The police were suspicious, so they started trying to beat a confession out of them. When they went to search their room by the wharf, they found a gun and some ammunition. The two brothers and their father were all arrested and sent to the prisoner-of-war camp at Huzhou to dig coal. The two boys had been buried in the collapsed mine, while their father, and the Colonel, who was on the same team, ended up safe.

"That's what it means to be a father," the Colonel said. "For ten days after the cave-in, he was digging. When they switched shifts, he just stayed down in the pit. He slept where he fell. A few steamed buns were all he needed to keep going. He kneeled and thanked the men that kept working alongside him. He told them to keep going, no matter how long it took. He would say – and he never stopped digging at the rock during this time – to the people working alongside him, 'If you help me get my boys out, I'll owe you a debt of gratitude. I will be at your service, the rest of my life.' He was shouting that the whole time, until finally his voice gave out. If they had any humanity in them, anyone that saw the old man down in the hole threw everything they had at the job." But the collapse had taken down a massive portion of the mine, and, even with hundreds of men working for ten days, there wasn't much progress. It seemed that it would be impossible to save the buried miners. Finally, the head of the camp told them to give up. He wanted his prisoners back at work. The old man was dragged out of the pit. During the day, he did whatever he was told, but at night, he went back underground to dig for his boys. Everyone told him to give up, that his sons couldn't have survived. They told him that he was going to kill himself trying to get them out. All he could do in response was whimper, since his voice had already been wrecked by yelling in the tunnel. When they saw his empty bunk each night and the rats cuddling up there to spend the night, the prisoners knew that he hadn't listened to them. The prisoners watched the body of the man wither. He had worked on the docks most of his life and the muscle on his chest was so thick it would have turned away a rifle round. But it seemed like layers of flesh were being carved off him. He was getting thinner by the day.

One night, the Colonel was woken up to tend to some men that had been injured in a fight. It was already late, but as he went out into the yard, he glimpsed under the light of a big winter moon, the silhouette of a man staggering towards him. When the figure drew closer, the Colonel realised that it was the father. He had been like that for several days, going out every night, even after the nights had grown cold, headed for the collapsed mine. But that night, the father of the trapped boys was walking like a drunk, stumbling across the yard. He took a few steps forward and staggered backwards. The Colonel got some steamed buns and ointment and went for him. He thought he might be able to persuade him to spend a night indoors. The father of the boys kept going, staggering towards the entrance to the mine, vomiting up the contents of his stomach, and finally collapsing.

"I figured he wanted to die near the resting places of his sons," the Colonel said. "He was using his last ounce of strength to drag himself down there, to be buried alongside his sons. He had been a mountain of a man, and he still looked it, wrapped up in a parka. He looked a bit like you" – and the Colonel pointed to my father. "But when I went to help him, I realised he was as light as you are" – and the Colonel pointed to me. "I knew he had lost a bit of weight, but I never figured he had wasted away to a skeleton. All the meat had been scraped from his bones, and even his bones seemed to be being eaten away. I was ready to use all the strength I had to lift him into the cave, but when I lifted him up and found out how light he was, I dropped him. I couldn't help myself from crying. It's not as if I had never seen death. I had watched many lives slip away on the battlefield. But his death was sadder than all of those. I picked him up and carried him into the mine. I cried all the way. I cried while carrying him and I cried when I set his body down on the rocks. And I feel like crying now."

In the three years after I first went to visit his house, I had heard many types of stories. Some were scary, some were strange, some were funny, and some, like that one, were sad. After he told it, I could see that his eyes were wet with tears. His stories were fascinating, and I often found myself spellbound. My head burned for hours after some of them. But he never told the stories that I really wanted to hear. He would never tell the story of what happened that night with the Old Constable's mistress, for example. He only hinted at sleeping with his commander's wife. And he never actually explained why he was chosen to be a medic. And was there any truth to the rumours that Grandpa had mentioned, about the reasons the People's Liberation Army had just let him go? Whenever I pressed him to talk about those things, he would either ignore me more or start cursing me.

One time he asked: "Where did you hear about all that crap, you little bastard?" Another time he told me: "If you keep asking me stuff like that, I'm going to sew your mouth shut." And I didn't even ask him what I really wanted to ask him, which is whether he was actually a eunuch. I knew that was completely off-limits. All I would get out of even hinting at that was a slap across the face. If my imagination was a vast black ocean, rather than being sunk to the bottom, this was floating right on the surface. But Blindboy's lesson was still fresh in my mind.

XV

I listened to Grandpa more than anyone else. You probably already know that by now. Whenever I heard a new story from the Colonel, I went straight to Grandpa to tell him. They seemed to inspire him sometimes. He sometimes filled in the blanks that the Colonel had left behind, like with the story about the spy giving birth in the ruined temple…

Grandpa had always said that the Colonel had been a clever boy. The precocious cleverness had grown into an adult intellect. If he put his mind to it, the Colonel could pick up any skill. That's how he became a medic, even though he didn't receive any formal instruction. It was all because of the injury that had given him his second nickname. During his long recovery, he watched the doctors and nurses working. Eventually, he figured that he could do it himself.

During the war, most of the casualties came in with bullet and knife wounds. Most of the battlefield medics were surgeons in their civilian lives. They were adept at all the blood medicine required near the front line: putting in stitches, pulling out bullets, setting broken bones, and wrapping bandages. Most of the time, the field hospitals were fairly tranquil, but when the fighting started, the casualties came by the truckload. After the surgeons triaged the casualties, some of the most severely wounded were shuttled to the side and left to their fate. The pleas of the dying men were like the howling of wolves, but the doctors had learned to harden their hearts and get on with their work. When the Colonel had recovered enough to get around by himself, he started treating those badly wounded men that had been cast aside by the doctors. Even when they knew, the doctors had no objections, since they were busy working on casualties that had far greater chances of survival. The Colonel set up his own operating room. That was how he trained to be a medic. He even saved the lives of a few of the triage patients. The doctors eventually recognised his talent, and he was given a formal assignment.

With a formal assignment as a medic, the Colonel was suddenly buried in casualties. He was working on men from many different battlefields, some from the front line of the assaults by the Japanese invaders, others from fights with the Communists, and quite a few also from skirmishes with local bandits and gangsters. Bullets and knife points don't discriminate – they pierce and stab everyone the same way. The casualties the Colonel treated included every sort of person, from every level of society, from privates to generals, from the wealthy to the poor... He looked after them all the same. The soldiers thanked him sometimes by bowing deeply or even getting down to kowtow, but the high officials and rich merchants sometimes offered him some money, maybe even some gold or silver, and he was offered promotions and ceremonial titles. One year, when he returned to the village at the end of summer, he had with him a chest full of gold. His mother was shocked when he opened the lid and showed her the ingots and bracelets and bars of pure gold. She told him to get rid of it right away.

"Why didn't she want it?" I asked Grandpa. "It must have been worth a fortune."

Grandpa could always explain these kinds of things, but sometimes he liked to take a more circuitous route to this conclusion. "Because she didn't want a fortune," Grandpa said. "A fortune is an invitation to disaster, just waiting for larceny, embezzlement, or outright robbery... That's what it brings. You pull a chest of gold into your house, and all the scoundrels and ruffians outside your walls are already counting it for you. Could you put your head down and sleep soundly with a fortune under your bed? And she's a widow!"

The Colonel dragged the chest back to his barracks. It sat on a shelf like a box of assorted junk. He had only his old mother to look after, and no sons or grandsons to give it to. The gold was basically useless to him. Finally, he had a goldsmith make him a set of gold surgical tools: various scissors and shears, tweezers and forceps, scalpels of various sizes, and lancets. The goldsmith had mixed in some other metals to make the tools hard enough to work with, and the additional alloy made them shine even brighter. The entire set, laid out on the surgical bench, gleamed. They were shiny enough to blind you. The Colonel and his gleaming instruments came to be known across the country. The fame seemed to take wing and fly. The sick and injured that had been written off by other doctors arrived in his operating room. They seemed to never stop coming. They were as persistent as leeks: even when they seemed to have been taken down to the roots, they sprouted again. When they left, they told more people about the lifesaving medic and his golden scalpel, his ability to bring people back from the brink of death, and his complete refusal of any reward. He was treated as close to a god, for he seemed capable of divine feats. Nobody called him the Colonel back then, since that would have been a confusing nickname for an army man – they called him the Golden Blade. The nickname referred to his instruments, but it made him sound like a hero, wielding a sword. While other swords cut men down, the Golden Blade resurrected them. Even if he was a eunuch then, he was as powerful and respected as the eunuch that had once stood around the emperors.

Grandpa said: "Everything has a reason. Everyone has their fate. There are people resting in coffins right now that regret not being able to get an audience with him."

Four

XVI

Grandpa knew a lot about the Colonel, but there was plenty he didn't know.

My father was the best source of information on the Colonel. He told me once: "Grandpa gets everything he tells you second-hand. He only knows what he hears from me. Half of what he tells you is bullshit."

I had realised myself that Grandpa didn't always have the full story. My father was the one that usually really knew what had happened. When he talked about the Colonel, he could shade in events with more detail than Grandpa had. My father knew the exact times and places things happened. It was usually more interesting to hear my father talk about the Colonel than Grandpa. Sometimes Grandpa would get halfway through a story, then trail off. When I asked what happened next, he would tell me to ask my father. My father had been the one to tell me about the Colonel making friends with a People's Liberation Army cadre, and he'd told me about the Colonel's cats, too. Unlike Grandpa, my father wasn't much of a talker. I had to drag the stories out of him. If I hadn't asked him, he would never have told me about the cats and the PLA cadre.

The Colonel's first cat had been given to him by the wife of a KMT general.

It was the fall of 1946. After the Japanese surrendered, the Colonel went back to being a medic. He was tired of killing people, my father said. He wanted to save lives. The Colonel was working out of a field hospital in Fushun in the northeast. One day around noon, a young woman arrived, chauffeured in an American jeep by a pair of orderlies. The woman had on a wool beret, and a peach-coloured cape. It was clear that she was a woman of some rank and importance. When she met the Colonel, she gave a deep bow and thanked him for saving her man. When the Colonel asked who the man was, she wouldn't answer directly, but gave enough hints to suggest that it was a KMT general. It was unclear whether her vague answer was because of the man's rank or because of some top-secret cover. All the Colonel knew was that this woman was thanking him for saving some anonymous high-ranking KMT official that would have been unlikely to survive if not for his care. She had prepared a gift, as well. Whatever it was, it filled a rattan box in the back of the jeep. The Colonel waved her off, refusing to accept it.

"I know what's going on," the Colonel said. "Anything valuable you've got was probably expropriated by the Japanese at some point. I don't want it."

"You don't need to worry about that," the young woman said. "I can assure you that it's of sound provenance."

"I need to travel light," the Colonel said. "We're in the middle of a war. I can't cart around things I don't need."

"What I'm giving you is something that you can keep with you for a long time," the woman said.

"I'll be happy to hold onto my life," the Colonel said. He refused to take the rattan box. But the woman was persistent. She would not give up trying to persuade him. When she got her escorts to lift the rattan basket out of the back of the jeep, the Colonel picked it up and put it back. He got the surprise of his life when he looked into the back of the jeep and saw a cat sleepily curled in the backseat. It was a plump, handsome tabby with a pair of coppery eyes. "If you really want to give me something," the Colonel said, "how about this cat?"

The young woman smiled, bent into the jeep to get the cat, and passed it to the Colonel. From that moment on, the Colonel always kept cats. He had no children of his own, but the cats seemed to serve the same purpose for him.

XVII

The cat provided a happy distraction to the Colonel, and it was the reason that he had missed his chance to surrender to the Communists.

The KMT kept losing ground to the Communists, my father explained, so the Colonel kept being shuffled between different units as they retreated south. In the winter of 1948, he ended up stationed with a naval unit at Zhenjiang in Jiangsu, about a hundred and fifty miles east of Shanghai. Their base was near the Jinshan Temple. The sound of the monks tolling the bells mixed with the bugles of the base. The Colonel worked at the hospital during the day, and went back to the barracks at night. It was only a few minutes' walk between them. One night, just as he had fallen asleep, two men dressed in dark clothes burst into the room, tied him up and loaded him into a car. The car dropped him off to be loaded into a boat, and when the boat stopped, he was loaded into another car. This car drove deep into the Dabie Mountains, where the PLA had a base. When the Colonel was unloaded from the car, he was told that he had been brought there to perform surgery.

This senior cadre had been shot in the chest, and the bullet was still stuck somewhere in there, between his heart and his lungs. He had already been that way for twenty-four hours when the Colonel arrived. The senior cadre's life was hanging in the balance. The Colonel knew very well that there was no way out. If he didn't do the surgery, he'd be shot. If he failed, he would probably be shot, too. If the senior cadre died while he was operating, the Colonel knew that they would suspect he had done it intentionally. The cadre had a bullet in his chest, but the Colonel had a gun to his head.

Fortunately, the operation was a success. The senior cadre lived. His men rejoiced. The PLA treated him as a distinguished guest. They also gave him the chance to defect to the PLA. At that moment, the KMT was already retreating, and the PLA was about to use the Dabie Mountains to launch their decisive Huaihai campaign, which would let them capture large swathes of land and major cities. The Colonel realised that the KMT was on its heels, and he would have stayed – if not for the cats. After getting the tabby, he had added a few more strays to his menagerie. He couldn't bear the thought of them starving to death or being abandoned. He chose to return to the KMT.

The decision was tantamount to choosing to walk into the gates of hell.

My father told me that when the Colonel had first joined up, he had been sent to the front lines in Jiangxi. At that time, the KMT was encircling the retreating Red Army. They chased the Communists all the way to Longyan, about a hundred miles west of Xiamen. The Colonel couldn't help but wonder what kind of war they were fighting. They would sometimes spend a day fighting or chasing the enemy, then have an entire day where they could carouse or amuse themselves however they pleased. Even in a war, there was time to eat and drink, or gamble, or pay a girl for her company. The Colonel spent his leisure time in a different way. He studied military tactics, bushcraft, and marksmanship. The way he saw it, carpentry was a trade to get by in life, and the battlefield had its own trades – but those trades could save your life. The Colonel trained in the necessary skills to keep himself alive. He watched his comrades get killed or mutilated, but he relied on his own skills to stay out of harm. He was a deadly shot, too. He could hit nine bull's-eyes in a row, while others were still loading their magazine. He had all the makings of a star soldier. During the fierce fighting in Longyan, the Colonel became a hero. He even made the papers.

Later, when his unit defected to the PLA, someone from the KMT dug up the articles to show to the Communists. The PLA was not bound on revenge, though. They investigated the account and then made ready to put him on trial. Fortunately for the Colonel, the senior cadre he had saved in the Dabie Mountains was put in charge of his case. It wasn't a big deal for the senior cadre to pull the necessary strings, since all he had got for the Colonel was a chance to go to the front line. He could atone for his errors by meritorious service. It was better than being executed, which was one of the possibilities.

When I told Grandpa about that story, he shook his head so hard I thought I could hear a rattle. He sighed and said: "It's always women." He suddenly grew serious. "His life was ruined by women. It was always women."

I figured there was some truth in that. He had lost his manhood because a woman had seduced him. He had been sent to Shanghai as a spy because he had saved the woman in the ruined temple. He had been captured by the Japanese because of a woman. He had ended up in a PLA cell because of a woman, too – if that young woman hadn't given him a cat, he would have defected to the KMT. If he had defected to the KMT earlier, he wouldn't have suffered so much later. I found it sad, thinking of the Colonel suffering so much because he couldn't bear to part with his cats.

Grandpa said: "And he still keeps the damn things. He

never learned his lesson. He's a hard-hearted man. He might be intelligent, but he's too arrogant. He'll never bow to anyone. Everyone needs a certain amount of fear in their heart. It's a big world. Knowledge is limitless. There is always something over the horizon. You need to know when to give in. You have to admit when you're wrong."

XVIII

While Grandpa was lecturing me in the front room, my mother and sister were in the kitchen wrapping glutinous rice in reed leaves to make *zongzi*. A pair of hens strutted through the yard and paused to smell the sweet fragrance of rice steamed in mountain spring water. They pecked around in the dirt, waiting for a chance to get their share of the *zongzi*. I had two older brothers and an older sister. My sister was the oldest of all the kids. She'd already got married by then. She was visiting us for the Dragon Boat Festival. My eldest brother was older than me by seven years. He was already working with my father on the production brigade. They went out together every morning to work the crops, spread fertiliser, build waterworks, fell timber, catch fish, or do whatever was required that day. I had another brother that was five years older than me. He was working as an apprentice painter in town, so he wasn't around much, except during the busy seasons around planting and harvest. We used to call those seasons "double time", rushing to get the crop in the ground, then rushing to get it off the land.

The day I'm describing, with Grandpa lecturing, and the chickens pecking, and my mother and sister making *zongzi*, was before the Dragon Boat Festival, 1967, and my fourteenth birthday. We always added a year, though, since we started counting from conception, so I thought of it as my fifteenth birthday. Many years before, when that day came around, my mother would say, "This is the day I gave birth to my two little *zongzi*." And sometimes, when times were bad, she would say that she wished she actually did have a pair of *zongzi*. It sounded like she would have traded in her kids for two bundles of glutinous rice.

I had a twin. She was a girl. But she got sick and died when I was five years old. That was the last time my mother ever talked about her two little *zongzi*. It hurt her to talk about my sister. She had given birth to another girl, as well, before me, who had died shortly after being born, but she wasn't emotional about that. She almost seemed to have forgotten it. Losing a child of five years old is far different, though. She often brought up my younger sister – younger only by half an hour – and it was clear she was still mourning the girl. Losing a younger and older sibling left me spoiled. Grandpa especially was worried that their spirits might haunt me. Even though our family was poor, there were always extra preparations for Dragon Boat Festival: there was always *zongzi* and rice wine, which was offered along with incense to any hungry spirits, gods, or ancestors. Grandpa wanted to make sure the spirits of my two dead sisters ate their fill, so they wouldn't bother me. I didn't think of it as anything but a superstition. I wasn't that worried about ghosts haunting me. The dead were nothing to fear, especially compared to the living. My father and the Colonel were scary enough – and they weren't dead – not to mention my teachers! To me, the very alive Blindboy was just as frightening as the ghosts were supposed to be, even if I never let on how scared I was of him.

The day after the Dragon Boat Festival, four kids disappeared. Among the missing were Blindboy and my cousin, and also Phoenix Blossom's boy, whom we called Wild One, the stone mason's third eldest boy, whom we called Meathook. Some money and food were missing from each of their homes, so everybody assumed they must have hatched a plan to sneak off somewhere together. Their families went looking for them, but when night fell, there was no sign of the kids. My aunt was crying when she came to see my father that night, begging him for help to find her boy.

Grandpa wasn't at home that night. He was over at his second youngest daughter's place, a few villages over. My father was his only son, but Grandpa had four daughters. Except for his youngest daughter, who still lived in the village, all the rest had married and left. Every month, Grandpa would go visit one of his daughters and spend a few days. That was why the Colonel was over at our place when my aunt showed up.

The Colonel looked at my aunt, took a drag of his cigarette, and said: "Don't bother looking for them. They'll be back." He took another drag. He turned to my father and said: "That's exactly what I'm worried about. That's when the trouble is going to start." Nobody had any idea what he was talking about.

"What do you mean by that?" my father asked.

"It's got nothing to do with you, anyways," the Colonel said, chuckling. "I'll worry about it."

"Just tell us where they went."

The Colonel responded with this: "The wind is going to blow. The rain is going to fall. People are going to suffer." It was like the sorts of riddles that fortune tellers give. It wasn't an answer, exactly, but once you untwisted it, maybe there was some truth hidden inside. It didn't satisfy my father or my aunt, though.

"What do you mean, the wind is going to blow?" my father asked. "Where's this rain supposed to come from?"

"A red wind," the Colonel said, finally, "and an insurgent rain."

I had no idea what he meant by that, but my father seemed to know. My father started cursing. I wasn't even sure who exactly he was angry at. It seemed like he was angry at whoever or whatever the "red wind" and the "insurgent rain" were. At the time, I sort of assumed those might be another pair of nicknames. I found out later what it meant: the red wind was the conservative faction, who wore dress shoes, and the insurgent wind was the rebel faction, who went everywhere barefoot. There was a pair of factions vying for power in the county. At first, the war had been fought with megaphones and what they called "big-character posters". They had put up banners and held meetings. During that time, the conservative faction had been winning the battle of words. Later, with the help of a leftist faction within the PLA, the rebels had organised a Red Guard suicide squad with the goal of seizing power through violence. The first shot had been fired in front of the county government buildings, and the factional battle had quickly shifted in favour of the rebels. Eventually, the rebels began wresting power from bureaucrats and factional rivals at all levels, and sending their enemies into hiding. The rebels might've been barefoot yahoos, but they had the benefit of youth. They weren't content with what they saw, and they wanted to carry the revolution through to the end. They wanted to completely wipe out the conservative faction. The front lines of the battlefield had eventually shifted out into the countryside, where they had started recruiting middle-school students into the Red Guard ranks. With their numbers swollen, the rebels set about cutting the grass and pulling out the roots.

XIX

My cousin and the others had joined the revolutionary cause. They had run off to join a countywide assembly of Red Guards that would travel from town to town, and village to village. They descended like a swarm of locusts. They shouted murderous slogans, smashed things, put up big-character posters, and grabbed people to interrogate and parade through the streets. It was the same in our village, too. The first thing they did was go house to house to search for members of the conservative faction.

And they pretty quickly turned up a prize in the haystack in our principal's pigsty: the section chief of the county Party committee's propaganda department. He had been one of the ringleaders of the conservative faction. He was a gifted writer, whose every word had been like a dagger stabbing at the heart of the rebels. With his essays alone, he had nearly wiped out the rebel faction. Since such a mighty villain had been found in my principal's haystack, our village became the focal point of the grand assembly of Red Guards. Captain Hu of the Red Guards arrived by bike to lead away our principal and the propaganda department chief. He ordered a Red Guard branch established at our school. The first task of the branch would be to conduct mass revolutionary cleansing and education in the village.

That afternoon, an assembly was held at the school. We were told that regular classes were suspended. Following that, a solemn ceremony was held to welcome all of the junior high students into the Red Guard. The new recruits swore allegiance to the rebel faction and were given their own red armbands. The sixty-seven new recruits, led by a boy and a girl that I didn't recognise, turned to the big red flag and shouted their slogans, challenged their enemies, and repeated the oath. Everyone looked as if they were ready to lay down their lives for the cause. The battle they were fighting was not a distant struggle against an invader, but was taking place right in our village. The enemy was landlords, rich peasants, counterrevolutionaries, and the bad elements that had fallen in with rival factions. Some of the first targets were temples and the ancestral hall. There were two temples in the village: Guande Temple and the Guandi Shrine. They were both on the slopes of Tail Mountain. The Guandi Shrine was close to the entrance to the village, right at the crook in the tiger's tail. It was a small, stone structure that didn't house anything but a red-faced, elaborately moustachioed statue of the deified general Guan Yu. The Guandi Shrine usually only had visitors on festival days, when people would burn incense in front of the statue. The much larger Guande Temple was at the nape of the tiger's neck. There was a slabstone courtyard out front, a little bigger than a basketball court. To get up or down the mountain, you had to go by the temple. Over the years, the narrow path up to it had been worn into a wide road by the footsteps of pilgrims, monks, and pious villagers, so that there were parts of it wide enough to drive a tractor down. The road terminated in a stone staircase with eighty-one steps to represent the eighty-one sufferings required for Buddhahood attesting to the merits of the temple's monks, and built with the alms that they had collected. As intricate and extensive as the staircase and the courtyard were, you can imagine the temple itself. It was far larger than the ancestral hall in the village. Its shrines looked like mansions. In the first shrine, there was a statue of the Buddha Maitreya. The Bodhisattva Guanyin was housed in a central shrine. There was a monastery in the back of the complex, as well, where seven or eight monks lived. There was no way to keep a garden up there on the mountain, but the monks raised chickens and ducks, which they traded for grain and vegetables. I had seen most of the temple's monks but I had never seen the old monk that served as their abbot. He never came down from the mountain and he rarely left his quarters to walk around the temple. Rumour had it that he had his own small room, with red walls, where he spent all day every day in meditation or practising martial arts. Grandpa said that when the Japanese had come to our village, they had gone up the mountain to the temple. The abbot waved his horsetail whisk to signal for help from his fellow monks. But the commander of the Japanese unit intervened before his men could attack. The commander was from a samurai family, and he wanted to test his martial arts skills against the abbot. The Japanese commander and the abbot agreed to a fight. If the abbot won, the Japanese would give up, and if the Japanese commander won, he would burn the place down and kill everyone that had taken refuge inside. Of course, back then, the old monk was not very old at all. He was quick of eye and deft of hand, strong as an ox, and he fought with his horsetail whisk. Within seconds of facing off, the abbot had forced the commander's katana out of his hand. The commander admitted defeat and bowed to the abbot. The temple was spared.

The fame of the abbot spread far and wide. The monastery and its temple grew in prestige. Pilgrims came from all over the country to burn incense in its shrines. Villagers went up the mountain to pray for healthy children, safe lives, and good fortune. The Colonel's mother went up to the temple nearly every morning to burn incense to the Bodhisattva Guanyin, and to deliver firewood, rice, oil, and salt to the monks.

Grandpa said: "She treats the monks better than she ever treated her parents."

Fortunately for her, she was away at Mount Putuo Temple when the Red Guards arrived. If she had been there, she would have seen her place of worship smashed and her beloved monks beaten. She probably wouldn't have been able to take it. Perhaps Guanyin knew what was coming and made sure the Colonel's mother wouldn't be there to see it.

XX

After their assembly at the school, the Red Guards went to destroy the Guandi Shrine. They burned the statue of Guan Yu and then went up the mountain to attack Guande

Temple. They burned every image of the Buddha and every statue, tore up the sutras, and smashed up the carved pillars and niches. I was among those watching, and it felt like seeing a fortress razed. The sky was full of smoke. The monks cried out and prayed for help, and cursed the Red Guards. It was a chaotic scene.

A fat monk had laid an iron rod across the gate, attempting to stop the Red Guards from entering the monastery itself. The young rebels regrouped and started shouting slogans, preparing to charge the door. We were all nervous, prepared for the worst, but right at that moment, the abbot appeared. That was the first time I had seen him!

The old monk didn't speak but motioned for the fat monk to remove the iron rod. The fat monk refused to step aside. His face turned red and he stamped his feet. Finally, the abbot pressed his hands together reverently, closed his eyes, and very quietly said the holy name of the Buddha Amitabha. The abbot walked to where the fat monk stood and slapped him twice on the neck. The fat monk dropped the iron rod and froze. He looked like one of the statues. He knew he was about to see the place destroyed. Later, while the temple burned, he wept and wailed. His cries were so loud that my father said he could hear him all the way down in the village.

When I finally fell asleep that night, I had a nightmare. In my dream, I was a Red Guard. I was surrounded by rebel comrades, and we were setting upon the fat monk. The iron rod flew across the courtyard in front of me, but I wasn't afraid. The next thing I knew, the iron rod had smashed into my forehead. Blood ran down my face and dripped onto the ground. I felt no pain. I kept my head held high. I kept pushing forward, charging like a bull. And then I was a bull. I drove my horns into the side of the fat monk's neck. The fat monk screamed. I woke up.

The events of the day had been shocking, and they had followed me even into my dreams. In my nightmare, the horror seems to be magnified – the murderous rush, my head split open, blood everywhere, flames licking the sky, black smoke rising, a bull charging through the crowd, ghosts wailing, wolves howling, people fighting for their lives... That night at dinner, before the nightmare, everyone was talking about what they had seen that day when the Red Guards had smashed the temple. The Colonel arrived while we were still eating. "I guess I was right," he said. "I told you there were bad times ahead."

"You were right," my father said. "What do these bastards think they're accomplishing?"

"I'm trying to stay out of their way," the Colonel said.

"What do you mean?"

"I figure I'll be one of the bad elements they'll grab tomorrow," the Colonel said. "They'll parade me around."

"You've been through worse," my father said.

"A wise general knows when to retreat. I'm going to make myself scarce for a while, and we'll see how things shake out."

"These little fuckers don't even have hair on their balls," my father said. "What are you so scared of?"

"There's an old saying, 'Fear the child, not the old man. The young ghost makes mischief, and the old ghost sobs.' You don't know what these little bastards are getting up to in the city. They're hauling bodies out of the river every day. They're kids – they don't even realise what they're doing. I'm going to do my best to steer clear of them."

My father wasn't a talkative man, but the one person he would open up to was the Colonel. He begged him not to go. "You're getting worked up for nothing," my father told him. "I don't think these little bastards have it in them to mess with you." He paused for a moment and then a thought came to him: "Hey, you should be fine, since your mother has an in with the Bodhisattva. She's always burning incense, praying for you..."

"I hope she's burning some incense for my two cats, too,"

the Colonel said. "I'll look after myself, but they might need some help." From his pocket, the Colonel took a pair of keys on a red string and a ten yuan note, and passed them to my father. "My mother is still over at Mount Putuo Temple. Those cats are counting on you." When my father waved off the keys, the Colonel put them down on the table. "They're picky. They'll beg for dried fish. If you run out of money, just fry up whatever, though."

"I'll catch some mice for them," my father said.

"Those cats will catch mice themselves, but they won't eat them. Mice are filthy. Would you eat something that had been down in the sewer? They wouldn't, either." As he spoke, he was already walking out the door. He planned to leave that night and there were still things he needed to prepare. I watched him go, his head held high and his shoulders square. I thought he looked like a ghost, walking out into the gloom...

XXI

My cousin arrived close on his heels. He was looking for Grandpa. There was going to be a struggle session at the ancestral hall the next day, and he knew Grandpa had been classed as one of the "poor and lower-middle-class peasants" after Liberation, so he wanted him to speak on behalf of the oppressed classes. Grandpa could give a speech and he was well respected in the village, so my cousin thought he'd be perfect for the job. Grandpa was still at my aunt's house, though, and he'd been held up there looking after one of her pigs that had got sick. My cousin was disappointed, but he wasn't discouraged. He told my father to go find Grandpa and bring him back. My father pretended not to hear him and went back to eating. "The Colonel was right! He saw all this coming."

"So, what?" my cousin demanded. "We're still going to make him atone for his crimes."

"Take all that crap about 'struggle sessions' and cram it up your ass," my father said. "You little bastards aren't worthy to wash that man's feet."

"You better watch your mouth," my cousin said. "You're starting to sound like a counterrevolutionary."

"What the hell are you talking about?" My father set down his chopsticks and pointed at my cousin: "You're the one who better watch out. I'll give you a slap upside the head!"

In the past, my cousin would have been intimidated, but that night, he was unmoved by the threat. He leaned towards my father and his nostrils flared menacingly. He pointed at the red armband he wore and said, "We're the ones that slap people now. You wouldn't dare."

My father stood up and was about to hit him, but my mother and older brother held him back. My father didn't hit him, but he told him to fuck off. The way my cousin left, he didn't look at all like he was fucking off – his head was held high, and he was taking his time. Even though he had only been away from home for a brief time, my cousin already seemed to have grown into a man. He wore a handsome military uniform, decorated with the red armband, and on his chest he had pinned a Chairman Mao badge the size of a hen's egg. He walked with his shoulders back, his arms swinging. When he spoke, he gestured in the air with his right hand, like my teacher conducting us when we sang. I had no choice but to follow him. I ignored my father when he called me to come back.

I didn't go home that night. I stayed with my cousin. Anyways, with Grandpa away, I would have been sleeping alone. I asked my cousin to tell me what he had been up to, starting with the day he had left home to link up with the Red Guards. He told me the whole story, ending with me joining him. Listening to the voice in the dark, it didn't sound like my cousin. The stories didn't sound like they could have possibly happened to him. The stories sounded like they were from a novel. A soft breeze rustled the mosquito net and I smelled the familiar body odour of my cousin.

"You talk different now," I said.

"I've experienced the revolution," he said.

"The revolution is good," I said.

"The revolution is great," he said.

"I want to join the Red Guards, too."

"You're still a freshman. You're not old enough. You can join the reserve team, though. We're setting it up for freshmen and sophomores in junior high. I can talk to Blindboy and see if he can get you in."

That's when I realised Blindboy outranked my cousin. Blindboy was the head of the village's Red Guard team, and my cousin, Meathook, and Wild One were serving under him as lieutenants. Blindboy was the meanest kid in our school. He was notorious for stealing everything from light bulbs to chalks. The teachers had caught him peeking into the girls' bathroom. He was the one that told us all the best dirty jokes about our female teachers. Blindboy was in trouble almost every day. Not long before he'd run away from home, there had been an incident on our school sports day, where he'd buried a shot put ball in the sand pit, thinking he could come back and steal it later. The PE teacher found out and ruthlessly scolded him. The day after that, Blindboy went around to the PE teacher's house, grabbed two of his chickens, and threw them in the cesspit behind his house to drown. When the PE teacher's poor old mother had gone out to discover them, she sat down by the cesspit and cried. Blindboy was hiding around the corner, laughing about it. I had seen the whole thing myself.

"Why did they put him in charge?" I asked.

"The Captain wanted him," my cousin explained.

"Who's that?" I asked. I had seen a boy and a girl that I didn't recognise leading the assembly at the school. "Was it those two I saw at the school? Which one is in charge?"

"It's neither of them," my cousin said. "The Captain hasn't arrived yet. He'll be here tomorrow morning."

I was fourteen that night, when I first experienced real insomnia. It felt like the gloom was pressing down on me, as if it had a form and a smell and a shape. I no longer felt as if I was lying on the bed, but had somehow floated up into the night air. My mind instead of resting was being churned by feverish, twisting thoughts. And then those thoughts seemed to take shape, too, as hateful men in black uniforms, slowly encircling me. I was powerless. I couldn't sleep but neither could I wake up. When I forced my eyes shut, I was trapped in a twilight mirror world. A shape emerged: tall, with square shoulders and square head, wearing the same uniform as my cousin, a leather belt around his waist, a red armband – that's how I imagined the Red Guard Captain.

Five

XXII

The Captain was nothing like I had pictured. He was short, with a pale round face, and he looked gentle and frail. His arms were thinner than mine, and they looked like a pair of broomsticks – uniformly skinny the whole way down, with not an ounce of muscle on them. I noticed the sneakers he had on were even tinier than my mother's shoes.

Grandpa said: "If you have small feet, you'll never get that tall. A tall guy with small feet would fall over. There's no foundation to build from."

The Captain did have a massive head, though, and a wide forehead. His head was full of dreams and poetry. Before joining the Red Guards, he had been the head of his school's poetry circle, the Blue Sky Club. He fancied himself not a bad poet, too. Whether the name of the poetry circle had been chosen by him or not, the Captain always seemed to be gazing up at the sky, although that was maybe because he was short and always seemed to have his neck tipped back, looking up at something. What impressed me the most about the Captain was his full, dark moustache. The moustache made him look like a poet. He also had a nice smile, with big white teeth, but he rarely showed it. I heard that the only time he smiled was when looking at himself in the mirror. My cousin told me that the Captain used to grease and trim his moustache every night before he went to bed and when he got up in the morning. The Captain would stare at himself in the mirror for a long time while he worked, smiling in silent self-satisfaction. It was like he was holding a twice-daily meeting with the man he saw in the mirror.

There was no guesthouse in our village, so the Captain and his underlings crashed in one of the classrooms at the school and slept on desks pushed together. The Captain had brought one girl and three boys with him, all former classmates from the county town. We didn't know their names, so we just called them the Four Mighty Guardians. They had a girl with them, so to avoid any misunderstanding, they kept the lights on in the classroom and the door open. There were no misunderstandings, but the Four Mighty Guardians and the Captain were assaulted all night by mosquitoes. When they emerged the next morning, they were covered in welts. It looked like they had come down with measles overnight. They eventually changed their sleeping pattern, so they went to bed in the morning and slept until the afternoon, when they went to work. Their work consisted of eliminating any traces of the conservative faction, spreading the cause of rebellion, rooting out feudal superstition, and struggling against the last vestiges of the landlord and rich peasant class, and exposing counterrevolutionaries and bad elements. They hung from the school gate a placard that read: "Fuchun County Revolutionary Rebels Union Headquarters, Seventh Branch". Our principal's office became the office of the Captain, and his Four Mighty Guardians put a Red Guard flag over the door to announce his occupation. Everyone entering and exiting the office had to salute the flag. Later, we found out that the Captain was actually related to the Captain Hu of the Red Guards that had arrived by bike to lead away the bad elements found in the pigsty. They even had the same last name. He loved being addressed as Captain Hu, even though it was a bit confusing at first. Eventually, the other Captain Hu was promoted to Commander Hu, which solved that problem.

Captain Hu's work in our village never seemed to end. During the day, he would oversee the writing of big-character posters and banners, and sometimes lead a team door to door, interrogating whoever he suspected of being a bad element, and ransacking their homes. They were looking for signs of feudal superstition at first, which might be religious books or idols. Those were all immediately burned or smashed. There was no reasoning with the young rebels, or convincing them to spare a devotional item. At my house, they found a small sculpture of Guan Yu, a pair of Zhong Kui pictures that we hung up at New Year's to chase out ghosts, and my grandmother's old prayer beads. The Red Guards rarely missed anything, but, miraculously, they never managed to find Second Grandpa's statue of Jesus. That was their work during the day, and they were even busier when the sun went down. They started each night with a rally to denounce bad elements, and to mobilise the masses to expose their own counterrevolutionary crimes. After that, anyone that had not joined in with enough enthusiasm or whose reactionary crimes seemed serious enough for further attention were dragged into Captain Hu's office for personal interrogation. Those brutal sessions could go all night.

Captain Hu said again and again that his work in our village was going to take a long time. Our village was big, it had a long history, and evil forces had long been given free rein. When it came to feudal superstition, there was the temple on the mountain, the shrine at the village entrance, the ancestral hall, military memorials, and honorific archways for great local men. The KMT's influence in the area had been extensive, too, which made it hard to carry out the work of class struggle after Liberation. Captain Hu told his Red

Guards to prepare themselves for ideological warfare and long-term class struggle. They would be required to endure many hardships in the task of mobilising the revolutionary enthusiasm of the masses, rooting out class enemies, and carrying through to the end the Great Proletarian Cultural Revolution.

XXIII

During Captain Hu's interrogations, there were always people peering in the window or trying to listen in. I was usually there with them. It was the best entertainment we had. Many of those hanging out for the interrogations were also kids that wanted to get into the Red Guard reserve team. They thought of their voyeurism as a revolutionary act, lending support to the Red Guards.

The interrogations always started the same way. Captain Hu would remove his belt, pound on the table, and say: "Our great leader Chairman Mao has told us to carry through the Great Proletarian Cultural Revolution to the end. The full force of this revolution has focused itself on you. You are the enemy of the people. Do you realise that?"

I admired Captain Hu's intimidating routine in the office. He could successfully tame any sort of bad element. The foulest counterrevolutionary would bow their head and answer his questions with complete honesty. When I saw my father being escorted to the office, I was scared. I knew my father had bad-mouthed Captain Hu and called him a "little bastard". I wondered if my cousin had sold him out.

That turned out not to be the case.

Captain Hu had gone through most of the remaining bad elements, but the Colonel had slipped through his net. He had learned that the Colonel had been a KMT officer. Even though he had been set free by the PLA, the Colonel seemed not to have learned his lesson. The Colonel refused to work, and he persisted in a lazy, bourgeois lifestyle. On top of that, his mother was involved in feudal superstition. Those ignorant and backward beliefs seemed to have been passed on to her son. The Colonel and his family were a stumbling block on the revolutionary road. Captain Hu couldn't let that continue. He dispatched Blindboy, the head of the village's Red Guard team, to track down the Colonel and drag him into a struggle session. Blindboy took three of his best men and put them on a twenty-four-hour watch of the Colonel's house. That was why my father had been brought to the office – he had gone to the Colonel's house to feed the cats. Blindboy reported this to Captain Hu, who ordered my father be brought in for questioning. He suspected that my father might know where the Colonel had gone.

Captain Hu was uncharacteristically polite to my father, asking him to take a seat and offering him a cigarette. Watching from the window, I felt like I was dreaming. I couldn't understand how what I was seeing could possibly be real. Later, I found out that it was because my father was from a poor peasant background. People like my father were the ones that supported the Red Guards, so they couldn't afford to mistreat him. Captain Hu very politely asked my father where he could find the Colonel. It was clear that it wouldn't be the usual overnight interrogation.

This time, I knew my father had to be lying. He answered casually, but I thought there was a hint of aggravation in his voice: "How would I know? If I did know," my father said, "I would have gone to see him." My father said more firmly this time, "He said he was going to be gone for a day or so, and he'd be back. He left me a couple dried fish to bring those two cats he keeps. Once they ate those, I went over to the reservoir and caught a couple fish for them. It's been a real pain in the ass."

At that point, I was sure my father knew where the Colonel

was. The story about going to the reservoir was a complete lie! He hadn't caught any fish. It was bullshit! We had plenty of dried fish at home. My father didn't betray any emotion in front of Captain Hu. He was completely calm. I was disappointed to see my father return Captain Hu's kindness with lies. I realised that I was rooting for Captain Hu over the Colonel. It was confusing to me: adults always told kids to tell the truth, but they had no problem lying themselves.

But I had my own reasons for hoping that the Colonel would be interrogated by Captain Hu – I thought I could finally hear all the stories that the Colonel didn't want to tell. I wanted to know why the Colonel and the Old Constable had remained friends. I wanted to know what he had between his legs. I wanted to know where that ten yuan note he gave my father came from. How did he have money, even though he didn't work? Maybe the rest of the kids sitting outside Captain Hu's office were thinking the same thoughts. Maybe Blindboy, Meathook, and Wild One were even more curious than I was.

We got our wish. Blindboy was the one that lured him back with a cruel trick. Only a mean little bastard like Blindboy could have come up with it! He realised that the cats were what would bring the Colonel back. Everyone knew that they were his sweethearts, like children to him, his whole life... The cats were more important to him than anything else. Blindboy got approval from Captain Hu to trap the Colonel's cats. He planned to use the village public address system to broadcast a ransom message, announcing he had seized the cats.

Blindboy trapped the cats and brought them to the school. After the message was broadcast, the Colonel returned, just as they had expected, and went straight for the school to look for the cats. He was carrying a black leather satchel. When Captain Hu searched it, he found a pair of slippers, a facecloth, half a carton of cigarettes, and two aluminium boxes. Inside the first box was a set of gleaming surgical tools, and inside the second were rotten fish bones.

"Arrest him!" Captain Hu shouted.

The Four Mighty Guardians and a gang of skinny Red Guards moved to seize the Colonel. At first, the Colonel tried to evade them. He looked like a cornered cat, batting at them with his big hands. He slapped any Red Guards that got within range, and he managed to knock a few to the floor. From the way they wailed, it looked like it must have hurt. The Red Guards didn't give up, though. They attacked in waves. Even after they were knocked down, they kept fighting. I don't know whether the Colonel was scared or he knew he couldn't beat them, but he eventually stopped fighting. The Red Guards grabbed him and pushed him to the ground.

"Tie him up!" Captain Hu ordered.

But there was no rope. They hadn't had to tie up any of the bad elements taken in for interrogation before. Blindboy glanced around and then had the bright idea to get a length of butcher's twine from the school kitchen. He passed it to Captain Hu. He did the job himself, wrapping it around the Colonel and knotting it. In the few months that he had been part of the revolution, he had tied up quite a few people. He knew exactly what he was doing. He motioned for the Four Guardians to help him, and they led the Colonel out into the village.

XXIV

The Red Guards had led some bad elements through the village before, but this was a special occasion. This time, there were the usual shouted slogans, but also a gong and drum to accompany them. The drummer sometimes drowned out the crashing of the gong, but neither was ever as loud as the howling of the Red Guards. All the birds in the village took to the sky at once and flew towards the hills. It was a grand ceremony to mark the capture of the last bad element. The Red Guards had caught all of their targets. During the previous parades, when the bad elements came by, everyone had solemnly bowed their heads. It was sort of boring, like watching a silent movie. The Colonel was much more fun. He performed for the crowd, cursing at them, straining at the twine, and dodging blows from the Red Guards.

The Colonel always held himself so arrogantly. He walked through the village with his head held high. In the winter, he wore high-top boots with nails in the soles that clattered on the snowy cobblestone like the hooves of a warhorse. To see him reduced to a mangy dog on a leash, a loathsome creature bound and dragged by a gaggle of rowdy students – it was shocking.

Grandpa had come back by that time, and when he saw the Colonel, he shook his head and said, "I think it's hopeless. The Eunuch might not be blameless, but I've never seen him treated this badly by anything... These little bastards are..." – and he had already returned home before he came up with something to end the sentence – "...no better than beasts."

"They're worse," my father said. "They even destroyed the temple."

"Guande Temple stood for two hundred years. Plenty of evil people have looked up at the mountain and seen it standing there, but they left it well enough alone. These wild animals had to go up there and tear it down. Beasts! Swine!" Grandpa cursed the Red Guards for a long time. It was as if he was expelling all the hate that had built up in him – it looked like he thought that if he cursed enough, he might be able to curse them to death.

Grandpa seemed to detest the Colonel, but in this situation, it was clear that he sided with him over Captain Hu and the Red Guards. I was just the opposite. Once again, I couldn't understand adults. I couldn't figure out why older generations could join together so quickly against young people. It was like they were raising us just so they would have someone to fight against. Grandpa, I wanted to ask, don't you see what's really happening? Is a temple being torn down any reason to curse Captain Hu and his Red Guards? Don't you realise that's counterrevolutionary, Grandpa? Do you want to be dragged up on stage and denounced? How can I join the Red Guards if I have a counterrevolutionary in my family? I just couldn't figure out how Grandpa and my father could be so selfish and short-sighted.

While Grandpa was cursing the Red Guards, they were dragging the Colonel back to the school. They looked like orderlies trying to get a straitjacketed madman back into a locked ward. The parade through the village should only have taken about an hour, but it took them far longer to get the Colonel to march his circuit. The Colonel dug in his heels, fought back, and resisted them each step of the way. The sun had already set by the time the parade had ended. Usually, that would have been the end of things. After a struggle session, most of the bad elements were set free. They would go home and eat their dinner and go to bed – back to life as usual. But Captain Hu suspected that the Colonel had not been broken. The Colonel didn't look like a man that had admitted his guilt. Special treatment was required. Captain Hu ordered that he be held there as a prisoner.

Blindboy had been just about to untie the Colonel. He was ready to let him go. But he was happy to hear the command from Captain Hu. "Perfect," Blindboy said. "I'll leave this on him, then."

At that point, Captain Hu wasn't sure exactly where to keep the Colonel locked up. He tipped his head back and stroked his moustache, deep in thought.

Blindboy once again offered the solution: "Lock him up with the cats."

Blindboy had no shortage of cruel ideas, and Captain Hu respected him for it. "Two jackals can share a lair" – I'd just learned the idiom in school that year, and it came to mind when I saw them plotting. But I knew that wasn't an appropriate phrase to describe them, since it was supposed to be derogatory. Blindboy might have been a jackal, but Captain Hu definitely wasn't one. I always thought that Captain Hu would eventually realise that Blindboy was a mean little bastard and kick him out of the group. If he did that, maybe my cousin could take over as the head of the village's Red Guard team.

That was what was on my mind that night as I fell asleep to the familiar sound of Grandpa's snoring, steady as a bellows.

XXV

The Colonel's two cats were locked up in the school's woodshed, which had once housed the shop run by the mistress of the Old Constable. The small shack was full of firewood, but also charcoal briquettes, straw, broken desks and blackboards, and all sorts of other junk that was headed for the fire. There was even a coffin stored in the woodshed, although nobody remembered who had left it there. The place stunk to high heaven. It was the smell of rotting wood and straw, but also the fermentation of piss and shit. The school had a bathroom, but the canteen cook had put a pair of buckets – one for piss, one for shit – in the woodshed. He didn't want to waste anything that he could spread on his own fields later. In a brief time, the cats had picked up the noxious stench of the woodshed, and their fur was blackened from soot and dust.

It was hard to see the cats like that. It was hard to tell the white cat from the black cat, since they were both equally filthy. Each time they flicked their tails, they raised a fresh cloud of dust. The cats had been pampered since they were young. They could never have imagined that one day someone would tie a nylon rope around their necks and drag them in a filthy woodshed to starve. When the Colonel saw them, it was like he was watching his whole world collapse around him. He sobbed. Snot ran down his chin. He cursed everyone and everything. He didn't try to conceal his anger and hatred for those that had put his cats in the woodshed.

Blindboy was mystified. That afternoon, as they had led the Colonel around, he had cursed them and fought back, but he had never cried out, even when he was beaten. The Colonel had resisted but he hadn't complained. Seeing the cats in the woodshed, he couldn't hold back his mad grief. The only thing restraining him was the twine wrapped around him. Blindboy had been looking forward to sitting in on the interrogation. Like all the other kids in the village, Blindboy was curious about the Colonel. He thought that his curiosity might finally be satisfied. Blindboy thought he might be able to get in some of his own questions. But when he saw the Colonel reduced to madness, all thoughts of interrogation evaporated. After he was in the woodshed, Blindboy turned away without saying anything. He looked like he was deserting the fight just as things had turned in his favour.

"Don't go," the Colonel called after him.

"What do you want?" Blindboy said. He was already walking out the door. "Just say it!"

"Let the cats go. If you want to pull me in front of a struggle session, what do you need the cats for?"

Blindboy grunted and said, "Who do you think you are? I don't have to listen to you."

The Colonel turned around and patted his back pocket with his bound hands. The Colonel told him that there was ten yuan in his pocket and Blindboy could take it. He told Blindboy that with ten yuan, he could buy a hog, salt it, and feed his whole family for a year. Blindboy was suspicious, though. He thought that the Colonel might be trying to lure him in close enough to do something to him. The Colonel had military training, after all, and he had only been subdued at the school because he gave up the fight. Blindboy was tempted, but finally, he turned to the Colonel and said, "You think you can buy me off, you fucking eunuch? Just wait until I tell Captain Hu. We'll add bribery to your list of crimes against the revolution."

When Blindboy got back to Captain Hu and told him what had happened, he got another pat on the shoulder.

"We need to mobilise the masses in the struggle!" Captain Hu said. Captain Hu continued in a solemn tone, "To simply drag him in front of a struggle session is not enough. He's an arrogant man, impudent, contaminated by the counterrevolutionary poison of the KMT... We need to harness the power of the dictatorship of the proletariat to cleanse him of that poison. We need to wipe out his power and prestige. I want him to be afraid to lift his head. I want him to think twice before he lets out a fart. He needs to bow down to the masses! I want him to be a slave to the people!"

When Captain Hu had first arrived, I hadn't thought much of him and his skinny arms, but I admired his firm tone, his perfectly standard Mandarin, and his eloquence. I figured it must be because he was a poet. I heard that he carried a thick notebook with him, and when everyone else was asleep, he was writing poetry in it. If they weren't too long, they were sometimes copied onto the blackboard. This was one of them:

> Among the grass, there are weeds
> Among the people, there are enemies
> Some mountains impede the rise of others
> Some people stand in the way of revolution
> Let us climb to the mountaintops

Let us swim in the ocean
Revolution is not a dinner party
The Cultural Revolution is great

The night before Captain Hu left the village, he personally copied this poem onto the wall of the school, facing the highway. Every character in the poem was as big as my father's fist. He wrote it in red on the white wall. You could see it from a long way away. The red was spectacularly bright. It was said that he had mixed blood with the ink – some people said it was chicken blood, or pig blood, and others said it was the fiery blood of Captain Hu himself... Normally, that was the kind of thing people would ask the Colonel about. Not only was he considered one of the most experienced and knowledgeable men in the village, but he had plenty of experience dealing with blood. But the Colonel seemed to have disappeared.

Six

XXVI

But we aren't at that point in the story yet. Let's step back to the Colonel in the filthy woodshed, locked up with his cats, waiting for a tremendous struggle session to begin. While I was eating dinner that night, I heard the girl from the Four Guardians get on the village PA. She told all the villagers to report to the school for a struggle session. Since the Red Guards had arrived, there had been nightly broadcasts like that. The girl from the Four Guardians made the initial announcement, and then Captain Hu would get on to his piece. The message was always about the same: big assembly, everyone should, every household must send at least one adult representative.

The Colonel's struggle session began with the usual overwhelming chorus of slogans from the Red Guards. When the shouting died down, the Colonel was led onto the low stage by a pair of Red Guards that had come from the city. It was only the Colonel being struggled that day. He looked completely alone – not only on stage, but in the world. The Colonel had his hands tied behind his back, and he wore a tall, conical paper hat on which had been written "Enemy of the People" and "Evil Beyond Redemption". There were paper placards hung around his neck, all bearing slogans similar to the ones on the hat. Someone had painted a big red X on his chest, too, as if he was going to be dragged in front of a firing squad after the struggle session.

Captain Hu took to the stage. He began telling the story of how the Colonel had attempted to escape justice at the hands of the masses, and his speech eventually returned to the great victories that the Red Guards had already scored in the revolution. Finally, Captain Hu walked to the centre of the stage and pointed at the Colonel. Filled with righteous indignation, he roared: "Now, we struggle this man, who is guilty of the most heinous crimes. To this very moment, he denies his guilt. He knows exactly what he has done, but he refuses to change his behaviour. He has vowed to fight against the revolutionary masses until the very end. Our great leader Chairman Mao teaches us that the man that confesses to his crimes should receive a lighter sentence, and refusal to confess is grounds for harsher punishment. As for this kind of die-hard bad element, seemingly irrevocably set against the revolution… We must firmly reject their influence. Comrades, what do you say?"

A chant of "Reject! Reject!" started among the Red Guards around the sides and at the bottom of the stage.

The Red Guards raised their arms to pound their fists along with the chant, but only a few hands went up among the rest of the crowd. Captain Hu was disappointed by the response. He took a few steps closer to the edge of the stage and looked out past the phalanx of Red Guards. With his gaze fixed out beyond his devout followers on the broad revolutionary masses, he called again for a response.

Once again, it was disappointing. Beyond the Red Guards, there didn't seem to be many people out in the audience. The revolutionary masses were not being obedient. Captain Hu turned away, disappointed, and began to pace the stage, stroking his moustache. Finally, he lifted his head and walked back to the edge of the stage. He grimaced and wiped sweat from his brow. The gesture was meant to be stern and dignified. Captain Hu began to deliver the most impassioned speech that I had ever heard. Even without the military cross-strap belt around his waist, and the crimson armband, he would still have looked like a revolutionary general. It was an inspiring performance, and you couldn't hear it without being moved.

"Comrades of the commune!" – Captain Hu was shouting over the heads of the Red Guards, waving his arms, his voice droning like a gong – "I must tell you, just now I smelled something. It stunk like a latrine pit. It was a poisonous smell! Do you know what it was? It was the stench of sympathy for class enemies. Where's your class consciousness? The man on this stage is a running dog for KMT reactionaries! When we talk about cow demons and snake spirits – those most evil of evildoers – we are talking about this man! The revolutionary winds have blown across the land, and class enemies are trembling with fear. They gave up their fight! They surrendered. But what about this man? He is absolutely unrepentant. Why do you think that is? Because he has support behind the scenes. He has powerful people backing him! Who are they, you ask? The Kuomintang! Chiang Kai-shek! CIA spies! Soviet revisionists! He thinks they can save him, even still. That's why he will never repent for his crimes against the people. He will fight against us until he draws his last breath. It's a joke, isn't it? It's absurd! Our great leader Chairman Mao teaches us that the world is ours, the future belongs to us, and we will rule the world! The counter revolutionaries are nothing but paper tigers. Down with the paper tigers! Down with Chiang Kai-shek! Down with American imperialism! Down with the KMT reactionaries! Down with the Soviet revisionist Brezhnev!"

The slogans came one after another, like waves crashing on a beach. The birds nesting in the eaves were startled into the sky. The air above the school was full of birds, wheeling madly through the sky. The birds started colliding with the bats that came out every night at dusk. The tiny bats, when they were hit by the flock of birds, started to fall to the ground, hitting people in the crowd and causing a small amount of panic.

XXVII

I had been to all the rallies, but that one was the best. I will never forget it. Captain Hu didn't usually talk that much. He spoke with the force of justice, each phrase ringing out like the crash of a gong. The words flowed out of him. He was absolutely clear and logical. Captain Hu didn't seem like a kid from the county town, or even the provincial capital – but someone straight from Beijing. Even though I respected the Colonel, I liked his stories, and I knew he was close with my father, but I wanted to join the crowd's chants. My mother once told me that her happiest moment was the day the production brigade distributed grain and she loaded it up into a wheelbarrow. Standing in the crowd, chanting down with this or down with that – that was my happiest moment.

After the shouts died down, Captain Hu asked people to come on stage to expose the Colonel's crimes. Blindboy was the first to jump up, followed by Meathook, my cousin, and Wild One. They had been the first in the village to be swept up in the revolutionary wind. They had become the core of Captain Hu's local team. Their status was second only to the Four Guardians. In private, we called them the Four Little Guardians.

After the Four Little Guardians had finished denouncing the Colonel, Captain Hu called on members of the commune to take the stage and continue the struggle.

Captain Hu tried to encourage the crowd: "Don't be afraid. Say whatever comes to mind. If there's been an injustice, let's sort it out now. If you bear a grudge, we can deal with it. If revenge is what you want, you will get it. We need to get to the bottom of his case. I don't care if it's financial, or historical, or political, or something else. We will uncover all of his crimes. This is a revolution and a revolution is not a dinner party. Revolution is merciless. Revolution is struggle. We need to unmask our enemies. We need to let the whole world see their true colours."

The crowd did not stir. They pretended not to have heard. There was complete silence when the Captain finished. He wasn't discouraged. He kept going, using every oratorical trick in his arsenal, coaxing and cajoling his audience, then baiting and goading them. Finally, someone stepped from the crowd. It was the Old Constable. He was already in his seventies, but his back was still ramrod straight. He could still eat a roast chicken and drain a *jin* of *shaojiu* in a single sitting. Grandpa was always saying he was jealous of the Old Constable for staying in shape. I heard them one time, talking in the ancestral hall...

"Old Perv," Grandpa said to him, "you're a year younger than me."

"Goddammit, Sorcerer," he swore back at him, "you've held that over my head our whole lives, that you're a year older than me! You're a bully."

"Bullshit I did," Grandpa said. "You used your rank. It was the other way around – you were bullying me."

"I wasn't the constable most of that time, was I? You were the bully."

"Well, even if I was, those days are over. I can barely bend over to pick something up off the ground. By next year, I'll probably be bedridden." Grandpa pounded his lower back and sighed sadly. "I'm old. I'm an old man. You look at least twenty years younger than me."

"I wish that were true," the Old Contable said, chuckling. "But I'll tell you, when I get a girl in bed, I feel like I'm twenty years younger."

I remember another time, too, over at the mill... Grandpa and I were threshing rice. I was running the machine and Grandpa was scooping the unhusked rice out of an old sack. My job was quite easy, since all I had to do was twist a handle. But I was only eleven years old, so I tired out quickly, and my hands started to hurt. I was dripping with sweat. Grandpa told me to keep going. I held on for a while, but my strength finally gave out, and I sat down on the ground. Just then, the Old Constable was walking by. He called out in a sing-song voice: "The harder you work, the stronger you'll get. The more a little girl rubs her tits, the bigger they'll get."

"Ya Old Perv!" Grandpa said. "Don't go around talking like that." Grandpa took a couple stalks of unhusked rice and smacked him.

"I thought I was helping," the Old Constable said, chuckling.

"He's just a kid," Grandpa said. "Watch your mouth."

"He might be a kid, but we're old enough. If I don't shoot my mouth off now, pretty soon I won't be able to. I was telling the boy the truth. But once you get old, it's different. Every ounce of strength is precious. I'm not wasting it on anybody but a woman."

That's just how the Old Constable was. He couldn't go more than three sentences without mentioning girls, fucking, or tits. He was the Old Perv and his nickname was well-earned. Grandpa used to say that the Old Constable had treated women so poorly that he'd be reborn as a mule – it sounded bad, but I didn't fully comprehend the curse. Grandpa cursed people in his own way. He cursed at a high level. The Old Constable cursed at a low level. They each mastered their own form. Just like Captain Hu had mastered his: preaching revolution.

XXVIII

That's what Captain Hu was doing on stage at the struggle session for the Colonel. The Old Constable was walking to the stage to join him. The Old Constable's usually steady appearance was gone, and it looked like he had been drinking. The way he walked, it looked like he was about to fall down. He leaned one way and then the next. When he faced the audience, his face was red and his voice was hoarse.

Liquor had given him courage and loosened his tongue. "I want to say a few words," he slurred, pausing to pick snot out of his nose. The aroma of booze rolled off him. He didn't bother with the microphone that was offered to him, but he was loud enough that even the people in the back could hear him. "Just now, Captain Hu said, 'Say whatever comes to mind.' These Red Guards said their piece, so let me say mine."

The Old Constable made sense at first, but he slowly went off the rails. He drifted from topic to topic. He sounded like one of the old ladies gossiping at the ancestral hall. He started out okay, but he eventually moved into territory that was either completely irrelevant or seemed contradictory to the message of the struggle session. Captain Hu and the other Red Guards began to get angry.

"What I want to say is," the Old Constable slurred, "these little bastards have got it all wrong." Blindboy and the Four Guardians were not impressed with his choice of words, but the Old Constable hadn't meant anything by it. "They said he slept with my woman. That's not true at all. That's a load of crap. Everyone knows that. You ask any stray dog and they'll tell you. He couldn't do it. He's a goddamn eunuch. How do you expect a eunuch to fuck a woman? It's impossible. Don't slander him. One of you guys said he was in the KMT, right? That's true. How do you think he got the nickname, the 'Colonel'? Because he was an officer in the KMT. But that doesn't mean he's a reactionary or a counterrevolutionary! He once saved the life of a senior PLA cadre. Would a reactionary do that?"

The Old Constable burped and the force of it seemed to knock him back a step. When he steadied himself, his voice was even more forceful: "Even if he was a reactionary before he saved the guy, he wasn't after that! Take me, for example... You know who put me in charge? The collaborators! My family used to be rich. We owned half the farmland in this village. But after Liberation, when the Communists decided our status, I was categorised as a 'farm worker'. I was one of two given that status. How did that happen? My family was rich, right? But I lost all that money long before they ever came to divide us up. I gambled it all away. I staked my house as collateral and had to live in the ancestral hall. I had to go to the temple and steal whatever people offered at the altar. I was as poor as any of the people they called 'poor peasants'. So, when they gave us our status, I was called a 'farm worker'. If they had come along a few years earlier, I would have been called a 'big landlord'. I should have been shot! But they didn't. They were reasonable. They saw how poor I was. They saw that I was homeless, nearly starving to death... They gave me clothes, a blanket, and something to eat. If not for them, I wouldn't be here today. I've got plenty to eat and plenty to drink! So, quit talking about what he was – talk about what he did later! He saved the life of a senior cadre, he fought against the KMT and the American bastards. Look at the man's entire life. That's the Communist Party way."

The Old Constable turned to face Captain Hu. "You want to talk about what went on back then?" he asked. "If you want to talk about that, then you better lock me up, too. Look at what the man did with the rest of his life. Let him go."

"Let him go?" Captain Hu thundered. He started removing his belt, thinking he could scare the Old Constable.

"What's going on here?" the Old Constable said. "You

want to start slapping people around?" He was unmoved by Captain Hu's attempt at intimidation. "Let me tell you something, you little bastard... If you lay a finger on me, I'll get the Communist Party on your case. They'll let you rot in prison! The Communist Party protects people like me. The Communist Party are the only people that make any sense. I listen to them. Everything I just said, it comes from the Party. If you want to get up on stage and talk a bunch of bullshit, that's fine with me, but I'm going to start digging into your background, and we'll see what comes up. I'll go back eight generations and see what you came from. Are you a farm worker? I read in the paper that only a farm worker can denounce a farm worker – even the poor and lower-middle-class peasants aren't allowed!" He walked to the front of the stage. "Comrades," he said, "is anything I just said untrue?" While he spoke, the crowd had begun to grow restless, muttering to themselves, and his call from the front of the stage ignited them.

The majority of the crowd called back: "You're right!" After that, the Red Guards completely lost their audience. They broke into excited murmuring, laughter, and chitchat. Eventually, a few people walked out, each followed by a few more, until nearly everyone was leaving.

When Captain Hu saw where things were headed, he snatched back the microphone and ordered the assembly adjourned.

XXIX

I wasn't happy. I had been enjoying the struggle session. It was a shame to see it break down into chaos halfway through.

I went home and was feeding the rabbits I kept in the pigpen when Clubfoot's grandson Stumpy Tiger ran up.

"The Colonel escaped," he said. "They're going to hang him. Captain Hu wants to send a message. Everyone's going to watch."

Apart from my cousin, Stumpy Tiger was my best friend in school. Whenever I got into trouble, I was usually with him. We were like brothers.

When I heard a bunch of people were going to see the Colonel, I had to go, too. I finished feeding the rabbits and followed Stumpy Tiger. We ran towards the school as fast as we could. There was only one tree there, and it had died the year before, so it was completely bare. There wasn't much moonlight, but we could tell that there was nobody hanging there.

"We must be too late," Stumpy Tiger said. He didn't want me to think he'd brought me there for nothing, so he wanted me to climb up and look for a noose. Before we could do that, we heard a horrible yowling sound. It was followed by another tortured feline squeal, as if two cats were fighting. I understood immediately what had happened. I knew what Captain Hu was going to do to send a message. He was going to target the thing the Colonel loved the most.

I thought of another idiom I had learned at school that year: "like carving my heart with a knife". It meant to feel a pain like a knife being twisted in your heart. I figured the Colonel must be experiencing exactly that.

Stumpy Tiger had been right about one thing: a lot of people had come out to watch. We followed the sound of the yowling in the direction of the canteen. There was a crowd gathered in front of the woodshed that the Colonel and his cats had been locked up inside. They were crowded around, hooting and yelling, like they had cornered a wild boar. We didn't have to sneak up on them, because nobody would have noticed us coming, anyways. When we got closer, we realised there were no adults among them, only Red Guards. There were about twenty or thirty altogether. They had something cornered, but it wasn't a wild boar – it was the Colonel. He was wrapped like a *zongzi*, bound with twine, and was being hung up from the ceiling of the shed.

While the Red Guards were still working on securing the Colonel from the rafters, Captain Hu was already slipping off his belt. He motioned for the Red Guards to give him room, then, in a well-rehearsed performance, he swung the belt around his head twice. The third time the belt came around, it connected firmly with the Colonel.

Crack! Crack! Crack! It was a clear, sharp sound, like a piece of bamboo snapping in a fire.

Captain Hu cursed the Colonel while he beat him: "You think you can run? The Red Guards are everywhere. You can run to the ends of the earth and we'll be there. You can't escape us. Let's see if you run again after I break your legs. If you run, we'll get you. And we'll beat you again! Beat you, and beat you, and beat you..."

Crack!

Crack!

Crack! I thought about that night a lot, and I always remembered that horrible sound. I remember how Captain Hu was panting from exertion, but the Colonel was completely silent. The two cats were not as dignified. Each time their master was struck, the two cats yowled, as if they could feel each blow. It was impossible, of course, but somehow it seemed like the cats were absorbing the Colonel's pain. They were an unusual pair of cats, but I didn't think they had that power. While the cats cried out in pain, the Colonel convulsed, and he would grit his teeth or open his mouth about to scream. Blood dripped to the floor below him. There was no doubting the ferociousness of the beating. But he didn't make a sound, not even a groan or a sigh. He looked like a scarecrow having the hay beaten out of it. I'll never forget that. His eyes were still very much alive, gleaming in the gloom, and seeming to glow even brighter with each blow he received. They looked like cat's eyes.

I don't know what would have happened if my father hadn't led Clubfoot, the Old Constable, Grandpa, and a bunch of other older folks in the village to stop the beating. Would he have beaten the Colonel to death? Was it considered murder to kill a KMT counterrevolutionary? That night, I started to feel uneasy about Captain Hu and what he had done. I once again feared him, and did my best to avoid him, hoping that he would leave the village. Grandpa said: "For his next eight lifetimes, he'll be peeling his skin off on a rock." I knew Grandpa meant that he would be reborn as a snake, the lowest, most hateful creature in existence, cursed to crawl around blindly on its belly, making meals of mice and corpses...

Seven

XXX

The morning after, I learned two more things.

The first was that the Colonel hadn't returned home that night. My father said it while his face was still buried in his rice bowl. I kept washing my face, trying to figure out what it meant. Was he still in the woodshed? That would mean that Captain Hu wanted to torture him some more. Had he been shot? My father had intended the comment for Grandpa, hoping the old man might be able to use his seniority to get some answers. Grandpa made use of the right that all elderly people have, which is to feign confusion.

The second piece of news came from the Old Constable. My father had invited him over for lunch. My father passed the Old Constable a pack of cigarettes and asked him to take some food over to the school. Because of the Old Constable's status, and his class background, he would have the best chance of being given access to the Colonel. The Old Constable agreed and left, carrying the bundle of food my father had prepared. He reappeared a short time later, still carrying the food.

"Motherfuckers," the Old Constable swore, shaking a cigarette out of his pack. "They've got it in for me now. The little bastards wouldn't even let me in." He lit the cigarette and took a long drag. "What's this goddamn world coming to? The lunatics are running the asylum. They were threatening to slap me around again. They missed their chance yesterday, and they weren't getting it today. I had to run out of there. These old legs saved me again." He erupted into a fit of coughing that left him even redder in the face. "Bring me something to drink. Pour me some tea." He took a long drink and continued, "I don't know if it's true or not, but on the way back, I heard Phoenix Blossom saying the Moustache" – he was referring to Captain Hu – "is supposed to be headed out later this afternoon, or he might be gone already."

If that turned out to be true, it would be good news for the Colonel. The source of the information was Phoenix Blossom. The Old Constable considered the news to be reliable, since her son – Wild One – was one of the Four Little Guardians. My father hoped it was true, but it was up to me to confirm it for him. He went to a cupboard beside the stove and produced two pieces of candy wrapped in wax paper.

"You go over to the school," my father said, pressing the candy into my hand. "I want you to find out if the Moustache is gone or not."

Before leaving, he suddenly bent down to kiss me on the forehead. He had never done that before. And then he hurried me out the door.

I ran so fast it felt like I barely touched the ground. The kiss had given me wings. That spot in the middle of my forehead had always felt like it was missing something. It prickled and itched. But maybe my father knew all along how to soothe it. When I finally ran into my cousin, I felt like my heart was going to jump out of my throat. I was worried he would tell me that Captain Hu was still there. I didn't want to disappoint him.

And I wouldn't have to.

My cousin said that Captain Hu and the Four Mighty Guardians had left minutes before I arrived. There were two theories as to why they had suddenly decamped: the first was that they were going to report the situation with the Old Constable, since there was no precedent for denouncing someone of his class background siding with a counterrevolutionary, and the second was that they just needed a shower and a change of clothes. With the second theory, there seemed to be some issue with the female member of the Four Mighty Guardians...

But, anyways, once I heard about Captain Hu leaving, I snuck over to the junior high classroom, where Stumpy Tiger and some other kids were eavesdropping outside the window. Blindboy was reading a newspaper to the assembled Red Guards. With Captain Hu and the Four Mighty Guardians gone, Blindboy was in charge. The Four Little Guardians had replaced the Four Mighty Guardians. Blindboy was following the schedule left behind by Captain Hu, so Blindboy was leading a political study session. That was why he was reading the newspaper. The Red Guards that were not already snoring were fighting to keep their eyes open, looking like they were on the verge of dropping off to sleep.

All the kids waiting outside the classroom eventually got tired of listening and left.

It started to rain a bit. The school was mysteriously quiet. A pair of jet-black crows squawked in the dead tree. The previous week, it had felt like we were living in a propaganda poster. Our lives had resembled the slogan we chanted: "The Four Seas boil with anger, the Five Continents shake with excitement." At that moment, though, the Four Seas were deathly still, and there was no seismic activity on the Five Continents. It was a nice change. It was quiet and cool, with the Red Guards dozing in the classroom, and the rain chasing the heat away. The revolutionary wind had blown through, chasing off anyone that would tell us where to go or what to do. We were the swaggering masters of the campus.

I asked Stumpy Tiger if he wanted to go check on the Colonel. I saw how he had been beaten the night before, so I knew he must be a mess. I was scared to go by myself, but I didn't want a bunch of people around, either. We slipped out of the bathroom, where we had taken shelter, and headed for the woodshed. As we left shelter, the rain came crashing down, raising a cloud of steam and dust. The two crows in the dead tree were startled and flew away. We ran through the rain like it was gunfire, shrieking the whole way to the woodshed.

XXXI

After the Old Constable's mistress abandoned her shop and ran off, there was no reason that it should have been abandoned to become a woodshed. It was in a good location, right by the school, and it had been well-built. But it had been contaminated. Nobody had much use for it, knowing who had lived there. The Old Constable had dumped his meagre savings into building what would eventually become a woodshed. It had fallen into disrepair over the years. The windows had been busted out. The door had fallen off its hinges and been replaced by a sheet of bamboo rods, like the kind people used for their pigpens. I didn't think there was any way to lock it, but when we got up to the door, we saw a rusty padlock had been jammed through. That must have been to keep the Colonel inside.

There was a big window at the front, where the Old Constable's mistress had her counter. She would stand in the window, taking money, and getting whatever people asked for. That type of window is too big to put glass in, but there was a groove in the counter, so you could slide a slatted shutter across it. The groove had long since rotted away, and some of the slats in the shutter had disappeared, too, so kids our size could have slid inside. I'd heard that the Colonel had tried to escape that way the night before. His cats had ruined his plan, though. He got them out between the slats, but they had uncharacteristically disobeyed his commands and gone running to catch a pair of mice that were loitering beside the latrine buckets left by the canteen cook. The cats were hungry from a couple days in the woodshed, so they thought they'd eat a quick meal after getting their freedom. That was why they had started beating the Colonel that night.

Crack!

Crack!

Crack! That was the sound that was ringing in my ears as I approached the front window. The missing slats in the shutter had been reinforced with scrap wood from the woodshed. The whole thing had been filled with nails, hammered in seemingly at random. There was a length of nylon cord left tied up under the eaves, and it looked like it might have the Colonel's blood still on it. Stumpy Tiger and I stretched out across the windowsill to try to get a look inside, but it was too dark to see anything. It smelled like a whole brood of rats had been left to rot inside.

We weren't the type of kids to be put off by a bad smell. We kept trying to see if there was anything moving in the woodshed. But the Colonel seemed to be gone.

Meow!

It was just a cat, but it scared us both so bad, we fell from the windowsill. It was like hearing a ghost calling out to us from inside the darkness. We got back up to listen and heard what sounded like a yawn. Suddenly a voice was calling me. I knew it was the Colonel.

"What do you want?" I asked.

"Get in here," the Colonel said. "I want you to take these cats. Give them to your father."

"The door's locked."

"Just bust it off," the Colonel said.

I found a rock and gave it to Stumpy Tiger along with one of the pieces of candy. He took the rock but he wouldn't take the candy. Stumpy Tiger held the rock in his hand for a long time, staring at the sky. Finally, he tossed the rock to the ground and said, "I can't do it. Captain Hu is going to be back eventually."

From the darkness came the sound of the Colonel's laughter. "What the hell is he the captain of? He's never even held a pistol. I wouldn't even have let him be one of my orderlies."

"You had orderlies?" Stumpy Tiger asked. He had gone back to the front window.

"I had a few," the Colonel said. "I had one to wipe the sweat off my forehead, one to wash my hands, one to put my shoes on for me, and another to wash my clothes." He started laughing again. He seemed to be in a good mood.

"Were you injured?" I asked.

"I've been in more battles than I can count. I've taken more bullets than you've eaten sweet potatoes. What do you mean, was I injured? Of course I was. My body is one big injury. I'm full of shrapnel."

"I mean last night," I said. "Did you get hurt? I saw them beating you."

"Did you see the arms on that little pussy? I barely felt a thing."

"But you were bleeding."

"Superficial wounds," the Colonel said. "You ever chase a chicken out of the yard with a broom? If it loses a couple feathers, would you call that an injury? When someone says 'injury', I assume that they mean flesh wounds and broken bones. That mutt has barely enough strength in him to scratch my back." The Colonel broke out into laughter again, then gleefully sang a folk opera, accompanying himself with sound effects to mimic the drums and gongs. He really did seem to be in a great mood.

I put my eye to a crack in the bamboo door and peered inside. His singing seemed to have dispelled the darkness. I could see the Colonel in one corner of the woodshed. His hands were still tied behind his bed. Two cats were curled up between his legs. I saw their eyes beaming back at me. I could see the cords still tied around their necks.

"It's too bad," the Colonel said, "I used to have a black cat and a white cat, and now I've got a pair of black cats. Whitey already turned black. Say hello to him, Whitey." One of the cats meowed. "And, Blackie, you, too." The other cat meowed. "You can hear it in their voices, can't you? They aren't taking this well." I watched him bend down so that he could stroke them with his chin.

"Are they sick?" I asked.

"They're homesick. I have to get them out of here. This place is filthy. They can't handle it."

I thought it was an impossible request. With Captain Hu gone, Blindboy was in charge, and locking up the cats had been his idea in the first place. There was no way he would agree to let them go. I knew what kind of kid Blindboy was. He was the meanest kid in the whole school. I told the Colonel what the situation was, but he didn't seem worried. He told me to go and get Blindboy.

"I'll have him wrapped around my little finger," the Colonel said, "just like these cats." He chuckled to himself. "You don't believe me? You'll see. The cats will be going home tonight."

I figured the beating must have knocked something loose in his head and he was just talking nonsense. When I got home, I didn't bother telling Grandpa about the cats. But I told him about the Colonel singing and laughing in the woodshed. I wanted to know why. Grandpa's haemorrhoids were bothering him, and he wasn't in the mood to talk. All he said was: "Whatever could make him feel bad, he's already felt bad about, so there isn't much left…" I wasn't really sure what that meant.

XXXII

That evening, when I saw my cousin appear at the door with the two cats, I felt like I was dreaming. I was shocked. I thought I was hallucinating it, until the two cats darted past me, meowing, and stroking their tails on my ankles as they went. I felt like I was going to cry. I was overjoyed. Even though it was just the Colonel's cats free from the woodshed, it felt more like seeing two members of my own family being released from prison.

The two cats recognised my father, so they went to him right away. They circled him, looking up at him, and my father spoke to them like the Colonel would: "Are you two hungry?" They bent down to lick the tops of his feet, as if they were about to feast on his toes. "You two must have got hungry in there." He called for my mother to make the cats something to eat.

I asked my cousin what had happened, but he wanted to talk to Grandpa and my father. "We're going to interrogate the Eunuch," my cousin said, "but we agreed to his one condition. The cats are free to go. He said he wouldn't talk to us, unless the cats were dropped off here. He said we could beat him to death but he wouldn't say anything. So, here they are."

"You're going to beat him again?" my father asked.

"The best thing for him now would be for you to go and talk to him," my cousin said. "Tell him not to prolong things. We want the truth from him."

"That man is capable of many things," Grandpa said, "but telling the truth is not one of them."

"Now that the cats are here," my father said, "you don't have anything to hold over his head. You won't get anything out of him."

"We'll beat it out of him, then," my cousin said.

"Don't do it," my father said. I couldn't tell for sure, but it seemed like my cousin nodded slightly. My father went over to him and said solemnly, "What do you think it means that he gave me the cats? It means I'm the person he trusts more than anyone. I'm the closest person he's got. If you slap him, if you beat him up, that's the same as beating up me. If you do that, if you raise your hand against your own uncle, I'll destroy you."

Grandpa cut in and said: "A man ties a length of cord around his waist to keep his pants up, and he can't complain, since it does the job, and it didn't cost much, anyways... But then the government comes around and gives him plenty to eat and a nice play to stay, and they give him a belt, too. Pretty soon, that length of cord doesn't look so fancy, anymore." As Grandpa went on, his voice became louder and harsher. "I've been telling you for a long time to steer clear of Blindboy. It's too late now. The pair of you are stuck together like a couple lumps of snot. Sooner or later, you'll get what's coming to you."

The Old Constable used to call my mother a scaredy-cat. Even when she was forty, she acted like a fourteen-year-old girl, blushing every time she opened her mouth to say something. My father was like a tiger – he could roar, but he was content to keep his mouth shut most of the time. Grandpa was the one that liked to talk. He didn't mind being the bearer of bad news, and he was content talking about happier things, too. That night, the way he talked to my cousin, it was something different. It hit my cousin like a flash-flood, soaking him all the way through. He left without saying a word, and I could tell by the way he walked that all the fight had gone out of him.

I chased after my cousin and walked with him for a while. I wanted to comfort him. I could feel the anger and pain radiating from him. I wasn't sure what to say, so I just made small talk. I babbled away but he didn't seem to be listening. I could tell that he was quickening his pace. And then he seemed to erupt. At first it was just curses, but then he said, "They're all insane! Can you imagine, treating a class enemy like your own flesh and blood? They've lost their minds. They have no class consciousness, no revolutionary mindset, and it's going to come back on us. I'll never be the head of the village's Red Guard team, and you'll never even make the team in the first place. I might even be branded a counterrevolutionary."

We walked in silence for the rest of the way. His bad mood was infectious. It felt like we were walking in a funeral procession. The moon rose overhead but there was not enough light to pierce the darkness of the alley. It was so dark that I could barely see the ground I was walking on. The only sound in the world seemed to be from our heels on the cobblestones and their echo answering back from the walls. When we stepped out of the alley and onto the highway, the moon seemed to glow even brighter, lighting up the gravel road like it was a sunny day. My cousin finally spoke again. "Captain Hu might not be here," he said. "But we're going to get something out of the Eunuch tonight."

XXXIII

The "we" my cousin was referring to was the Red Guards. They had assembled in the classroom that Blindboy had used that afternoon for the political study session. Sprinkled among them were kids like me, too young to join the Red Guards, and others that just wanted to watch. Blindboy was the podium at the front of the class. There were too many people to even get inside, so I had to stand way at the back, with all the other late arrivals, trying to peer in the classroom window, and straining to hear what was said.

As I was standing there, a rush of excitement swept through the crowd and they parted to make way for someone to get in the door. It turned out to be the Colonel. He was led through the crowd by Meathook and Wild One. He was greeted by Red Guards shouting slogans. They were the same slogans as usual – down with this or down with that. Even though there weren't as many people at the school that night as had been at the rallies, the chanting seemed even louder because it was bouncing off the walls of the classroom. It was nearly deafening.

While the Red Guards chanted their slogans, everyone else tried to get into a better position to watch the show.

I managed to get right against the window. I could see and hear everything going on in the classroom. I could tell that the Colonel seemed to have lost weight. His forehead and his eyes looked bigger. His eyes weren't bright anymore. The gleam was gone. I noticed something else: there were black smudges all over his face. When I looked closer, I saw that he was covered in grey and black marks, each roughly the size of a prune.

I realised they had to be paw prints.

The Colonel was led to the podium, his hands still tied behind his back. His white shirt had been blackened by the paws of the cats and the dust of the woodshed, so that he almost blended into the blackboard at the front of the classroom. Someone had written on the blackboard: "Jiang Zhengnan Denunciation Rally."

I guessed that must be the Colonel's real name – Jiang Zhengnan – but I'd never heard him called that before. On that night, nobody would address him as the Colonel, either, for obvious reasons. On that night, he was the Eunuch, a monstrous beast, a KMT spy, a paper tiger... It got ugly fast, with the crowd jeering the Colonel, and Blindboy fighting to maintain order. When it was time to denounce him, everyone seemed to get up at once. Blindboy tried to get people to come up, one by one, but nobody paid any attention to him. Captain Hu had given Blindboy his authority, but with the leader gone, he was just another Red Guard. Wild One got up and started arguing with Blindboy, and that was the end of it. Blindboy called the meeting to a close and started leading the Colonel out of the classroom.

We crowded around Blindboy as he led his captive out, and eventually his path was blocked. Blindboy yelled at the crowd to disperse, and he tried pushing the Colonel through them. The Colonel refused to move. He turned back to Blindboy and said: "I want to go home. My clothes are dirty. I want to go home and change."

"Go home?" Blindboy asked. He was in a bad mood already, and he took it all out on the Colonel. He pushed him hard. "I'll put you in the ground first."

"As long as I can change my clothes. You have to bury people in clean clothes. Go home and ask your father about that."

"Clean clothes? That's not your problem," Blindboy said with venom. "You need to scrub your brain."

The Colonel was going to continue arguing with Blindboy, but, when he saw me, he stopped. "I want you to tell your father to bring me a set of fresh clothes," he told me. "He knows where my stuff is." It sounded like a command. He was talking to me like we were related.

My heart was pounding. I was blushing. I felt like everyone was looking at me. I wanted to say, "I'm not doing it," but I couldn't manage to speak. The Colonel fixed his gaze on me and I couldn't look away. I saw the old glint in his eye return for a moment. I started to feel dizzy. I still couldn't speak. I wanted to shrink myself down and slide into a crack in the wall. It was Blindboy that saved me, forcing the Colonel forward, into the crowd.

Blindboy surprised me by turning back and saying, "It's fine. You can go get him the clothes. Anyways, it's like Captain Hu said at the struggle session: your father has no class consciousness. Even if he is helping him, he doesn't know what he's doing." He paused, and I thought he was going to reconsider, but he said, "You bring the clothes, though. I don't want him here. If it wasn't for him showing up last night, we would've already got a confession out of this bastard."

I thought Blindboy had saved me, but all he had done was drag me further into things. I felt even more like I was being stared at. I wanted to scream, I wanted to cry, I wanted to slap someone, I wanted to do something... But I had no choice. I turned without speaking. I felt the weight of a million eyes were on me. My knees felt as if they were about to buckle. I didn't know shame could weigh so much that it could break someone.

XXXIV

My father went to the Colonel's place and collected a change of clothes. He packed it into my schoolbag, along with a bottle of liniment and two packs of cigarettes. He told me to hurry up and go straight to the school, but I didn't listen. I went to get Stumpy Tiger. I was too shy to go back by myself.

When we got to the school, I was surprised to find that there was nobody guarding the door. I wondered if the Red Guard sentry usually posted there had just wandered off, or if he'd been told to stand down. I had no way of knowing. But the schoolyard was empty, too, and the classroom was dark. The place seemed deserted. It was a creepy feeling, as if it had just been hit by some sort of natural disaster.

"Where is everyone?" I asked Stumpy Tiger.

"They must have gone home," he said. "Nobody was listening to Blindboy."

"But Captain Hu put him in charge," I said.

"Do you know why? Blindboy gave him a cigarette. That's how it started. After that, Blindboy was always buying him cigarettes."

"Really?" I asked. I was sceptical.

"I saw it myself!" Stumpy Tiger said. "Twice!" Since Stumpy Tiger's family ran the only shop in town, I figured he must know.

That made me like Captain Hu even less. I felt cheated. I felt a sudden sympathy for the Colonel, and I regretted how I had thought of him for the previous couple days. I hugged the schoolbag to my chest and quickened my pace. I didn't want anything to happen to the clothes that had been entrusted to me. I didn't want the Colonel to have to go around like a beggar. Everywhere was dark, and there was nobody around, so Stumpy Tiger and I decided to look for the Colonel in the woodshed.

The door of the woodshed was slightly open, and a stray dog was inside, eating some leftover food. The dog was spooked by our arrival. He ran out of the woodshed and hung around outside, watching us. He seemed to be waiting for us to leave. Stumpy Tiger picked up a stick and went to get revenge on him for scaring us.

Stumpy Tiger earned his nickname because he was as ferocious as his namesake, even if he was short. He wasn't afraid of anything. He'd pick up a rattlesnake by the neck.

He chased the dog to the edge of the schoolyard, where it snuck through a crack in the wall. When he got back to the woodshed, he said, "I saw a light up there, in the principal's office, the one Captain Hu took over. Blindboy must be interrogating him."

"Or they're just beating him up," I said. "Captain Hu told them before he left that they could slap him around, if he didn't tell them the truth." I quoted Grandpa, "He's capable of many things, but telling the truth is not one of them." I was really starting to worry about the Colonel. I knew that Blindboy was just waiting for an excuse to lay into him.

The had two wings jutting out from a central rectangular building. There was a series of pillars in the main walkway, made out of granite. Every year, they collected curse words and dirty jokes, and the principal would choose a few students to scrub them off with lime. The pillars had become a mottled blue-grey over time, but they looked impressive in the moonlight. The principal's office was at the end of the walkway. The door to the office had not been shut tightly, so we could hear everything being said inside. Stumpy Tiger and I couldn't resist the temptation to eavesdrop. We didn't want to be discovered, so we stepped back and sat down behind the last pillar before the doorway to the office. Blindboy was questioning the Colonel, who seemed to be in a candid mood. He answered every question that Blindboy asked. It was fascinating, and we strained our ears so that we wouldn't miss anything.

Eight

XXXV

"According to reports we've received" – it was the voice of Blindboy, coming from behind the door – "you receive yearly stipends to conduct covert operations. You also travel frequently to meet with other spies."

"Bullshit! Bullshit! Bullshit!" That was the Colonel's voice, louder and clearer than Blindboy's own. "That's the stinkiest load of bullshit I've ever heard. I'll tell you again: I'm not a spy, I've never met with any spies, and nobody's paying me to do anything for them." It sounded like the Colonel was probably facing the door, so Blindboy must have his back to the door.

"If nobody's paying you, and you don't work, then where do you get your money from? It looks like you lead a pretty comfortable lifestyle."

"Who said I don't work? I'm always working."

"I've never seen you out on the fields," Blindboy said. "Even if you did want to, we didn't find any equipment or tools at your house."

"So, if I don't go dig in the field, I'm not working? What about your father? Was he a farmer? He had his own ways of making money, didn't he?"

Blindboy's father was called the Blind Man. He was blind in both eyes and walked with a cane. He made a living mostly by being a big talker.

"My family's broke," Blindboy said.

"You don't look like you're starving," the Colonel said.

"I don't even eat as well as your cats do."

"Me neither," the Colonel said and laughed. "I treat those cats the same way your father treats you: I go hungry and all the treats go to them."

"Why do you treat them like that?"

"It's like I said, a father-and-son relationship... They're like my children."

"My dad tells people's fortunes for money," Blindboy said. "What do you do to make money?"

"Look in that satchel you took from me. It's right there on the desk. What's inside there is how I make money."

"What's inside?"

"Open it up," the Colonel said.

"What is this stuff?"

"Those are my 'equipment and tools'. That's how I make a living. Those are the tools of my trade. I save lives. If I was a fucking spy, don't you think I'd have a pistol in there, at least, and probably some bullets, too, maybe a knife?"

"You probably hid those things at home," Blindboy said.

"Then get someone to go search it. If you find anything like that, feel free to put me in front of a firing squad."

"We will search your house. We're just waiting for Captain Hu to get back."

"You might as well go look now," the Colonel said. "Go search for yourself, then let me go home."

"You're dreaming. All you need to do right now is answer my questions truthfully."

"I'm happy to answer each and every question with complete honesty, but I need you to untie me first."

"Don't play games with me," Blindboy said. "We had an

agreement." From outside the room, we heard Blindboy's chair creak, as if he was straightening himself up. "A man that confesses to his crimes will receive a lighter sentence, and refusal to confess is grounds for harsher punishment! Captain Hu told me before he left that I was within my rights to beat a confession out of you. It wouldn't be considered a crime."

"First of all, I haven't lied to you once. I'd love to answer your questions. But it's painful having my hands tied up like this. I can't focus. If I can't focus, I can't answer your questions truthfully. Second, if you want to beat me up, go ahead. It's not like I've never been beaten up before. And anyways, didn't we agree to all of this beforehand?"

"When the hell did I ever agree to that?" Blindboy demanded.

"You agreed to have somebody get me a change of clothes. Therefore, you agreed that I could change into those clothes. And therefore, you agreed to untie me. It's not like I could get dressed with my hands tied behind my back, right? Not to mention, I need to go to the bathroom. You're not going to forbid that, are you? Even Captain Hu let me take a break yesterday."

XXXVI

They went back and forth for a while, but the Colonel finally agreed that he wouldn't attempt to escape, and Blindboy agreed to take him to the bathroom. In the time between untying him to the time they led him out, Stumpy Tiger and I had more than enough time to hide out in a classroom. The darkness in the classroom matched my mood.

I was trying to figure out two things...

Where was my cousin and the rest of them? I could

understand the regular Red Guards not being present, but the Four Little Guardians being dismissed was unthinkable. But how could they just wander off? What would Captain Hu think? He'd be furious of course. Later, I learned that they were still in the school, but they were over in the canteen. Captain Hu had the habit of working until dawn, and he would usually eat a big meal late at night. So, my cousin, Meathook, and Wild One had decided to prepare a feast for themselves in his absence. Blindboy had extorted some salted pork and bamboo shoots out of a former landlord's wife, and Meathook had stolen some *shaojiu* from home. The feast was set to commence when the interrogation of the Colonel was complete.

The other thing I was trying to figure out was why the Colonel hadn't escaped. Now that he was alone with Blindboy, he could have easily made a run for it. Blindboy was perfectly suited to the task of being one of Captain Hu's subordinates – he was a black-hearted, evil little bastard – but he wouldn't have been much of a match for a man like the Colonel. If the Colonel decided to run or fight, Blindboy might as well just give up. The Colonel could beat him with one hand tied behind his back. I was conflicted: even though I hoped the Colonel would escape, I dreaded it at the same time. I asked Stumpy Tiger what he thought.

"I hope he doesn't run away," Stumpy Tiger said. "I'm having fun listening."

The Colonel was true to his word. He didn't escape. On the way back to the office, I heard him asking Blindboy when I was coming with the clothes. Stumpy Tiger and I stayed in the classroom for a while, trying to listen in, but we couldn't hear the full conversation, so eventually, we crept out again to hide behind the pillar. We could hear the Colonel asking Blindboy for a cigarette. Blindboy said he didn't have any to give him.

"There are cigarettes and matches in my satchel." The

Colonel had sounded exhausted since he had returned from the bathroom, as if he had been in a fight with Blindboy. "Let me have a look. If I find out they're gone, I'll know who to blame. If Captain Hu would stoop so low as to steal a man's cigarettes..."

"Shut up! Your cigarettes are right here."

"Hurry up," the Colonel said. "I'm surprised you didn't try to confiscate these, too."

"Take them. Who would want to steal your stinking cigarettes?"

"'Stinking cigarettes'? They smell fine to me." I heard the Colonel laughing to himself. "You know what they say: liquor and cigarettes are two things you should always share. Take one. Oh? You can't smoke? You better learn. Real men smoke. A cigarette in a man's mouth is like a flower in a girl's hair. You know what I mean? It makes a man look like a man."

"You call yourself a man? You've got nothing between your legs!"

"Are you as blind as your father? Take yours out and I'll take mine out, and we'll compare."

We had no way of knowing whether the Colonel actually took it out, but it seemed like he might have. After that, the interrogation started to turn nasty. There was real bitterness between Blindboy and the Colonel after that exchange, and it had Blindboy on the back foot. The Colonel worked him into a rage.

"Who cares if it's bigger?" Blindboy asked. "I can tell it's fake. It's rubber! It's fucking useless."

"Get your mother in here and I'll show you how useless it is."

"Fuck you," Blindboy roared, pounding the desk.

"Oh, that's right," the Colonel said, "you didn't have a mother. I guess I'll fuck your grandmother, then."

"Fucking disgusting eunuch. How about you go fuck yourself with that thing?"

"That's something you know a lot about, right, fucking yourself? I know you've never even touched a girl. When I was your age, I had my pick. I ran through them."

"And then someone cut your dick off," Blindboy said. "Now you have to piss sitting down."

"I think you're mistaken. I forgive you, though. You didn't have it easy. You didn't even have a mother to breastfeed you. You had to drink goat's milk." That one cigarette seemed to have recharged the Colonel. He was in high spirits. His rant was like listening to a string of firecrackers going off. "Don't think that red armband is going to save you. You're the worst off in this whole village – no mother, raised by a blind man, never knowing where your next meal was coming from. When this is all over, you go ask your father about me. Ask your father what I did for him. And still, after all that, you despise me, you lie about me, you try to frame me for things I've never done... How could I be a spy? The Old Constable said it himself, didn't he? I saved the life of a senior cadre of the Communist Party. In turn, at the end of the war, that senior cadre saved my life. If it wasn't for him, I'd probably still be rotting in prison."

"Why would they lock you up?"

"I was in the KMT!"

"Then they would have been right to lock you up! That's why we need to investigate you now."

"Go ahead. Investigate. Put me on trial." The Colonel's voice was muffled slightly as if he was putting another cigarette in his mouth. We heard the snick of a match being struck. "Anyways, just don't lock me up in that woodshed again. It stinks worse than a latrine! As long as I have smokes, I can sit here all night. Ask me anything. I'll answer you. I could tell you what went on with your parents, even."

XXXVII

We already knew that story, though. Blindboy had been raised by his father, without any brothers or sisters. It was an unusual situation in our village, and, thinking back, I think he was the only kid that grew up like that. Wild One was a different story, since he'd been adopted from outside the village. His mother was barren.

Blindboy's mother had never been around. Even before giving birth to him, she had run off with someone else. What kind of woman would marry a blind man? I heard that his mother was somewhat attractive, too. She had a pretty, round face, with bushy eyebrows and plump lips. I never saw her, and neither did Blindboy, but I'd heard stories. The rumour was that his mother had been tricked into marrying the Blind Man. When they set up the marriage, the Blind Man's younger brother had stood in for him. On their wedding night, the Blind Man's brother led her into the bedroom, flicked off the light, and the Blind Man went in to take his place. I thought she must have been an idiot to fall for it.

Grandpa said: "Don't blame her. It was an elaborate scheme. Even the Bodhisattva Guanyin would have been fooled."

The Old Constable was the one that explained to me that all brides are nervous on their first night. When the lights go out, they don't know what to expect. As long as the person getting on top of them doesn't have horns or hair, they won't put up a fight.

The next morning, the Blind Man woke up and pretended to cry. The Blind Man told his new bride that sleeping with her had somehow robbed him of his vision. At first, she believed him. She started crying. She dragged him all over the place looking for a doctor to cure what she believed to be a sudden onset of blindness. But he had been blind long before he met her, just as he had been a liar long before she arrived. His treachery might not have been discovered if his younger brother had not come back. When work outside the village dried up, he was forced to screw up the courage and return home. When he got there, he saw that she was already pregnant. He greeted her sweetly and enthusiastically, hoping he could dispel her suspicion and convince her to stay.

Why did she stay? Her son's wickedness was not inherited solely from the father. She was a cunning woman, even if she didn't show it. She was a wolf in sheep's clothing. Behind everyone's back, she started sleeping with a peddler that came through every now and then to sell barley sugar. They would sneak off together to the edge of the village and make love in a haystack. At the same time, she was stealing every bit of money that the Blind Man made telling fortunes. One day, she went to the commune clinic and came home with some sleeping pills. When she made dinner that night, she crumbled them into the rice porridge. Everyone in the house fell into a deep sleep. Even a thunderstorm raging outside couldn't wake them up.

Grandpa said: "Women's hearts are a black hole of evil."

She disappeared that night, streaking out of their lives like a bolt of lightning. There was no trace of her. Suddenly, one evening, she snuck back into the village. It was the middle of the night. She wandered in like a lonely ghost. That night, the Blind Man was awakened by the sound of a baby crying. It was Blindboy, swaddled, and left on the doorstep. There was a note attached, which gave the child's name and said, "This is your seed, Blind Man. Raise him as you see fit. This is the parting gift of his mother. She is already dead."

Nobody ever saw her again. It seemed like maybe she really was dead. Blindboy was raised on goat's milk. Like his mother, he became a wolf in sheep's clothing.

XXXVIII

There was a sound like a slap and a cry, but it was just the chair creaking. It sounded like Blindboy was shifting uncomfortably in his seat. When the sound stopped, Blindboy went back to interrogating the Colonel: "What's your relationship with the Old Constable? I want the truth this time. Don't jerk me around, either. I'll let you have it."

"How would I jerk you around? Everyone knows the story. When I was younger and more naive than I am now, I slept with his girl. There was a grudge."

"But last night, he got up to support you," Blindboy said. "He even said that you didn't sleep with the girl."

"Why would he get up in front of everyone and say I slept with her? He wants to hold onto his dignity. That's why he did it. He just wanted to make himself look better. He was covering up his own lies. That's why he called me a eunuch. That's the gravest insult you can make. There's a grudge. The man hates me, which is the only reason he got up to insult me like that."

"But everyone says you're a eunuch."

"I thought we were talking about me being a spy," the Colonel said.

"You are, though," Blindboy said.

"Not at all." We heard another match being struck. "People call you 'Blindboy', but you aren't blind, are you? Idle chatter can become a fearful thing, as the saying goes. And the second half of that saying is about how the hearts of men are unfathomable, right? Some people have wicked hearts, and they use that idle chatter to hurt other people. My flaw is that I like to show off. That draws attention, and sometimes it's the bad kind of attention. People make up stories about me. But I'm not a spy, and I'm not a eunuch, and you aren't blind. I'm a real man. I smoke. I drink. When I was younger, I fucked whores and I gambled and I fought.

I did it all. The times have changed, though, and I'm older, too. I've given up on gambling and whoring. I don't fight anymore. But I'm still a real man."

"A real man? Who do you think you're kidding? I saw it myself, when we were in the bathroom… You squatted down to piss. Does a real man squat to piss?"

"I was taking a shit," the Colonel said. "I didn't know you were watching me take a dump."

"Why didn't you wipe after?" Blindboy asked.

"There was no paper. Did you want me to use my finger? That's worse than not wiping at all. You can't smell it? It stinks in here. I didn't wipe my ass. Hey, I had no idea that I was being watched by a deviant. Is that one of your hobbies? I hope for your sake you're usually watching women. You make me sick. Really sick! I'm telling you this for your own good: you'll never get a girl if you act like that. Women like sophisticated men. If you want to know what sophisticated is, just look at me! When I was younger, I always had women around. I could, still, if I wanted to…"

"Stop bullshitting," Blindboy said. "You never even got married!"

"A man like me doesn't need a wife. A wife would be like a cop over my shoulder all the time. I'll give you a piece of advice: if you really want to be free, don't get married. I'm a romantic. I can't change that fact. If you want to say never getting married proves I'm a eunuch, I mean… You've got to be joking. But all right, you can say I'm a eunuch, go ahead. Is that part of the interrogation? Is that a political problem?"

"Then let's get to your political problems."

"I don't have any. You won't find anything there. I'm not a spy. I was in the KMT, but that doesn't mean I'm still working for them. I'm not a reactionary. I support the Communist Party. I support Chairman Mao. I support New China. I fought in the war to Resist America and Support Korea.

I was given medals for defending New China. I was a model soldier. I gave speeches all over the country."

"How did you end up back here, then?" Blindboy asked.

"I let the little head do the thinking for the big head. I wasn't leading a healthy lifestyle. I haven't led the cleanest life, but you won't nail me on anything political. If you want to criticise me for my lifestyle, I can accept that. But I think you're barking up the wrong tree with the political stuff."

"Tell me about your lifestyle, then."

"I wouldn't even know where to start. Do you want to talk about now or in the past? I'd tell you about it, but I don't think you want to hear it. You probably wouldn't even understand half of what I told you. I know you like looking up skirts, but have you ever seen a pair of tits? How big were they, like pumpkins or pears? Are we talking about a pair of saggy old tits? Have you ever seen that before? Have you ever grabbed a handful of tit? Have you ever buried your face in tits? Have you ever sucked on them? What was that like? How good did that feel? Did you ever—"

"Shut up!" Blindboy said. "You're perverted."

"See?" the Colonel said. "I told you that you wouldn't want to hear it…"

We couldn't take it either. Stumpy Tiger and I were writhing like we were on hot cement. Listening to the Colonel was like having a hot poker plunged into our chests. I tried to swallow and I couldn't. I felt like I was going to choke. We both stood up at the same time, fighting back the urge to cough. Finally, Stumpy Tiger couldn't take it anymore. He ran down the walkway, hacking and coughing the whole way. I couldn't follow him, though. I had to deliver the clothes. Blindboy burst into the hallway like a watchdog startled by the rattling of a gate. "Who's there?" he barked. He rushed for me and I thought he was going to hit me, but he saw the clothes and snapped them up. "Where have you been?" he asked. Before I could explain, he said, "Were you out here listening?"

I said I hadn't been. How could I have told him the truth? The Colonel called my name, but Blindboy was already chasing me off. I think he was worried that the Colonel would give me another task. He didn't want me hanging around eavesdropping, either. If I had known what was about to happen, I might have tried to hang around a bit longer... But as it was, I was relieved to be sent off, since I was covered in mosquito bites. All the way home, I was scratching. When Grandpa saw me, he brought me some bayberry wine to rub on the bites. I counted twenty-seven red bumps, all over my body.

Grandpa said that most mosquitoes died off in hanlu, which was the name for the season around the middle of October, when the dew started to freeze in the morning. But the mosquitoes that had feasted on human blood would have the energy and the wits to survive right through hanlu. For them, the cold season coming was a sign that they should find a warm place to hide out. If they bedded down in the right place, it was possible that they could survive right through the cold season, then re-emerge in the spring to wreak havoc. That night, between Stumpy Tiger and I, we must have given one extra year of life to dozens of mosquitoes. They might even survive long enough to bite us again...

Nine

XXXIX

As far back as I can remember, I never went upstairs to sleep with my mother and father. I slept downstairs with Grandpa in a little addition off the main house. Directly across from his addition was a separate addition, off the west side of the house, which was our dining room. In the area between the main additions, in front of the main house, was a small courtyard. If you went through the front of the house to the back half, there was a small kitchen and the steps to go upstairs, and there was also a door to go into the backyard. We had a woodshed and a pigsty in our backyard, which was where I kept my rabbits. There was an old stove in the back half of the house, which faced a set of steps that led upstairs. The stairs were made out of rough boards, so they creaked anytime someone went up or down. In the front half of the house, separated from the rear by a thin partition, was a hall and a small room with a table, three benches, and a pair of armchairs. That was where we used to hang a picture of Grandpa's parents, my great-grandparents, who I both called A-Tai – but that picture was gone, since we had hung up a portrait of Chairman Mao. All around the picture of my great-grandparents, there used to be an altar where we could put offerings or put some symbols. Those had disappeared, too. My mother had managed to save some, but most of the religious items had been carried off by the Red Guards, who probably burned them.

I rarely went up into the attic over the back half of the main house. That was where we stored grain, so it was always full of mice. The mice didn't have it easy up there, though. My father had put traps around, baited with soybeans. When I saw them, I could imagine the beans calling to the mice: "Please, come and eat me. I'm far tastier than that grain over there." My sister used to live upstairs in the eastern addition, right over me and Grandpa. When she moved out, my eldest brother moved in. My parents lived in the upper half of the western addition. The attic over the front half of the house had a few rooms, and my two elder brothers had occupied it over the years, but it was empty by that time, since my eldest brother was in the western addition, and my second eldest brother was busy in town, working as an apprentice painter. If you wanted a good place to see Tail Mountain, the attic over the back half of the house had a great view. Looking at it from up there, it felt like you could reach out and touch it. Grandpa said he used to climb up to the attic of the west addition to look at Head Mountain. At the time, you could even see the creek from there, since there was nothing around. By that time, with everything in the way, you couldn't even feel the breeze blowing down from the mountain.

I didn't go over to Head Mountain very often. It was too far. I was very familiar with the creek, though. I'd usually go along the riverbank on my way to school, and when I got off school and went out into the fields to cut weeds to feed the rabbits, I'd go along it again. In the summer, I could spend all day down by the creek, swimming, catching fish, pulling up reeds... The creek had a name: the Great Source. As the name suggested, it was the headwaters of rivers far downstream. It was fed by water coming off Head Mountain. The mountains were so vast that they might have contained as much water trapped in them as an ocean. That's why it was called the Great Source, instead of just "the Source". Through the winter, the creek was a sickly trickle, but when the spring thaw came, it seemed to rise higher with each day, until summer came. Floods were not uncommon, either. In a bad year, the creek turned into a raging torrent, uprooting trees and wrecking crops. A few miles down, the creek emptied into the Fuchun River. In bad years, the water would be too high in the river to catch the run-off from the spring melt, and the creek would back up, flooding the land around it, including the village.

Grandpa said that there were lots of fish in the Fuchun River. In the twelfth year of the Republic, which would have been 1923, the Fuchun River had a hundred-year flood. The water was three-feet deep in the village. You could take a boat through the lanes. He went fishing that year from the attic of the house. He told me that he caught a fish that weighed seventy-eight *jin*. It was supposedly longer than Grandma was tall. The fish had white scales that gleamed so brightly they lit up the entire back half of the house. But the fish was a bad omen. It ended up sticking around longer than Grandma did. Grandpa said it had been sent from hell to test him. If he had set it free instead of eating it, Grandma might still be alive. As it was, she was dead before he was even done carving fillets off it. After that, he always burned incense at the table in the front half of the house, put up a statue of Guan Yu, and made offerings to his ancestors. He wanted to be sure that no more evil spirits would be sent his way. He couldn't have foreseen that one day Red Guards would carry all that stuff away. And after that, it did seem that the family's luck got worse! There was no doubt that our bad luck, and Grandpa's offerings and statues being confiscated were connected.

The table in the front half of the house was usually used for making offerings, but since the Red Guards had come, it had been put away, along with the benches and chairs. Before that, I used to sit at the table to do my homework. A few times, I would wake Grandpa up from his nap. He was over in the eastern addition, but he could still hear me reading aloud – probably as clearly as I could hear him snoring. If he saw me working on homework when he was planning to have a nap, Grandpa reminded me not to read anything aloud. Before he went to bed each night, Grandpa went to the front hall to see if anyone was in there. If they were, he would chase them out. You could only stay if you promised not to make any noise, or to at least talk in a whisper.

Grandpa said: "When you're asleep, you're like a dead pig. Even thunder and lightning can't wake you up. Me, I sleep like a squirrel. You know how a squirrel sleeps? If a single leaf drops from the branch, they're wide awake."

But that night I guess the "dead pig" had some life left in it. What I mean by that is that I was suddenly woken up sometime in the middle of the night.

XL

I don't know what woke me up – maybe it was some itch I couldn't scratch, or maybe it was just the way the moonlight hit my eyes – but I just couldn't sleep. After that came the sound of some people whispering, then sobbing. The sound was not constant, but came in fits and starts. When I heard it, I felt like something inside me had been ignited and sat up straight in bed. I realised Grandpa was no longer in bed with me. I imagined Grandpa being whisked out on the beam of moonlight that came in through the crack in the door. The crack in the door let in more than moonlight – that was how I heard the sound of crying. It seemed to be louder. All at once, I felt fear, curiosity, and excitement. The sound of sobbing seemed to writhe in the darkness.

I could tell it was an adult. It was a man.

But it wasn't my father, and it wasn't Grandpa. It wasn't one of my brothers, either.

Who was it? My curiosity won out over my fear. I crept across the room, quiet as a cat. The door was open just enough for me to slide out. I sidled towards the sound of the crying, as slowly and carefully as if I was walking along the edge of a precipice. The sound was coming from the back half of the house, near the stove. Who would be in a place like that in the middle of the night? The lights were all off. I got closer, but it was too dark to see anything. It was as if it was too dark even to hear the crying anymore. The sound disappeared, and came again, as if made by a ghost. It sounded at once familiar and unfamiliar. The strangest thing was that whoever was crying seemed unable or unwilling to actually give voice to the sound. It was just as much choking and moaning as it was crying.

Who was it? I felt like the sound was going to split me in two. It was so sad and so painful.

The door to the back hall was shut. I didn't want to open it and go in, so I looked for one of the many holes and cracks in the partition that separated the two halves of the house. Just as I pressed my eye to the crack, I heard a match being struck. Light ripped through the darkness. It only lasted an instant, but it was long enough to see a few things. It had been Grandpa lighting the cigarette. He was seated on a small bench, facing the partition. He looked solemn, as if something very important was taking place in the back half of the house. I could see a man's back, too. He was a tall man, leaned forward, sitting on the stool that my mother often sat on while watching the food cook and stitching shoe soles, with his elbows up on the stove, and his head buried in his hands. The man's shoulders were heaving. He was the one that I had heard crying. He looked exhausted and broken. He seemed frozen in his position. My father was standing beside that man. He looked tired, too, and scared out of his wits.

Who was the man?

Before the match went out, I saw enough to know that it was the Colonel sitting on the stool. He was wearing the clothes that I had brought him that night. There was no mistaking it, since the undershirt I had brought him had "12" on the back of it in big red letters.

I remembered that shirt so clearly because Grandpa had told my father not to bring it to him. Grandpa told my father that there were too many mosquitoes, and that he should take him a long-sleeved shirt. My father explained that the shirt had been brought by the Colonel's mother from Mount Putuo. He figured it might have some special blessing that could protect the Colonel. Even though I had only seen the shirt for an instant by the light of the match, I was sure it had to be him in there.

But how was the Colonel reduced to the tortured wreck on the other side of the partition? My image of him was turned upside-down. He was completely different! In my mind, he was a proud man, who seemed to strut when he walked, his back always ramrod straight, fearless... I never could have imagined him as I saw him in that moment, by the light of the match. He looked broken! He looked defeated! He looked helpless!

Was it really him? Of course it was. I knew the shape of his shoulders, I recognised the sound of his voice, and there was no mistaking that shirt.

XLI

What had happened to him?

At first, I thought something must have happened to his cats – either they were dead or they ran off.

But if they had run off, everyone would be out looking for them.

Even if they were dead, I knew the Colonel wouldn't react so dramatically. What about his mother? She was an old woman, and she had been unwell. She also seemed not to have returned to the village. The way she burned incense and prayed, it seemed like she was expecting her life to end at any moment. Considering that possibility put my mind at ease. If the Colonel's mother had died, it didn't have anything to do with my family. I watched the tip of a cigarette glowing in the dark like a will-o'-the-wisp. The strained sobbing started again. It was like listening to a ghost moan. If it really was the old woman that had died, I was thinking, it was one less old bag hanging around. She had always been a pain in the ass. When they caught us doing something we weren't supposed to, some old people would start yelling at us, but she was even worse: she'd start chanting the holy name of the Buddha Amitabha. All I could do was fantasise, though, since I had no idea what had actually happened. All I could do was wait for somebody on the other side of the partition to speak. It was almost like Grandpa had read my thoughts. He cleared his throat. "Don't purposely go down a dead end," he said. He said it clearly and calmly. There was no emotion in his voice. He spoke with all the authority and experience that a man his age had earned. "You have to go now, before the sun comes up. If you wait until dawn, it'll be too late."

I heard my father's voice next. It came between the sobs of the Colonel. He spoke deliberately and firmly, but there was a downcast, sad tone to his voice. "He's right," my father said. "You need to go. That little bastard isn't worth dying over." By the light of the cigarette, I could just make out my father struggling to get the Colonel to his feet. The Colonel didn't want to go.

Grandpa stood up. "Hurry up," he said. "You still have

stuff to get ready. You don't have time." He was trying to get the Colonel to his feet, too. "Get up. You have to go."

The Colonel looked like he had just woken up from a dream. He staggered to his feet. "Go?" he asked. His voice sounded as if his soul had left his body. He sounded robotic. "Where would I go?" It was the voice of a man whose bravery had completely deserted them. Once again, he seemed nothing like the Colonel that I knew. Usually, he was the one giving commands and solving problems. He was always so calm in moments of crisis, but standing there in the back hall of our house, he looked as if he was about to collapse. He looked like a fly trapped against a window.

"This is a great big world," Grandpa said. "Go wherever you want. But don't go down a dead end."

"You have friends out there, right?" my father said. "Just go somewhere. Anywhere is better than hanging around here waiting to die."

"There's no time to wait," Grandpa said. He turned to my father. "Drag him out of here. If he's still here when the sun comes up, he's never getting out alive."

Grandpa took a drag on his cigarette and for a moment, I could see my father dragging the Colonel to his feet. I ran back to the eastern addition and hid behind the door. From there I could see the front door of the house and the courtyard. A short time later, the three of them emerged, illuminated by the moonlight. The moon was bright that night, and I could see the Colonel clearly, one arm slung over my father's shoulder, being dragged off, with Grandpa behind them, prodding them to hurry. The Colonel's head lolled on his chest, and he slumped against my father, walking unsteadily. When they got to the front gate, the Colonel seemed unable to lift his feet to get over the threshold. Since I last saw him in the school, he seemed to have aged decades. He looked even more fragile and decrepit than Grandpa.

That was the last time I saw him in the village. But the way he looked that night, was nothing like the man I knew: his face under the moonlight looked lifeless, he could barely lift his feet, his back was slumped, and he seemed unable to raise his head. If he had been a roaring bonfire before, he had been reduced to embers. Comparing him to the man I had known before was like comparing night and day, a corpse to a living man, a crystal-clear spring to a stagnant pond... As they stepped through the gate, I lost sight of them, but I could still hear Grandpa. "Go," he said.

The Colonel said: "Where are the cats?"

My father said: "The cats are fine. Don't worry about it. I'll look after them for you."

"I want to take them with me."

Grandpa said: "You can't."

My father said: "If you take the cats, they'll know you came here."

Grandpa said: "I don't want to end up in prison because of a couple cats."

"We'll look after your cats for you. When the time comes, I can send them to you."

Grandpa said: "Hurry up!"

I heard the Colonel break down again. He sat down on the threshold of the back door, but Grandpa shouted, "Go!" They prodded him like a disobedient child. Finally, the sound of their footsteps faded.

Grandpa didn't return immediately. He stood at the gate for a while and finished his cigarette. I couldn't tell if he was keeping watch for someone or trying to settle his nerves. As soon as he came back into the room, he knew I had been eavesdropping. If he had been trying to settle his nerves, it had been for nothing. He erupted at me. I had never seen him like that before. Unlike my father, who wasn't shy about a curse or a slap, Grandpa had always spoiled me. While my father and sometimes my mother scolded, he was the one that comforted and protected me.

Grandpa didn't hold back that night. He slapped me hard and roared, "Listen and listen good, you didn't see anything! You were dreaming."

I had no idea what he meant. I decided he must be confused, so I repeated to him everything that I had seen. That made him even angrier.

Grandpa grabbed my ear and twisted hard. "Forget everything you saw and heard," he said. "Every single thing! Pretend you saw nothing! Do you understand?" He twisted my ear so hard that I thought he was going to rip it off.

I screamed for him to let me go, but he wouldn't.

"This is nothing," Grandpa said. "If you go around running your mouth, you're going to get us killed. They'll wipe all of us out."

At that moment, I realised that something serious must have happened, even though I had no idea what it was. Whatever it was, it was a life-and-death matter. I was horrified. When I thought about my ignorance and recklessness, I felt sick. I felt like I deserved to die.

XLII

Sometime after dawn, I was awoken by a nightmare. I saw that Grandpa was gone again. I found him out in the courtyard, smoking a cigarette. The ground around him was littered with smoked butts. I knew he was waiting for my father to get back.

My father returned while everyone was sitting down for breakfast. He was soaking wet and carrying the carcasses of a pair of wild hares. He paused in the doorway, smiled, and said in a loud voice, "Look what I got up in the hills last night. I set a couple traps and got lucky." From where he was standing and how loud he was talking, I knew he was putting on a show for the neighbours. When you catch an animal in a trap, there's bound to be some blood, but his hares were spotless. He must have bought them off a hunter on the way home from wherever he took the Colonel. The fact that my father was going to such great lengths to conceal the truth proved to me that Grandpa's warning had been deadly serious. I had to forget everything I had seen and heard. If anyone asked where my father had gone the night before, I would say that he was trapping in the hills. Everything else – the Colonel hunched over the stove, my father urging him to go, Grandpa prodding them out the door and catching me – had never happened. It was nothing but a nightmare. Grandpa's warning was burned into my mind.

I needed to know what had happened, though. It felt like a black curtain had come down, right at the point where I had eavesdropped on the conversation in the back hall. I knew everything that had happened after the curtain had fallen, but there was no way of knowing what had gone on before. All I could do was stare at that black curtain separating me from the truth, feeling fear and helplessness. I had a feeling that I had been cut off from something incredibly important, which had the power to destroy my world. I felt like one of my rabbits, hauled from its pen, waiting for something terrible to happen.

The mystery was solved two hours later, when the Old Constable emerged from the school, calling for everyone in the village to come and see what he had found.

The Old Constable didn't have a wife to make his breakfast for him, so he usually went over to Phoenix Blossom's shop in the morning and bought *youtiao* and fried dumplings. He walked by the school on the way and saw that it was open and unguarded. There were no Red Guards, which he thought was unusual, so he went inside to look around.

"Scared me half to death!" the Old Constable said. "As

soon as I stepped into the woodshed, I smelled it – shit and blood. It smelled like someone slaughtering a pig. I thought, 'The fucker's dead.' They must've beaten the Eunuch half to death, I thought, with the amount of blood that was in there. He must have started shitting and pissing himself when the beating started. It was pitch black in there, and I didn't want to go a step further. I was worried I'd step on his head or something. I managed to find the pull string for the lights, though. I saw that there was somebody curled up in the corner. He had his back to me. He wasn't moving. I started hollering, but there was no answer. I was sure he was dead. Bad fucking luck, right? Imagine getting up in the morning and winding up dead before noon. The Eunuch wasn't my best friend in the world, but he didn't deserve something like that. I wanted to go and check on his body, and make sure somebody looked after it. But when I got closer… I got the shock of my life. It wasn't the Eunuch at all. It was the Blind Man's son. He looked pretty dead, so I didn't want to get too close. I ran out of there to call for help. Just think, what if he wasn't dead and I ended up doing something to him. The Red Guards would come looking for me. I don't need them making accusations against me. I've seen a lot of soldiers in my life, and they're about as bad as it gets. You can't reason with them. I didn't want to have to plead my case to them. They're like talking to a brick wall."

Blindboy wasn't actually dead, though. He was just unconscious. When the Red Guards dragged his body out of the woodshed, a breeze and some sunshine were enough to rouse him. When Blindboy tried to talk, all that came out was a tortured moan and clotted blood. Whoever had attacked Blindboy had gone so far as to cut out his tongue. Nobody could understand him. The whole time he was trying to talk, he was waving his arms around, too. But whoever had cut out his tongue had also gone to the trouble of severing the tendons in his hands, so that they hung off the ends of his wrists like steamed chicken feet, curled up, twisted, and useless. He looked like a monster. He wasn't dead, but the sight of him was enough to knock you down.

He had to be taken to the hospital, the sooner the better.

Someone called for the tractor to be brought over, but it had already been taken out into the fields. As the man ran towards the fields, he shouted out what had happened. The news spread fast. When the tractor finally pulled up at the front of the school, a huge crowd had formed. There were far more people there that morning than at the Red Guards' usual assemblies. I was one of them. As soon as I saw Blindboy, I was sure that the Colonel must have done it. It seemed fairly obvious to me. As Captain Hu said later, "Evidence of his guilt has not been hard to find."

The first piece of evidence was that the Colonel had escaped. Captain Hu reminded us that those were not the actions of an innocent man. The Colonel had a motive, as well, since he had hated Blindboy ever since discovering it had been him that had come up with the scheme to catch the cats to lure him back. On top of that, Blindboy had been bound with the same rope that they had used to tie the Colonel up in the woodshed. My cousin explained to me that even though they locked him up in the woodshed and he was tied with twine, they still tied him up with a length of rope just to be certain. As Captain Hu saw it, the Colonel's disappearance, his hatred of Blindboy, and the use of the rope were enough to convict. But there was more evidence to come. At around noon, word came from the hospital. Blindboy's tongue had been completely severed, and it had been stitched up after. The doctor said that if the tongue was cut and not stitched up that Blindboy would likely have bled out. The severing of the tendons in his hands had also been complete and thorough. The positioning and depth of the cuts had been perfect. The injuries to the hands and tongue would have required expert knowledge and professional tools. That seemed to be ironclad proof that it was the Colonel that had done it. It wasn't some random attacker with a butcher's knife or a cleaver, but someone with a scalpel. The only man in the village that could have pulled it off was the Colonel. He had once made a living as a surgeon. The Golden Blade was what they had called the Colonel in the war, because he could bring people back from the brink of death with his scalpel.

Captain Hu reported the case to the Public Security Bureau and made ready his Red Guards to pursue the fugitive.

The PSB sent two officers, accompanied by a dozen or so militia members. They searched far and wide, checking every house in the village, then going up into the hills to look. They came to our house first. My father and Grandpa sat across from them at the table in the front hall. My father answered each question calmly, relying on the story about trapping in the hills on the night of the incident. He could back up the lie: he had the traps, he had wild hares, shoes still muddy from mountain trails, and the testimonies of the neighbours that had heard him return. He had material evidence and human testimony – and animal testimony, too, since the Colonel's two cats were still there.

My father dragged the two cats out of where they had been hiding, and said, "Everybody knows he lives for these. If he showed up here, he wouldn't have left without them."

"He'd rather die here than leave his two cats behind," Grandpa said, then went into a long soliloquy about the situation and the Colonel's psychological state: "Therefore, knowing that he left the cats behind, according to my understanding of the man, he did not in fact escape, but is likely already dead, or at least preparing to die, so all that you and your men are likely to find is his corpse, which seems barely worth hunting for." Listening in from my room, I was trembling with fear, expecting the police to find some flaw in the story they had concocted. I didn't want to be dragged in front of them to be cross-examined. Luckily, these particular representatives of the PSB and the militia were particularly stupid and lazy. They drank the tea and smoked the cigarettes that my father and Grandpa offered, then they left. They didn't bother going upstairs or out into the backyard, or any of the other places where somebody could have been hiding. When I heard them go, I realised that my father and Grandpa had pulled it off.

You can't imagine what that was like. When I heard the police leaving, I started crying tears of joy. I'll never forget that moment!

PART TWO

Ten

XLIII

That was a bloody summer. It was a summer of unanswered questions.

For a long time after, I wondered why he did it... Why did the Colonel cut out Blindboy's tongue and sever his tendons? Why did he stitch up the wound left behind when he cut his tongue out? It made no sense to me. When I asked my cousin what he thought, he told me to mind my own business. My cousin had changed after the situation with Blindboy. He didn't come over to my house as often, and he seemed withdrawn, almost like he was sinking in on himself. The same thing was happening to Meathook. Both of them kept to themselves, after that. It seemed like Blindboy getting hurt had done some emotional or spiritual damage to them, too. They withered like leaves in the autumn. The first frost of the year had come, and they were dying on the vine. But Wild One seemed to be thriving. He and Blindboy had never been close. They'd even fought a couple times. I don't know if Wild One was gloating over Blindboy's misfortune, but when we asked him about it, he didn't avoid our questions. In fact, he seemed to relish talking about it. Wild One was happy to tell us his theory that the Colonel had stitched up Blindboy because he was scared he might bleed out before help came. If Blindboy died, the Colonel would be facing charges that carried the death sentence. The Colonel knew that even if he was brought to justice, he would be facing a lighter charge – or, at the very least, charges that wouldn't have him in front of a firing squad. The Colonel was willing to risk time in jail, but he didn't want to lose his life over Blindboy. It was very calculating and systematic, I thought, and worthy of the Colonel. But, on the question of why exactly he cut out Blindboy's tongue and severed his tendons in the first place, Wild One was willing to pontificate, but he didn't have any definite or particularly compelling answers.

I would have usually gone to ask Grandpa... He would have been able to tell me. Grandpa was different from most old people: he was experienced and knowledgeable, and he had a way with words. He was a folk philosopher and a professor of the people. I learned almost as much from him as I did at school. We were close, Grandpa and I. We even slept in the same bed. He kept my feet warm at night, and I kept his heart warm. On long, humid nights and chilly winter evenings, I asked him all the questions that were swimming around in my head. He answered everything I asked him. But I knew I couldn't ask him about the Colonel. Grandpa had told me to forget all about him. I knew I couldn't ignore Grandpa's words of warning on the night that Colonel left.

Since that night, the Colonel's name was rarely raised in my house. Anyone that tried to bring him up was met with an eye roll, or even a slap. It was as if his name had been cursed – or maybe like we were just too good to sully our household with mention of him. My father's best friend had suddenly been cut out of our lives. He was taboo, poison, a landmine waiting to blow up and kill us all... We had to tiptoe around him. I started to resent him.

Goddamn you, Colonel. It was because of you that I had that horrible secret locked up in my head. What the hell did you actually do? Where did you run off to? Why did you treat Blindboy like that?

Nobody knew where the Colonel had gone. Captain Hu's Red Guards couldn't find him. The PSB put up wanted posters all over town. He seemed to have simply evaporated, just like Blindboy's mother – like a fart, like a puff of steam... That night, when I watched him leave, we were like two ships passing in the night, tossed by the same raging waters. All I could do was watch him be swept away. The Colonel's mother seemed to have disappeared, too. Wild One told me that Captain Hu and his Four Guardians had left for Mount Putuo as soon as he learned that the Colonel's mother might be there. They marched overnight to get there, but it was all for nothing. Captain Hu tracked her down to a hostel near the temple, but all they found in her room was a pair of reading glasses and an incense burner. The ashes in the incense burner were still warm – proof that she had narrowly escaped and that the Bodhisattva was protecting her. I had seen the incense burner many times at the Colonel's house. It was brass, about as deep as a soup bowl, with three four-clawed dragon feet on the bottom, and a pair of phoenixes as handles on the rim. I picked it up once and it was so heavy I was sure that the Bodhisattva's very soul was buried in the ashes it contained.

Like the incense burner, that summer had a mysterious weight to it, as if it had swallowed up more unexpected emotions and strange events than it could comfortably hold.

Various theories circulated through the village as to what had possessed the Colonel, but nobody could be quite sure what exactly had happened in the first place. The more people talked, the more far-fetched their explanations became. The only way we could know for sure was to wait for Blindboy to recover. Even if he was never able to speak again, at least he should be able to write out an account. Blindboy's condition was not improving though. He was taken on a medical tour, spending time in the county hospital, the provincial hospital, clinics devoted to Chinese medicine and clinics devoted to Western medicine, and with all manner of specialists and experts. His family even resorted to hucksters and quacks. All of the money that the Blind Man had earned telling fortunes was spent. As the Old Constable put it, it was squatting on a latrine for a big, burbling fart, and then nothing coming out.

Blindboy might've lost his tongue, but the Old Constable sure hadn't – he ran his mouth more than he ever had. He stuck his nose in every issue that came up, ready to say his piece. I knew he was going to end up sticking his nose somewhere it didn't belong.

XLIV

I had often heard the Old Constable say things like this: "Let me tell you about the Eunuch. He's an extremely intelligent man, and a fine soul. But everything has a balance. God took what he had between his legs, but blessed him between the ears. There's no beating him. When he put his mind to saving lives, that's exactly what he did. If he ever put his mind to the opposite, the gods themselves would run for cover. You could send Blindboy up to heaven to consult with the immortals, and they couldn't do a damn thing for him, either."

Grandpa might have advised the same, once. After that night, though, you couldn't pay him enough to talk about the Colonel. "Bring me a sack of gold…" I imagined Grandpa saying. "I'll just keep my mouth shut. My life is more valuable." He had forced me to forget everything that happened that night, but he was still living in the terrible shadow of those events. He didn't have to be a legal scholar to realise that he and his son had committed a crime. That was common sense. At the Red Guard assemblies, Captain Hu had said over and over again that those that concealed crimes were just as bad as the perpetrators. But because my father didn't understand the law, it seemed to be magnified in his mind into something horrible and magnificent. It was oppressive. He was withering under the weight of it, barely able to lift his head, fighting to breathe... You couldn't bribe or threaten him into talking about the Colonel. When the topic came up, his tongue might as well have been cut out, too. The Old Constable made up for his silence, though. I often saw the Old Constable holding court in front of the ancestral hall, telling everyone his theories on the Colonel and Blindboy.

The Old Constable would tell people that asked for his theory, "Just fucking think through it yourself. It's all so clear. The Eunuch wanted to shut him up, and shut him up for good. Blindboy must have had something on the Eunuch. What it was that Blindboy knew, if it got out, the Eunuch would have been ruined. Cutting out his tongue and wrecking his hands were to shut him up. It's like a murderer shooting the witnesses before he leaves, but the Eunuch didn't have to kill him to get away with it. It was a brilliant move, if you think about it. He's a smart man."

One time Grandpa was there to hear him offering his theory, and added, "The Old Perv is right. There are plenty of cases in history of a murderer killing the witnesses. There's an old saying about this, 'The more money in your chest, the better, but tying up loose ends will earn you more in the end.'"

"How much money have you saved up your little box?" the Old Constable asked.

"I don't have any money, but I'm not the type of man that worries about loose ends, either." Grandpa gestured at his chest with a calloused hand. "At my age, I'm just waiting around to die."

"You have a bit longer to wait," the Old Constable said, laughing. "Either way, I'm behind you. I know you'll go before me. People like you think too much. Worrying about things takes years off your life. The King of Hell made that rule, so don't blame me." He laughed again. "But you're not even at the head of the line anymore! The Eunuch cut in. He might not have killed the kid, but when he decided to run, he made himself a fugitive. That's a capital crime. When he gets back, all he has waiting for him is a pretty little piece of brass and lead. They'll put it right through his heart for him. I didn't make that rule, either, so don't blame me."

Grandpa knew he had already crossed the line, so he just smiled and said nothing.

The Old Constable seized on Grandpa's seemingly content silence. He wouldn't let him go. "Look at the way you're smiling," he said, "like a man slipping into bed with the blushing bride on his wedding night. I know you hated the Eunuch. I know you wouldn't have mourned his death. But look at your son, going around crying. Everyone in the village knows how close they were. They were so close that they would die for each other, wouldn't they?"

"Bullshit!" Grandpa said. He was furious. "A man in your seventies, and you still don't know how to speak like a civilised person. What does my son have to do with any of this? You're the one that got up at the struggle session to tell everyone how great he was. God only knows what was going on with the two of you." Grandpa walked off, panting. He didn't have it in him to take on the Old Constable in a war of words.

I knew Grandpa was afraid of letting slip things that he shouldn't say. When he saw me standing there, watching, he dragged me away, too. He didn't want me to become a pawn in whatever was going on in the village, or to be pressed to talk about what had happened on the night that the Colonel had left. If anything came out, it would be the end for my father and Grandpa. I had to keep everything I knew locked away deep inside me. Since that night, Grandpa had been very careful when the topic came up. He reminded me and warned me, and he even threatened me.

For a long time after the night the Colonel escaped, every night when we went to bed, Grandpa would say the same thing: "If you can't keep it a secret, I'll drink pesticide before they can take me." I used to see it in my nightmares, the old man chugging pesticide, foaming at the mouth, his eyes rolling back in his skull... It was all the Colonel's fault.

Goddamn you, Colonel. What the hell did you actually do? Where did you run off to? Why did you treat Blindboy like that?

XLV

Compared to Grandpa, my father was less cautious. The clearest example was how he treated the two cats. When my cousin had first brought them to us, while the Colonel was still locked up, Grandpa hadn't opposed the idea, since he assumed it would be a temporary arrangement. Grandpa also told the Colonel to let the cats stay with us on the night that he left. That was only because taking the cats would be proof that the Colonel had visited us before escaping. Nobody had ever intended for our home to become the permanent residence of the cats. Grandpa was haunted by their presence. He crept around the house as if the two cats might transform into tigers at any moment. He was sure that they were harbouring evil thoughts.

Although Grandpa might have been overreacting, I too noticed that the cats had become more feral since arriving at our home. They often went out of our gate to run around. We didn't have as much room around the house as the Colonel did. The Colonel was usually around to look after and spoil his cats, but my father spent most of the day working. The cats were bored at our house. When they had enough to eat, they went out to play. If we didn't feed them enough, they went out to hunt, or they would steal the fish drying on the eaves. The bigger problem was that they were the most tangible legacy of the Colonel. When people saw the cats, they thought of their former master and his close relationship with my father.

Grandpa was tortured by the cats. He threatened to stomp them to death, to drown them, to steam them... If it hadn't been for my father, the cats would long ago have ended up tossed out into the street for the stray dogs to eat. My father and Grandpa argued about the cats frequently. One time, it got so bad that Grandpa grabbed a knife and threatened to stab them. My father held back the white cat with his right hand and the black cat with his left hand. "You'll have to get through me first," my father said. Another time, after a particularly vicious argument, my father said: "If any harm comes to them, you'll be next." That guaranteed the cats wouldn't be harmed. And they lived on, always with the spectre of the Colonel hanging over their heads, constantly tormenting Grandpa. But one day the cats finally disappeared. That somehow made Grandpa even more anxious, though. It happened in the middle of winter, when all the grain had been put into storage and farm work had ended for the year. At that time of year, the men of the village went to work on the dam and the reservoir. My father was sent to Cockscrow Mountain in the northern half of the province. The journey to the job site was treacherous and conditions were even worse when the workers got there. Everyone had to bring their own cookware, bedding, and grain. My father was worried that Grandpa was going to kill the cats, so he brought them with him. It was sort of ridiculous – my father explained that the cats were going along to guard his grain. My mother asked if he'd lost his mind. She didn't support the idea, at all. Grandpa didn't say anything, though. He just watched my father getting ready to go. If, as my mother had suggested, my father had lost his mind, then Grandpa was content to let it happen. As far as he was concerned, it would be better for everyone if the cats didn't come home. He hated those cats.

At the end of the year, when my father was sent home, he came back with two sacks. One contained the things he had carried there, and the other contained some New Year gifts that had been either given to him by the production brigade, picked up in the mountains, or purchased in town. He presented a red silk scarf to my mother. My father told my mother that he didn't want her to wear it, but to keep it around for when my brother was looking for a wife. My father gave me a pair of white cotton socks. They looked just like the thick socks that the workers at the power plant wore. When I held them, I felt warmth spreading through my body like I was a loaf of bread in an oven. That was exactly what I wanted as a gift. Everyone was so wrapped up in the New Year celebrations that they forgot about the cats altogether.

Grandpa noticed first. "Where are those two little monsters?" he asked my father.

"I ate them," my father said. "I thought you hated them."

"Tell the truth," Grandpa said.

"They're dead."

"How did they die?" Grandpa asked. He didn't believe it.

"It was too cold up there," my father answered flatly. It sounded like he had rehearsed the speech. "The cats couldn't stand it. Before long, they were sick. And then they died."

I thought Grandpa would gloat about it, and maybe say something like, "Good to hear it," or "They deserved it." But he was silent. After a long time, he said, "That's life. We have to move on." Instead of gloating, he sounded sympathetic. It was the kind of thing you would say to comfort someone that had lost a friend. I couldn't figure him out.

A little while after the New Year, I heard my father and Grandpa fighting. I was out in the yard, feeding my rabbits, as I always did before bed. The soft, snow-white fur collected from the four long-haired rabbits was enough to cover my school fees. Every day when I was done school, I went to cut weeds for them. They got fed twice a day, no matter what else was going on in my life. There was no light over the pigsty, so my father and Grandpa had no idea I was hiding out there in the dark.

"I want you to tell me," Grandpa roared, "where those two cats really are!"

My father looked as if he had just been woken up from a sound slumber. "What are you yelling about?" he asked peevishly. "I already told you, they're dead."

Grandpa spit in the dirt. "You think you can outsmart me?" he asked viciously. "I see everything that goes on around here."

"What the hell do you know?" my father asked.

"I know those two cats are still alive," Grandpa said.

"Where the hell did you hear that?" my father asked.

"Don't worry about that. You just tell me, where are they? Where did you go that night?"

"What night?" my father said, then paused. He wasn't willing to confront the issue head-on, but he didn't want to completely avoid the question. "I was working. Where do you think I went?"

"I ought to slap you!" Grandpa said. "A man your age, still trying to get through life lying through his teeth! Are you going to tell me or not?" Grandpa started walking towards him in the dark, forcing my father to retreat. "Fine, I'll say it for you: on the fifteenth day of Layue, there was a heavy snow, work was shut down for a couple days, and you disappeared with the cats. You came back the next afternoon, without the cats. So, tell me, where did they go?"

My father suddenly giggled, as if an ice cube had been stuck down the back of his neck. "You've got it all wrong," he said, still laughing. "I already told you: it was too cold up there, and the cats got sick. I did take them to see a vet that day, and I got them something to eat. But they both died that night. I found a nice spot and buried them. I didn't take them home and eat them, though. I couldn't bear the thought of that."

Grandpa seemed to believe him. "Are you telling the truth?" he asked.

My father seemed outraged that Grandpa would even ask. He swore and adopted an impudent tone. "What do you think happened?" he said. "I told you what I did. Everyone I was working with there assumed I went off somewhere and ate them. That's where the gossip started. How could I do something like that? Didn't you ever stop and consider that? They were like his children. Even if I was starving, I wouldn't have eaten them. I'm sure you can understand that. Those guys I was working with started talking, the bastards..."

Grandpa seemed to have no doubt left in his mind. "Do you know what they were saying?" Grandpa asked, sounding concerned.

"I know," my father said. "They all said I must've known where the Colonel was hiding and went looking for him. They assumed I was bringing him the cats."

"If the PSB gets wind of that story," Grandpa said, "they're going to show up here asking questions."

"What do you want me to do about it? I can't stop those guys from running their mouths."

"You just keep your own mouth shut. I'll deal with them myself." Grandpa sighed and lectured my father sternly, "You need to learn how to look after yourself. Times have changed. You need to be careful not to give offence where none was intended. That's a good way to get yourself killed."

My father passed a cigarette to Grandpa and stuck one between his own lips. Grandpa struck a match and lit my father's cigarette and then his own. They walked back into the house together. The darkness seemed to cling close to them. They looked like two brothers. I had never imagined that such a bitter argument could end like that, but it made me happy. It was a cold, dark night, but my heart felt as warm and bright as the flame of Grandpa's match.

After that night, I heard rumours, and people whispered that the Colonel was still alive, that my father knew where he was hiding, that he had gone to see him... The Colonel was still a fugitive, and if those rumours got to the PSB, they would come to question my father. But it seemed that Grandpa had actually got to the right people in time, since the gossip seemed to die down a short time later, without attracting the attention of the police.

XLVI

Grandpa said everyone had four seasons to their life, just like the village had four seasons. Childhood was spring: full of vitality, but essentially useless. Spring brought flowers but no fruit. Spring was the season when more people starved to death than at any other time of the year. Adolescence was summer. The hot season. Summer was when the snakes and worms came out. Summer was the time for planting seeds, and adolescence was the time for finding a mate. It was the time to work yourself to the bone. Manhood was autumn: the season of the harvest. The autumn was a time to fill the granary, to admire your work, to relax on mild nights... Old age was winter. Winter was coldness, fear, and boredom. This is all double meaning, but some of it makes more sense in our local dialect. When we said the "hot season", it could mean either the season or the time of life – summer was hot, but we said the same thing when people's blood ran hot, too. "Summer was when the snakes and worms came out" was a good example, too, but unlike the first example, it mostly meant something negative. I mean, it could be meant literally, in that snakes and worms did come out in the summertime, but it was also the season of gossip. When the days grew long and hot, everybody wanted to get out in the evening to enjoy the cool. They went out in groups of three or four, maybe five or six, and gathered in front of the ancestral hall, or they took up positions in the lanes. They had something to eat together, played cards or chess, maybe watched a play, and they talked, chatting about this or that – and that was how rumours started. The summer was the season of gossip.

The summer that the Colonel disappeared, his name came up a lot. Rumours sprouted like mushrooms after the rain. There were whispers everywhere. The snakes and worms were coming out. But in the fall, the gossip seemed to subside, and it seemed to have hit its low point by winter. But the next summer, the rumours started again. It was like watching a balloon being blown up, with every whisper adding to its size. But I figured it would deflate again. After all, there was nothing new to add to the rumours about the Colonel. People could do their best to improve on old gossip, but it was always stuff everyone had heard before. What was required was something fresh – the Colonel had been arrested, or there was some new evidence in the case, or Blindboy had finally spoken... But there was nothing. Everyone assumed that the Colonel must be a long way away by then.

One day someone had something fresh. I don't know who started the rumour, but it spread like wildfire in dry grass. It was quite shocking, actually, what they were saying... According to the rumour, the Colonel had never been a eunuch at all, but a sodomite! He had been lying all along. We could pity him for being a eunuch, but there was no pity for a deviant. It was a bolt of lightning from the blue. It didn't take long to spread from one person to the next, then out into the entire village. It blew through the village like a typhoon.

I spent a lot of time with Stumpy Tiger hanging out in his grandpa's shop. I called Stumpy Tiger's grandpa Clubfoot when I was talking to Grandpa, but I usually called him

Mr Seven in public. His little shop, like the ancestral hall and the public bathroom, was one of the hubs of gossip in the village. People came and went from the little shop, picking up and dropping off fresh rumours. I must have been among the first to hear the rumour, when I heard Clubfoot – or Mr Seven – telling the Old Constable, while Stumpy Tiger and I were out front of the shop, trying to fix a slingshot. The Old Constable laughed and said, "What kind of goddamn nonsense is that! Everyone knows he's a eunuch. Ask anybody! Ask that stray dog picking through the garbage over there!"

"Right," Mr Seven agreed. "I thought it was kind of strange, too. But it sounds like it might be true."

"Bullshit," the Old Constable said. "You must be going soft in the head in your old age."

"You're the one whose brain is pickled from all the drinking," Mr Seven said angrily. "I'm pretty sure this is true, since it came straight from Blindboy."

"Wait," the Old Constable said, the smile fading from his lips. "Blindboy said it? He's talking?"

"Not yet," Mr Seven said. "He used his feet."

The Old Constable's doubled over laughing. He laughed so hard that he started coughing and had to sit down on the bench beside the shop counter. "Fuck me, Clubfoot," he said, "I think you've finally lost it. The boy's talking with his feet now, is he? How the hell did he do that?"

It was a good question. But it was true – Blindboy was using his feet to talk. I saw it myself. He looked right at me and Grandpa and wrote with his toes in the mud: "Fuck your mother."

But I'm getting ahead of myself.

That day with Mr Seven and the Old Constable and the slingshot was a few weeks before, in July. Mr Seven went out front of the shop, followed by the Old Constable. In the dust, with his big toe, he wrote a single character: 大.

Mr Seven said to the Old Constable: "That head of yours

is only good for two things: figuring out where your next lay and your next drink are coming from." He gestured at the character he had written in the dust, and said, "That's how you can use your feet to talk."

"What the hell do you know?" the Old Constable said, laughing. "You spend too much time cooped up in that shop. Unlike you, I've been past the gates of this village. If you told me that the Eunuch was some kind of a rapist, I might believe you – but a goddamn sodomite?"

The Old Constable and Mr Seven were the perfect pair to broadcast the story. Apart from both being enthusiastic gossips, the Old Constable was always over at the ancestral hall, chit-chatting with the old folks, and Mr Seven oversaw one of the rumour hubs of the village. Between the two of them, they knew pretty much everything there was to know about goings-on in the village, even if they sometimes couldn't agree on the details. The Old Constable usually won out in those disagreements. He was fearless, especially when he had a couple drinks. The Old Constable was willing to say things that nobody else would say. He wasn't scared to drag anybody's family into the rumours, either. Mr Seven was the opposite – in other words, he wasn't called Clubfoot only because of his peculiar way of walking, but also because he tended to tread carefully around sensitive issues. The Old Constable would go hunting for gossip, but Mr Seven would wait for it to come to him. Also unlike the Old Constable, Mr Seven believed in projecting an image of dignity in his old age. He was happy to gossip but he didn't want to get down in the mud. That was why the Old Constable always managed to beat him in verbal battles.

The Old Constable losing out to Mr Seven in their disagreement over the Colonel being a sodomite was a rare occurrence. Mr Seven was seen as the more reliable source, with the Old Constable being written off as an unreliable old drunk. Grandpa was the only one that agreed with the Old Constable that the story was bogus. That was rare, too, since Grandpa rarely took the Old Constable seriously. But on that occasion, he took him seriously. That was part of the reason Blindboy lost his mind and started biting people.

That was how Blindboy and Grandpa came to have a fight.

XLVII

This happened to take place on the fifteenth day of – going by the old calendar – July. That was also the day of the Ghost Festival. Grandpa said that on the day of the Ghost Festival, ghosts could reach into the world of the living. The tradition was to offer steamed sponge cake and sweet osmanthus bread in the shrine at the ancestral hall. The shrine was the point where the world of the dead intersected with the world of the living. Not many people ventured into the shrine, since it had an undeniably creepy atmosphere, but everyone had to go on the day of the Ghost Festival. If you didn't go to make offerings, it was considered disrespectful to your ancestors. That sort of affront was an invitation to hauntings. Even if the shrine was creepy, the once-a-year visit was preferable to vicious ghosts seeking you out. The only way to get out of visiting the shrine was to send someone as a representative. The visitors to the shrine on Ghost Festival were mostly the elderly, or kids and young women, sent by their families. It started to get busy around noon. At its busiest, the shrine looked like a chopstick holder crammed full of chopsticks. There was always a buzz in the air during that time, as if people were expecting their ancestors to suddenly burst out into the shrine to thank them for their offerings.

Grandpa took me there at noon. It was as busy as it always was, with the front hall crowded with people coming and going, and the air filled with the intoxicating perfume of osmanthus and rice wine. The sun blazed down from overhead, obliterating the shadows. As we went into the front entrance, I caught sight of Blindboy, sitting off to the side of the door. He had a basket in front of him, filled with steamed cake and sweet bread. They had been a gift from his neighbours and friends. In the past, nobody would have bothered stopping by with Ghost Festival offerings for the family, but people had started to take pity on Blindboy. He had no mother, his father was blind, and he was crippled, so the family would have had a hard time getting together their own offerings. Blindboy was there to deliver the offerings to the shrine, and also to soak up any further beneficence he could.

Grandpa said: "Most of the time, it's a man's circumstances that decide his conduct. Blindboy was happy to strut around when times were good, but now he has to suck it up and find a way to feed himself."

After Grandpa made his offerings in the shrine, he went back out front to where Blindboy was seated. Grandpa took a pair of steamed sponge cakes out of his own basket, and placed them in Blindboy's basket. He said: "How do you know he's a sodomite?"

Blindboy moaned incoherently. He clearly hadn't understood.

"How about this," Grandpa said, "I'll ask you a question and you nod your head or shake your head. It's very simple."

Blindboy nodded.

"You told someone he's a sodomite? Did he rape you or not?"

Blindboy shook his head.

"So, you didn't catch him in the act?"

Blindboy shook his head again.

Grandpa laughed loudly. He raised his voice, hoping to draw in other people waiting outside the hall. "Sodomy isn't like a normal disease," Grandpa said solemnly. "It's not like

being blind, or crippled, or a hunchback, or paralysed – you
can see those with your own eyes. It's more like being deaf,
or being a whore, or impotent, or barren, where you can't
tell just by looking. It's a disease you can keep secret. If he
didn't do anything to you and you didn't see him doing it to
anybody else, why would you accuse him of it?"

Blindboy tried to struggle to his feet. He moaned, trying to
form words with his absent tongue.

Grandpa motioned for him to sit down. "Just sit down.
Don't try to speak. Nobody can understand you. I'll speak
and you listen. Everyone in the village called him the Eunuch,
right? You've called him that yourself, right? Right? Just nod
your head."

Blindboy flushed red, and he moaned even louder. He refused
to nod or shake his head. He seemed to realise it was a trap.

"So, you're not telling the truth now, are you?" Grandpa
said. "Why didn't you nod when I asked you if you've ever
called him the Eunuch? Everyone in the village knows that's
what he is. Even kids know that. You heard what the Old
Constable said at the struggle session. It's a fact. He's never
produced any evidence to disprove it. You're the only one
that's ever disputed the facts. Why is that? The next question
is, if he was tied up in the woodshed, how did he do this
to you? Are you saying this guy was actually the Monkey
King in disguise? He used his superpowers to bust out of
there? Who untied him? Why did he cut out your tongue and
wreck your hands? Why?" Grandpa didn't wait for Blindboy
to answer. He knew that he couldn't. So, he kept going: "As
I see it, there is only one conclusion that can be reached.
That conclusion is that you are the sodomite. You wanted
to fuck him, didn't you? That's why you untied him. That's
why he fixed you up like this. He didn't want you spreading
around your own version of what had happened. But he also
didn't want you to end up dead, or suffering too much. The
Eunuch loves helping people, even when it's not in his best

interests. It's fortunate for everyone that he went through with it, though. God only knows what wicked things you would have got up to..."

The crowd around Grandpa and Blindboy started to grow. Blindboy moaned pathetically. Even though nobody could understand him, they could tell that he didn't want to hear more. But Grandpa was only getting warmed up. Blindboy started to slap his hands on his thighs, groaning and roaring incoherently, foaming at the mouth, snot running down his face... Finally, he ran. He went through the crowd to a patch of dust, took off his slipper, and used his big toe to write in the dirt. Blindboy was shaking too much to write clearly.

Grandpa comforted him. He told him to take his time.

By the time Blindboy had managed to write anything, his big toe was dripping blood. What he had written was this: "Fuck your mother."

Grandpa was angry but he laughed. "My mother died a long time ago," he said. "She's nothing but dust now. You want to fuck a ball of dirt? You really might be a sodomite!"

Blindboy charged at Grandpa. With his hands useless at his sides, he wasn't much of a threat. Grandpa quickly sidestepped him, and Blindboy fell face first into the dirt. "I thought you wanted to fuck the dirt," Grandpa said, "not eat it!"

Grandpa let him lie there. "Is that any way to treat me?" he asked. "I just brought you some steamed sponge cake, and I was just trying to figure out what had happened between you and the Eunuch, offering my own analysis... And you started cursing my family and trying to fight me. Is that how you treat a man of my age? Where's your respect for your elders? Even if you thought I was wrong, it's no reason to start attacking me. You can't go around acting like a common street hoodlum. There are some perverted thoughts running around in your head, aren't there? I wasn't sure at first, but I'm pretty sure now – you're a sodomite!"

Eleven

XLVIII

I knew what a rapist was, but I had no idea what a sodomite was. I asked Grandpa and he just glared at me and told me to mind my own business. "It's a filthy thing," Grandpa said. "Don't even say the word. It's shameful." From the way he said it, I realised that a sodomite had to be worse than a rapist, and being one was far more shameful than being a eunuch.

I still couldn't figure out why Grandpa took the accusations against the Colonel so seriously, though. The way I saw it, whatever Blindboy said was fine, as long as it didn't implicate my family in any way. It's not like anything Blindboy could say at that point could further harm the Colonel, either. The Colonel had already escaped. The other thing I couldn't figure out was why Grandpa suddenly wanted to talk about the Colonel. He had warned us repeatedly not to bring him up. So, what was he doing drawing a crowd, shouting about the Colonel? On top of that, he seemed even to be defending the Colonel's honour! I was a bit sceptical that Grandpa was taking the right course of action.

That was only the beginning, though. Things were about to get even stranger.

Starting from the day of the Ghost Festival, Grandpa started spending more time on a circuit between Clubfoot's shop, the ancestral hall, the hair salon, the tailor shop – places where gossip was spread. He was like a candidate on the campaign trail, promoting his theory that Blindboy was a sodomite and had raped the Colonel. It was all part of his plan to smear Blindboy. He didn't merely spread the story, but had his own logic and evidence to give it an air of truth. He pointed out that Blindboy had sent away the other Red Guards that night, so he could be alone with the Colonel. It was a complete break from the practice established by Captain Hu. The reasons for getting the Colonel alone were clear: he wanted to do something shameful to him. Another piece of evidence was that Blindboy had a habit of sneaking peeks in the public bathroom. We'd heard of guys peeping on women on the toilet, but Blindboy was different – he peeped on the Colonel. Stumpy Tiger and I could attest to that. Blindboy's upbringing was additional evidence for his homosexuality: he had never known a mother's love, and, deep down, he hated all women. Because his mother wasn't around to breastfeed him, Blindboy had grown up on goat's milk – in other words, he had been raised by beasts. He had the blood of a wild animal, not a human being. Grandpa also presented plenty of evidence that the Colonel wasn't a sodomite, like his playboy days in the army, and – most definitively – the fact that he was a eunuch. Everyone knew those stories about the Colonel.

Grandpa was doing his best to clear the Colonel's name – of being a sodomite, at least – and implicate Blindboy. The sodomite smear was like the Monkey King's golden band, placed on the demon's head and locked in place by the Bodhisattva. Even though I didn't know quite what the word meant, or why Grandpa was going out of his way to make the case, I became convinced that Blindboy was a sodomite. Still, I was dying to ask him what a sodomite actually was, and why it mattered so much to him that Blindboy was one.

I wanted to ask why he suddenly wanted everybody to know that they were all wrong about the Colonel.

None of Grandpa's efforts amounted to much. He was fighting an invisible enemy. Each time Grandpa won a small victory, the enemy would blow through the lanes like a gale. By the start of August, the gale became a typhoon. Grandpa went out to brave the storm, but he and the Old Constable both ended up getting blasted back home, soaking wet. He had made a fool of himself.

It all ended on the day that Blindboy showed up at the ancestral hall with his father and his uncle. The Blind Man and his brother beat a gong and hollered for people to come and watch. It was as if Blindboy was about to put on a show – in a way, he was. The Blind Man and his brother carried props with them: a placard, a bag of fine sand, and a bamboo carrying pole. Blindboy's uncle put the placard on the ground and poured the sand onto it. He got down and used one of the flat sides of the pole to scrape the sand even. He sat down across from the placard and took out a sheet of paper and a brush. Blindboy was the star of the show. Supported by his father, he walked to centre stage, shook off a shoe, and began writing in the sand with his big toe. Blindboy's uncle copied down each character that Blindboy wrote in the sand. It was fine, soft sand, and easy to write in. I figured they must have practised the performance many times at home. The characters Blindboy scratched out in the sand were ugly and rudimentary, but you could always make out what they were supposed to be. The Blind Man kept yelling the whole time, drawing in more people to watch. Eventually, a large crowd had gathered to watch the performance. The late summer sun blazed overhead. Sweat dripped down Blindboy's face. The crowd watched with rapt attention. It was better than any busker's show.

When he was done, the passage copied out by Blindboy's uncle was pasted up on the wall of the ancestral hall. There were a few characters written wrong, but I could get the gist of it. This is what it said: "I said the Eunuch is a sodomite because he has a tattoo on his stomach that says, 'Sodomite bastard.' I saw it with my own two eyes. Giraffe and Meathook can back me up." The "Giraffe" he was referring to was my cousin. There were many miswritten characters: one of the characters in "Eunuch" had been miswritten as one meaning "salt", the character for "tattoo" had a superfluous stroke that turned it into the character for "slashing", Giraffe's name had been transformed by the substitution of an unrelated character, and he was missing strokes in the character for "eyes" and one of the characters in Meathook's name.

XLIX

At that point, I hadn't seen my cousin for a while. He had gone off to work in town. At first, Captain Hu had put him in charge of forming a revolutionary committee for our commune, but there wasn't enough work to keep the young revolutionaries occupied. Captain Hu offered to get him a job at the middle school, working as a gate guard. The job paid thirteen yuan a month. The low pay wasn't what was holding my cousin back, though. Rather, he was worried that being a gate guard wasn't a fitting task for a young revolutionary. It lacked prestige. But the only alternative was staying in the village and joining the militia as a full-time member. As a full-time militia member, he would've still had to do farm work for the commune, and he would be paid in workpoints instead of money. Eventually, he took Captain Hu up on his offer.

When my father and Grandpa got word of Blindboy's performance, they immediately summoned my cousin and started questioning him. I positioned myself outside to listen. Nobody had expressly forbidden me from listening, but I decided it was better to keep a low profile. The interrogation started with Grandpa angrily warning my cousin to make sure that he told the truth. "Don't try to hide anything from us," Grandpa said. My cousin realised that he wasn't going to get out of answering their questions. He hemmed and hawed for a bit, but he started talking eventually...

As my cousin told it, he had been in the canteen kitchen with Meathook and Wild One that night. They got dinner ready, then went to call Blindboy, who was interrogating the Colonel in the office that Captain Hu had formerly occupied. My cousin said that they had no idea what had happened during the interrogation. I knew that was true. My cousin said all four of them escorted the Colonel back to the woodshed. He wasn't tied up at that point, since he was going to change into the clothes I had brought him. Their plan was to take him back to the woodshed, let him change his clothes, and then tie him up again. Before they got back to the woodshed, though, the Colonel had asked if he could wash up in the canteen. He was filthy from spending the night in the woodshed. Blindboy had immediately disagreed with the suggestion. "You must be dreaming," he had said. They pushed the Colonel into the woodshed and Blindboy ordered him to get changed. Blindboy stepped out to let the Colonel get changed, then went back in, rope in hand. He was going to tie up the Colonel so the four of them could safely go off to get something to eat – but he paused before binding him again. He agreed to let the Colonel wash up.

"At the time, I thought it was strange," my cousin said. "But Blindboy told me later that his plan was to spy on the Eunuch washing up in the canteen. The Eunuch had claimed not to be a eunuch. Blindboy wanted to know for sure. I figured it was a waste of time, since the Eunuch wouldn't be dumb enough to show us what he actually had down there. I didn't say that to Blindboy. I let him go ahead with it."

That had to be a lie. My cousin made it sound like he

was an innocent bystander, but he must have been curious. I would have been curious, too. If he didn't want to watch, he didn't have to. Maybe Wild One could be considered lucky for getting in a fight with Blindboy over something else and being excluded from the peep show...

To avoid the problem of the Colonel trying to hide himself, the boys came up with a plan.

Once again, it was Blindboy that came up with the scheme. He ordered my cousin to move the canteen kitchen's water tank closer to the window, so the Colonel would have nothing to hide behind. They knew the Colonel might want the lights off, so Blindboy tied a length of cord to the light pull and ran it out the window. They could lead the Colonel to the canteen, promise him privacy, then wait until he had got undressed, then hide outside the window and switch the lights on. Wild One's job was to sit by himself on the other side of the wall from the Colonel, in one of the dining rooms, and make a bunch of noise, like everyone was in there drinking. He would clatter stools and clink glasses and shout, "Come on, you bastards, drain it! Finish that glass! Let's get another bottle."

There were no curtains on the window, but, at first, it was too dark to see anything. All the moonlight was being blocked by a tree. The Colonel would have thought that he was safe in the darkness. Maybe Wild One's ruse had worked, too, and he figured that his captors were getting drunk in the next room over. He let his guard down and got completely naked. That was when Blindboy switched the lights on. The Colonel got the fright of his life.

At that moment, the Colonel made the decision to rush for the light switch near the door which allowed the three of them – Blindboy, my cousin, and Meathook – to get a clear look at everything. They were shocked to see that his body was covered in tattoos, including a bright red arrow, with two columns of characters on each side of it, pointing down to physical proof that the Eunuch was not a eunuch at all.

"It was mostly writing," my cousin said. "There were big characters, about the size of my fist, and little characters, all over his belly, mostly. I couldn't really read it, though. Blindboy told me what one of the tattoos said, but I didn't actually see it clearly. The Colonel got dressed right away. But Blindboy asked him about that tattoo."

As soon as Blindboy asked, the Colonel realised that they hadn't seen his tattoos clearly. "You're done with your drinks already?" the Colonel had said, mocking them. "If you could spare a glass for me, I'd be happy to tell you..." Blindboy fell for it and brought the Colonel to the dining room. Once the Colonel had eaten and drank his fill, Blindboy asked him again. "You couldn't read it?" the Colonel asked. "It says, 'Your mother's a whore.'" Blindboy lost his temper and was about to hit him.

"I told him not to," my cousin said. "He wasn't tied up, and I knew he could beat us up."

At that moment, the Colonel could have escaped. But he didn't. He didn't see the need. He was freshly showered and fed, with plenty of cigarettes to smoke. His beloved cats were safe by that time, too. He had not been found guilty of anything at that point. Running would make him a fugitive. He went willingly to the woodshed and let them tie him up again. After that, my cousin, Blindboy, Wild One, and Meathook went back to eating and drinking. They discussed what they should do with the Colonel. They were all certain at that point that he was not actually a eunuch. All of them, except for Wild One, had seen proof.

According to their schedule, my cousin and Meathook were supposed to take the first watch, with Blindboy and Wild One taking over for the second half. But before they switched off, Wild One went home sick with a stomach ache. So, Blindboy was alone with the Colonel. Whatever happened during that final watch, only the Colonel and Blindboy could know for sure.

"All that stuff he wrote in the sand," my cousin said, "if it's true, it had to have happened on the final watch."

"What do you mean 'if it's true'?" my father demanded. "Of course it's not true! It's all lies."

"So, you know what happened?" Grandpa asked. His tone seemed to be prodding my father to reveal something.

"How would I know?" my father said angrily. "Who the hell knows?" My father pushed upon the door as if he was about to storm out, then turned to say to my cousin, "I told you to stay away from that little bastard, but you wouldn't listen. You followed him wherever he went, and now look where he's led you. Someday I'm going to fix it so he never talks again."

My father charged out, looking like he really was going to go looking for Blindboy. As for fixing it so that he could never talk again, I wasn't sure how he would do that... Blindboy already had his tongue cut out and his hands paralysed, so my father would have to cut his feet off. I still couldn't figure out why my father and Grandpa were so obsessed with his particular part of the Colonel's story, though. I figured I'd have the missing piece of the puzzle whenever I figured out what a sodomite actually was. Without understanding that detail, I couldn't be sure if everyone was overreacting, or if this really was a major issue. Hiding in the dark, I felt all alone in the world. I had nobody to turn to.

L

My cousin slept at the middle school's worker dormitory and only came back on weekends.

He had come back to the village earlier in the summer vacation for a few days, but his father had put him to work in the fields. He hated farm work, so he ended up going back to the dormitory in town. The school was empty, and so was the dormitory. He had the place to himself. It was better to stay there than to return to the village and do chores for his father. He invited me to spend the night with him. It was my cousin who finally told me what sodomy was.

He waited until the lights were out, like he thought it was too dirty to discuss with them on. We were in complete darkness, with no moonlight coming in the windows. The darkness had an inky, shiny quality and it seemed to be swallowing me up inside of itself. But it was not even close to as frightening as what my cousin was telling me.

As I listened to him explain, I started to shiver. I had goose bumps breaking out all over my body. I wanted to vomit, to cover my ears, to run from the room... The thing he was describing was revolting – nauseating, ugly, savage, more obscene than any pervert, more brazen and shameless than a rapist, more repulsive than a eunuch... Without even thinking, I reached for the light pull.

"Why did you turn on the light?" my cousin asked. He was sitting up in bed, looking at me.

"I got scared," I said. My hand was frozen on the light pull.

My cousin kept staring at me. "You mean," he said, "you didn't know?"

"Know what?" I asked, my hand slipping from the light pull. I turned to look at my cousin.

"Your father..." he said, turning to me.

"What about my father?" I couldn't figure out what it might have to do with him.

"You didn't hear?" my cousin asked. He lay down again, rolled onto his side, and turned his back to me. "Forget about it. I don't even feel like saying it. It's disgusting."

How could he stop at that point? I had to know. I begged him to tell me. I went over to his bed and sat down beside him. I grabbed his hands and pulled him towards me. If he didn't tell me, I knew I couldn't sleep.

"How can you be so stupid?" he asked. "You can't just have one sodomite. It's two men. The Colonel is one, and they're saying your father is the other one."

"What are you talking about?" I said. "That's impossible."

"That's what everyone's saying, though," my cousin said. "But you better keep your mouth shut when you go back there."

My cousin wasn't in the village often, so if he had heard the rumours all the way in town, it would mean that the rumours were growing fierce. But I hadn't heard anything. I realised eventually that it was intentional: everyone did their best to avoid that particular element of the gossip when I or anybody from my family was around. They were scared. Grandpa told me that, if I ever heard someone talking like that, I should start hitting the person – and don't stop. Grandpa said that if somebody talked about our family like that, jail or death was preferable to letting them get away with it.

My cousin hurt me deeply that night. I could lay out plenty of evidence to disprove the things he had said, but I didn't bother. His words that night coiled around my heart like a viper. I knew that the fangs of the snake were always waiting for me. I saw them in my nightmares. In my nightmares I was fighting back against everyone, beating and kicking, running away... One night I woke up Grandpa with one of my nightmares. I was shivering so much that he thought I was having a seizure. He took me lovingly into his arms. He tried to wake me up. The only reason I told him anything was because I thought I was still dreaming. If not, I would have kept my mouth shut. I was a mature kid. I was already fifteen. I felt like I was alone in the world. I was at the age where I could tell good from bad. I could adapt to just about any situation the world threw at me. I had taken a lot on my shoulders. I was going to take on even more. I wasn't ready to give up. I would have kept my mouth shut.

But I didn't even know I was awake. I thought I was still dreaming. I told everything to Grandpa...

I'll never forget Grandpa's reaction. It was like a dark cloud rolled across his face. I couldn't tell exactly what he was thinking. It was a mixture of shock and fear, and also anger and embarrassment. He seemed at first like he didn't want to hear it – what I was saying was too revolting and too shameful – but he kept pressing me for details, demanding to know who had told me about my father. If I had known what I was saying, if I was fully conscious, I might have held out longer, but eventually I gave up my cousin.

When he heard who had told me, his eyes sparked to life. He clenched his fists. I hated myself for failing to keep the secret. I hated myself for driving the hateful rumour into his heart like a dagger. Grandpa was a strong man, though. The dark cloud rolled away as quickly as it had come. He smiled. He comforted me. He gave me strength. Even if I knew he was faking it, it made me feel better.

Grandpa said: "The Colonel couldn't be a sodomite. Back when he was a younger man, I saw him with dozens of women – busloads of them! Blindboy's lost his mind. That's the only explanation. You'd have to be crazy to say those things. You know the tendons in your hand are connected to your brain, right? Something must have gone wrong in that head of his when they sliced the tendons. He's gone insane. And I know your father doesn't help things. He goes around barking at everyone. He offends people, then he wonders why they talk about him behind his back..."

Grandpa kept talking, even though I didn't believe him and I didn't understand half the things he said. His words fell like a summer rain pattering down on the roof of a shack. The words were his warm blood, shed to comfort me. His fists were still clenched tight, and I could hear his joints cracking. The two of us – an old man beaten down by the world, and a boy that didn't yet understand the ways that the world could beat me down – spent the night together, cradling a secret so humiliating that it could destroy our family, shouldering a weight that threatened to crush us both...

For the next several days, Grandpa followed me everywhere I went. Sometimes he made his presence known, but, other times, he would try to blend into the shadows. He was scared that someone would try to pull me into the rumours about my father and the Colonel. My sister had already got married and moved away, so he wasn't that worried about her, and my two elder brothers were already grown up and they could look after themselves. If anybody tried to drag my brothers into it, they wouldn't hesitate to put up a fight. I was the only one that needed to be looked after. If somebody provoked me, Grandpa knew that I might say the wrong thing. He wanted to protect me, and at the same time, he wanted to see who was spreading the rumours. He even armed me with a long, sharp file. He told me that if anybody started talking about my father being a sodomite, I had his permission to stab them to death.

Grandpa said: "I'd let the sky fall before I let anybody smear my family as sodomites."

Grandpa entered into a sort of siege mentality. He was like a soldier prepared to go down fighting for his family. He was willing to die fighting to keep anyone from smearing his family as sodomites. He had already done everything he could, though. He had said what needed to be said. He had done what needed to be done. He had comforted me. The shame had faded. But there were things that he could not do. Shame beckoned like an abyss. When the first day of school came around, I couldn't force myself to walk out the door to face my classmates. I didn't want them talking about me or my father. I knew that they were going to talk. That was what they loved to do. They were experts at finding weak points. They would figure out where you were vulnerable, and focus on that point. When they were done, they sprinkled salt on the wound.

Grandpa felt my pain. He had comforted me and told me not to be ashamed, but he had taken all of my anxieties and fears onto himself. He couldn't stand it. He got sick. He was confined to his bed for days. He only sat up to take his herbal medicine. He seemed to wither away. It looked like he was going to die in his bed.

LI

When it looked like my Grandpa wasn't going to last much longer, my mother went to get the doctor. My father and brother were out working, so it was just me and Grandpa in the house. It was a rainy afternoon and I was in the kitchen, brewing my Grandpa's herbal tea. The house was filled with the bittersweet smell of liquorice root. As I watched the mixture simmer, I wished for some of my own life essence, some scrap of hope to float up out of me and get infused in the tea.

When I heard a knock at the door, I thought my prayers had been answered. I thought my mother was finally back with the doctor. But it was just the Old Constable.

He was drunk. He had pounded at the door and then came staggering in, headed directly for the back hall. I was just coming out into the front of the house and he almost ran into me. The smell of herbal tea mixed with the stench of liquor breath. The Old Constable was a mean drunk. He told me to dump out the tea and get him a cup of water. He didn't care that I was angry. He turned and walked away after giving his command, going to look for Grandpa. "Sorcerer," he yelled, "I heard this is your last day on earth. I came to see you off." The Old Constable looked down at Grandpa, who was curled up in his blanket like a sick kitten. "I don't see you for ten days, and I come back and you're thin as a stick bug.

What've you got that blanket on for? It's hot outside! You're not really going to die on me, are you?"

Grandpa managed to sit up in bed, and said weakly, "I'm ready to go. The King of Hell moved me to the top of his list. I'm just waiting for him to give me the word. The waiting's the worst part. Right now, it feels like I'm caught in the middle."

"So, are you going to die or not?" the Old Constable said.

"I'm ready to go."

"Don't go yet," the Old Constable said, chuckling. "Get out of bed and have a cigarette first."

To my surprise, Grandpa started to cry. "I'm not getting out," he said. "Wait until I'm dead, and you can drag me out."

That made the Old Constable laugh even harder. "I'm not going to let that happen," the Old Constable said. "How am I going to go on living without you to kick around? My life wouldn't be worth living if I didn't have you around to curse out. I'm telling you right now, I'm not letting you die. I'm here to save your life. I'm saving my own life, too! You always told me I was doomed, didn't you? You said I wasn't living right. So, how are you going to go and die before me? I have to save your life, don't I?"

Grandpa rolled his eyes. "You came to watch me die," he said.

"You're hurting my feelings, Sorcerer," the Old Constable said. "I came to save your life." He noticed that I'd brought back a cup of water for him, and he drank it in one gulp. He sat down on a stool beside the bed, panting. He seemed to have actually had his feelings hurt. "Sorcerer," he said, "I'm telling you the truth, I'm here to save your life. We spent our whole lives bickering, but we did it together, didn't we? Even if we were sworn enemies, we were meant for each other. We're like a pair of shoes – you're the right and I'm the left. We go together! I can't let you die like this."

"I heard you tell him to dump out my tea," Grandpa said, trying to catch his breath.

The Old Constable laughed and lit a cigarette. "What's bothering you can't be fixed by any medicine," he said. "It's not the King of Hell that put you at the top of his list – it was Blindboy! You've been like this since his uncle tacked up that paper in the ancestral hall. That little bastard knew exactly what would happen. He knows your weakness. He knew you already suspected the Eunuch and your son were over there fucking each other in the—"

"Shut up!" Grandpa said. He slapped his hand down on the bed. "Just shut up." It sounded more like a plea for mercy than a curse.

The Old Constable went on, though. He wanted everything dragged out into the open. He took a long inhale of his cigarette and said, "You thought that, didn't you?" He exhaled into Grandpa's face and puffed out a single smoke ring. "You suspected the Eunuch had picked up something when he was out of the village. You knew he was a deviant. You thought he might have passed it on to your son. That's why you were trying to tell everyone that he fucked my girl, right? You were talking about how he fucked busloads of girls, right? You didn't want anyone saying he might be a sodomite. Why might that be? Because you thought your own son might be involved. You know better than anybody what the pair of them are like. You didn't want anybody else to figure out what you already knew. But nobody believed it. And, fuck, that must have made you even more suspicious! You must have wondered why they called him the Tigress. Blindboy knew what people were saying, and he knew it would hurt you and your family."

Grandpa had been silent through the Old Constable's rant, but he suddenly asked, "Why did he want to hurt us?"

"Ask your son," the Old Constable said flatly. "Ask yourself. What did you do to him? How many times did you stand in front of the ancestral hall and insult him and his family? That's why he wrote all that stuff. You brought this all on yourself."

"I said he was lying," Grandpa said. "But he was spreading the story long before that."

"Go ask your son," the Old Constable repeated. "Ask him what evil things he's done." The Old Constable told me to get him another cup of water and turned back to Grandpa. I could still hear them talking from the back half of the house. "What I expect to happen now is that the Tigress will go after Blindboy. He has to do something. Fuck, just think... Blindboy turned his brother into a fugitive. He has to get revenge, doesn't he? I don't know how he's going to do it, but it's going to be fucking harsh. Blindboy was getting his own revenge, though. He couldn't fight, and he couldn't curse, but he came up with a plan that played perfectly into what everyone already suspected. If the Eunuch was a sodomite, who was his partner? It had to be your son, right? If it wasn't your son, then who would it be? Blindboy realised that. When you went after him, he made the rumours even worse. They spread even further. That's what he wanted. Now everyone believes it's true. Your family's name is ruined. He put you on your deathbed. I only came because I knew that. I knew that this was going to eat you alive. But I'm here to tell you that you've been had! You were fooled! That's right, Sorcerer. You might be clever sometimes, but you're still plenty stupid. You can sit here talking about dying, but I'm here to tell you that it isn't worth it." The Old Constable took out his cigarette pack, glanced inside, then put it back in his pocket. "I came to save your life, and you can't even offer me a cigarette?" I knew where the cigarettes were, so I rushed back into the room to get them out of the cabinet. Before I offered the Old Constable one, I glanced at Grandpa to make sure he approved.

"You mean," Grandpa started to say, then paused, watching the Old Constable light his cigarette, "Blindboy is... lying?"

"Of course," the Old Constable said, sending a cloud of smoke into the room.

Grandpa sat up a bit straighter. He shot an anxious glance at the Old Constable and said, "But he does have writing on his belly."

"I don't think so," the Old Constable said. The Old Constable took a drag of his cigarette and went on, "Maybe he had something written there. Maybe I could believe that. But it's not what Blindboy said it was. I'm sure of that. You could tell me he carved his name in his forehead, and I might believe you. You could tell me that a corpse climbed out of a coffin, and I might believe you. You could tell me that after I die I'm going to be met in hell by a hundred pretty ghosts just waiting to suck me off – but I don't believe for a second that the Eunuch is a cocksucker. Trust, but verify, I always say. That's my approach. I always go off my own experience first. What I'm about to tell you, the only reason you're getting it out of me is only to save your life. If the Eunuch knew I had let it slip, he'd grind me into mincemeat."

LII

When the Old Constable saw me lingering, he told me to get out. He didn't want me hearing his secret. But it was raining outside, so I didn't have anywhere to go. Grandpa told me to go up to the attic in the back half of the house. I knew I wouldn't be able to hear what was being said all the way over in the eastern addition. I stomped up the stairs, making as much noise as possible, then I took off my slippers and crept as quiet as a mouse through the attic, until I got to the portion where the ceiling of the main house met up with the addition. From there, I could creep out in a crawl space that was directly over where Grandpa and the Old Constable were talking. The floorboards had been laid down a century before, and they had warped with time, so that there were plenty of cracks and gaps. I would be able to hear everything – if the Old Constable ripped a fart or Grandpa sighed, I wouldn't miss it. I loved hearing stories about the Colonel. The idea of a story so secret it could get the Old Constable chopped into mincemeat was too tempting to pass up. I lay down on the attic floor and settled in. The rain outside had started to come down heavier, and I could hear it running along the eaves-troughs and pitter-pattering down into the courtyard. As long as I didn't sneeze, I would be safe.

The Old Constable told stories differently than Grandpa did. Their styles matched their personalities. The Old Constable always spiced things up with dirty jokes or curse words, and his stories were notoriously short on details. Everything was "that year", never "such-and-such year of the Republic" or anything. He started the story in the autumn that the Colonel had returned to the village with a chest full of gold. At the time, the Old Constable was a much younger man. He lived in a big house with a pair of stone lions at the gate. He kept a yellow dog tied up out front. The dog would wag its tail when it saw someone it knew, and it would bark to warn the Constable if any strangers came by. The dog functioned like a doorbell. When the Colonel came by, the dog barked and the housekeeper came out. He was from the village, so he knew of the Colonel, although he'd never met him before. The housekeeper suggested to the Colonel that it was best if he left. He was aware that the Constable hated the Colonel. But the Colonel insisted on going in.

"What are you doing here?" the Constable asked when he saw him. "Looking for a woman? I heard that in the state you're in now, they wouldn't be much use to you."

"I didn't come here for you to insult me," the Colonel had said. "I'm here to settle my debt. I left without paying you back."

"Pay me back?" the Constable asked him. "You owe me a life!"

"I don't owe you a life," the Colonel said. "I owe you a woman."

"You must have forgotten who the fuck I am. Who do you think runs this place now? I could arrest you and take you to the county capital. You'd get the death penalty." At the time, our county was under the control of the Japanese. The Constable was a collaborator. Since the Colonel was fighting the Japanese, the Constable was obliged to hand him over to them, or to their puppet government.

While he was ranting, the Colonel took a gold ingot out of his pocket and set it on the counter with a thud. "That isn't a coating. It's pure gold. I'm paying you back for the woman I took from you."

The ingot was about three inches wide and two inches high. It looked like a glob of flame. Its glow reflected up from the dull varnish of the table.

The Constable looked at the ingot, his mouth watering. But his dignity was worth more than a chunk of gold. He was waiting for the Colonel to say something – anything to convince him. Even though he wanted to grab it off the table, the Constable told himself to wait. But the Colonel turned without speaking. He thought it was better to turn his back on the Constable, and not watch him take it. He thought it would help the Old Constable preserve his dignity, but the Constable took it as an insult. He took it as the Colonel flaunting his wealth, slamming down the gold and walking out… The Constable picked up the ingot and hurled it at the Colonel's back.

It hit him between the shoulders and then fell to the ground. The Colonel winced and reached down to pick it up. He put it in his pocket and drew his pistol. The Constable sprang back, but the Colonel cornered him. "You're making a mistake," the Colonel said. "I should be dragging you to the firing squad. You know what I do for a living? I hunt down traitors like you."

The Colonel cocked the pistol and the Constable's knees

gave out. He realised that the Colonel had changed. His manhood had been taken, and he had nothing else to lose. The Constable put on a brave face. "You owe me for a woman," he said. "What am I supposed to do with this? This is an insult."

The Constable knew he was beaten, but he wasn't willing to give up. Facing death, he clung to his dignity. "If you want a woman," the Colonel said, "I'll get you one." He took out the ingot again and held it up for the Constable to see. "With this, you can sleep with a dozen girls prettier and younger than your village whore. Come with me."

Where did they go?

Shanghai, of course.

The Colonel's description of the place sounded unbelievable to the Old Constable: trams running between skyscrapers, bright lights, parks bigger than the biggest fields in the village, streets paved with gold, crowds swarming all over like an ant colony, each woman prettier than the last... Everything in Shanghai was improbable, impossible, like something out of a painting. In Shanghai, you could go to see a matinee at noon, go for a stroll in the park, then go dancing and get a massage at the sauna. On hot days, you could sit in front of an electric fan, and when it was hot, there were radiators. All you needed to get by in Shanghai was money and power – available to any man willing to seize it. If you had those things, Shanghai could be a paradise.

The rain reached a crescendo as the Old Constable sighed and said to Grandpa, "The way he described it, I couldn't get it out of my fucking head. I had to go with him. We left three days later, in the middle of the night. I remember it was pitch black that night, no moon in the sky. We met up on the bridge and I followed him like his shadow. When I think back on it now, probably the only one that realised I was leaving was that yellow dog. That dog followed me all the way to the bridge, but wouldn't come across. He howled for me, like he was begging me to come back."

Twelve

LIII

By my calculations, it would have been the fall of the thirtieth year of the Republic – that is, 1941 – when they left. That winter, the Pacific War between the United States and Japan started. When the Colonel and the Old Constable arrived, Shanghai was full of Japanese soldiers, but it was still technically an international city, carved up into foreign concessions. People from all over the world were thrown together. The dregs of society mingled with the wealthy and famous. Warlords and soldiers sat down with bureaucrats and diplomats. The puppet government claimed authority, but the Green Gang and the mob held the real power. In the fragrant port of Shanghai, fortunes were won and lost with violence, gambling, and prostitution. Things were especially interesting along Yuyuan Road. The street ran through what looked like farmland, but it was lined with teahouses and whorehouses. It attracted a strange mixture of people, who ranged from venerable heroes of the Republic to ghoulish thieves and monstrous villains. On Yuyuan Road, life roared by at a wicked pace.

After a two-day voyage, the Constable and the Colonel arrived in Shanghai. They travelled there by train and ferry and truck, and finally got pulled into the city by a rickshaw. They arrived at dawn on an eerily calm Yuyuan Road, with a light rain falling. They turned down an alley and were swallowed up by the city. The Constable was seeing it all for the first time. He studied the layout of the city: the streets surrounded lanes that surrounded alleys. The alleys ran like a maze through the interior of the city, joining up or dead-ending seemingly at random. Down the alley they were riding on, the Constable saw windows looking out on them, but they were all seemingly abandoned. The early morning sunshine scarcely penetrated the depths of the cities. The alleys were gloomy. At the end of the alley, there was a golden rain tree inside a high wall. The rain of the night before had shaken the pale yellow blossoms from the tree, and they stuck to the soles of the rickshaw puller's sandals as he ran. He stopped a short distance away, under the shade of the tree. The Constable got down and the Colonel led him to a door marked with a red cross. Below the cross was written: "Private Clinic". The Constable wondered why the Colonel was taking him to see a doctor.

"I thought we were going to get some women," the Constable said. "What are we doing here?"

"We'll stay here until tonight," the Colonel said. "I'll take you to your women tonight." The Colonel showed the Constable around the clinic, told him where he could eat and where he could go to the bathroom, then handed him some money, got back in the rickshaw, and left. Even though the sun was already rising overhead, the alley was dark. The Constable went in and slept on the hospital bed. He woke up and went out to get something to eat, then returned to the bed. A few times, he dreamed that the Colonel had come to get him. The agreed-upon hour came and went, and the Colonel didn't return. The Constable fell back to sleep. When he woke up again, the Colonel was standing over him with a white suit, a peach-coloured felt hat, and black dress shoes.

In one hand, the Colonel held a cigar as thick as a thumb, and in the other, a lacquered rattan box. In the rattan box was an outfit for the Constable to wear out. The Constable looked like a new man. The clothes fit him fine, but they didn't suit him. He looked like a rich man possessed by the soul of a farmer. The Colonel taught him how to walk. He demonstrated his own strut, with his shoulders back and his chest out. The Colonel clicked his heels together, tilted his head back, and gazed into the distance.

The Constable couldn't master the walk. The Colonel couldn't decide whether to laugh or cry. In the end, the Colonel broke down and gave him a pep talk in the village dialect: "Think of this as your village. You are the Constable. You rule over the place with an iron first. The woman you are going to see is your mistress. She does whatever it takes to please you."

When the Constable came close enough, the Colonel led him out the door to the waiting rickshaw. The moon was up, but the golden rain tree cast a long shadow on the alley. The rickshaw took them back the way they had come, but everything was transformed. The empty windows and seemingly abandoned homes had come to life with bright lights. People had dragged stoves out into the doorway and were cooking along the alley. The farther they went, the brighter it got, with more shops, more people, and more rickshaws. The smell of smoke and fire was strong. When they emerged out of the alley, the neon lights exploded like fireworks above them. It was enough to make someone dizzy. The street was full of cars and people and rickshaws. The sound of the street was like the tides, rushing in and then rushing out again, seemingly on its own schedule. The windows on both sides of the street were full of food and clothes and everything else – inviting you to reach out and touch, but protected by glass. Glass, there was so much glass! Lights, everywhere! It was like all the light and all the glass in the world had been concentrated in one place. The Constable's head jerked around, trying to take in everything. He simply couldn't, though. His head was abuzz and his eyes darted around.

The sense of being overwhelmed only increased as the rickshaw pulled them onwards. The Constable had been curious and excited at first, but he was slowly filled with a helpless, lonely fear. He felt like a man being led to his death. The rickshaw puller had seen men react like the Constable, so he pulled off the main road and into the lane. The lights and the chaos disappeared. The lane he chose had been built in a more modern style. It was wider than the dark lanes he had been down in the morning, and lined with ivy-covered walls enveloped with oleander or razor wire. It was absolutely quiet. The heavy iron gates of the homes along the lane were shut tight. Some of the gates even had guards posted outside. The only way you could get in was to shoot your way through. Each wall and each gate protected its own section of the city, but it was the uniformity of the fortifications that gave a sense of security.

There weren't many people around, and the rickshaw puller picked up speed. It was quiet enough to hear the scraping of the rickshaw puller's sandals and the sound of the wheels grinding. The canopy of the rickshaw fluttered in the breeze. The Constable started to wonder where he was being taken. To him, the houses along the lane looked more like prisons than whorehouses. He wondered if that was how women were kept in Shanghai – locked up by the rich and powerful like pets? On the journey to Shanghai, the Colonel had done his best to reassure the Constable, and they had come to an understanding. They trusted each other. The Constable couldn't back out at that point, even if he wanted to. The rickshaw kept going, deeper and deeper into the lane. The extravagant homes with their forbidding gates might have comforted the people who lived within, but they unsettled the Constable. He started to imagine the type of woman that would be waiting for him in a place like that. He was being taken to see a vampiress, he decided. He imagined the vampiress sinking her teeth into his neck, then sucking out his blood. He'd heard similar stories. He'd heard it was actually a pleasant experience.

The Old Constable said to Grandpa: "You know, when I was given the job as Constable, I was working for the puppet government, but I never actually dealt with any Japs directly. I probably heard more about them than you would have, though. I heard they had women that did that sick stuff. Men would die at war and leave everything they had to them. They had good lives and they never went hungry. They idled away their time, just waiting for the next man to come along. You know what they say, the best food can't beat soupy rice, and it's fine to play games against yourself, but the real fun is playing with another person. You wouldn't understand, Sorcerer! You weren't there. I was. I went to Shanghai looking for it, and I found it. I didn't get into the stuff with biting necks, though. That wasn't for me. That was the kind of fucked-up shit that the Japs were doing. Have you ever heard anything like that? Even going back to ancient times... Nobody has ever treated women like the Japs treated them. They'd take six-year-olds, seven-year-olds, and even old crones in their sixties or seventies. They put them out to work in daytime, night-time, anytime, right out on the street. You could do whatever you wanted to them. They were worse than livestock. I saw it in the county capital, first. I saw it with my own eyes. The Japs didn't care about their dignity. The women they had were even more shameless. I told you, someone would even suck your blood! They would bite your neck and keep sucking until you couldn't even stand up. It's disgusting!"

Vampires and monsters ran through the Constable's head, and the rickshaw puller kept going, running faster and faster.

As fast as the rickshaw went, the visions of ghouls spun around in the Constable's head even faster. The lane kept going, seeming to piece right through the heart of the city. The Constable imagined that instead of going through the city, they were descending down into another, subterranean world. The walls and the gates of the underworld seemed to look the same, but there were long red tongues concealed everywhere, stretching out towards the Constable, threatening to suck him dry. He trusted the Colonel, but he was starting to lose his resolve.

"Can you imagine how scared I was?" the Old Constable asked Grandpa. "When we finally stopped in front of a gate, I tried to get out of the rickshaw, but I could barely walk. My knees had just about given out. It was like trying to walk on cotton balls. But even worse, I grabbed my dick to make sure everything was in place – my balls had sucked back up inside my body, and my dick was halfway in, too. I could barely feel it. Just a bit of the head was sticking out. You know how it is, though. That's the part of your body that can take the least amount of pressure. One little scare, it's gone, like a turtle going in its shell."

LIV

The gate and its wall looked much like the others along the lane. The gate's massive door split in the middle. When he got closer, the Constable realised that it wasn't iron at all, but a thick slab of catalpa wood, lacquered and painted a deep crimson. Each half of the door had a knocker in the shape of a lion. The knockers looked like they would be used to summon the King of Hell to drag you down to the underworld. The Colonel seemed not to see the look of panic on the Constable's face. He walked confidently up to the lion's head, knocked once, paused, and then knocked again. The door opened wide enough for the bald man to stick his head out and look at them. Seeing the Colonel there, he opened the door and let him and the Constable inside. The bald man nodded and bowed deeply to the Colonel in the same way that the Constable had heard the Japanese greeted each other in the county capital.

The courtyard was not large, but the path from the gate had been paved with bluestone and lined with carefully manicured holly bushes. The path ended at a flowerbed and a sprawling magnolia. The path forked there and led to a pair of modest mansions. One was larger than the other, about three stories, while the smaller was only two stories. The tree was taller than the bigger of the two mansions and spread out luxuriantly to shade the entire courtyard from the moonlight. The lights were on in the big windows of the two mansions. The Colonel motioned for the Constable to follow him. He seemed to know his way around the place. The Colonel didn't bother taking the path, but went straight towards the larger of the two mansions.

Just as they were about to go up the steps to the mansion, light spilled out onto the stairs, and a silvery voice called from inside, "Where have you been? How long has it been, ten days? I thought you jumped in the Huangpu."

The timbre of the voice had the quality of moonlight. It belonged to the hostess of the place, the whore-in-chief of the brothel, the madam. Everyone called her Little Mama. Her make-up was too thick to figure out how old she might be. Her clothes, on the other hand, were thin to the point of being transparent. Every curve of her pale flesh was revealed by her translucent gown. She was in charge of nearly a hundred young women. A few of the women were there to greet them at the door, and many more lounged on sofas or looked down from stairways. Like their mistress, they all wore translucent gowns and heavy make-up. They shrieked with delight when they saw the Colonel and welcomed him back like a member of their family. They even called him Papa.

He spoiled them like they were his daughters. He pulled out a bankroll, slapped it into his palm, then smacked it down on the table. "Everybody take one," he shouted. "There's enough for everybody." The girls shrieked and laughed. They ran out into the main room of the mansion like they were doing a fire drill. In an instant, every woman in the place was gathered around the stack of cash.

The Old Constable said: "You should have seen him that night! He had style! The man knew how to carry himself. Until that night, I still thought of him as a village carpenter. I had seen a few KMT officers before, but none of them would have been fit to fetch his slippers. That night, I saw things I couldn't even have dreamed of – stacks of money, women all over the place... I couldn't believe that people actually lived that way. I saw it all myself, but it still feels like a dream."

The Colonel led the Constable and Little Mama to the private reception room. The Constable was immediately hit with the aroma of the place: the smells of liquor and perfume, cigarette smoke and cosmetics, and disinfectant, all blended up together. The Colonel took a seat on the sofa, pulled Little Mama down onto his lap, and stuffed the gold ingot into her generous cleavage.

Little Mama wrapped her arms around the Colonel's neck and said, "What are you up to?" The diaphanous sleeves of her gown slid down to her shoulders, revealing a peony tattooed on her upper arm. The Constable admired the red flower against the pale flesh of her arm. The Colonel told her all about how he had offered the ingot in return for the Constable's mistress. He explained to Little Mama that he was giving it to her in exchange for the services of her girls, paying back the Constable for taking his woman.

Little Mama looked over at the Constable and laughed. The Constable got a good look at her breasts, spilling out of her lace top. "You're going to kill him," Little Mama said in her soft northern accent. "He's not a young man. You think he can take it?"

"Don't worry about that," the Colonel said. "Just keep him happy. Make sure he enjoys himself. I owe him."

Little Mama produced a photo album and set it down on the coffee table. She flipped through it, letting the stiff pages clatter. "Everything I've got," she said to the Constable. "It's all in here. Each girl has a number. There's no number four, number thirteen, or number fourteen. There are sixteen girls altogether, but numbers nine and fifteen are unavailable. You've got your pick of the litter for one month. If we get fresh meat in after you choose, feel free to switch. They are at your service, for as long as you need them, for as long as you can take it…"

"Where's Number Nine?" the Colonel asked.

"She caught something."

"Then why is she still in the book?" the Colonel asked. "You're going to get someone sick."

"That's exactly why I keep her," Little Mama said.

"That's evil," the Colonel said.

"Nobody comes here with a pure heart," Little Mama said.

That night, the Constable went through five girls, and had dinner sent over twice. Early the next morning, Little Mama called him over to the other mansion to eat breakfast with her. She interrogated him over the meal, asking how he had met the Colonel, what he did for a living, how much money he made, where his hometown was, and where he was staying. The Colonel had prepared him for that, and told him that he shouldn't answer any of her questions truthfully. Their chat was brisk, and quick. Nothing genuine was revealed. The Constable assumed that her man was sleeping upstairs in the mansion. He suspected that man might be the Colonel.

When he left that morning, Little Mama told him: "Five

girls in one night... You have powerful appetites. If you can keep this up for three days, I'll know you're not human. If you really have it in you, I'll be happy to give you a freebie."

The Old Constable laughed. "That fucking slut uses her whores to figure out which men are worth taking out for a ride herself."

Grandpa had grown weary of the Old Constable's adventures in Shanghai. "What's the point of all this?" he asked. "I don't want to hear about this stuff."

"Everything has its source," the Old Constable said. "You have to peel it all back. If you don't hear this part, you won't understand the rest. You don't even know where the story is going. If I hadn't lived it myself, I probably wouldn't even believe it."

I could barely follow the story. Why did the girls all have numbers instead of names? What did it mean that he got five in one night? What did Little Mama train them in? I knew the numbers four and fourteen were unlucky, because they sounded like a character that meant "death", but why was Number Thirteen taken out, too? What kind of disease did Number Nine catch? It had to be something contagious. I assumed she must have got tuberculosis. But why did Little Mama want to use her to get other people sick? I couldn't figure it out. The Colonel's role in all of it was incomprehensible to me, too. I thought he was a special agent for the KMT. What were the other members of his team doing at that time? Why was he hanging out in a brothel instead of hunting down targets?

LV

"I spent the next month that way," the Old Constable said. "During the day, I was at the clinic, then I went over to the brothel at night to eat and fool around. I could order whatever I wanted, drink as much as I want, pick a girl... It was an easy life. If I ever go to heaven, I doubt it'll be as good as that month was. But he – the Eunuch, I mean – wasn't around much. It was almost like he was avoiding me. Maybe he was busy with something. Whenever I saw him, he was always in a hurry to get somewhere. He always had that satchel with him, with his medical tools in it. I couldn't figure out exactly how he ran his clinic. It was open at strange hours. Most of the time, someone would just show up looking for him. They weren't regular people. Special people. They all dressed nice, but most of these guys had a shoulder holster with a pistol in it, or a knife strapped to them. He didn't let me meet some of them. He'd send me out on an errand, so I wouldn't be there when they showed up. Most of the time, though, I acted sort of like an assistant to him. I'd greet whoever came by, pour them some tea, and see them off when he was done. Even though some didn't look it, they were all willing to spend big for the Colonel's services, and there were often generous tips for me.

"So, like I said, I was over at that brothel most nights, fooling around. You know what I was doing? Let me tell you, nothing goes together like whores and gambling. That's how I got hooked on gambling. The first couple years, I actually did okay, but the losses started building up. You know how that ended. I ended up losing everything I had. I remember this so clearly... It was the last year of the war against Japan, sometime in May. I staked my house as collateral for a loan. I went all in on one final bet. I decided that if I won, I'd give it all up and buy a post as a county magistrate, and if I lost, I'd drown myself in the Huangpu. In the end, I didn't do either. I lost everything and I went back to the village to live like a stray dog. I had some kind of a bad spirit trapped inside of me. When I was winning money, that spirit started burning like a flame. When I started losing, that spirit lost all its spark. That's what gambling was like for me."

"All right," Grandpa said. "I've got it: you were gambling and whoring."

"Just quit interrupting me," the Old Constable said. "So, one day, I had gone through every girl in the place a couple times. I spent the rest of that month with just one girl: Number Seven. I was sick of all the other women, but she scratched an itch. That's how it is, sometimes. You find your perfect match. Number Seven is the reason I ended up gambling. She took me to the card table. Whatever I lost came out of my pot, but she got half of whatever I won, so she was raking it in, and that put her in a good mood. I guess it was fate that brought us together. She was aimed like a bullet at my heart.

"All right, so, Number Seven eventually started talking about the Eunuch. When I had been going through the other girls, I always asked them what they knew about him. None of them would talk. Little Mama had told them to keep their mouths shut up about him. Me and Number Seven had a certain trust between us. I wore her down and she eventually started to open up. She told me a lot of strange things."

Grandpa leaned back on the bed, reassured that the Old Constable was finally getting to the Colonel.

"It turns out that the clinic was a cover," the Old Constable said. "Did you know that? You know he was an agent for the KMT. He didn't work directly for Dai Li, the chief of the KMT intelligence services, but for one of his key operatives. It was a woman, actually. Beautiful woman, too, but fierce... Some people said she was Dai Li's mistress. One time she was on a mission in Shanghai and ended up getting hurt. The KMT got her out of Nanjing, and they called for the Eunuch. He ended up saving her life and delivering a baby she didn't even know she was pregnant with. You've heard that story before, right? The Eunuch used to tell it himself."

I'd heard him tell the story, too. There were three bullet holes in her. The Colonel delivered the baby and it survived, even though it was only about the size of a kitten.

"She went to Dai Li and got the Eunuch sent to Shanghai," the Old Constable said. "He was a capable doctor already, and they trained him as a spy. It had to be Shanghai because that woman had her cover blown in Nanjing. I mentioned that before, right? When the Eunuch pulled the gun on me, he told me he was tracking down traitors for the KMT. I jumped up when he pulled the gun on me and he started—"

"Get back to Shanghai!" Grandpa interrupted.

"Shanghai?" the Old Constable asked. "Where was I?" He thought for a while, then reached for another cigarette. "Oh yeah, I was going to tell you about that filthy whore. I'll tell you, she was far more than a common slut – she was a traitor to the nation!" The Old Constable puffed on his cigarette. "I'm talking about Little Mama. She was a pimp for the Japs. Just down the road from that brothel I went to, she ran another one, just for them. She reserved her best girls for the fucking Japs. I tried to walk in there and they gave me the boot. The place was guarded by two big, strong guys with a pair of German shepherds. Running dogs with running dogs! If you got anywhere close to the gate, they'd tell you to fuck off. If you kept going after that, they'd either slap you or sic the dogs on you. I watched the place for a while. The Japs were coming and going in big cars. Big walls, everything covered in gold and silver – it was enough to make me sick!"

The Old Constable was back on track. He stubbed out his cigarette and went on, "Basically, what I'm saying is, that fucking whore was running two brothels side by side. It turned out that the one I went to served as a training ground for the other one. She took a girl, dumped her in the first brothel, got her all trained up, then sent her to the Japs. But some girls didn't make the cut. They weren't good enough for the Japs. Those were the ones that stuck around, for the most part. Sometimes it would be a situation where the Jap brothel didn't have enough girls, so the girls at the other brothel were like troops in the barracks, just waiting to be sent to the front line – serving the Japs. There were no Chinese people allowed in the Jap brothel, except for the girls. In the first brothel, anyone could go in, as long as you had the money. That's how it worked.

"According to what Number Seven said, the Eunuch had appeared at the beginning of that year, right around Spring Festival. I figure he must have got word that there was a Jap brothel being run on the side, and he figured he could use the madam to infiltrate it. The Eunuch was a popular man, right from the start. There was something unique about him. He had skills. You can see what I'm getting at, right? It wasn't really him that became famous – but that cock of his earned a name for itself!

"Number Seven had seen it herself. Yes, she'd been with him before me. She told me all about it. The Eunuch's dick was unlike any other she had ever seen, and she had seen plenty. It had been rebuilt! What I mean is, it had been cut off, and when they sewed it back on, it changed. There were stitches here and there, but the texture of the entire thing had changed – it had got thicker, longer, and it was as rough as a walnut shell. It's hard to explain but it's like all the scar tissue built up. Number Seven told me that the top half was covered in grooves and bumps. It's like rebuilding anything: you make it stronger than it was before, but it never ends up looking quite the same. It looked strange, but it worked. If these girls knew anything, they knew dick. All the girls said it was the best they'd ever had. The feeling was incredible. It drove women wild."

Grandpa couldn't take it. "Enough about that," he said.

"All right," the Old Constable said. "But you get my point. We heard he got it cut off, but we never heard what happened after that. We didn't get all the facts. People were just making things up. That includes me! I hated the guy. I was the one that started the rumour that a KMT officer castrated him. I knew that he'd got it cut off, but I didn't know he stuck it on again. None of us knew. None of us realised that his dick was legendary! All the girls in the brothel ran their mouths about it. Everyone had to try it. He knew how to use it, too. That's what they told me, at least. He fucked every girl in there. So, if you want me to believe he's a sodomite... There's no fucking way! There are a hundred whores in Shanghai that would testify on his behalf."

LVI

The Old Constable was drunk when he arrived, and he'd been drinking water from the time he came in the door. He went to take a piss and came back to continue, "The madam trained all her whores. When she heard rumours about the Eunuch, she wanted to try him for herself. He was as good as all the girls said. She lost her mind. After she fucked him, she called a meeting. She set two rules: don't fuck him and don't tell anybody about fucking him. She kept him for herself, only sometimes lending him out as a sort of prize. You know who got him? Female Japs and foreign devils. Some of those Jap women, their husbands got killed on the battlefield, but they inherited all the money their husbands had looted and the power they'd accrued. These were no ordinary widows, either. They were young, they were hungry, they were reckless. They couldn't just sit at home.

"That fucking whore – that traitor to her people – she was pimping Chinese women to the Japs, making a fortune off it, and she dealt with them directly, too, so she started making connections. That was how she came to learn about the war widows. She was willing to help them out. That business, though, wasn't like the brothel. The brothel operated out in the open. But the stuff with the female Japs was all secret. She already knew a few men who were willing to do anything for money. These were not good men, of course. But they were shameless. A brothel attracts men like that, like a piece of rotten meat attracts flies."

The Old Constable seemed to anticipate a question from Grandpa and said, "I'm not including the Eunuch with them. He had integrity. He had great ambitions. He was patriotic. He hated the Japs! Just look at what they'd done to him: they killed his father, and they almost robbed him of his manhood. You better believe he had it out for the Japs! He'd fought them right on the front line. And he was willing to risk his life in that den of ghouls in Shanghai to kill them and anybody who worked for them. He was loyal to the nation, and he was looking for more personal revenge. That's why he had got mixed up with the madam. When the chance came to gather intelligence for his superiors on goings-on at a Japanese brothel, it was a chance he couldn't pass up. It was exactly what he'd been hoping for. As the old saying goes... What was that one again? If you aren't a tiger, don't something something..."

I knew what he was trying to say. It was: "If you aren't willing to go into a tiger's den, you'll never catch his cubs."

There were all those legends about Tiger Mountain being a tiger that escaped from Sea Dragon Mountain. Grandpa told them to me. He liked idioms about tigers, too. There was one that went, "a newborn calf isn't scared of a tiger," "the family of a general will produce tiger cubs," "fear a wolf that you can see and the tiger that you can't," "one mountain is never big enough for two tigers," "if there are no tigers in the mountains, the monkeys will call themselves kings," "a man at forty-five is like a tiger descending from his mountain," "leopards and tiger can always be found in the mountains, and good men always emerge in trouble times," "a hunter must walk in hills where he knows tigers hide," "to catch a dragon, go to the sea, and to catch a tiger, climb a mountain," and on and on... I could quote them back to you all day.

I couldn't shout down from the attic to correct the Old

Constable, but Grandpa was there to guide him back on track: "You mean, 'If you aren't willing to go into a tiger's den, you'll never catch his cubs.' There's another one, 'a hunter must walk in hills where he knows tigers hide.'"

"That's the one," the Old Constable said impatiently. "He knew there were tigers, but that's exactly why he was going up the mountain. The Eunuch knew exactly what that whore was up to. He was taking a risk getting involved with those foreign women, too. They weren't toothless old crones. They could have got him in trouble, too. There was always the chance he would have his cover blown. If someone found out he was sleeping with the enemy or traitors to the cause, he could be exposed. He was committing two crimes: whoring around and sleeping with the enemy." The Constable paused and thought for a second before continuing, "You know, it's one thing for a woman to sell pussy. That's a crime. But if a man sells his dick, that's even worse. If a woman sold pussy to the Japs, that made her a traitor, on top of everything else. If a man was selling his dick to the Japs – what would that make him? He wouldn't even be considered human. It's, like, legally, you couldn't even charge him with a crime! To do something like that, he'd have to be a subhuman monster... When the Japs showed up on the doorstep, every able-bodied man should have gone to the front lines. Whatever a man had done, if he was willing to fight and die for his people, we could forgive him. But if he stayed behind and crawled into the beds of the enemy's women. His family would be cursed for generations.

"The Eunuch was an intelligent man. He must have known that. He must have stepped into that pit of snakes knowing that he might not drag himself out alive. If anybody ever found out what he'd done, nobody would understand. At that moment, he separated himself from all the good people of the world. He could've jumped in the Yellow River and the stain would still be on him. But the Eunuch knew he had to do it. It was his job. He was willing to risk everything. That's how the Eunuch had always been, though. Once he set his mind on something, he went through with it. He was brave and he was stubborn as an ox. The whore hatched her evil plan to use him, and he went along with it. He went right into the tiger's den. She sent him straight to the barracks a couple times to entertain some Jap women. When I got to Shanghai, that's what was keeping him so busy. Little Mama thought she was using the Eunuch, but he was actually using her. At the same time, he had to keep his cover as a doctor. He had to look after me, too. That's why he was always rushing around. He kept up appearances, though. Like I said, all the girls at the brothel called him Papa. They considered him their boss. Like I said, I didn't see him much in those days. But I heard plenty of rumours from the girls. Half the time I was over in the brothel, he was in the mansion next door…

"But, of course," the Old Constable emphasised, "I had no idea what was going on. I didn't even know what the KMT or the Communists were up to at the time, either. He avoided all my questions. I asked him directly a few times, but he'd just say, 'It's better for you if you don't know.' You know how he talked. He said to me one time, 'While you're here, just listen to your little head. Your little head might get you in trouble, but nothing you can't get yourself out of. If you start thinking with your big head, that's how you get yourself mixed up in something that can't end well.' Life was good, so I took his advice. I was living like a god. I let my little head do the thinking."

I had no idea what the Old Constable was talking about. Who has a big head and a little head? I could figure out about half of what he was talking about, but a lot of it made no sense. "He knew there were tigers, but that's exactly why he was going up the mountain" – I understood that part clearly. It meant the Colonel was like a hero, going up into the mountains to hunt tigers, even though he knew it was dangerous. There was nothing shameful about that – it was shameless, in the best sense of the word! The Colonel was willing to go into the lair, even though, if anybody found out what he was doing, it would mean he would never be able to hold his head high again. I couldn't figure out why the Old Constable considered this a dark secret. It was the story of a hero!

LVII

When the Old Constable started talking about things I didn't understand, I started to tune out. My attention fell on the slanted dormer window. The way the rain was blowing, it was falling at an angle perpendicular to the window's angle. For some reason no rain seemed to blow inside. There was no glass in the window, but it was set so far back into the eaves that it stayed dry. It would take a typhoon to blast the rain far enough into the eaves to get the attic wet. That day, there was barely enough wind and rain to moisten the eaves.

A hacking fit drew my attention back to what was happening below me.

It was Grandpa coughing. The Old Constable was smoking the place out. I was struggling, too, but Grandpa must have been nearly asphyxiated. But at that moment, I was more worried about the cigarette supply running out than I was Grandpa's suffering. Just as I expected, the Old Constable paused and said, "I'm out of smokes. You got another pack in there?"

Grandpa motioned for him to get it himself. He had held onto the cigarettes in the cabinet for years, smoking them sparingly. He seemed happy enough to have the Old Constable smoke his way through them, though. It was like a final gesture on his deathbed. The thought of Grandpa dying made me lose interest in the Colonel's story. But Grandpa wanted to hear it.

Grandpa rushed him to rip open the fresh pack. He was dying to hear the story – literally, it seemed. It was like Grandpa was waiting for the Old Constable to finish his story, so that he could roll over and die in peace. The Old Constable wasn't in a hurry, though. He lit his cigarette then went to get some more water and take a piss. When he returned, the Old Constable didn't bother to take a seat. He stood to tell the story, as if delivering a speech.

At this point in the story, a year had passed since he'd arrived in Shanghai. He'd actually gone back to the village at least once, to celebrate the New Year. But he was drawn back to the big city again... "Things had changed there while I'd been gone," the Old Constable said. "Big changes! None of the girls were talking about him" – referring to the Colonel – "and he seemed to have disappeared. I went looking for him at the clinic. Everything looked normal from the outside, but when I got inside, I saw the place was abandoned. I hung around the brothel and eventually I heard some of the girls talking about him. But they sounded different. They didn't call him Papa anymore. Suddenly, there were all sorts of nicknames for him: the Witch Doctor, the Prick, Walnuts... You could tell they didn't respect him anymore. When I first showed up there with him, he was like a member of the family. Things had changed, like I said. That's actually when I heard all that stuff about his dick. Number Seven had to explain to me why they were calling him Walnuts. Before that, she wouldn't dare. She and the other girls still respected him. Something had happened while I'd been away. But what was it? Number Seven wouldn't tell me. I figured she had to know something, though. She just didn't want to tell me.

"I went back and forth between Shanghai and home a few times that year, and I was doing pretty good at the tables. I'd win a bunch, take it home, then come back to do it all again.

I was making bigger bets every time. I didn't know I was just falling deeper into the trap. I remember one time I won a bunch of money, and I was drinking with Number Seven in a room at the brothel. I think that was on my third trip to Shanghai that year. We were both drinking heavy that night. Number Seven ended up passing out. I ran next door and started looking for Little Mama. I wanted to get out of her where the Eunuch had gone. But I ended up running into one of those Number Seventy-Six bastards.

"You know what Number Seventy-Six was? I'm talking about Seventy-Six Jessfield Road. That's the place Wang Jingwei's puppet government had their intelligence agency headquartered. It was notorious. I didn't actually end up there, but I ran into one of their guys. The Seventy-Six crew were far worse than the average collaborator. Wang Jingwei was backed by the Japanese, and both of them were getting the mob to do their dirty work. The criminals could do whatever the hell they wanted, as long as they were available for whatever the puppet government and the Japanese needed. They were ruthless! They'd skin you alive without thinking twice about it. I don't even remember what happened that night. I was too drunk. The next thing I knew, I was waking up in the hospital. I didn't even recognise myself in the mirror. It was like staring into a boiled pig's head. Half of my face was purple. I had big lumps leaking pus... I must have offended the guy somehow, but I was lucky he didn't kill me where I stood. The Bodhisattva was looking out for me.

"In the meanwhile, Number Seven had woken up and went looking for me. She was worried I was going to see the queen whore and ask about the Eunuch. That was why she ended up telling me everything. Everything I'm telling you now, Number Seven told me after the night I got beaten up by the guy from Number Seventy-Six. It turned out three of the Jap women had conspired together to keep the Eunuch as their own. They couldn't bear the thought of him spreading that walnut-shell dick around. What they were really concerned with was him fucking Chinese women. They thought of the Chinese as dogs, and that included the madam of the brothel. That's what she got for trying to please the Japs. They turned on her! No gratitude at all. The Eunuch and the madam were thick as thieves at the time. Little Mama and Papa, right? The Jap women didn't know how to separate them. Finally, they decided to send a spy. That was Number Nine. They paid her off.

"She was sick, right? She caught something while working there. So, she wasn't earning. That made her vulnerable. As soon as she saw the money the Jap women were offering, she went along with whatever they told her to do. Can you fucking believe it? Selling out like that? It's revolting. But the madam had her own connections – she was running a brothel for the Japs, after all, right? She knew people at Number Seventy-Six and some of her customers came straight from Jap headquarters. She never expected those Jap women to come for her. But once she realised what was going on, she called in some favours. They couldn't punish her directly, so they decided to attack the Eunuch. He was faced with a choice between blowing his cover or going back to those Jap women and bravely taking his punishment. Do you know what that punishment was? Can you guess? They got someone to tattoo him, right on his stomach – a warning to him, but also a message to the madam to keep her hands off him."

The Old Constable stopped there. He sat down. He seemed to be savouring Grandpa's reaction, waiting for him to ask the question that he knew he was begging to ask.

"What did they tattoo on him?" Grandpa asked, finally unable to restrain his curiosity.

"I don't know," the Old Constable said. "I told you everything Number Seven told me. She said the madam got drunk one night and told her. She said that the Jap women had a tattoo artist that worked for them. Number Seven said the madam had a peony on her arm that had been done by the same artist. I saw it myself. Blindboy, Meathook, and even your nephew said he had a tattoo on his belly. That would confirm it. As for what he has written on him, I don't actually know. I've thought about, though... Why did the Jap women tattoo him in the first place? They didn't want him sleeping with any Chinese women, right? So, they had to have written something that would scare off anybody that he climbed into bed with."

The Old Constable started telling Grandpa what he knew about the custom. He said he'd known about it even before he went to Shanghai. After he became the puppet government's local constable, he had been invited every year to a meeting in the county capital. All the local bosses got treated like kings. The Japanese even let them use their baths. In the baths, everyone was naked, and the Old Constable noticed that many of the Japanese officers had tattoos all over them. They were mostly Chinese characters – things like "courage", "loyalty", "endurance" – so he could read them. "Sometimes they were on their chest," the Old Constable said, "or on their shoulders or their arms... Usually dark blue, but sometimes black, sometimes red, sometimes—"

"Enough!" Grandpa said. He wanted to hear more about the Colonel.

The Old Constable stood up, scratched his ass, and headed for the door. "'Enough' is right. If the Eunuch knew what I'd told you already, he'd have my head. The rest, well... Let's just say the past is past, and the future is unknown. Forget about it!" He paused in the doorway and turned back. "Get out of bed," he said. "Whatever they wrote on his belly, it's not what you or Blindboy think. You can be sure of that."

He walked out without saying anything else.

Grandpa and I both wanted him to keep talking. But that was it.

Grandpa started to make a slow recovery. The night after the Old Constable visited, he drank a bowl of rice porridge. After that, the colour returned to his cheeks. He got out of bed and went to sit on the stool that the Old Constable had sat on that afternoon. He lit the first cigarette he had smoked since falling ill.

When my father smelled the cigarette smoke drifting out of the eastern addition, he said to my mother: "Whatever medicine you got him seems to have worked."

Thirteen

LVIII

Grandpa slowly recovered, and his relationship with his son improved even quicker. He even called my father by his nickname again. In the past, he'd never called him by any name – just "Hey!" or "Get over here!" or he'd get me to call my father for him. The transformation warmed my heart, but my father seemed not to have noticed. Since the sodomite accusation became public, Grandpa and my father had acted more like enemies than father and son. At best, whenever they ran into each other, they would exchange a scowl. With them, it was either a cold war or a full-blown firefight. If the house wasn't covered in an inch of ice, it was a raging inferno.

Grandpa said: "Both of us hold grudges. For me, it's out of shame. For him, it's out of resentment."

Grandpa's shame had been alleviated, but he still had a guilty conscience. Calling my father by his nickname was the perfect example. That was Grandpa's way of trying to tell my father that he was sorry. One day he sat my father down and told him everything that the Old Constable had told him. My father had always been close with the Colonel, but he had never heard those stories. "Why didn't he tell me about any of that?" my father asked angrily. "How did he hide all of that from me?"

"There's more where that came from," Grandpa said. "The Constable knows…" Grandpa sighed mournfully. "But I guess you don't know anything about it," he said. From that moment on, Grandpa and my father were on the same side again. Their shared goal was getting more information out of the Old Constable.

One afternoon, Grandpa took out a wad of cash and sent me to Mr Seven's shop to buy two *jin* of *shaojiu* and four packs of cigarettes. When I got back, my father made a pan of fried peanuts and put them in a tea mug. They packed it up with the liquor and cigarettes, and headed out for the Old Constable's place. Maybe the past was past, as the Old Constable had said, but a few drinks would loosen his tongue.

The Old Constable lived in a lonely old stone house near the entrance to the village, right at the tip of the tiger's tail. The house had once been an outbuilding on a landlord's property. The landlord had stored his coffin inside. The house was built like a tomb: it had only a single small door, and no windows, except for a pair of small transoms up near the ceiling on either side of the main room. The Old Constable had lost his fortune in Shanghai. He went from a wealthy and powerful man to a homeless wretch stealing offerings from the temple altars. The stone house had been assigned to him after the Communists had arrived to liberate the village.

Grandpa said: "That's the perfect place for a man that needs to keep secrets. Nobody's going to catch him doing something he should be doing. It's like living in a coffin."

It was the perfect place to try to get secrets out of someone. That was what Grandpa and my father thought, at least. Even with the door open, you could talk as loud as you wanted and nobody would hear you. They had no idea that someone was listening to everything they said. That was me, of course. I climbed to the top of the woodpile beside the Old

Constable's house, so that I could hear what was happening inside through one of the tiny transoms. That was one time when I really surprised myself. There was no hiding from me, if I really wanted to know what was going on. Even then, I thought I might have a future as a spy.

LIX

"What the hell is this?"

"*Shaojiu*," my father said. "Two *jin*."

"I know it's *shaojiu!*" the Old Constable said. "I could smell it when you came in. I'm saying, what the hell are you bringing it to me for? You're up to something, Sorcerer. You told him everything, didn't you? And now you want to get me drunk and have me tell you the rest."

"No," Grandpa said, "that's not it at all." I couldn't see, but I knew Grandpa must be grinning. "I came here to thank you. You got me out of bed. You were right when you said there was no medicine that would cure me. I believed I really was set for a date with the King of Hell. You knew exactly how to fix me up. You really did save my life. I thought I should come and thank you."

"Right," the Old Constable said. "You owe me. I won't turn down a drink, either."

"And some cigarettes," my father said. I could picture him pressing the packs into the Old Colonel's palm.

"Sure," the Old Constable said. "I won't turn those down, either. But you're going to be disappointed if you think you can get me drunk so I'll spill my guts. You've both seen me drunk before. But as drunk as I've been, I've never even hinted at those stories before. I only told you" – he was talking to Grandpa – "to save your life. That was the first time I ever told anybody. You" – he was talking to my father – "probably never heard any of that before, right? You two were so close people thought you were fucking each other – why did he never tell you about what happened in Shanghai? He couldn't tell you! And I shouldn't have told you anything, either. You had better keep your mouths shut."

"He told me about being a spy in Shanghai," my father said. He passed the Old Constable a cigarette and lit one for himself. "He told me all those stories. He was serving his country, killing Japs and traitors. What's wrong with that? He told me a bit about the brothel, too. I never heard about the madam and the Jap women, though, or the tattoo…"

"There's plenty you don't know," the Old Constable said firmly.

They were all standing in the small room, but Grandpa was still not quite recovered yet, so he pulled out a stool to sit on. "So, tell us," Grandpa said. "It'll never go further than these four walls."

"I'll tell you," the Old Constable said, pulling out his own stool, "but I want your boy to tell me what he knows."

"What do you want me to say?" my father said, chuckling. "You already know everything."

"Not everything," the Old Constable said.

"Like what?"

"Where is he?" the Old Constable said. "Right now." From his tone, I could picture the Old Constable glaring and jabbing a finger at my father. "You went to see him, didn't you? I want the truth." My father didn't reply. "You know, but you don't want anybody to find out," the Old Constable said. "Don't worry about that. I want to go see him, too. I'm worried about him. He's the only thing left that I have to worry about."

My father remained silent.

The Old Constable sounded emotional as he continued, "Let everyone in this village drop dead tomorrow, but he doesn't deserve it… This is an evil fucking world. That's the only way I can explain it – a man like that reduced to a fugitive, and his poor old mother left to skulk around... I blame Blindboy, that little bastard. If I was still running this village, I would have executed him. He ruined a good man's reputation. He deserves a bullet between the eyes. Do you know what that man did for the country? Do you realise what he went through? You can't even imagine! It was like a living death. He's a hero. Do you even realise that? This is... It's... I don't even know what to call it... Everyone has a path laid out for them by fate. His life was always going to be hard. His fate was to be built up and then torn down. The fact that he's still suffering – it makes me sad." From the quaver in his voice, I realised he was crying. The room was so quiet that I could hear Grandpa wheezing.

After a long time, the Old Constable spoke again. His spirit had returned. "Sorcerer," he said, "tell your son he can tell me. I just want to go see him. I'd die before I tell the Red Guards anything."

Before Grandpa could say anything, my father said, "He's fine. Don't worry about him."

My father's words went off like a gunshot in my head.

I don't know what Grandpa was thinking at that moment. I don't know what his expression looked like. I was scared. I had just heard my father confess to a crime. The police had been hunting all over the place for the Colonel, and my father seemed to know where he was, and might have even been to visit him. It was a crime. That night the Colonel had come to our house, it had been like planting a bomb under our family. Once I heard the confession, I was holding the fuse. I immediately regretted climbing that woodpile to eavesdrop.

Everything could have gone smoothly if my father had simply told the Old Constable what he wanted to know. Instead he seemed to want to provoke the Old Constable. "It's better if you don't know," he said. "If you knew, you'd be just as guilty as me. Let me keep my secrets and you keep yours."

"What are you trying to do?" Grandpa said.

My father kept going, perhaps hoping to goad the Old Constable into saying something. "I know everything," my father said. "One of his men was caught by Number Seventy-Six. They tortured the guy until he talked. That's how they caught him. They sent him to a prison camp in Huzhou to dig coal. That was in the thirty-second year of the Republic, right?"

"What about after that?" the Old Constable asked. "How did he get out of the prison camp?"

"He saved some Jap commander," my father said.

The Old Constable laughed in my father's face. "Is that what you think? You think the Japs needed a doctor? We're not talking about the New Fourth Army. The Japs had the best doctors in the world. Let me tell you, I was running a fever one time... I was burning up, three days straight, ranting and raving. All the whores thought I was going to die. Number Seven took pity on me and went to the madam. Two pills – that's it! Two little green pills. I started feeling better almost right away. It was like the fire was going out. At the time, I thought it was like some kind of magical elixir. It saved my life. So, let me ask you again, do you really think the Japs needed doctors? Why would they send for a guy like him to save one of their top guys? Are you really that stupid?"

"Then you tell us," Grandpa said angrily. "Tell us, please," he said, trying to temper the harshness in his tone. "How did he get out of there?"

"It's better if you don't know," the Old Constable said. "Isn't that right? I'd be committing a crime by even telling you. Say what you want, but it's for your own good that I'm not telling you. It's for your family's own good. Why do you want to take this onto your shoulders? You think you can take it? You want to be like me? I held onto those secrets all by myself. Here I am now, just waiting around to die, still holding onto the secrets. Even now, when I want to go see him, you" – he was talking to my father – "won't tell me where he is. That's fine. As long as you know where he is, you can take him something for me. Take him that liquor you brought me. I want you to take it to the Eunuch."

I was terrified of what would happen if my father gave in and led the Old Constable to the Colonel. I knew the police would follow them all the way there. I had snuck up on the woodpile because I wanted to hear stories. All I was hearing down in that coffin house was bad luck. It felt like a nightmare.

A deal was struck between the Old Constable and my father.

LX

Even though the latter half of the Colonel's story seemed to hover over our heads like a sword, Grandpa was not flustered. His heart had already been put at ease. All of his suspicions had been for nothing. He was a happy man. The stories the Old Constable had told him had made Grandpa so happy that he couldn't keep them to himself. He wanted to show them off. He took them out, one by one, and passed them around. The stories started to spread – from the ancestral hall to Mr Seven's shop to the tailor...

The Old Constable showed up at our house almost immediately. He was always among the first to hear the latest gossip, and he knew the source of these particular rumours had to be Grandpa. At first, Grandpa denied everything, but he was finally forced to admit it. He told the Old Constable that he wanted to "restore the family's dignity". They squared off like two gamecocks in the courtyard, squawking back and forth. I was on Grandpa's side at first, but the Old Constable had a good case.

"I know they aren't sodomites," Grandpa said, "but what good does that do me, if everyone in the village is still saying they are. You must have heard them. What's wrong with trying to tell the truth?"

"I've heard them," the Old Constable said. "I've heard more than you have."

"Then let me tell them the truth! You want me to just take their abuse lying down? We're talking about my family's reputation. It's humiliating!"

"It's useless. The second you finish telling someone the truth, they run around the corner and tell someone else that you were just there trying to spread rumours. The whole thing gets twisted back on you."

"I told everyone that you said it," Grandpa said.

"But I can't admit I said it," the Old Constable said. "I promised the Eunuch I wouldn't say anything."

"Blindboy is still spreading lies," Grandpa said. "I just want you to tell everyone he's making it up. Please, Constable, I'm begging you." He rarely called him anything but Hooligan – that meant he was begging him for help. "We've been through a lot. I need you to tell them the truth. I can't die with this hanging over my family. Gossip is a fearful thing, Constable. Help me undo all of this. Let me die with some dignity."

"It's not that I don't want to help you, Sorcerer. I broke my promise to the Eunuch to save your life. But I can't help you now. I could walk up to the front of the hall and tell them everything I told you, but it wouldn't matter. They know we've always been close. Everyone knows that. They'd say you put me up to it. They'd assume you had paid me off to cover for your son. You're always so rational – can't you imagine what would happen?" Grandpa didn't reply. "Sorcerer," the Old Constable said, "I told you to forget about it. The past is the past. Don't waste your time twittering like a fucking magpie, trying to get these people to change their minds. It's only going to make things worse. You're going to humiliate both of us. There are some things you just have to accept. That's fate. Sometimes you can't fight it."

"Tell me how to fix it," Grandpa begged. "Tell me what I should do."

Seeing that he had wasted his words, the Old Constable stood up and headed for the gate. "I'll tell you how to fix it," he said, "just shut up and let it go away." The Old Constable was already walking away. "Your problem is that you're too damn selfish. All you care about is your dignity. What good does dignity do you? Fuck, look at me… Once upon a time, I was living like a stray dog. The Eunuch was an officer in the KMT and now he's a fugitive. Nothing means shit. Look at Blindboy! He's a fucking cripple, writing with his toes. But none of that matters to you. All that matters is your dignity, like the world revolves around you."

Grandpa was dumbstruck. He was confronted with the idea that he could do nothing about all of the smears that had been dumped on his family. He just had to swallow them. I knew he couldn't accept it, though. A short time later, he called me over to accompany him to see Blindboy. He was going to bring a basket of corn as a gift.

"I thought you hated Blindboy," I said. "Why are you going to see him?"

"I need to talk to his father."

He waited until he knew Blindboy had left to go over. Grandpa passed a cigarette to the Blind Man and asked how he'd been. Grandpa admitted that he'd been spreading rumours about Blindboy being a sodomite. He apologised. He explained that he was simply trying to deflect the rumours about his own son. I wanted to drag Grandpa out of there. I tugged at his shirt but he just ignored me.

The Blind Man said nothing. But he seemed to have noticed the corn. He couldn't see it, but he could smell it. "That corn smells fresh," he said.

"I just picked it this morning," Grandpa said. Seeing

Grandpa grovelling like that, I wished that I had thought to piss on the corn before we brought it.

The Blind Man was two years younger than Grandpa, but he looked much older. His hair and beard were a dishevelled grey mess. He looked like he hadn't eaten a good meal in a long time. His shirt was missing buttons, and he had on a pair of old underpants with a stretched out waistband. I wanted to pity him, but I knew I couldn't. Blindboy and his father had done their best to hurt my family. It made me happy to see his household in such a state.

"I wouldn't need to be a fortune teller to know you aren't coming to have your future read," the Blind Man said. His blind, white eyes were fixed on the ceiling. He looked like he was toying with something in his hands, even though they were empty. Maybe it was Grandpa's heart he was toying with. "I assume you're here to see my son. He's out. Tell me, and I'll pass it along to him."

Grandpa was rarely at a loss for words, but that was one of those times. It took him a long time to get to his point, but it was this: he knew Blindboy had seen some words written on the Colonel's belly, but Grandpa thought Blindboy was lying about what was written there, and he hoped Blindboy would tell everyone what he had actually seen.

"The Eunuch treated you well, didn't he?" Grandpa asked. "He doesn't deserve to be insulted like this."

"Why do you think my son's lying about what he saw?" the Blind Man asked.

"I know he's not a sodomite. I have someone that can prove it."

"Who's that?"

I motioned for Grandpa to keep his mouth shut. Grandpa thought for a long time and then said, "It's the Old Constable." My eyes rolled back into my head, just like the Blind Man's. I couldn't believe he had revealed it.

"Him?" the Blind Man said. "Two bowls of *shaojiu*, a

pack of cigarettes, and a pair of thighs, and you can get him to say whatever you want him to. Don't drag him into this." Grandpa was impervious to the hostility in the Blind Man's tone.

"If that's what the tattoo said, the Eunuch wouldn't have cut out his tongue. That's not worth doing that over."

"That's ridiculous," the Blind Man said, chuckling. "Anyways, what does it have to do with you?"

The laugh sent chills through me. It sounded like the Blind Man knew exactly what Grandpa had in mind. I pulled Grandpa to go, but he held back. I couldn't believe it. He came to the Blind Man in peace and the Blind Man had spit in his face. It seemed like Grandpa was completely unaware. I left Grandpa standing there. I have no idea how the rest of the conversation went. To me, what Grandpa was doing was shameful. It reminded me of something he had said to me once: "If you don't pull your head out of your ass, you'll eat shit for breakfast."

Grandpa came home from the Blind Man's house in a rage. "He must have been cursed – the Heavens cursed him to be a blind man. I opened a dog's mouth looking for ivory! I'm just as blind as he is!"

I wanted to remind him of what he had told me about pulling my head out of my ass, but when I saw how angry he was, I kept my mouth shut. More than angry, he was desperate. He looked like a wounded animal.

Grandpa used to say that life and death were only separated by a thin sheet of paper, and I realised that the separation between humans and animals was just as thin.

LXI

That road that went along the creek followed its twists and turns. I'm talking about the highway. It ran along the creek towards the mountains. As it approached the mountains, there was a fork in the road: one route led to Yongkang, Dongyang, Yiwu, and Jinhua, and another route led to Xiaoshan, Zhuji, and Shaoxing. If you got on the road beside the Fuchun River, you could get to town, the county capital, and even as far as Hangzhou, Suzhou, and Shanghai. The county capital was on the north side of the river and the village was on the south side, so you had to take a ferry to get there. It was an old steam ferry with a deck that was about as big as a basketball court. You could drive a jeep right onto it.

Grandpa told me that the Japanese had brought the ferry and built the road. The Qiantang River Bridge in Hangzhou had been blown up to stop the Japanese from crossing, so they had gone upstream looking for somewhere to cross the river. They found the ideal place near the county capital. The river was narrow there, and both banks were fairly flat. They built a wharf and started running a ferry. That was how they brought across all the tanks and soldiers. They pillaged and looted their way towards Yongkang and Jinhua. That was where the provincial government had been temporarily relocated, along with some units of the KMT's army. When the Japanese troops arrived, the KMT knew that they were no match, so they ran for the hills, slowly retreating towards Jiangxi. The mountains were the perfect place to hide, and they could occasionally mount a counterattack or plan an ambush. When the Japanese figured out – or were tipped off about – exactly where they were being attacked from, they called in air and artillery strikes. The all-out assault managed to knock a few peaks off the mountains, and the rest were left scorched. The planes flew away after dropping their bombs, but the tanks stayed behind. The tanks kept shelling for over a week. Most of the villagers escaped, and those that couldn't flee sought refuge in the Guande Temple. That was the time that the Bodhisattva in the form of the abbot had intervened to save the temple. The abbot had fought the Japanese commander and beat him, so the temple and everyone inside was spared.

But when the tanks and troops left, the villagers returned to find that the village had been looted. All the grain had been eaten, the animals slaughtered, and everything of value stolen. Grandpa said that was their policy in whatever village they occupied. I learned from the Old Constable that it was even worse: not only did they take grain, livestock, and valuables, but women, too. The village was cleared out before the Japanese troops arrived, but they caught a dozen or so women and girls up in the hills. They locked them up in the ancestral hall and took turns raping them. When the villagers returned, there were two corpses left behind in the ancestral hall. One was the body of an old woman and the other was a young girl. They were completely naked. They looked as if they had been fucked to death.

The Old Constable said: "There's an old saying, 'A baby can't cry itself to death, a man can't work himself to death, and a woman's never been fucked to death.' But those two were fucked to death. Look at who they chose to do it with – one was a little girl, a virgin, and the other was an old woman, already all dried up... The Japs weren't human. They were worse than animals!"

Grandpa never told me about stuff like that. I think he was worried that it would contaminate me somehow. Grandpa told me that the path of the highway had originally been carved out by the Japanese tanks. The tanks steamrolled through, leaving a rough trail that got pounded into a road by the tracks and tyres of the trailing vehicles. At first, the highway was just tamped earth that turned to mud in the rainy season and dust in the summer. In New China, when the workers became the masters of their own domain, the government called on people to build and repair roads. Dirt roads like the old highway were covered in gravel. Granite was blasted out of the mountains, then smashed to pieces by rock crushers. The pieces of gravel were all mostly grey and brown, with every hundredth piece white, and every thousandth or so piece the same colour as the blueish-grey cobblestone in the village. When the sun shone on the road, each colour seemed to show its true hue. When it rained, all the colours seemed to fade into one uniform, nameless shade.

Grandpa took the road a few times a month. He went up towards the mountains to visit his eldest daughter and his youngest daughter, and towards the river, to visit his second eldest daughter. When he went visiting, the Colonel usually appeared on our doorstep. Grandpa still went out to visit, but the Colonel no longer came. Nobody knew where the Colonel was at that moment, except for my father. I lived in constant fear that the Public Security Bureau would either follow my father to the Colonel's hiding place or show up to interrogate me.

As the seasons passed, Captain Hu's revolutionary poem slowly faded from fiery red to light pink. It faded even quicker when we started firing balls against it in gym class. On rainy days, the wet balls would leave a dark stain behind. Most of the ball prints were washed off eventually, but some seemed to have been permanently baked into the wall by the sun. Seeing that poem on the wall, faded and scuffed, I would sometimes think of Captain Hu. When I thought of Captain Hu, I thought about the Colonel, and then my mind would always drift towards my nightmare of the PSB using my father to track him down.

My courage was wilting as I got older, even as I got stronger. A year earlier, I couldn't lift Grandpa, but by that time, I could carry him upstairs on my back. He didn't actually need to be carried. He had no reason to go upstairs, either. But I could have carried him upstairs, if I needed to. My courage had wilted, though. Grandpa had shrunk a bit since the time when the Old Constable had saved his life. His clothes were baggy and flapped in the breeze like a sail.

Grandpa said: "The tail always looks bigger on a skinny horse, and the same goes for a man's mouth." It seemed to hold true for him. Even if he'd been physically diminished, he was as smart as ever. He still went out every morning to stroll to the ancestral hall or Mr Seven's shop. He still took trips to see his daughters. My life went on as it always had, too. I entered my third year of junior high school. I did my homework and looked after my rabbits. My grades weren't bad, but not good enough to get into high school. I figured I wouldn't get in, so I didn't exert myself much in my final year of junior high. I ticked off each day like a monk tolls a bell. I tried to spend as little time in school as I could, often getting there late, then finding an excuse to leave early.

One afternoon in October, Stumpy Tiger and I came up with a plan: he would fake an injury and I would volunteer to take him home. We waited until gym class, and Stumpy Tiger collapsed in the sand pit. Our acting was perfect. I volunteered right away to take him home. I tossed him onto my back, and we left. As soon as we left the gates of the school, he jumped down and ran alongside me. We headed out past the tiger's tail, and up into the hills. There was a superstition in the village about cutting down trees in the section that they called the tiger's ass. It had remained virgin forest. The big trees were covered in vines and surrounded by thick brush. Plunging into that section of the forest was like entering another world. In the spring, we went there to collect raspberries. In the summer, we picked wild peaches. And in the autumn, there were wild persimmons. By October, the persimmons were just turning from green to red, and the mouth-numbing astringency faded to a tart sweetness. We climbed the trunk of the tree and gently shook the branches until the ripest persimmons fell. We knew not to shake too hard or the green persimmons would fall, too. We considered that immoral. It's hard to explain, but we understood that rule clearly: to benefit yourself at others' expense was permissible, but it was forbidden to do things harmful to others without benefiting anyone. It was a basic moral rule that had been passed down to us like a birthmark by our ancestors. Basically, eating the ripe persimmons was benefiting ourselves at nature's expense, so it was permissible. If we shook down unripe persimmons, it would be harming the forest without benefiting anyone – even pigs wouldn't eat green persimmons, and all they would do is attract mosquitoes.

We were too early. Only a few persimmons fell, and none of them were sweet. Eating unripe persimmons is like rubbing sandpaper on your tongue. We decided to wait two days and try again. On our way back to the village, we ran into Blindboy. It was over by the Guandi Shrine. He moaned something at us. We couldn't understand him, but he seemed to be happy about something. I wondered if he had just gone to the shrine to confess his guilt and Guan Yu to heal him. But I knew that the statue of Guan Yu was already gone from the altar inside. Blindboy and the Red Guards had smashed it. I knew there was no hope of him being healed, either. For that, he'd have to wait until he was dead. The King of Hell would give him back his body. Grandpa and the Old Constable had both said that. They rarely agreed on anything, but they were unanimous on that. I finally realised that Blindboy must have snuck into the shrine to steal offerings.

Grandpa said: "You can tear down a temple and people will still go to make offerings, even if the only people that take them are beggars."

Over the previous year, Blindboy's family had spent their savings on his medical treatment. His condition didn't improve. The family was so poor that they struggled to feed themselves. An empty stomach is shameless: he went to the shrine to steal the offerings. When he had raided the shrine, he went hunting for salted pork and bamboo shoots drying on the eaves of houses in the village. He would sometimes root in the garbage and take home whatever he could scavenge. If he could still climb trees, he probably would have taken all the wild persimmons. His belly was a bottomless pit. He was always hungry. He must have found something good on the altar that day.

When I got home, dinner was already on the table but nobody was eating. Grandpa was in the east addition, smoking a cigarette. My father was across the courtyard. I looked into the western addition and saw him, his head low, and a cigarette burning between his fingers. I knew something horrible had happened. The courtyard between the two additions might as well have been a moat of bloodstained water. I had no idea what I had missed. Later that night, I learned that the Colonel had been arrested.

Fourteen

LXII

About an hour's walk from our village was another small village, called Qinwu. If you kept walking for another hour into the mountains from Qinwu, you would come to a larger village called Luo Village. That was where Grandpa's three eldest daughters lived. Every Spring Festival, I went with Grandpa to visit each of my aunts. I hated going to see my Third Aunt because it was such a long walk to get there. I had to go, though. It was tradition. I ended up learning a bit about Luo Village... For example, I knew why it was called Luocun. At first I thought it was because everyone there had the surname Luo, but that turned out not to be the case. "Luo" means "camel", and the village got the name because the people there were like camels. Our village had plenty of water from the Great Source, but Luo Village seemed to be in a constant drought. Even when the spring thaw came, the streams there would often run dry. The people of Luo Village had to dig deep cisterns to store their water.

Grandpa told me that the problem in Luo Village was that it was in the wrong place. None of the mountains nearby held much water, and the area around the village was dominated by one narrow ridge – Leech Ridge. It was long and skinny and formed from dark stone. It looked like a leech and it seemed to suck up all the water from the land around it. A leech isn't like a mosquito, which sucks blood until it's full or it gets chased off. A leech is stupid – you can't shoo it away. A leech just keeps sucking. You have to tease and tickle it off.

Leech Ridge was like a leech. People from outside the area would try to get across it, thinking the trail over it might be a shortcut. They found themselves regretting their decision just as they reached the spine of the Leech, running low on food and water...

The mountains of the area were a field of peaks that looked like a choppy ocean with its waves frozen in stone, and Leech Ridge jutted into the waves like a peninsula. It served as a boundary between our county and the neighbouring county, called Xiaoshan. If you crossed over Leech Ridge into Xiaoshan County from Luo Village, you'd find yourself in the valley that was home to Little Chen Village. On the ridge of the valley was Great Chen Village. By the time you got to Great Chen Village, you were already on the edge of what was called the Hangzhou-Jiaxing-Huzhou Plain. Out on the plain, the villages could spread across the landscape, unencumbered by the mountains. Great Chen Village had a population of about ten thousand people, and it was about twice the size of my own village. It was the largest village in the province, in fact. I didn't know any of that for sure, but it's what Grandpa told me.

Grandpa said: "If you want to hide a leaf, put it in a tree. If you want to hide a person, put them in a crowd."

The Colonel was an intelligent man. He knew where to hide.

He went to Great Chen Village with his mother and they settled in a local temple. The Colonel's mother had met a monk from the temple years before at Mount Putuo. The monk had a malignant tumour growing on his spine. The tumour looked like an old woman's tit hanging off his back.

It swayed side to side as he walked. When it was time to run, he remembered the story his mother had told him about the monk. He went to the temple, offered his assistance as a surgeon, and bargained a place to hide out.

He was out of the reach of the police. Our local county's Public Security Bureau hadn't circulated their wanted posters there. Nobody knew he was a fugitive. He spent more than a year in the temple, sweeping the floors, and sitting beside his mother while she chanted sutras. After a while, he could recite more sutras from memory than even the monk. He shaved his head and dressed as a monk. He even learned the local language. Nobody suspected his true identity. He was well respected in Great Chen Village, just as he had been in our village, and he got along with everyone he met. When the Public Security Bureau arrived to arrest the Colonel and his mother, they found a gang of monks blocking the gate to the temple. At the end, the Colonel himself had to tell them to back down. He and his mother surrendered to the police and were loaded into a jeep.

On the way back over Leech Ridge to the county capital, they had to pass through our village. The PSB parked their jeep in front of the ancestral hall, then escorted the Colonel back home, so that he could pick up whatever he might need while in jail. At the same time as the Colonel was pulling up in front of the ancestral hall, I was up a persimmon tree with Stumpy Tiger. We might have been the only people in the village to miss the scene. Even Blindboy had seen him.

Grandpa said: "He was pale and fat. His head was shaved and he was still wearing the robes. He looked like a real monk."

He was only a fugitive, though. He stepped down from the jeep in handcuffs and was forbidden from speaking to anyone. My father tried to approach him and got shoved away by an officer. Blindboy tried to spit on the Colonel, but a cop knocked him out of the way. The Public Security Bureau was there to stop him from running, but their most important duty in the village might have been to stop anyone from attacking the Colonel. He was the state's prized possession. The Colonel's mother remained in the jeep. Her head was buried in her hands and she was sobbing quietly. Whenever she was loud enough for an officer to hear her, she got told to shut up. She never showed her face. Everyone looking in from the outside could only see a mess of tangled white hair. She looked like a sheep being carted off to slaughter. Her hands were cuffed, too. The way the handcuffs peaked out of her sleeves, it looked like she was wearing silver bracelets.

That night, everyone was asking the same questions: How did the Public Security Bureau find him? Grandpa assumed the Old Constable had told them. My father had taken the Old Constable to see the Colonel, after all.

"You know what's like," Grandpa said, "pour some liquor down his throat and he'll tell you whatever you want."

"I don't believe that," my father said. "You know how long he kept the secret of the tattoos."

"That's true," Grandpa said. "More than twenty years…"

"You could cut his throat and he still wouldn't open his mouth," my father said.

"Did you tell anybody else?"

"You think I'm an idiot?" my father said.

"What do you need to yell for?" Grandpa said. "You want the whole world to hear you? You need to keep your mouth shut, especially now. If the police know you kept his whereabouts secret, you're going to be arrested, too. Look at what happened to his poor mother. They arrested her for aiding a fugitive. That's a crime. Do you even realise that?"

I wasn't there to see it and nobody would talk, but I had an image in my head of the jeep pulling up to the ancestral hall, the Colonel being led away, and a crowd forming, waiting for him to return… Everyone would have been staring at him, looking at the spot on his belly where they imagined those horrible words were written. That's not to say that they didn't sympathise, or they wanted to have a laugh at his expense – they were just curious. I was the same. When I heard how the Public Security Bureau men had led him through the street like a mad dog, I hated them for it. But if they had stripped him naked in front of the ancestral hall, I would have wanted to be there. The way I imagined the scene, only his belly appeared, hiding behind the monk's robes. I didn't even imagine his face. I fell asleep listening to the wind blowing outside and trying to image the Colonel's tattooed belly.

LXIII

My Colonel was an intelligent man. He hadn't expected to be arrested, but he had intentionally not taken anything with him from the temple, even though the police had given him the chance. He wanted to return home so he could get word to my father. There was no way he could talk to him directly, of course. He had to find a way to pass a message. When the Colonel was leaving his house, he purposely dropped a towel in the doorway. He also left the gate open. To make sure he got the message, the Colonel had taken advantage of Blindboy trying to spit on him... "Filthy animal!" the Colonel had cursed, emphasising the second word, while also looking meaningfully at my father. When the Colonel had been driven away, my father went back, found the open gate and the towel.

At first, my father thought the towel meant that the cats were at the Colonel's house, but he looked around and couldn't find them. He realised that the Colonel must have left them at the temple. My father went the next day to Great Chen Village. He came back with the cats, and something else, in a box, wrapped in paper. I didn't know what was

in the box, but he hid it at the Colonel's house. The two
cats stayed with us. They quickly ate their way through
the dried fish that we had hanging from the eaves. If there
was anything I didn't like about the Colonel, it had to be
those two cats – or that gossipy old mother of his! I did feel
bad for her, of course… But can you imagine going around
bragging about how the Bodhisattva Guanyin is personally
looking after you, then getting into that kind of trouble? The
Bodhisattva didn't keep her out of jail!

After the cats got settled in, my father went to the Old
Constable and asked him to accompany him to the county
capital to see the Colonel.

The Old Constable had run afoul of the Public Security
Bureau in the past, over his gambling, but he had also made
friends with a senior cadre that was in charge of logistics.
The Old Constable took my father to visit him. The cadre
received them warmly. He led them into his office and passed
out cigarettes and poured out tea. He was perfectly polite,
but there was no budging him on matters of the law. When
they asked about seeing the Colonel, he just shook his head.
He was firm on that. He looked like a teacher lecturing a
pair of school boys on their naughty behaviour. They came
back disappointed. My father went straight to bed when he
got home. His expression showed all the liveliness of a wilted
head of cabbage. He didn't even eat his dinner. Grandpa
brought out a bottle of *shaojiu* and invited the Old Constable
to stay. He wanted to find out exactly what he knew.

The Old Constable was only too happy to share, especially
after he'd had a couple drinks.

"I learned a lot today," the Old Constable said. "Before,
I thought crimes were divided by severity. Now, I know,
they're divided up by type: there's civil law and criminal
law. Basically, whoring and gambling, fights where nobody
gets injured badly, corruption, adultery – those are all civil
offences. If you commit a civil offence, you can get visitors.

The Eunuch injured somebody, which puts him into another category. He can't get any visitors before he goes on trial. He can't get out, either. On top of that, the person he injured was a Red Guard. And he went on the run for over a year! They looked into his background, too... So, he's been classified as a dangerous serial offender. That means he could get the death penalty."

Grandpa didn't know much about the law, but he didn't see how the Colonel could get the death penalty. The cost of taking a life was forfeiture of your own life, but the Colonel had not killed anyone. The Old Constable said, "The revolutionaries are in power now!"

"You have to kill someone to get a death sentence," Grandpa said. "It's the law."

"Says who? You don't make the law."

"He'll be sentenced to life in prison," Grandpa said.

"Maybe it would be better for him if they killed him," the Old Constable said.

"A good death is not as good as a wretched existence," Grandpa said.

"Life in prison... It's not even living! You'd be better off in hell."

"The only thing guaranteed in this world is suffering," Grandpa said.

"The only time I suffer is when I run out of liquor and smokes," the Old Constable said.

The two old men went back and forth, their conversation slowly veered further and further away from the topic at hand.

Grandpa had said once: "Young people are reckless with their hearts and old people are reckless with their mouths."

My father couldn't take it anymore. The line about running out of cigarettes and liquor had been the final straw. He jumped out of bed, pushed open the window, and threw a shoe at the Old Constable. The Old Constable felt bad for him. He knew he had said the wrong thing. He dumped the rest of the liquor on the ground, and left. I realised that my father had got his heart broken. He was never a talkative man, but, after the Colonel was arrested, my father seemed to switch off completely. He wouldn't talk to anybody but the cats. When I saw him talking to the cats, I couldn't help but wonder if he would ever recover. It made me sad to see him like that.

One afternoon, on my way home from school, I saw a crowd around the front of the ancestral hall. Everyone was looking at something that had been posted up on the front wall. I knew it had to be a big-character poster. Who would be putting up big-character posters at that time, though? I thought it had to be Blindboy. But what did he have to say? Maybe he was making the sodomy charge again. Grandpa had done his best to dispel that rumour, but with the Colonel locked up, Blindboy might have thought it was the right time to go on the offensive. I decided not to go over and look. If the big-character poster was directed at my family, I didn't want to invite abuse. I knew it was all a lie, anyway. Nobody wanted to hear the truth. I'd heard a line once about that... I forgot who said it. Maybe Grandpa or one of my teachers... The line went: "Truth always rests with the minority."

I remembered my Grandpa had said: "Every word is a light."

Most people in the village were illiterate. No matter how big they wrote the characters on the big-character poster, they couldn't read them. Even if they could read, it wouldn't have made a difference. Grandpa had wasted his time trying to tell them the truth. People prefer to hear lies. Nobody wants the truth. Nobody even called each other by their real names – it was always a nickname, instead.

I tried to slip away, but Stumpy Tiger noticed me. He swooped on me like a magpie that had spotted something shiny. "Come and look!" he said. "The Public Security Bureau posted an announcement: the Colonel wasn't a sodomite. He was just a traitor!"

I ran over to look at the poster. It was written with black ink on clean white paper. Every character was written clearly and every sentence was excellently composed:

> Announcement: In recent years, a rumour has spread in your village that Jiang Zhengnan, alias "the Eunuch", has tattoos on his lower abdomen indicating that he was engaged in sodomy. After careful investigation, we have determined that this rumour is false: his tattoos refer instead to having served as a running dog for the Japanese devils. This man was a traitor to the nation. Our hope now is that the masses will not allow this misunderstanding to spread further. For a man guilty of the most heinous offences to be reduced to nothing more than being the butt of crude jokes is a grave error and could serve to undermine our revolutionary fighting spirit.
>
> Long live the Great Leader Chairman Mao!
> Long live the Great Proletarian Cultural Revolution!

At the bottom was the date and the bright red seal of the Public Security Bureau.

I read it through many times, as if I was chanting a sutra. It seemed to have some sort of hold over me. It felt like the words of the announcement were being drilled into my mind. I had mixed emotions, but I was overjoyed that the announcement would put to rest any rumours about sodomy. It had been a stain on my family. It was a rumour that was impossible to fight – trying to refute it only added fuel to the fire, and silence was like an admission of guilt. Grandpa had even armed me with a long, sharp file. I had his permission to stab to death anyone that insulted the family. The shame was like a tail that I had grown, and that announcement severed it completely. The days of anxiety and worry were gone.

LXIV

When the news came, Grandpa killed a chicken and ordered a feast. He had been looking forward to that day. My mother steamed the chicken in a clay pot. It was fat, and juicy, and even the cats got to enjoy it. They usually ate their fish heads and tails out in the courtyard, but on that day, he let them have a few choice morsels of the celebratory chicken.

But, like I said, I had mixed emotions. I couldn't figure out why the Colonel was suddenly being called a traitor. The announcement from the Public Security Bureau had confirmed "tattoos on his lower abdomen", but what did they say? Why did the PSB bother putting up an announcement to tell everyone what they knew? It almost seemed like it had been done to spare my family more shame. But why would they care about that? Grandpa was just happy that the sodomy rumour had been dispelled. My father wasn't satisfied, though. He still wanted to know why the Colonel was accused of being a collaborator.

"It's clear what's going on," Grandpa said. "The Colonel is helping you." It was one of the few times Grandpa had ever called him that nickname. "He's helping himself, too. You told him about Blindboy's poster, right, when you went to see him?" My father nodded. "So, he knew what Blindboy was doing! He was insulting your family. That's why he's helping you. Being accused of sodomy is more shameful than just being called a criminal. A criminal is still human – a sodomite is an animal. Who would willingly go along with being humiliated like that? He doesn't want that hanging over his head. The Public Security Bureau must have agreed to put up that announcement."

"Why would they agree to it?" my father asked.

"You still don't get it, do you? He's an intelligent man. That was probably easy to get them to agree to, anyways. Just think, they have him locked up, and they want him to talk... All he has to do is say, 'Sure, I'll talk, but these are my conditions.' One of the conditions must have been dispelling that rumour, clearing your name... For the police, it was no big deal. All they had to do was write up a poster and send a guy over here on a motorbike to paste it up. If it gets him talking, why not do it?"

I thought Grandpa was probably right.

That was exactly the type of thing the Colonel would do. He was willing to sacrifice himself for my father. They had grown up together. They were like brothers. He didn't want my father to go down with him. The Colonel was a responsible, reasonable man. He was as responsible as Grandpa was insightful. And what could I say about my father? I could say he was a man of few words. As Grandpa celebrated the resurrection of our family's dignity, my father was nearly silent.

It was a cool fall night. The mosquitoes had died off or found places to hide. The summer stench of the gutters in the lane had faded. Grandpa and I sat together after dinner, talking, and peeling corn for tomorrow's breakfast. My father sat with us, but stayed out of our conversation. He was talking to the cats, while brushing them. The white cat seemed to glow under the autumn moon, and the black cat became a pit of darkness, darker still than the night itself. There was something sinister about the way they meowed, as if they had heard about their master's fate. Everyone was celebrating, except for my father and the cats. I looked down at the corn husks that had piled up in front of us. I could smell their green, grassy smell. It was an aroma, I thought to myself, that the Colonel would probably never experience again.

Grandpa had been sure that the Colonel wouldn't get the death sentence, but, once the announcement was posted, he wasn't so sure. It would all depend on what exactly the Colonel had done to earn the label of "traitor". Grandpa told me that after the Japanese surrendered, the collaborators had been lined up and shot. Grandpa said that people had started picking up the shells left behind and turning them into whistles to scare the sparrows. Nobody used them anymore, though. They put scarecrows up instead. If you went to the rice paddies in autumn, you'd see crowds of scarecrows.

Autumn was the season of sparrows. Grandpa said that sparrows dressed like thieves, always in dull grey or brown. Sparrows, he said, are the natural enemy of the farmer. You can kill as many sparrows as you want, and they'll always come back. Swallows, though, were the natural ally of the farmer. They were like hired hands. They wore black, which was, Grandpa said, a respectable colour. Farmers let swallows make nests in their eaves. There was a saying: "Neighbours are dearer than distant relatives, and hired hands are dearer than neighbours."

LXV

After the announcement, it seemed like the Public Security Bureau had established some indirect line to our village. From time to time, we got word about the Colonel. It was hard to say what was true and what wasn't, though. Nobody was sure who to believe. One story had it that the Colonel had resisted the interrogation and been hung for a few days from the ceiling in an isolation cell. They said he had been kicked so hard that his ribs were broken, but he had still refused to talk. A conflicting story had it that the Colonel was putting his intelligence training to use and, even though he refused to talk, his interrogators didn't dare strike him. Someone else claimed that the local PSB had brought in experts from the provincial government. The experts administered a drug to the Colonel that made him powerless to resist their questioning.

All kinds of stories circulated. Maybe all of them were true. Maybe none of them were true. We had no idea.

There were theories about the tattoos, too. It became like a guessing game. Some people guessed that the tattoo read: "I am a Dog for the Imperial Army". Others said it might be "Long Live the Imperial Army" or "Collaborator Scum" or "The Imperial Army is Great" or "Never a Eunuch, Always a Traitor"... Some people started saying that there was actually a map tattooed on his belly, which gave out the liaison points for spies in Shanghai.

Grandpa asked the Old Constable what he thought about the speculation. The Old Constable always cursed and said: "Bullshit."

The Public Security Bureau wanted to stop people from spreading rumours and picking fights. When a serious fight broke out, the PSB sent a few of their men out to deal with it, and to issue an authoritative statement. They didn't confirm whether the Colonel had been beaten or drugged. If that was part of their interrogation, they weren't going to reveal it. But they did confirm that the Colonel had confessed to his crimes, and would, as the policy promised, receive a lighter sentence. What crimes had he confessed to? He admitted that he had harmed Blindboy. What were his motives? Blindboy saw the tattoo on his belly. What did the tattoo say? Something offensive. Why was it offensive? They couldn't say. It was too offensive. It was something so filthy that to simply say it out loud would poison your mind. However, the PSB reminded us, the actual content of the tattoo was not important. The real problem was that it indicated he was a traitor.

Grandpa said: "You can't see the people on the radio. You can't hide something in a glass box." It was hard to explain, but he meant that if you try to talk around the truth, you're giving people an opening to make things up. If you don't tell the truth, you can't blame people for lying.

The speculation about the words on the Colonel's belly

became even filthier. There seemed to be no limit to what people would say. It was disgusting! Some people said it was actually a picture: maybe a thick, veiny cock, or a vivid red cunt. I got goose bumps whenever I heard people describing it… It was just like the man from the PSB had said: so filthy it could poison your mind. Just hearing the description seemed to set my ears on fire. I was only sixteen at the time. Grandpa used to say: "Boys with hair on their balls still blush."

One night, not long after the PSB had come, as I was getting into bed, the Old Constable showed up at our gate. Grandpa had been just about to shut it for the night. The Old Constable was drunk. He wouldn't stop yelling until Grandpa gave him a cigarette. "Who was stupid enough to get you drunk without giving you cigarettes, too?" Grandpa said. He saw that the Old Constable still had a full pack, unwrapped, in his breast pocket. "What's this?" he asked. "You forgot about these? You should be the one handing out cigarettes instead of me."

"I can tell you a story instead," the Old Constable said.

"What kind of story?"

"About the Eunuch."

"I'm not going to fall for that again," Grandpa said. "I wasted two *jin* of *shaojiu* on you! You didn't tell me a damn thing."

"I had a deal with the Eunuch," the Old Constable said. "I kept my promise. He didn't keep his side of the deal. You didn't hear? Everyone's talking about it. The whole village is talking. They're saying disgusting things. But it's all fucking lies! I don't know what he said, but I owe it to him to tell the truth. I want to cram the truth down everyone's throats."

The Old Constable hollered for my father to come out.

"You don't have to keep it a secret this time," the Old Constable said. "Tell whoever you want! They're all lying, but I know the truth."

My father came down, pulled out some stools, and poured

tea. Usually, they would be sitting out in the courtyard, but on that night, they went to the front half of the house. Maybe they didn't want to wake up the rest of the house, but I thought it might also be because they didn't want me to hear. Of course, though, I *was* listening. I had followed them all the way to the coffin house, and sneaking to listen to them talking in the front hall was much easier.

Even if I hadn't wanted to listen, I would have had no choice. The Old Constable was so loud that the whole house could hear. Grandpa and my father would get him quieted down, but he'd almost immediately start up again.

Grandpa said: "A drunk man that wants to be heard is loud enough that they can hear him in hell!"

LXVI

M y father reminded the Old Constable where he was in the story... It was the thirty-second year of the Republic and the Colonel was in a prison camp in Huzhou. "That was the fourth time I'd been to Shanghai that year," the Old Constable said. "I heard that the Eunuch had run into trouble. His men betrayed him and he was sent to the prison camp. We were very close at the time, so when I found out that he was arrested, I wanted to go see him. I planned to detour through Suzhou and take a ferry across Lake Tai. I was too late, though. It was the middle of winter and the lake had frozen over. I couldn't go through Hangzhou either, since there was no train or bus from there to Huzhou. The only way to get there was on foot. I had plenty of money at the time, so I thought I'd hire a carriage. Nobody would take me, though. It was the middle of winter. It was too far to carry feed for them, and everything was covered in snow. All I could do was wait.

"I waited until March, when the spring came. I took a

boat to Hangzhou first, spent the night at an inn, then hired a carriage. I got to Changxing a day later. It took a couple more hours to get up to the prison camp in the mountains. Once I got there, I still had to find the Eunuch. I ended up talking to the warden. The camp was run for the Japs, but there weren't many around. Most of the people running the place were Chinese – traitors that the Japs had bought off. I slipped the warden two silver dollars. That was all it took. Even if he couldn't find the Eunuch, he would've sliced his own nuts off for the right price.

"The Eunuch was already gone. I was a month late. The warden told me that he had been taken out of the camp right around Spring Festival, chauffeured out of the mountains in a big sedan. The warden treated me well, since he thought he might be able to get more money out of me. I talked to him in the work shed for about an hour or so. He told me that the man that had come to get the Eunuch was a fancy guy in a suit and a bowler. The guy had a certificate from the Jap headquarters in Nanjing and the car had Jap plates on it." The Old Constable jabbed his cigarette in my father's direction and said, "I thought the same as you, at first. He was famous as a surgeon, after all. But if that was the case, they would have returned him to the prison camp. The warden said that the only way out of the camp was to die and go to heaven. So, where did the Eunuch go? The warden didn't know. He was in charge of hell, so he didn't know much about heaven."

The Old Constable paused to chug some tea. "I went back to Shanghai," he said. "Number Seven told me that the Eunuch was in Beijing – they called it Beiping at the time, though. I asked her what he was doing in Beiping. She said, 'Where else would he go?' The madam – Little Mama – was involved in it all somehow, but Number Seven mentioned another name, too. It was a Japanese woman. She asked me if I'd heard it before. I might've heard the name before, but I didn't remember it. I couldn't even tell you any of those whores' names! I didn't even know Number Seven's name. Japs have fucked-up names. All the women are called whatever '-ko' and the men are called whatever '-taro', '-kami'... Number Seven said that woman was Chinese but she'd been adopted by a Jap, who gave her a Jap name. Her stepfather was a very powerful man. Even Wang Jingwei had to bow to him. Now, his stepdaughter was a smart girl. She knew how to use her stepfather's influence. She knew all of the important Japs. She could order people around. It was nothing to have someone killed – or get someone out of prison."

"I had no idea who she was, but Number Seven pointed her out in a newspaper one time. She was beautiful! She was thin as a twig, with a cute face. She was all made up like a Western woman, too. I wondered how she had ever got mixed up with the Eunuch. But it turns out she was a fucking ghoul. She was a traitor with a sick mind. Number Seven told me – and Little Mama had told her – she was a notorious slut. She even fucked her stepfather. She was like an animal. She'd fucked and sucked her way through Beijing, but once she had the Eunuch's dick, that was all she wanted. Nobody else was good enough for her. She kept the Eunuch like a pet. She put him up in a house with high walls and a German shepherd out front. He had anything he wanted. There were servants at his beck and call. But he was like a prisoner. When he went out, she sent a bodyguard to look after him. After ten or fifteen days like that, he started to get restless. Even if he was living like a king, he had a job to do. She was a traitor and his job was to kill traitors. He knew he had to report back to his superiors at some point. He didn't know how he would explain becoming her plaything."

"He should have cut her throat," Grandpa said.

"I guess he didn't think of that," the Old Constable said sarcastically. "You think this woman was dumb? She knew he was a spy. As soon as he fell into her grasp, she left her mark on him. She got her name tattooed on his belly. Your nephew saw it. That first group of Jap women had tattooed something on him. They put a big red arrow and a row of characters on his stomach. So, this woman put her name on both sides of the arrow. She took a picture of it after and locked it in a safe. Even if he killed her, the picture would still get out, so he couldn't touch her. If the picture got out, everyone would know he was fucking her. They'd assume he was in love with her or something, not that he was running an intelligence operation. It was hanging over the Eunuch's head... He knew there was no way he could ever explain it.

"I'll get to that later." The Old Constable sipped his tea. "But he figured he might be able to use her. If he could get back in touch with his superiors, the information might be useful. That's what he had done with the first bunch of Jap women. If he could do it again, he could take down a notorious traitor. He thought it was worth a try. Everyone figures they can be Zhuge Liang, but it's harder than it sounds... The Eunuch had big dreams, but it turned out to be a disaster. A year went by and he couldn't get in touch with his superiors. Nobody knew him in Beijing. The National Government ended up picking him up. All they knew about him was that he was the companion of a notorious traitor, so they locked him up."

The Old Constable paused and turned to my father. "You knew about Beijing, right? You knew he was locked up for a while there..."

I couldn't see my father, but I imagined he was shaking his head.

"Well, he was," the Old Constable said. "He didn't like to talk about it. It's messy. He told the Public Security Bureau, though. I figure that rumour about them drugging him has to be true. He wouldn't have said anything otherwise."

"How did he end up going back to the KMT, though?" my father asked. "How did he go from prison to the KMT?"

"How did he join the Communists?" the Old Constable

asked. "How did he join the People's Volunteer Army? Times change, right? The poor bastard spent time in a Japanese prison and a National Government prison, and now the Communist Party has him locked up. I hope he makes it out this time..." The Old Constable burped. "That's just how things are. After the Japanese surrendered he got locked up in Beijing, at the prison on Paoju Hutong. The KMT military and intelligence services ran the prison. I only know that because they took me in to interrogate me."

The Old Constable stood up and went out back to piss. When he came back to the front hall, he turned his stool around to face the back half of the house and I couldn't hear him clearly. I got out of bed, opened the door a bit. I moved Grandpa's recliner closer to the gap and settled in to listen.

It was a moonless night, and the wind blew in through the crack in the door and chilled me to the bones. I pulled the wool blanket Grandpa kept on the recliner over me. He had rheumatism in his joints, and kept it to warm his knees. The blanket smelled like Grandpa's feet. I knew the smell well. I had grown up at his feet. When I was a boy, I fell asleep hugging his feet to my chest. The warmth of the blanket and the smell of Grandpa lulled me to sleep.

Fifteen

LXVII

Most of the old people in the village couldn't tell you what year they were born, but they all knew what year the Japanese surrendered: it was the thirty-fourth year of the Republic of China, or 1945. Grandpa told me about how the Yankees had dropped the atomic bomb on the Japs. Two days later, the Japs surrendered. The Old Constable said: "There were two big mushroom clouds. The Yankees barbecued them." That was also the day that the Constable's luck ran out.

The Japanese surrender hadn't hurt business at the brothel. There were plenty of people looking to blow through their ill-gotten gains. The Constable didn't even realise how deep in the hole he was until a couple weeks later. At first, he wasn't willing to accept it. He borrowed money, thinking he could win it all back. He went broke again. He borrowed more and lost it again. He had nothing to his name. The loan shark was scared that he'd run, so he stripped him naked, told the brothel to keep him there, and sent for Number Seven to bail him out.

Number Seven never came. The Old Constable said: "Never trust a girl you have to pay to keep you company."

The Constable had no choice but to wait for the inevitable. But his liberator was already on her way. One calm, cool morning, while everyone was still asleep, and nobody was stirring except for the flowers sprouting in the garden, the red wooden gate of the brothel was smashed open. The first person through was a woman that everyone addressed as Commander. She was a stunning, ferocious woman in her early thirties. She fired two warning shots in the air as her team stormed the gate. Two rounds downed the German shepherds. Her team was already at the back door to cut off escape. They started rounding people up. The madam was in the bathtub, so none of the soldiers were willing to disturb her, but the female commander kicked in the door, wrapped her in a blanket, and dragged her out. The female commander started interrogating her immediately, then handed her over to her men, who bundled her into a car.

The female commander stayed there and ordered her men to arrange the tables and chairs in the main room of Little Mama's mansion. Everyone from the main mansion was lined up and led in one by one to be interrogated. The female commander had two aims: the first was to expose Little Mama as a collaborator, and the second was to figure out where the Colonel was. By the time the female commander got there, the Constable had already been locked up in the basement for three days. When the soldiers found him, he was starving and could barely walk. He looked as if he was about to keel over and die. The soldiers raided the kitchen of the brothel and gave him whatever he wanted. He had all the cookies and cakes and cigarettes and liquor he wanted.

"I ate everything they put in front of me," the Old Constable said. "I ate until I couldn't eat anymore."

The female commander interrogated him last. It was late in the afternoon, and the sun had tinted the flowers in the courtyard a deep pink. By that time, the Constable had already faced death twice, so he was no longer afraid. He knew what to expect from the female commander, since he had already heard some of the girls from the brothel returning from their interrogations. They had described the female commander as a tyrant. Her eyes seemed to cut through you, the girls had said. She had supposedly taken out her pistol and tapped it menacingly on the lacquered top of Little Mama's dining table. The Constable took a seat at the table, too. He bent his head and waited. When the female commander came, he saw her face reflected up at him in the red lacquer.

"But I didn't want to look her in the eyes," the Old Constable said. "I just kind of took a glance to make sure she didn't have a gun or something worse."

He studied her reflection in the tabletop. He could see a pair of elbows in a floral blouse and her face, warped by dull spots in the lacquer. When he leaned back, he could see her legs under the table. Her left leg was crossed over her right. The Constable didn't really understand women's minds, but he knew their bodies. From a glimpse of her ankle alone, he knew she was a thin, pretty woman, probably in her thirties...

"Look at me," the female commander said. "What do you do here? Why do you stink like that?"

The Constable finally raised his head. He glanced around. He could still barely believe he wasn't dreaming. He felt like he was going to eventually wake up again down in the basement. He saw how the light of the setting sun hit the window of the mansion. He had seen it before while sitting down for dinner with Little Mama in the same place. He looked back to the female commander. As she looked back, her fiery gaze cooled. She was a bit perplexed by the Constable.

LXVIII

When I pulled the recliner to the door, it had been dark outside. I thought it was a moonless night, but the clouds had just blown across the moon. It was October, going by the old calendar, and the night was quiet. All the insects and animals that had provided a soundtrack to hot summer nights had already died off or taken shelter for the season. The moon emerged from the clouds and the Old Constable paused. It was so quiet I was sure I could hear the sound of the moonlight spreading out across the land, shooing away the darkness, tiptoeing across the courtyard, and dancing across the roof. And then it was quiet again.

Grandpa said: "The moonlight sleeps on the top of the wall, like we sleep on beds."

He'd said that to get me to go to bed. Grandpa had an explanation for everything. There was a reason for everything. There was a reason to wake up, and a reason to get out of bed… If you asked him the "why" of something, he would always have an answer. Nobody could beat him at that game. But when it came to storytelling and bickering, the Old Constable was the king. If you got into an argument with the Old Constable, you had to know he was the best. He knew the best curse words, and he wielded them like a pair of pistols. He could torture a man to death with words alone, or get the already dead so angry that they'd crawl out from their grave to try to get the last word. When he told a story, he could take you on a voyage. You could be at the gambling table one second, then rolling into bed the next. He could rhapsodise on the gleam of a silver dollar, then compose an ode to the softness of a particular body, then launch into the most lurid, masterful description of a brothel whose rooms had never seen sunlight. The stories were better when he'd had a few drinks, and he was at his best when he was hammered. He had told his stories countless times, but buried within him were stories that he could never tell. Even after he lost his fortune and his home, he kept it sealed up inside him. He had somehow never let it slip before. He was sitting on a gold mine that he never dared venture inside. Setting a storyteller like the Old Constable to guard such a valuable cache of tales was like setting a drunk to guard a distillery – but somehow, the stories had stayed locked up, until he had used them to save my Grandpa's life, and until that October night. I admired him for it. There was something heroic in his secrecy.

The moonlight seemed to grow even brighter when the Old Constable paused. It was as if even the moon had stolen closer to listen in. The Old Constable knew how to use the silence. He knew when to pause at a key point, when to lean back and sip his tea, when to scrounge around for another cigarette... He knew that during those pauses, his audience was listening even more closely, silently urging him to go on, and hoping that the story hadn't abruptly come to an end.

When he had waited long enough, the Old Constable started his story again.

"Who do you think that female commander was? It was the spy that he had saved after her cover had been blown in Nanjing. He ended up delivering her baby, right? You remember that. I had seen her once before, in the Eunuch's clinic in Shanghai. She'd showed up in the middle of the night in a black limousine. I wasn't supposed to be there. She expected the Eunuch. But he was out. For whatever reason, that got on her tits. She started interrogating me like I was some common criminal, who she caught breaking in. And speaking of getting on her tits, she had a great pair... Great body on her. I could tell by the way she moved that she'd be great in the sack. I didn't have much of an appetite for that, at the time. She could have spread her legs, and I would have told her to pack it up. I would have turned down braised pork belly! I had got my fill working my way through the girls at the brothel. But there was something about her... She was a young woman, but she carried herself with authority. She knew exactly what she was doing. It wasn't her first time interrogating someone. But the Eunuch had prepared me for situations like this, so I played dumb and just kept babbling away in the village dialect. I stayed polite, though. I kept smiling to her face. She couldn't understand a word I was saying, so she gave up pretty quickly and started rooting through the drawers. She left with some ether and gauze. I realised that she must have come to get the Eunuch to operate on someone. She was going to do it herself, I guess. She told me: 'When he gets back, tell him Lady Jiang needs him.' My act had been so convincing that she was worried I might be deaf, so she took out a jade hairpin and left it on the hospital bed for me to give to the Eunuch. It was like a calling card, I guess.

"She had two hairpins stuck in her hair, actually, and she pulled them both out. Her hair suddenly came down to her waist. She transformed! She was wearing a tight green qipao, and with her shiny black hair cascading over it – all her fierceness was gone. It was like a piece of fancy lingerie, you know? You put a woman in a bra, it can be sexier than seeing her totally naked. Lady Jiang knew how to dress up. With two hairpins, she could completely change her appearance. There were girls at the brothel just about as pretty as her, but none of them were quite the same. I watched her walk out of there and admired every inch of her body as she got into the limousine. Fuck, I was thinking, I could get all the whores in the world and none of them would be as good as climbing into bed with her. Sometimes when I was fucking them, I was thinking of Lady Jiang. Whenever I couldn't get it up, I thought about what it would be like to peel off her qipao. When you're fucking, the pussy is secondary to what's going on inside your head."

I knew Grandpa couldn't take much more. "Enough, enough," he said. The Old Constable stood and was about to leave. But it was all an act. My father passed out cigarettes and got everyone calmed down. I thought it was all an act, but based on how the story progressed and how he told it, I thought the Old Constable might have actually got upset. The story didn't come quite as smoothly…

"There's not much more to tell after that," the Old Constable said vaguely. "She sent me to Beijing to look for the Eunuch."

"Wait," my father said. "Who sent you to Beijing?"

"You can't even figure that out? It was Lady Jiang."

"How did she know the Eunuch was in Beijing?" Grandpa asked.

"She just interrogated me," the Old Constable said peevishly.

"Is this at the brothel or the clinic?" my father asked.

"I'm talking about the brothel now," the Old Constable said. "She interrogated me for hours. She knew everything. You know those whores told her everything, first. They have no ethics. Especially Number Seven! If I had money in my pocket, she'd treat me like a king. But when I was broke, she was nowhere to be found. As soon as the military police got a hold of them, they spilled their guts. Basically, even before she got a hold of me, she knew that the Eunuch had gone to Beijing with the traitor. The woman had already been arrested, though. Her picture was in the paper. Lady Jiang assumed that the Eunuch must have been rounded up and put in jail, too. Think about it, what kind of man would be in the company of a traitor? Not a good guy, right? A vicious little mutt, at the very least, willing to bite the hand of its master. Why not arrest him? Who knew the Eunuch better than Lady Jiang, right? So, she wanted to rescue him. She told me to find him. I was sent to Beijing, which was called Beiping at the time—"

"Hold on," my father said. "Why did she pick you?"

"That's what I don't understand," Grandpa said. "She had plenty of her own men. Why did she send you?"

"What do you mean by that?" the Old Constable said, raising his voice. "He was mixed up with that traitor, right?

That's exactly why she sent me. It was a complicated time. She couldn't just send anyone in there... What if the Eunuch really was a traitor? She didn't want any of her men mixed up in that. But, to her, I was expendable. If I could save the Eunuch, that was all to the good. But if I couldn't... Well, that had nothing to do with her. Lady Jiang knew what she was doing. She knew exactly how to pull the strings without risking her good name. I was her only option. She knew that. If I didn't go, there was nobody else to send."

LXIX

The Constable was sent to Beijing with the cover story that he was the Colonel's uncle. The story he told was that the Eunuch's father was dead, and his mother had tiny bound feet, as small as *zongzi*, so she couldn't travel. Lady Jiang even sent the Constable back to the village to have a picture taken with the Colonel's mother. That shouldn't have been a problem, but the Constable had debts outstanding. He had put up the deed on his property as collateral, and he had to go back empty-handed. Once he got to the village, there were various procedures to take care of with transferring the deed. But in the time after the Japanese surrender, things were in chaos. The Constable had lost his position and gone broke, so nobody was willing to help him. The trip should have taken a day, but it stretched for more than a week. When he finally got back to Shanghai, it was already October (going by the lunar calendar). By the time he finally left Shanghai, it was the middle of the month. On the way to the train station in Lady Jiang's jeep, the roads were lined with people burning spirit money. The fires danced like sprites down every lane and alley. It was the Xiayuan Festival, one of the three big Ghost Festivals, when everyone went to burn offerings to the local Daoist gods.

Looking out the window of the jeep, the Constable was sure it was a bad omen.

As the train headed north to Beijing, it stopped many times along the way. Some of those were scheduled stops, but other stops were to check documents and search for collaborators. Any traitors that hadn't already been seized had hit the road. Many of them were riding the rails. The train was the perfect place to go undetected – or so they thought. The Constable had been given travel documents by Lady Jiang, giving him the same right of passage as any senior government officials. Sitting across from the Constable on the train was a middle-aged man, dressed like a scholar in glasses and a long robe. The scholar was courteous, and quick with a smile, but he was silent for most of the ride. When he noticed the Constable's travel documents, he immediately treated him with more respect. He passed the Constable cigarettes and offered to get him some *baozi*. There were many soldiers on the train. They ranged from the lowliest grunts all the way up to officers. They acted as if they were all war heroes. They terrorised the passengers, elbowed people aside and took whatever seats they liked. "These guys all act like they personally defeated the Japanese," the scholar said in a low voice to the Constable.

The Constable had been thinking the same thing. The two started chatting.

When the train pulled into the station at Zhenjiang, they had to wait a while for some more carriages to be hooked onto the back of it. A rumour spread through the train that the cargo of the carriages was full of gold, machine guns to protect the gold, and men to man the guns. Nobody knew where the gold had come from, but it was headed for Nanjing. The scholar and the Constable got out on the platform for a cigarette. The Constable strutted up and down, stretching his legs, and the scholar followed behind him like a servant. Before they got back on the train, the scholar took two packs of cigarettes out of his satchel and gave them to the Constable. He asked if he might possibly serve as a member of the Constable's retinue, perhaps as a personal assistant. The Constable was confused. The scholar took that as him hesitating over the manner, so he reached back into his satchel and took out two silver dollars. At that point, the Constable did indeed begin to hesitate. At such a chaotic time, there was no telling where the money had come from. But he had seen the military police checking the scholar's papers, and there hadn't been a problem, and he looked reliable... The Constable took the silver dollars and the cigarettes and patted the scholar on the shoulder. "Fine," the Constable said, "I can be your assistant."

"No!" the scholar said, shaking his head. "I want to be your assistant."

After that, the Constable did introduce him as his assistant, and the scholar called him "Boss". The Constable couldn't believe his luck. The train was slowed down by its constant stops along the way. Half of the passengers got off in Xuzhou. There were plenty of empty seats on the train after that, so the Constable and his assistant could stretch out. "This is riding in style," the Constable said. "Everyone crammed in here, it was like riding with cattle. They stunk the whole place up." The Constable's assistant advised him that it wouldn't last for long.

He was right: the carriage quickly filled up again. There were even children sitting up on the luggage rack. If they had tried to get down, they were in danger of being trampled underfoot. The Constable's assistant wasn't there to see any of that, though. He had already been taken away by the military police. The scholar had prepared documents, but the police recognised him from his wanted poster. The scholar – the Constable's assistant – was a collaborator on the lam. It was a good lesson for the Constable. He realised that anyone around him could be a traitor. From then on, he kept to himself. Even if somebody offered a cigarette, he would turn them down. He even handed the two silver dollars and packs of cigarettes back to the military police. It was evidence of the scholar's crime, after all.

The Constable was not short of funds at the time. Lady Jiang had given him enough to pay his travel fees and cover any unexpected expenses. She'd even given him a parka and a pair of shoes. He knew the parka and shoes were second-hand and they could very well have been pulled off a corpse, but he'd rather wear a dead man's clothes than freeze to death in Beijing. He'd felt it getting colder as the train steamed north. In Shanghai it was still late summer, but by the time he got to Beijing, it felt like winter had arrived ahead of him. A cold wind howled through the carriage.

The train got to Beijing in the middle of the night. The Constable spent the night in a small hotel near the railway station. He managed to bargain a discount on the rate, since it was so late, but the innkeeper put him in the coldest room he had. He woke up the next morning with a runny nose and his entire body numb from cold.

The Constable went to the courtyard house that Lady Jiang had told him to find. In the centre of the courtyard, there was a gnarled old pine tree. It was about as wide as it was tall. The way its branches curved, the Constable guessed that it had been artificially crafted by a master gardener. Most of the rooms off the courtyard had been sealed up, but the kitchen and the servants' quarters were still open. There were festive red paper cuttings pasted up on the windows, but he could see that they were not recent, and had begun to fade and curl. The old paper cuttings and the general atmosphere of decline gave the Constable the creeps. The guardian of the place was a man with a stump for a left arm. He greeted the Constable with a huge grin, as if he was the first visitor the place had seen in years. The Constable was smiling, too. He had the feeling that his luck was about to change again.

LXX

Lady Jiang had provided him with documents, photos, and money for expenses, but there was no guarantee that she could put him in touch with the right people. That was what the Constable really needed: someone who could get things done. He needed local help. Grandpa said: "A dragon far from home won't attack a snake on his own territory. Nobody in the world is more powerful than a bully on his own turf." Lady Jiang's turf was Shanghai, but she had connections outside the city. Before the Constable left, she prepared three letters, and gave him addresses to deliver them to. If he was lucky, one of the recipients would help the "uncle" to find his "nephew". If none of the recipients could help him, the Constable was instructed to return home, destroy everything he had been given, and keep his mouth shut. Lady Jiang would deny all knowledge of the plan.

The Constable got lucky. The first recipient he met offered to help. He set the Constable up with a place to stay. He knew exactly where the Colonel was being held and offered to take the Constable there to see his "nephew". The Constable was told to wash up first.

After that, he was led to an abandoned-looking courtyard, where he met a man named Lefty.

"When I got there, Lefty told me that the entire courtyard had been a den of collaborators," the Old Constable said. "That's why it had been sealed up." Lefty had kept living in the courtyard even after the police had sealed up most of the rooms. He was full of stories about all the traitors that had once been his neighbours. The Constable realised that Lady Jiang was right to be so suspicious. There were too many traitors. Even the Colonel had been taken in by one. There was nobody to vouch for the Colonel, and there would be nobody to vouch for Lady Jiang, if she got mixed up in the same business.

Lefty had his own story, too. He had been a pilot. He'd even been to the United States, and had flown in Burma. The Japs shot him down. He'd escaped the crash with his life, but he ended up losing most of his left arm. The Old Constable stayed with him for a few nights, sharing a *kang*. He could have kept talking about him all night, if Grandpa and my father hadn't interrupted.

"This sounds like a story for another time," Grandpa said. "You're getting off track."

"Where was the Colonel?" my father asked.

A couple days after arriving at Lefty's courtyard, the Constable took a rickshaw to Paoju Hutong. "They put me in an empty room to wait," the Old Constable said. "When they finally dragged the Eunuch in, I didn't even recognise him. He was dressed in rags and his head was shaved. He looked like a corpse they'd just dug up somewhere. He was so pale, too, I remember. He looked like something that had starved to death. His eyes were bulging out of his head. His cheeks were all sucked in. To tell you the truth, I couldn't tell if he was dead or alive. He recognised me, though. He wanted to know what I was doing there. I made a big show of saying, 'Oh, my nephew!' I pulled out the picture of Ms Guanyin" – he was referring to the Colonel's mother – "and me. 'Your mother sent me here to see you,' I said. He figured out what I was getting at and played along. He called me uncle and asked how things were at home… There was a guard watching us, but we were talking in the local language, so he wasn't really paying attention. We could talk about whatever we wanted. I gave him Lady Jiang's message and told him what he needed to do."

What Lady Jiang wanted from the Colonel was the truth. She wanted to know whether he had collaborated with the traitors. Either way, she was willing to help him. If he was innocent, she could get him out. If he was guilty, she could do her best to assist him, but there were limits. If his actions had hurt anyone, he would have to pay the price.

When he heard that, the Colonel had broken down and started crying. He looked like an innocent man being led to the gallows. When he recovered he told the Constable to take word back to Lady Jiang: "Go back and tell her that she has my word that I've never done anything to hurt this country or its people. I've suffered plenty, but nobody else got hurt. If I'm lying, may I be struck dead..."

"If everything you say is true," the Constable told him, "write her a letter. Explain everything. Tell her what happened. Sign it in blood. That's the only way."

The Constable returned the next day. The Colonel looked even worse than when the Constable had first seen him. He was even more pale and his eyes were bloodshot. He had stayed up the previous night writing two letters. The first letter was for his mother and the second was for Lady Jiang. He handed the first letter to the Constable. "I said everything's fine with me. So, I don't want you" – the Constable – "to tell her" – the Colonel's mother – "otherwise." He was hesitant to part with the second letter. He made the Constable promise that he would pass it directly to Lady Jiang.

"The letter was sealed," the Old Constable said, "but I took a peek. I sure wish I hadn't!" The Old Constable chose that moment to sip his tea. Everyone was on the edge of their seats. "There were five pages altogether, and every character on them had been written in blood. He even put five bloody fingerprints on the last page. I hadn't even read what he wrote in the letter, but I was already crying. Can you imagine? The Eunuch had a hard life. At that moment, if I could have, I would've traded places with him. I figured that my life was already over, anyways. I was broke and beaten. If I died in prison instead of him, my life might have amounted to something."

The day he handed the Constable the letters, the Colonel was in a good mood. The two men chatted for a while. The Colonel knew that the Constable was deep in debt. He had handed over the deed to the house he had put up as collateral on one debt, but there were others still outstanding. The Constable shook his head sadly. The men he owed money to were not forgiving. They would find him. "My life is worthless, but it's all I've got left," he told the Colonel. "I'll never have the money to pay off those debts." The Colonel was silent for a long time, and then he shouted to the guard to bring him a piece of paper and a brush. He started writing a third letter, addressed to Lady Jiang. In his letter he said that after his man had been arrested, he had moved his base of operations. He told Lady Jiang that all of his money and possessions were at the new place. The Colonel asked Lady Jiang to liquidate everything and pay off the Constable's gambling debts.

"As far as I know," the Old Constable said, "that's what she did. She took everything. I think she ended up giving him back some of the stuff, though. That's how he got those surgical tools back."

"How much did she pay off for you?" Grandpa asked.

"I thought you wanted me to stick to the Eunuch's story!" the Old Constable said. "That has nothing to do with him. I don't want to talk about it."

Grandpa told me later that after Lady Jiang paid off the debt, she took him into her office and slapped him twice across the face. Each slap was payment for a gold bar as thick as a thumb and as long as a chopstick. Grandpa said that even our house wasn't worth as much as one gold bar that size. I suddenly understood why the Old Constable felt the way he did about the Colonel. That was why he had dared to stand up to the Red Guards for him. For that much money, he owed him, Grandpa said.

LXXI

While waiting for a train ticket back to Shanghai, the Constable went back to Lefty's place. He heard lots of stories about his time in the air force, and he heard the history of the KMT's Central Bureau of Investigation and military intelligence branches. As Lefty told it, the Central Bureau outranked military intelligence, but the Constable found that hard to believe: Brother Number One, their contact from the Central Bureau, had to wait three days for a train ticket, but Lady Jiang – a member of military intelligence – had simply driven him to Shanghai Station and ordered the railway staff to let him on. Brother Number One had no problem getting the Constable into the prison, though. The Constable returned before leaving to see the Colonel. It turned out that Brother Number One was actually in charge of the prison, so he managed to get the Colonel held in better conditions and transferred to a different labour unit. When the Constable went to say goodbye, the Colonel seemed to have been transformed. He was steaming red, like he had just got out of a hot bath. The Colonel told him that he'd been transferred to the boiler room, which was the best job to have in wintertime.

"That last time I saw him there," the Old Constable said, "he told me to tell Lady Jiang that the Communists and the KMT were already fighting up north and in Shandong and Shanxi. He knew another war was coming. He wanted to join the fight. He knew he could save a few lives, even if he died out there."

The Colonel's prediction was accurate: a civil war broke out. Medical officers were in short supply. The Colonel returned to the front lines. All it took was for Lady Jiang to send an order to Fushun. The legend of the Golden Blade began to spread across the bloody battlefields of the northeast. He was celebrated in a poem that got published in the Northeastern War Report. The entire poem gushed praise for the Colonel. One particularly memorable part read:

> Savage Death came close
> Its gaping mouth blood-thirsty
> Flashing fangs like swords
> But the Golden Blade was at my side
> Roaring back at Death and his Ghouls
> The King of Hell rose up
> He ordered his Ghouls into battle
> But the Golden Blade blocked their path

The flames of war burned from north to south. The KMT stood no chance. The Colonel followed the retreat. He ended up stationed with a naval unit at Zhenjiang in Jiangsu. Eventually, parts of the navy defected to the People's Liberation Army. The PLA was not bound on revenge, though. Even those that refused to accept the doctrine of the Communists were not treated with bias. The men that refused to fight for the PLA were given travel expenses and sent back home. The only thing the Colonel cared about were his cats. He was willing to fight for the PLA as long as he could keep his cat. He was told that if he wanted to keep cats, he should take the deal to go back home. The Colonel went back to his operating room and started packing up his personal items, including the set of gold surgical tools. He had paid for them to be made, so it was within his rights to take them with him when he went. He took his cat and went to line up outside of the red brick barracks building, where men were waiting to get their travel expenses paid out. The cat started yowling fiercely, and the PLA man that was watching the line rushed over. He pointed his gun at the Colonel and was about to grab the cat and drop it off at the canteen. But he suddenly lowered the gun and laughed.

"They'd met before," the Old Constable said. "A few months before, he'd been one of the guys that grabbed the Eunuch and took him into the Dabie Mountains to pull the bullet out of one of their senior cadres. You already know that story, though."

I did indeed know the story. He'd fought the KMT all the way back across the Taiwan Straits, then he valiantly charged across the Yalu to fight the Yankees and support North Korea. Whoever was fighting, they needed doctors, and the Colonel was one of the finest military surgeons. Taking him into battle was like a warning to the King of Hell to stay far away. The fame of the Golden Blade spread far and wide. He returned from Korea a hero, and he should have been able to lead a good life, but his luck changed and he ended up discharged from the military. He went back to the village to take up farming again. As for how and why he was kicked out of the service, I had heard a couple things… Some people said he had accidentally killed a division commander during surgery, some people said that he got in trouble with a woman, and others said that a senior cadre that had taken him under his wing ran into some trouble and the Colonel got swept up in it. I wasn't sure exactly what had happened, though.

LXXII

The moonlight lay on the tops of the walls, then crawled down to slumber in the courtyard. I was ready to sleep, too. But I didn't want to leave the door, afraid that I would miss something important. From my bed, I could hear a bit of what the Old Constable was saying, but he was too drunk to keep his tone steady or his volume consistent. I had to return to Grandpa's recliner. It wasn't yet winter, but the night was cold enough to chill. I had got out of bed with just my underwear on. It was cold in the chair, even with the wool blanket.

The Old Constable was getting tired, too. "Fuck," he said, "my back is killing me. I better go." I heard the feet of the stool scraping across the floor as he stood, then the sound of footsteps in the courtyard.

"Stay a while," Grandpa said. "I want to hear the end. Just tell us what happened."

"I'm done," the Old Constable said. "That's it." He paused in the courtyard and looked up at the moon. "It must be midnight already. You go to bed. Your son has to get up early tomorrow. He earns the workpoints in this house, so he needs his rest."

Grandpa wouldn't let him go. "You didn't finish! I heard about Shanghai, I heard about Beijing, but what about the rest? Just tell us, then you can go."

"What do you want to know?" the Old Constable said.

"Don't play dumb," Grandpa said. "What's on his belly?"

"Ah, Sorcerer," the Old Constable said, "I thought I had you beat. I figured you'd forgotten all about that."

"You didn't beat me this time," Grandpa said. I could see him and the Old Constable standing together in the courtyard. A cigarette burned in Grandpa's fingers.

"Fine," the Old Constable said. "The police already have him. It'll come out eventually. I guess I can tell you. It says—" The Old Constable reached down and flicked Grandpa's dick.

Grandpa jumped back and said, "What are you doing? Sick old bastard. Pervert."

"I thought you wanted to know," the Old Constable said. "That's what the tattoo is. I might be called Pervert, but even I won't say it out loud."

My father appeared in my line of sight and stood beside the Old Constable. He looked at my father, then back at Grandpa. "Ah," the Old Constable said in a low voice. It was deathly quiet. I could hear everything they were saying.

"Sorcerer," the Old Constable said, "if I tell you, you can't blame me later…" He coughed twice, as if the thought of what was written there gave him physical pain. "I only know what I heard. You can choose whether to believe it or not. I don't know what's true and what's not." He coughed again, as if he were choking on his own words. Grandpa glared at him and he finally spat out: "From what I've heard, there are two things tattooed there. Those Jap women in Shanghai wrote something really disgusting there – 'This dick is the property of the Empire of Japan' – under his belly button, then there was a red arrow, pointing down at his dick. Then that woman in Beijing had written her Japanese name on there, too. It was four characters, arranged on both sides of the arrow. I forget what her name was exactly…"

I can't remember everything the Old Constable said, it was like a grenade tossed into the courtyard, momentarily stunning me. When I regained my senses, the Old Constable was already gone. I heard his sluggish footsteps out in the alley. Grandpa and my father were frozen where they stood, speechless, clearly still stunned by what they had heard.

Grandpa came to his senses before my father. He swore at my father, as if trying to shake him out of his stupor. "Monsters," he muttered under his breath. "There's nothing too evil for them, and they'll destroy anything that's good."

My father shuddered as if waking from a deep slumber. He stared blankly at Grandpa. He looked as if the moonlight had sucked the soul out of his body. Grandpa looked around, as if he was looking for his son's spirit. He swore under his breath again. He patted my father on the shoulder and said, "Get to bed. It's getting late." He walked out of my line of sight. I knew he was going out back to piss.

My father followed him. I could no longer see them, but I could hear him faintly. "Do you think," my father said, "it will hurt his case?"

Grandpa sighed and mumbled, "Who knows if it's even true?" There was silence for a moment. "Anyways," he said, his tone sounding lighter, "I wouldn't worry. He's a man with powerful friends. Just hope that they come in time." He told my father again to get to bed.

I was in bed when Grandpa got back. He fell asleep almost immediately. I was waiting for the sound of my father on the stairs, but it never came. The light of the moon started to fade. Everything went dark. I didn't know if it was because I fell asleep or if the clouds had just drifted over the moon. All I know is that when I ran to the back of the house to pee, I saw my father in the front half of the house, his head bowed, kowtowing where the pictures of our ancestors used to hang. The next morning, I saw a dark blue bruise on his forehead. When I saw it, I felt like crying.

Sixteen

LXXIII

Don't break the soil when insects stir,
Spring won't reach the mountains.
Mugwort dumplings on Tomb-Sweeping Day,
Baked cakes in the depths of winter.
The harvest looks promising in summer,
and heavy snows are an omen of abundance.
The eel rises to replace the dragon,
The God of Thunder enters the room.
The red clouds of dawn quickly fade,
The afterglow stretches for ten thousand miles.

Grandpa recited that to me, but he told many other
people. He told my cousin. He told strangers. I would
sometimes catch him ambushing my classmates with it. He
would ask them, "Why can't you break the soil when insects
stir?"

Nobody could answer the question. Nobody wanted to
answer the question.

But he would continue, "Insects come back in the third

solar term. The soil is full of delicate larva and fragile eggs. If you start ploughing, you'll kill them all. An insect is a life, too. We owe it to them to at least let them start their lives."

I have no idea where Grandpa got all his knowledge. But he always wanted to show it off, just like the Old Constable talking about women. People said that if you stopped Grandpa spreading his folksy wisdom, he'd get a headache. If you stopped the Old Constable from talking about women, his balls would ache. You know what that means, right? Grandpa was governed by his big head and the Old Constable was run by his little head. The big head is just your brain and the little head is... You can guess what the little head is. Some people say that if you let little kids talk dirty when they're young, they lose all sense of shame.

It's hard to explain, but Grandpa had a thing he said about that: "The bark on an old tree is plenty thick, but the thickest skin is on the face of a shameless man." See, because that's how we described someone that was shameless or brazen – the skin on their face was described as being thick.

Grandpa had another saying: "If your face is thick when you're young, it'll be gone completely by the time you're old." I'll let you figure that out for yourself.

The Old Constable said that if Grandpa had a silver dollar for every truism he spit out, we'd be the richest family in the village. As it was, we were far from rich. He was lucky that Grandpa never heard him say it.

Grandpa said: "A foolish man can sow but he will never reap. Even if he dresses in silk, he will be the same as the monkeys in the circus." He told the Old Constable once: "All you cared about was money and women, and you ended up a broke bachelor." He also told the Old Constable: "You spent your whole lifetime learning how not to feel ashamed." That was a very polite way of cursing him. It meant that the Old Constable was impervious to reality. The Old Constable was incapable of feeling shame. Even if he couldn't tell a story as well as him or curse as fluently, Grandpa could always beat the Old Constable at philosophy.

It was an abnormal winter. The sun never seemed to shrink. There was barely any frost. Almost no snow fell before the New Year. Heaven was taking pity on the Colonel, freezing in his cell. The government was taking pity on him, too. They hadn't yet pronounced a sentence. We heard rumours, of course, some sketchy and some more reliable. For a time, they said that the verdict would be announced at the commune's middle school. Some said that the announcement would be made on the winter solstice, and others said it would be a market day. Those days came and went, and nothing happened. People lost interest. In the cold months, the village was dormant. There was no farm work to be done, so the strongest men were sent up north to work on the dam and the reservoir. The old people and the women stayed inside, huddling around stoves and stitching soles. Only the children went outside. They ran around in the dry stream bed, looking for frozen mudfish, or they went up into the hills to catch weasels and hibernating snakes.

My father was sent up north with the labour team. The Colonel seemed to have drifted even further out of my life: my father wasn't there to mention him, and the cats disappeared. I mean, the cats were still there, but it was warmer upstairs, and they didn't have much reason to come downstairs to see any of us.

Things started to pick up again in the village when Spring Festival approached. Everyone was going around to visit one another. The older people had drinks around the table, while the kids ran underfoot, counting up the New Year money slipped to them by relatives. That would usually go on for ten days after the first day of the New Year, but a sudden heavy snowfall had put the damper on things.

It was the seventh day of Zhengyue, the first month of

the traditional calendar. The snow seemed to arrive as compensation for the arid months that had come before. The snow was so heavy that it collapsed one corner of the thatched roof over our pigsty. That morning, while I was sweeping the snow out of the courtyard, I suddenly thought about the Colonel. I remembered the way nails in the soles of his high-top boots clattered on the snowy cobblestones in winter. It was one of my earliest memories of him. It came every year, the sound of his boots on the cobblestones, sure and steady... I wondered if his jailers had given him a warm jacket or some cotton-padded pants. I didn't want to think about him freezing in his cell.

LXXIV

By noon that day, the snow was still falling. When the Old Constable appeared in our courtyard that day, he was absolutely covered in it. Some people had come over to visit Grandpa, so he and my father were in the front hall of the house. When they saw the Old Constable, they both stood up and waved him in to take a seat. The Old Constable only glared at them. He walked directly to Grandpa and slapped him twice on the cheek. "Fuck you," he said, "fuck your ancestors, fuck this family."

It wasn't acceptable behaviour any time of year, but cursing someone's ancestors during Spring Festival was considered particularly offensive. My father and the guests went for the Old Constable. My father pushed him up the wall, his hands around his neck, and said, "Tell me you're drunk, or I'll kill you right now."

"I'm not drunk," the Old Constable said. "I'm sending him a message, from your sworn brother. You ask him what he did!" He took advantage of my father's surprise to slip out of his grip and attack Grandpa again. "You son of a bitch," he roared, "you betrayed me!"

My father got between them and told the Old Constable, "Just say what you want to say. What did he do?"

The Old Constable grunted and said, "Ask him yourself. When I walk out of here, I'm never coming back. If I see him outside this gate, I'll let him have it again. I'll beat him to death. You can come ask me there. It's pretty funny, isn't it? He goes around telling everyone how to live their lives, but he doesn't know a goddamn thing himself."

The Old Constable was already pushing his way out the door. When he passed me, I was so scared I could hardly breathe, but at the same time, I wanted to kick him. I knew my father probably wouldn't have wanted me to, though. I didn't notice any hint of liquor or beer breath as the Old Constable walked by. I decided he must have lost his mind. He stumbled in the yard, and I wished he would slip and break his neck.

My father chased him out of the gate and into the lane.

I went to Grandpa's side and took his hand. I wanted to comfort him but I didn't know what to say. I was angry but it felt so futile. Since the Old Constable had slapped him, Grandpa hadn't said a word. He didn't curse him back or even cry out in pain. It was like he had been stunned. He seemed as if he had been barely conscious for the attack. I felt bad for Grandpa but I also thought that he might have been partially to blame.

My anger faded, but I was worried about whatever Grandpa might have done.

My father returned a short time later. He looked just as furious as the Old Constable had. He marched up to Grandpa and I thought he was going to slap him, too. Instead, he grabbed Grandpa and threw him up against the partition between the two halves of the house. "Tell me the truth," my father shouted, "did you go to the PSB? Tell me the truth!"

Tell him, Grandpa! Tell him it's not true! You never knew where he was hiding! Nobody told you, Grandpa. You have to tell him, Grandpa. Grandpa, if you really have any wisdom in that head of yours, you'll tell him you're innocent.

But Grandpa didn't say anything. He shut his eyes. Two tears ran down his cheeks and his nose started to run. My heart was broken. I started wailing, like I'd just seen Grandpa keel over and die in front of me. I cursed that day. The snow made everything look pure and clean, but I saw that everyone's heart was filthy. It was like no rules applied any longer: sons cursed fathers, the good were bullied by the evil. I felt like I was being suffocated. I wanted to cry myself to death.

LXXV

It quickly became clear that it had been Grandpa that went to the PSB and told them where the Colonel was. He had sent his youngest daughter – my Third Aunt – to follow my father, and she tracked him into Great Chen Village.

Every time my father went to see the Colonel in Great Chen Village, he stopped by Third Aunt's – his sister's – house. He knew it was best to get a good meal and stock up on water before heading out over Leech Ridge. On one of Grandpa's visits to see Third Aunt, she mentioned to him that my father had visited her several times recently, and he had even taken the Constable there. If she didn't mention this, Grandpa would not have noticed that. He quickly deduced that the Colonel had to be hiding somewhere fairly close to Luocun.

Grandpa told Third Aunt to follow my father. Even if she had wanted to, she couldn't have disobeyed him. The first time she tried to follow my father, she hadn't been expecting him to set off across Leech Ridge. She couldn't keep up, and he managed to lose her on the mountain paths. She sent her one of her sons – my Fifth Cousin – to follow him the next time. Fifth Cousin was nineteen at the time, light on his feet, and he had eyes like an eagle. He had no trouble following my father up over Leech Ridge and into Great Chen Village. Once he had an address for the Colonel, Grandpa went to Second Aunt. Her father-in-law ran a tofu shop in the county capital. He knew a lot of important people, including a senior cadre from the Public Security Bureau's logistics department. It turned out to have been exactly the same guy that the Old Constable was in touch with. Second Aunt's father-in-law had a fairly good relationship with him.

Grandpa managed to get in touch with him through Second Aunt's father-in-law, and he set up a meeting in his office. Grandpa explained how Blindboy had spread a rumour that the Colonel was a sodomite. Grandpa was never good at telling stories, so it took awhile for the PSB cadre to figure out exactly what he was getting at. When he put it all together, the cadre was still curious why Grandpa was telling him. "So, why are you telling me all this?" the cadre asked. "He's not in our custody. He's still on the run."

"If you promise to help me," Grandpa said, "I can tell you where he is."

"How can I help you?"

"I want you to see what he has written on his belly. I know there's something, but it's not what everyone's saying."

"And what then?" the cadre asked.

"I want you to make an announcement to the village," Grandpa said. "Tell them the truth. I've been trying to explain it to them, but it's not as good as you guys putting up a poster."

The cadre readily agreed to the deal. It was a mutual aid pact, nothing illegal or unethical. The Colonel was arrested and the announcement was posted. The deal was complete. Both sides were happy.

Another part of the deal was that the PSB had to keep

Grandpa's identity secret. Protecting confidential sources was perfectly in line with PSB regulations, so they agreed to it. When the Old Constable and my father went to see the senior cadre to ask to visit the Colonel, he had been polite but firm with them.

However, the senior cadre liked to drink. Spring Festival was the perfect time to indulge. He was a senior cadre with the PSB, so he had plenty of invitations. The day before the Old Constable showed up to slap Grandpa, he had been out visiting. The senior cadre just happened to be there, too. The Old Constable was friendly with the senior cadre, but they were still friends of friends. By chance, their mutual friend happened to be at the same place at the same time. The three men started drinking. It wasn't long before the senior cadre let slip that Grandpa was the confidential informant. The Old Constable passed out, slept until noon, then charged over to our house.

LXXVI

Even after the Old Constable slapped him and my father threatened him, Grandpa refused to admit the truth. Refusing to admit the truth was tantamount to saying he had done it, but my father wanted to know why he had done it. If Grandpa had been forced at knifepoint, that was a different story. My father went out in the snow and headed for Third Aunt's place to get her side of the story.

Third Aunt confessed everything right away. He broke down in front of her and cried. He was disgusted with what Grandpa had done.

It was already dark when my father got home. Grandpa was already in bed. He was like a fish waiting on a chopping block – just waiting for my father to bring the cleaver down on him. My father was exhausted from the trip to and from

Third Aunt's place. He sat down on a stool beside Grandpa's bed and smoked a cigarette. He smoked it very slowly. I didn't know that he was getting ready to say something so horrifying it would change my life forever.

He didn't raise his voice, but he seemed to spit each word out of his mouth like it had a foul taste: "You are an animal. From this day forward, you are no longer my father. I will never share my table with you. I don't care whether you live or die. When you die – and I expect that day to come soon enough – I will bury you."

When Grandpa finally spoke, his voice was weak. It sounded like they were the last words he would ever speak, as if he was speaking them with great effort: "I was trying to save you, save our family, save our dignity…"

My father sat up like a bomb had gone off under him. "Our dignity? We have no dignity now! Take a good look – we're no better than animals now! Our entire family is ruined!"

My father spoke rarely, and when he did, he would stumble over his words. But on that day, he blasted every word out like a machine gun. He had been rehearsing the whole way back from Luocun. Every single word carried the weight of a pronouncement from the Bodhisattva. Strange things started happening: a dead mouse was thrown into our window, two of our ducks disappeared and the feathers were scattered at our gate as if somebody had eaten them, my brother came home after getting in a fight with somebody that had insulted our family, and when I went to Mr Seven's shop, he kicked me out when I was just trying to play chess with Stumpy Tiger like I always did.

My father knew what was happening. One cold day that winter, he went to kneel in front of the ancestral hall and ask for forgiveness. He stayed there all day. He was treated to even more abuse. People said it was like the weasel showing up at the chicken coop to beg for forgiveness, or a whore putting up a memorial arch in honour of her long-lost virginity. They told him that if he wanted to make it right, he should take the Colonel's place in his cell. They knew my father couldn't do that, but they wanted him to know exactly what they thought of him, and of our family. The Old Constable was the only one that knew my father had no part in Grandpa selling out the Colonel, but he let my father suffer. He offered no sympathy to him. He even joined in with the insults.

"There's nothing I can do," the Old Constable told my father. "It's perfectly justified that a son pays for the sins of the father." He had learned that phrase from Grandpa.

Grandpa refused to go past our gate. He mostly stayed in bed. My mother had told him that it was better for him to stay home. It was better to stay home than to go out in the street and be cursed at and spit on. Eventually, people came looking for him. In Jesus' Name showed up first. He was allowed in because he was Grandpa's cousin. He was usually the most peaceful man in the village. He went around saying "Amen" this and "in Jesus' name" that, and generally staying out of everyone's way. But when he saw Grandpa, he rained abuse down on him. He took out the Jesus statue that the Colonel had paid for. He demanded that Grandpa kneel to it and beg for mercy. Grandpa obediently kowtowed to the Jesus statue, sobbing the whole time, crying out that he deserved to die. I'd never seen anything more undignified in my life.

"Do you even understand who he was? You call him the Eunuch, but to me he was a King. Everyone respected him! Everyone said he was a good man! Look at what he did for me. I had said bad things about him before, I had said he would die without sons... But when I was in trouble, he helped me, even though his own mother believed in the Bodhisattva and would be furious if she found out. He was like Jesus Christ, even if he didn't believe in Jesus Christ. You better believe, though, because He's the only one that can save you now."

I glanced over at the statue of Jesus. He had been placed on the table with his back to the wall. His head drooped at an angle. His hands were outstretched and his palms streamed blood. He looked like he was asking for help, looking for someone to save Him... Grandpa looked like he needed to be saved. I wasn't sure if Jesus was capable of it, but I kneeled down in front of the statue anyway, and asked Him to save Grandpa. Grandpa had once told me that it was better to die than to kneel. At that moment, with my father still at the ancestral hall, all three of the men of my family were on our knees. I felt sick when I realised that. I told Jesus to forget about saving Grandpa – just come down here, I pleaded, and strangle us to death.

LXXVII

As my fathering came staggering home from the ancestral hall, the snow was already melting.

Even Clubfoot could have beat my father's pace that day. His legs were both completely stiff. The next morning, my mother woke me up and sent me to my father's bed with a hot towel to put across his knees. Both knees were swollen, soft, and round, like a pair of steamed buns. As I rubbed the towel over his knees, I saw my mother preparing my father's things. It looked like he was planning to return to the work camp up north, now that the holidays were over. I figured it was all part of his plan. It was his way of doing penance.

But I learned that afternoon that he was going to the Colonel's house. He staggered behind my brother and me as we carried the two cats and a sack full of his things. The Colonel's mother had already cleaned up the front room and he set up a bed there. He slept with the cats at the Colonel's house and only returned home for dinner. Our house was nothing but a dining room for him. He still refused to share a table with Grandpa. He avoided him like the plague. When Grandpa talked to him, he ignored him, and when he cried, he pretended not to hear. My father was true to his word. He did everything he said he would. But the day he'd returned from Third Aunt's place, he hadn't mentioned anything about moving out of the house completely. I couldn't figure out if he was still begging for forgiveness from the village. Maybe he thought they would thank him for looking after the Colonel's house. I had no idea what he was doing.

But if he was begging for forgiveness, he was wasting his time. The village despised our family, including me. When school started, nobody agreed to share a desk with me. The teacher sent me to the busted desk at the back of the classroom. Later in the day, the teacher took me aside and said cryptically: "The desk might be broken, but that doesn't mean the man that sits in it has any excuse. Once upon a time, there was a young man who was too poor to afford oil for his lamp. It was too dark for him to read. He lived next door to a rich family, whose house was always bright. He used a chisel to chip through to the other side. He could study deep into the night with his borrowed light. He became a famous scholar and an example to future generations."

The next day, I found that my desk had been vandalised. Somebody – rumour had it that it was Stumpy Tiger – had carved a giant X into the top of it. As days went by, the Xs multiplied until they covered the desk. My teacher took me aside again. She told me that I needed to understand the situation. She had a sharp voice that cut like a razor. "Everybody knows," she said, "that an X is used to mark an error on a test. If there aren't any check marks, then you're a failure. On the big-character posters, they put it over the names of counterrevolutionaries and enemies of the people, to mark those who must be struggled against, even killed...

But what does an X on a desk mean? I don't know. I hope you do. Maybe you should go home and ask your grandfather. They call him Sorcerer, don't they?"

I realised I would rather have my family smeared as sodomites than snitches. When the sodomite rumour was circulating, nobody ever really did anything to me. They talked behind my back or looked at me strangely, but they didn't dare confront me. They knew I had the long, sharp file and permission to stab to death anyone that insulted my family. Before school started after Spring Festival, I asked my father for the file, but he refused to give it to me.

"This time is different," he said, weeping. "This is something you just have to endure. It's a lesson you have to learn one day..."

I tried to endure it, but I ended up just like my father – on my knees, begging for forgiveness. But I knew asking for mercy only made things worse. One day after school, things changed forever. I walked out of the schoolyard alone, with my classmates collecting in groups behind me. I was gloomier than the grey sky. I wondered when things could go back to normal. Loneliness and fear swept over me, and my thoughts turned to Grandpa. For the first time ever, I started to hate him. He had ruined my life and destroyed my family's reputation. It was like he was rotting alive, and the stench of his body was polluting the village. I couldn't take it anymore. I was thinking about moving to the attic of the addition, so I wouldn't have to sleep beside him anymore.

On my way home, I had to go by Clubfoot's shop and down the lane that led to the ancestral hall. The hall loomed over the narrow lane, blotting out the sun. I had walked down that lane countless times over the previous sixteen years. On that day, in that alley, my life changed forever.

A brick flew from the window of the ancestral hall. It flew soundlessly through the air, crashed into my lower back, and then fell to the ground and crumbled. I was lucky to escape with a cut and a bloodstain. If I had been a step too late or too early, I might have been dead.

I finally understood why Grandpa didn't dare venture past our gate. He was like a rat that was resigned to the pigsty because he knew there was a cat in the granary. Grandpa knew that bricks were just the beginning. And you could never know who threw a brick out a window. It might as well have been thrown by the wind. It could have been anyone. It could have been a cat... It could have been a rat... I suspected that Second Grandpa would have said only Jesus could know who threw the brick, and He would forgive them, too.

That night, I moved upstairs and slept on my brother's old bed. He was working as an apprentice painter in town, so used to come home only on rare weekends, but he hadn't come back since Grandpa's crime had been uncovered. Our house was like an enemy bunker. My brother knew he would be arriving under the gaze of snipers. I slept alone on my brother's bed, my back aching. I was used to Grandpa's snoring lulling me to sleep, and without it, I couldn't relax. I didn't want to sleep. I was afraid that if I went to sleep I wouldn't wake up. I felt like death was waiting for me in the shadows.

But I wasn't afraid of death. I was only sixteen years old. I was scared of simpler things, like my father slapping me and my mother cursing me. I wasn't scared of dying, but I know that the people who loved me were afraid to lose me! I might not have lived a life of luxury like the Colonel's cats, but I still had a family that loved me.

Grandpa said: "All parents love their children, like a tree sheltering someone from the wind."

The next day, my father told me not to go to school. I was forbidden from going past the gate of our house, unless I was with my brother. He left carrying an oil-paper umbrella and a sack of grain. He returned a few days later and told me he was sending me somewhere. It was early in the morning when I left. I didn't know that it was going to be a long time before I returned. My brother walked my mother and me to the highway, and I walked with her to the wharf in town. She hugged me tight and sobbed on my shoulder, praying for God to grant me safe passage.

"Please be safe," she said. "Come back to me when you can." In her voice, I heard her pain and her absolute exhaustion.

Only then did I realise I was going somewhere far, far away, and that there was a chance I might not see her again. The sun was just rising, staining the river red with its glow. The reflection of the sun in the river shone in my mother's shiny black hair. For the first time I noticed the silver hair at her temples.

At the end of a long voyage, I landed in a village beside the ocean. A fisherman met me there. His life had been saved by the Colonel, and he knew my father, too. I stayed there for a month before he put me on a fishing boat. I got on the boat at night and at daybreak, I saw that we were approaching a massive steamship. We pulled alongside and I was pulled aboard. The ship was loaded with some sort of rare mineral only found in China. Exposed to the ocean air, the minerals gave off an acrid, bitter smell. Someone appeared to lead me below decks. We walked for almost half an hour down lead-grey stairs, through iron gates to a hold filled with food. There were stacks of potatoes, radish, cabbage, dried noodles, and mountains of salted pork and dried fish. There were people seated and reclining along the walls of the hold. There were women and men, young and old. None of them bothered looking at me. At first, I thought it was contempt, but then I realised they might be just too tired to bother.

I was in a forgiving mood, even though nobody was willing to look at me, even though I knew I was running for my life, even though I knew I might not make it, even though I might die on the way, even though I might be tossed into the ocean to feed the fish... I had received good news before I set out on the fishing boat. My father had gone to the Public Security Bureau and ambushed the senior cadre in charge of logistics. He managed to get word through the cadre to the Colonel, and the cadre smuggled out a letter addressed to everyone in the village. In his letter, he explained the situation and begged for them to forgive Grandpa. He was eventually forgiven.

I heard that the last line of the letter read: "Everything that happens to us is fate."

All I cared about was whether the story about the letter was true. If it was true, there was no need to run for my life. If it wasn't true, I had to keep going. But maybe it was fate. I couldn't escape the ship, just like I couldn't escape my fate. Maybe it was my fate to run for my life.

Everything that happens to us is fate. Grandpa had said that many times before. That day, down in the hold, I regretted not saying goodbye to Grandpa. I figured he must have already died of a broken heart. Maybe that was his fate, too: to raise me for sixteen years, and then watch me slip away without saying a word. Grandpa told me once that a single kind word could erase a lifetime of resentment. I cried, but I couldn't even hear myself over the rumbling of the ship's engines.

PART THREE

PART THREE

Seventeen

LXXVIII

N ow it's second of December, 2014. I am writing this at nine o'clock Beijing time. It's three o'clock in Madrid. My life is divided into two time zones and two places. It feels as if I have been sliced down the middle: half of me is in Madrid and the other half is in China. I'm sixty-two years old, which means retirement age in China, but I'm still a busy man. A rising China gave me a chance to start my own enterprise. I started my first company at forty-nine, and now I have three, each with hundreds of employees. I go back to China a couple times a month to look after things there, but it's never enough time to get over jet lag. I am often awake in the dead of night. I worried that I would eventually collapse from fatigue, but my body adapted and became even stronger. We are all flesh and blood. None of us are made of steel. But I seemed to be composed of something even harder. I was made of pure diamond. Even though I worked until I fell asleep while standing up, I rarely had an ache or pain. Like jetliners have two engines, I seemed to have two hearts.

I read once in the newspaper that was the reason jetliners are the safest way to travel. Of course, there were always exceptions: a terrorist could take out a plane. Terrorists are to humanity what cancer is to the human body. I read that in the newspaper, too. I read the papers every day. When I was in China, I read *Reference News*, and when I was in Spain, I read *El País*, the Chinese edition of *Nouvelles d'Europe*, and *Overseas Chinese News*. The same four newspapers accompanied me through all four seasons, like shadows, like medals... I told my wife once that they were the medals I had won in my childhood battle with loneliness. But I am not alone anymore. I have my company, my wife, my children and grandchildren, and the rest of my family and friends. There are always demands on my time. I am too busy to be lonely. I forget what loneliness feels like. All I have left are my medals and my scars. Thanks to my Motherland, my business has grown larger and larger. Last year, I went to the Great Hall of the People and held a reception for overseas Chinese. My wife saw me on CCTV-4. When she saw it, she scared my grandson by breaking down in tears, and hugging him to her chest.

Life is like a dream. But even if I had another lifetime to dream, I never would have imagined I would end up here. My father was afraid that Grandpa's sins had doomed me. If I survived, my father thought, my life would still be ruined. That was why he took the risk to send me far away. My father made the right decision, even if he didn't know it then. It was better to go. After I left, my two brothers escaped, too. They took different routes than I had, though.

The first place I landed was Barcelona, a city on the coast of Spain, sort of like the Shanghai of Spain. The city was big and beautiful, and I was small and ugly. I didn't even have a name. During the daytime, I didn't dare go out into the streets. I shuddered every time I heard sirens. That's the life of a refugee. I was no better than the rats in the gutter. All I could do was keep going, trying to survive. I managed to find work at a shoe factory run by an earlier generation of Chinese immigrants. My job was putting buckles on dress shoes. I worked two shifts a day. Counting the first year, which was considered an apprenticeship, I worked for six years without seeing a penny. All the money went to the "snakehead". That's a modern word – snakehead – and everyone recognises it now, but I never heard it at the time. I only heard the smuggler referred to as the "dragonhead". The dragonhead was a capable man. He took me all the way across the ocean. But he had to be paid for his services. Many years later, my father told me that he had financed the trip with a gold bracelet that he had taken from the Colonel's house. The dragonhead claimed that he had never received it, though, so I had to pay him off. Where did the bracelet go? I have no idea. It's ancient history now.

When I finally returned to China, twenty-two years had passed. It was the year 1991.

The newspaper said that people had to learn to let go. That meant forgiving other people, but also forgiving yourself. I've let a lot of things go, but some things are harder than others to leave behind. I learned something from six years in a shoe factory: if you don't take a shoe off, it starts to hurt your foot. Some things stick with you, though. They grow to be part of you. Those things can only be let go when you die.

I hadn't gone into business yet in 1991. It was hard to scrape together the money for a plane ticket. Raising that money was like raising a child. I said before, it was difficult to return, but I knew I had to endure it. I had to let some things go, but I couldn't abandon that dream. I waited twenty-two years. My memories kept me going. While I toiled like a slave, my dreams took flight.

Everything I did, I did so that I could return.

In a way, I was living only for my return.

I waited twenty-two years for the day that I was handed my plane ticket back to China. I bought a round-trip ticket, flying to Shanghai and back. When I remember that moment, my heart still pounds. When I got home that day, I knelt on the floor, as if carrying the plane ticket home had exhausted me. I remember that moment like it was yesterday. I can still see my wife, and feel her hands gently wiping the tears off my cheeks.

Life is full of experiences. Some of those things are like a puff of air, and others are carved into you. Some of the things I had experienced felt like they had been burned into me with a soldering iron. The pain lingered.

LXXIX

Your hometown is where the bones of your loved ones are buried. In 1991, when I went back to my village, the tiger curled around Tail Mountain had three new tombs. They belonged to Grandpa, to my mother, and to my second eldest brother. If my sister-in-law counts as a relative – and I suppose she should, even though I never met her – then there were four. It was a grey, early spring day that I walked back into the village I had been away from for twenty-two years. I found my father sitting outside the eastern addition where I had slept with Grandpa. He was smoking a cigarette and watching rain drip from the eaves. He looked up when he saw me coming, then looked away again. "Who are you looking for?"

"Father," I said.

From his reaction, you would've thought I had only been gone overnight. He didn't seem particularly excited. Maybe he wanted to give me a moment to remember where I was, to let these old walls and old doors and old stones take me in. The place smelled sour and mouldy. There were cobwebs in the corners. The front hall of the house was stacked haphazardly with old chairs and stools, and the portrait of Chairman Mao had a corner ripped off. Everything was covered in a fine layer of dust. The only thing that remained clean was the square wood table. Its red lacquer top still glowed.

I thought maybe my father had lost his mind. I studied the deep, dark wrinkles on his face. He had shrunk in the time I had been away. His bony fingers were as skinny and fragile as the cigarette that burned between them. I called his name again. He flicked the butt of his cigarette out into the courtyard and watched it die out in the drizzle. "Grandpa's dead," he said.

I had figured as much. He was a man that could not live without dignity. The sodomite smear had nearly killed him, and that turned out to be only the beginning of his suffering. I read in the newspaper once that wise men can see the future in the past. I wouldn't call myself a wise man, but it was fairly clear where he was going to end up, even if it took a while to get there. After I escaped, I would write my family a letter at least once a year. At first, I had tortured myself waiting for their reply. When a few years went by without getting word, I kept writing, but I stopped waiting for an answer. Grandpa was the only one in the house that could have replied, so I knew he had to be dead. If he was alive, he would have written back. Even if he knew he was going to die, he would take the time to write to me. If he was still alive, and had just never written back, it would mean he was nearly a hundred years old. A man like him, beaten down by the world, could never hang on that long. He was dead within a few days of me leaving. He didn't wait for the Colonel's letter, either. He took his belt and hanged himself in the pigsty. Even though the Colonel had forgiven him, some people never would. The Old Constable held a meeting after Grandpa died, and he told everyone that Grandpa didn't deserve to be buried in our village. He said that Grandpa's body should be tossed out on the mountain and left for the scavengers to tear apart.

"Your mother's dead, too," my father said.

I had guessed that, too. My mother would never have let the house fall into such a state. She would never allow the dust and cobwebs to collect. Her house was her pride, and she worked hard to keep it clean. Even the pigsty stayed tidy. The mess was like a monument to her passing. I asked him when and how she had died. I hoped she had died a natural death, rather than it being a suicide or him hurting her.

My father continued without looking up, "Your Second Brother's gone, too. He died before her." My second eldest brother had died of leukaemia. I thought it had something to do with his job as a painter, dealing with varnish and lacquer and other chemicals for work. But my father thought otherwise. Of the three painters my brother worked with, he was the only one to get sick. He was closer to my father than either me or my brother, and he had the same personality. He was like a lump of iron. He endured everything and said nothing. "He looked like the men you see moping around because their wives are cheating on them," my father said. "He stopped smiling. He stopped talking. I think that's what killed him. He choked himself to death on all that stuff he couldn't say. Maybe we pushed him to it, me and Grandpa…" That was what my father told me later, too.

On that day, he kept listing death. "His wife died too. She went before him."

My brother was not an easy man to get along with, and he was thirty-two and alone when my mother and father bought him a wife from Guizhou. She was ten years younger than him. It was hard to say if it was the age difference or the language barrier, but they had an unhappy marriage. My brother was rarely home, but when he was, they would fight. He was happier at work, with his lacquer and his brush. His wife never learned the local language, so, when they fought, they would beat each other and throw things. One time, he slapped her hard enough to knock out a tooth. He walked out after that. She went and drank a bottle of pesticide. Their unhappy marriage produced a son. He was eleven years old. I slept together in a bed with him the night that I returned. He bore no resemblance to my brother. He was in primary school, then, and was at the top of his class. That was completely unlike my brother, too. My brother had failed most of his classes and left school early to learn a trade.

I felt like I was surrounded by the dead. I didn't want to ask about my eldest brother. I looked around at the house and knew they couldn't be there. I knew that if my brother and his wife were there, the place couldn't have fallen into such a state. But I didn't know where he was, or even if he had married.

"Your elder brother is gone, too," my father said. "But he's still alive." He paused. "If he hadn't left when he did, he would probably be dead, same as you."

I started to cry. It was like I was the lone survivor, left on a battlefield littered with corpses. I had proved myself, but at what cost? For my father, my return meant nothing. To him, it might have been better if I never came back. Nobody had returned my letters because he had hidden them. He didn't want anybody to know I was alive. He was sure that I was cursed, along with the rest of the family. If some wicked spirits knew where I was, they might come after me. He was worried that if I returned, there would be no hope for me.

LXXX

My elder brother had gone to Qinwu, an hour's walk into the mountains from our village. He had married a woman there and moved in with her family. He escaped with his life, but not his dignity. My brother, like my father, seemed incapable of standing up again after kneeling to ask for forgiveness. The people of the village had forgiven our family, but my father and my brothers and Grandpa had been unable to forgive themselves. They wanted to keep punishing themselves. Grandpa did it with a noose, my second brother did it by succumbing to his illness, my eldest brother did it by running away and taking his wife's surname, and I did it by spending two decades running for my life...

After my father recounted all of the disasters that the family had experienced in my absence, he said nothing. He was haunted. He was worried about revealing too much. He was still scared that those evil spirits were lying in wait for me. He didn't want to tip them off. It had become an obsession for him, rather than a fear. His haunted look, his dark, thin face, and his messy grey hair reminded me of my escape by sea. In those days, I thought every day about death. When I slept, I died in my nightmares. When I was finally taken ashore, it felt like I had aged years down in the hold of that ship. I knelt down on the docks with the other refugees, and we thanked Heaven and earth for letting us live. A flock of curious seagulls watched kneeling on the concrete. They swooped down on us, squawking and flapping. We did look like a bunch of birds pecking food off the ground, and they must have thought there was a meal available.

I read in the newspaper once that it doesn't matter how you live your life – the only thing that matters is how you remember it.

My father wouldn't let me stay at the house that time. He gave me the key to Colonel's place. When I asked what had become of the Colonel, my father would only say: "You'll understand in time."

I thought he meant that the Colonel would be home, and I could ask him what had happened. But when I got to his gate, I realised that nobody was living there. The garden that the Colonel's mother had kept was overgrown with weeds that stood almost as tall as me. What was left of the mouldering haystack in the yard was full of animal excrement and the skeletons of mice and birds. The cobblestones that once paved the Colonel's courtyard had been knocked loose by the tenacious labour of the earthworms. The house itself was becoming overgrown with vine. The old wooden recliner that the Colonel liked to sit out on in the evenings was in pieces on the ground, as if it had been struck by lightning. The key was useless since the lock had long since rusted away. The only way to get inside was to force the door open.

The house's interior had been preserved from damage, but there was a grim odour in the place. Every step I took sent up a cloud of fine dust, and I was worried I would walk into the cobwebs that hung everywhere. An old shirt hanging on a hook had been nearly completely eaten away by moths. In the room that the cats had once occupied, the velvet curtains were hanging by threads from their rods, scraping the floor. No one would have believed that the two handmade cat beds, filled with mouse shit by then, had once been home to the Colonel's two spoiled sweethearts.

I didn't go upstairs.

I was scared to go upstairs. My father thought our house was haunted, but I never felt it. It definitely felt like the Colonel's house was haunted, though. Standing there, I felt as if a ghost was about to leap out at me at any moment, waggling a long, bloody tongue. Maybe it wasn't that the house was haunted, but the house itself had somehow become replaced by some evil spirit. My father said that I would understand in time, and I realised what he meant. The Colonel was either still in prison or had already been executed. If the choice was between spending decades long in a cell, or facing a firing squad, then the latter would be preferable. I felt bad for the Colonel. I couldn't stand the house. There was so much humiliation and pain still floating in the air there.

There was no way I was going to spend the night there.

There was no way anybody could live there. It would take days to clean it out. The house was pretty much ruined, too. All the wood was rotting and the metal had rusted. There were trees growing from the roof. It wasn't much more than a rotting carcass, already picked over by scavengers. My father had probably not visited in a long time by then. He must have imagined it as he had last seen it. Maybe he thought a haunted house was the safest place for me. If evil spirits were after me, even they might think twice before going into the Colonel's house.

As I was walking out, I bumped into a cabinet that seemed to have been slid from its original position. It was close to the front door, and the way it was shifted, it looked like it had been edging towards the exit, begging someone to take it along with them. In the cabinet was a picture frame, about the size of a magazine cover. I had to blow the dust off to see who was in the photo. It was a portrait of a middle-aged couple. The couple was pressed shoulder to shoulder, and they were smiling. It looked like a wedding photo. I realised after a moment that the man was the Colonel. His happy expression was forced. The smile wasn't natural. That was why I hadn't recognised him. In my memory, the Colonel's smile was magnificent and unrestrained. He laughed easily and loudly. In the picture in the cabinet, he looked like he had a gun to his back.

The woman in the picture had shoulder-length hair framing a round face with a fleshy nose, a wide mouth, and a flat chin. It was hard to tell from the picture, but she looked younger than the Colonel. I wasn't sure how to read her smile, but compared to the Colonel's frozen grin, it looked sweet and innocent. It looked like she knew something that she wasn't telling us. From the style of the picture and the way they were posed, I knew the woman in the picture had to be his wife. It was an amazing coincidence that the picture had been left behind for me to find. One of the two people in the picture – either the Colonel or his wife – must have been preparing to take it with them when they left. That must have been why it was on the cabinet, near the door.

When I asked my father about the wedding photo, he

looked surprised and refused to answer. Finally, he told me that he'd tell me, but I had to go and clean up the Colonel's house first. As he spoke to me, he kept glancing around, as if looking for evil spirits tailing me. There was no way he could let me stay in the house with him. As I saw it, I would be haunted by evil spirits in my own house than face whatever haunted the Colonel's place. He stared at me blankly for a moment, then he started to cry. It was the first time I had ever seen him cry. When I had been a boy, he was a man of few words and fewer emotions, but he had changed in the time I had been gone. He had seen his family destroyed, and he had learned how to cry. The sound was like fabric being slowly torn. Tears dribbled down his face. The tears of an old man are the saddest thing in the world.

LXXXI

The next day, I went to town and bought incense, spirit money, and a Buddhist charm bag. I planned to go up into the hills to the graves of Grandpa, my mother, Second Brother, and my sister-in-law. It's custom not to go to an old tomb before Tomb-Sweeping Day, but for me, they were fresh graves. It was still early spring, the time when Grandpa said insects were stirring. In that season, the cold was gone, but the warmth had not yet settled in. It had been cold and rainy the day before, but the rain stopped and it warmed up for my trip to pay my respects. I slipped off my jacket on the way up. My father had refused to accompany me. He was sure that some evil spirits would be lingering there and might recognise me. It was a Sunday, so my nephew was out of school. He said he could guide me to graves. When we got there, though, we couldn't find them. The hillside was covered in the withered grass of winter and the fresh green of spring. He finally pointed out four graves. They were unmarked, so I had to take his word for it. I comforted myself with the thought that if my father was right, and evil spirits were lingering, they probably couldn't find the graves, either.

By the time we came down the mountain, it was already lunchtime, so I took my nephew to the food stall in front of the ancestral hall. A few people recognised me, and we got to talking. My nephew got bored and ran off with some classmates. I wasn't returning to the village in glory, and I didn't want to make a big thing out of my arrival. When I walked back past the Colonel's gate, I heard a pained moan. I looked through the gate and saw my father's head poking out the door. "Get in here," he shouted.

When I got inside, I saw that my father had already started tidying up the place. The seating area in front of the house's main door looked almost like it had twenty-two years before. My father had washed down the concrete floor and cleaned up a pair of bamboo chairs. The afternoon sun shined down on the concrete. My father and I sat down in the two chairs. Neither of us said anything, as if we had planned the entire thing. He took out a cigarette, lit it, and took a few puffs. "They all know," he said casually.

"What?"

"They know all about the Colonel. They know all about that woman."

He was not scared of whatever ghosts haunted the Colonel's house. Maybe he had already made friends with them. He didn't wait for me to ask what he meant, but immediately launched into the story. I could tell he had rehearsed this speech before. He was a man of few words, but he had twenty-two years to prepare for that moment. He still kept it brief, though. He told me that the Public Security Bureau had sentenced the Colonel's mother to three years in prison. She was locked up at the Hangzhou Women's Prison. The Colonel's case was held up for much longer. The county court passed it to the city court, and they passed it to the provincial court. I was already long gone by the time he was sentenced to death. The execution was set for May Day, in the commune's auditorium. The day before the execution, the radio broadcast reports inviting people to see the death of a man convicted of spying against the nation, betraying the people, perversion, and harming a Red Guard. Everyone knew who they were talking about, and the radio reports were just adding fuel to the fire. When the auditorium opened, people stampeded inside. A few kids ended up being trampled. Not many people from our village ended up going. They stayed away, out of respect for the Colonel.

My father said: "I didn't want to go, but I thought it might be the last chance I had to see him. I wanted to be the one to collect his body."

There was a row of dignitaries on the auditorium's dais that day, including the leaders of the county's Revolutionary Committee, Public Security Bureau cadres, judges, Red Guards, and ceremonial representatives of the masses. Captain Hu sat at the left side of the stage. He had already been promoted to the county Revolutionary Committee's propaganda department. His main role that day was to shout slogans. Captain Hu was full of revolutionary fighting spirit, but he was happy to see his own personal grudges being settled, too. He put all he had into it, quickly working the crowd into a fervour. When the Colonel was led onto the stage, the crowd hushed, as if waiting for the show to begin. The Colonel was unbound. There were two policemen beside him with pistols drawn. Even if he turned into a bird and tried to fly out of the skylight, he wouldn't have made it far.

My father said: "He was as skinny as an ape and he had a big, messy beard. I could barely recognise him."

It was hot that May. The Colonel wore only a light shirt and trousers. He had withered away to the point that he was on the verge of being blown down by the chanting of the crowd. The judge went to the podium and read out the charges. When the judge got to the part about having a tattoó that indicated he was a "sexual running dog" – and my father emphasised that this was exactly what the judge had said – for Japanese women and collaborators, someone in the crowd shouted for the guards to pull the Colonel's clothes off.

It was Blindboy's father doing the shouting. The Blind Man couldn't have seen anything, anyways. He stared up at the dais with his two dead white eyes, howling for them to strip the Colonel. Some people in the crowd started to chant, "Tear his clothes off! Tear his clothes off!" At that point, Blindboy's uncle and a couple of thugs they'd hired rushed the stage.

Captain Hu roared: "Long Live Chairman Mao! Long live the masses!" These were the usual revolutionary slogans, but it was clear he was trying to work the crowd up to charge the stage and strip the Colonel.

My father swore: "Those bastards wanted to strip him naked on the spot!"

The police that were escorting the Colonel weren't sure what to do. The dignitaries on the stage whispered to each other but no conclusions were reached. Blindboy's uncle and the two thugs seized their chance. They reached for the Colonel's trousers. At that moment, the Colonel seemed to detonate. He spun around, knocking down the two cops and sending the uncle and his thugs flying. At that moment, he was completely unbound and there was nothing to stop him from flying away. He wasn't sure quite where to go, though. The Colonel paced around the stage a few times, looking for an exit. Instead of retreating backstage, he jumped down from the front of the stage, right into the crowd. Everyone scattered, clearing a path for the Colonel. The Colonel roared like a madman, rushing through the crowd. He was like a wild horse. Some people were hurt again in the stampede, but their cries of pain were drowned out by the Colonel's howling. When the auditorium had been cleared, the Colonel did not leave. Instead, he walked right back to the stage, as if prepared to perform an encore.

My father said: "He had lost his mind."

LXXXII

The Colonel was too crazy to die and too crazy to be locked up. Within a month after the day at the auditorium, the Public Security Bureau sent for someone from the village to go and get him. The village Party secretary and the Old Constable returned with the Colonel. Along the way, the Colonel's mental state seemed to deteriorate even further. He howled curses at everyone they passed. People in the village wept when they saw what he had been reduced to.

From that point on, he was in the custody of my father. My father no longer had to do his regular work for the commune, and was instead given workpoints for looking after the Colonel. He was like the Colonel's nursemaid.

My father found it fairly easy to look after the Colonel. The only hard part was keeping him from having fits, and, if he did, keep him from hurting anyone or himself. The fits came on without warning. At those times, the Colonel seemed to lose touch with reality. One time, he grabbed a knife and stabbed himself in the stomach, but he usually attacked other people. Maybe he regretted not having used his surgical skills to erase the tattoo on his belly. Maybe that was what he was trying to do when he stabbed himself.

My father said: "Actually, I think he tried to carve it off himself a few times, but it didn't work."

My father made the Colonel wear handcuffs. He became as much a warden as a nurse. That went on for a few months, when a woman suddenly arrived in the village, looking for the Colonel. She looked very civilised and she spoke Mandarin without an accent. She started crying as soon as she saw the Colonel. Some people guessed it was his sister, but he'd been an only child.

My father said: "That's the woman you saw in the picture with him."

The woman turned out to have served with the Colonel in Korea. To prove it, she showed my father two pictures of them together on the front lines. She wanted to take the Colonel away from the village. She said she knew a doctor that could treat him. The village Party secretary held a meeting in the ancestral hall and let the old people that knew the Colonel vote on the matter. The woman and the Colonel left. They returned a year or so later. The Colonel had improved. He was no longer violent. He would sometimes even smile at people. Mentally, he was a bit sharper, too. After she brought him back, he was completely obedient. He would do whatever my father told him to do.

My father said: "When he lost his mind, it was like a fire was raging inside him, but after she brought him back, it was like the fire had burned down to coals."

When the woman returned, she brought a marriage certificate with her. She wanted to marry the Colonel and look after him. She needed the village to agree, though. Another meeting was held in the ancestral hall and nobody opposed the idea. Shortly after that, the photo I saw in the Colonel's house had been taken. That winter, the Colonel's mother was released. That was another reason the woman had brought the Colonel back. The Colonel's mother had never been in good health, and the time in prison had crushed her. Every step she took, she had to pause for breath. She couldn't keep anything down but rice porridge. The Colonel had to be cared for like a child, while the woman also had to look after his frail mother. But they both lived about as well as could be expected, given their conditions. They had their dignity, at the very least.

My father said: "Everyone in the village said that the

woman had been sent by the Bodhisattva Guanyin to repay the Colonel's mother for her devotion."

Everyone called the woman Little Guanyin. They treated her like a bodhisattva and she returned the favour. Later on, I heard people talking about her in the village... They said there was no woman like her on earth. They said they'd do anything to have a daughter-in-law like her.

About a year after returning to the village, the Colonel's mother choked to death on a spoonful of porridge. Little Guanyin sobbed at her funeral. She cried like a mourning dove. The sound of Little Guanyin crying was so sad and so sincere that everyone who heard it began to weep. She joined the men that carried the casket to the tomb, still crying. All the men that walked beside her were moved to tears, too. Little Guanyin's cries had been carved into people's memories. They recalled them through their own tears.

My father said: "This house must have good feng shui, I guess, to bring a woman like that into the Colonel's life."

That was why my father wanted to talk with me at the Colonel's house. I thought the place was haunted, but he knew there were no ghosts there. The only spirit haunting the place belonged to the Guanyin – the Bodhisattva herself and the filial nursemaid she had sent to accompany her follower and her son.

After finishing the seven days of prayer and mourning for her mother-in-law, Little Guanyin went back to the Colonel's house and started packing things up. What couldn't be carried, she gave away to the neighbours. She planned to bring the Colonel and his two cats back to her hometown. The cats were both too old to walk, and had to be carried in rattan baskets. They had been mostly impervious to all the great changes around them. Their relationship with their master had only deepened.

My father said: "He had become just as obedient to them as they used to be to him."

Hundreds of people walked with them down to the Fuchun River, where the Colonel, Little Guanyin, and the two cats boarded a boat. As the whistle blew and the boat headed out into the current, Little Guanyin even knelt on the deck to show her gratitude, thanking the village for everything they had done. Everyone there had wept, and my father wept while recounting it.

My father said: "That was the last time I saw them. I didn't want to pass on any of my bad luck."

I asked to see them, though, and my father gave me the address, which Little Guanyin had jotted down for him on the back of my old homework paper. It turned out that they lived near Zhu Family Corner in Qingpu. I had to go through there to get to Hongqiao Airport!

Eighteen

LXXXIII

At that time, there weren't many cabs, and, even if I could've found one, there's no way I could've afforded it. It was the age of the mototaxi. I negotiated with a driver for a ride from Zhu Family Corner to Mulberry Village, and jumped on the back of his bike. As soon as I got there, I realised why it was called Mulberry Village: it was guarded by a stand of mulberry bushes. They were still bare in early spring, and they had been trimmed into a low, square wall. It reminded me of a row of new recruits with their heads freshly shaved. A canal ran through the centre of the village, straight as an arrow, and as placid as the plains that surrounded it. The houses in the village were uniformly built of the same dark blue brick, and tiled with the same black roof tiles. All the homes were two stories, with conical roofs. It reminded me of the planned communities I had seen in Madrid.

The village had grown wealthy in the past by raising silkworms, and it still retained a youthful vigour.

My driver was from the village and he recognised Little Guanyin and the Colonel, even though the picture was more than two decades old. He was able to take me right to their door. Before I left him, he warned me that the man in the photo was mentally ill, although he praised the woman as gentle and kind hearted. I was about to knock on the door, but the driver beat me to it, hollering up at the house, "Granny, someone's here to see you."

It had started to drizzle on the way there. The early spring season in the area around Shanghai runs hot and cold. Whenever it rained, the wind would blow, and the chill would go right through you. My hands and feet were stiff. I was on my way back to Madrid, so I had taken my luggage with me to the village. Before I could unload the things – my bag and a box, but also a sack of bamboo shoots – that I had strapped to the back of the bike, the door behind me creaked open and I felt someone staring at me. I was a bit scared to turn around.

When I finally turned, I saw a thin old woman staring back at me. Her fine, grey hair had gone untrimmed for many years and waved in the breeze behind her. She was sallow and wrinkled. Except for the bags under her eyes, there was not an ounce of flesh on her face. She was bent at the waist and seemed to be held upright only by leaning on the doorframe. She looked nothing like the woman in the photograph. This woman had been completely drained of life. She must have thought I had gone to the wrong house, but her mood changed when she saw the picture, which I had tucked under my arm after showing the driver.

"Are you from Shuangjiacun?" she asked. When I nodded, she carefully picked her way down the stairs up to the door and started trying to help me with my luggage. "Whose boy are you?" When she heard my father's name, she grabbed my arm excitedly. "You were the one that went abroad, right?" I nodded. "I read your letters!"

In the first few years that I had been in Spain, I had written letters home every month. It was the only way to kill my loneliness. When I didn't get a response, I wrote fewer and fewer. At the end, I only wrote one letter a year. She had read those letters – from the first few years – aloud to my father, so she knew far more about me than I did about her.

She clasped my hand in hers and smiled warmly. "So," she said, "it's like we're old friends already."

She still had a sense of humour, at least. Her grip on my arm was strong, too, and her hands were big and rough. She carried my box into the house with ease, even though she was still bent at the waist. I saw that the walls of her house had not been whitewashed in many years, and the varnish on the door had faded and started to chip, but everything else was neat and tidy. On the right side when I entered, I noticed a small clinic had been set up, with a reception desk, a medicine cabinet, an IV stand, and a satchel prepared for making house calls.

Before I left, my father had told me to call her Auntie Lin. When she got me seated inside, she went to work pouring tea, stowing my luggage, and wiping down the table. As I sipped my tea, I kept looking around for the Colonel. When I'd finished my cup, I couldn't hold out any longer, and I said, "Auntie Lin, where's Uncle?"

It felt very strange to call him "Uncle", as if I barely knew him. In fact, I knew all his nicknames, and his real name!

"He's upstairs," she said. She turned to the stairs and yelled, "Come on down here, Old Man. You've got a guest." I heard the sound of quick, heavy footsteps upstairs. I stood to meet him when he came down, but Auntie Lin motioned for me to sit. She headed for the bottom of the stairs, but the Colonel appeared soon after. He resembled neither the Colonel of my memory, nor the man in the photograph. Standing in front of me was a plump, pale man, whose cheeks were flushed red. Even with a shock of white hair, the Colonel had the appearance of a child. He was like a little boy meeting a stranger, excited, but shy and unsure what to say. I said hi to him and he jumped behind Auntie Lin for cover.

"You're fine," she said, comforting him.

She put her hand on his shoulder, as if protecting him. They were both completely different from the two people I had seen in the photo: the timid young woman had become the mature guardian, and the stiff, middle-aged man had transformed into an overgrown child. I couldn't hide how puzzled I was by the whole scene. I felt myself staring, my eyes bouncing back and forth between them, but I couldn't stop. When I saw the fresh, childlike Colonel beside the old woman, I couldn't get over the impression that he had sucked all of the vitality out of her to use for himself.

I read in the newspaper once that life takes it out of you. They meant that life grinds you down, basically. But we grind each other down. We take the life out of each other.

LXXXIV

Auntie Lin told me that, in her medical opinion, the Colonel's illness had been caused by extreme stimulation for a very brief period of time. It could have been treated at the time, but she only learned about his condition months after the traumatic event. By the time she got him to a specialist, it was long past the optimum time for treatment. It turned out to be nearly useless.

"For example," she said, "let's say you cut your hand... If you go right to the doctor, you'll be fine. You might end up with a scar. That's it. But if you don't go to a doctor, that cut can get infected. If you let the infection go, it can only get worse. At a certain point, the entire arm has to be amputated. If you let it go past that point, your body becomes septic and you die. His father" – she meant the Colonel's father – "died that way."

I knew that story well. I got her point: an amputation was a radical solution, and far from ideal, but it was sometimes required to save the patient, and the Colonel had undergone some kind of radical treatment, too. It wasn't enough to restore him completely, but it saved enough of his mind to make him functional. He was left with the mind of a six- or seven-year-old. He was particularly nervous around adults and strangers, so Auntie Lin told me to treat him like a child, make friends with him, invite him to play... My two kids were ten and seven years old at the time, so I treated him exactly like I treated my seven-year-old daughter. We got along well. He loved listening to me talk, and he answered anything I asked him. When we played checkers, he was even better than my ten-year-old son.

He called Auntie Lin his wife, but she was more like his mother.

Later on that day, Auntie Lin went to the kitchen to make dinner. The Colonel seemed to be liberated. He shushed me and led me upstairs and to his room. He occupied the biggest of the three rooms upstairs. It was a long, rectangular room, completely filled with toys: marbles, slingshots, water pistols, wooden guns, and picture books. He loved drawing more than anything else. He had a chalkboard leaned against the wall, where he had drawn a girl with French braids, and he had a stack of paper hospital sheets that he had set up on a desk that was covered with a tablecloth. Beside the desk was a row of coloured pencils and crayons. He showed off all his toys to me, then he asked if I wanted to watch him draw. When I said yes, he pulled out a stool and sat down. He smoothed out the paper, chose a pencil, and started to draw. He worked in complete silence, peacefully but seriously. Except for his silver hair and wide back, he reminded me of my own kids at work. Up until that point, I hadn't even noticed what he was wearing. He had on a loose, dark brown sweater with frayed cuffs, navy blue corduroy pants, and a pair of slippers.

He was drawing an American soldier with a grey helmet, brown leather boots, and a black machine gun. I knew it was an American soldier because he drew a big American flag on his chest. Compared to my own kids, he was a better artist, and much faster. It looked like he had drawn this image many times before.

"Who's this?" I asked him.

"It's a Yankee," he blurted.

"Do you know him?"

He thought for a moment, then said, "I've seen him before." He paused again and then said, "When I was in the People's Volunteer Army in Korea."

I was surprised he still remembered. Without thinking, I reached out and took his hand. "You were a military doctor, right? You saved a lot of people."

The memory seemed to be balanced on the edge of a precipice. My gesture threatened to knock it into the abyss. "Doctor?" he said. "Who did I save?" His brow furrowed. "Where was this?"

"Korea," I said. "You just told me you were in the Volunteer Army in Korea."

"Don't make up stories," he said. "I never volunteered for anything. I was in the People's Liberation Army!"

Auntie Lin told me later that these memories were like fish in a pond. Most of the time, they were safely below the surface, but sometimes you got a glimpse of their shiny white bellies – or they would jump right out of the water! There was no rhyme or reason to them. The memory of his time in Korea had surfaced for an instant, but it quickly disappeared again, back under the water. It came and went so fast that I wondered at the time if I had heard him wrong.

He flipped over the page and told me he was going to draw the People's Liberation Army. The pencil was like a tranquiliser dart. He retreated into a world of fantasy. He seemed to relax as he worked. I tried my best not to disturb him. It was like watching a master at work. I knew he needed silence.

"I need to pee!" he said suddenly. He dropped his pencil and ran to the room next door.

There must have been a toilet in the other room. He didn't close the door behind him. When I heard him pee, I couldn't help but think about his old nickname. He had kept it a secret for his whole life, but at that very moment, I could have rushed in and taken a look. I needed to piss, too. In an instant, I could finally know his darkest secret. I knew how kids were, and I knew he probably wouldn't refuse. My own son was ten years old, and he had no shame about his body. When he went to take a shower, he would run around the house fully nude. But as soon as the thought came to me, I regretted it.

I had read in the newspaper that pity is what stops people from taking advantage of others. Pity is the only thing that can extinguish desire.

When he came back, the smell of the toilet came with him. He had run back into the room without doing up his pants. He held them up with one hand. He pulled down the waist and said, nervously, "Come and look. Somebody wrote something." He glanced at the door and said, "Don't tell my wife. She'd scold me. She always scolds me for showing people."

Once upon a time, he had pretended to be a eunuch to hide his secret. There was a time when he would do anything to hide it from the world. But at that moment, he was offering to show me. His only fear was being scolded by Auntie Lin.

I had been keeping it together up until that moment, but my heart finally broke. Without looking, I reached down and did up his pants. I hugged him and felt tears burning in my eyes. He was curious. He wanted to know why I was crying. I wanted to know how the world had been so cruel to him.

I regretted going to see him. I wanted to run away.

LXXXV

That night the rain came down like hammers on the roof. It sounded like some great monster was chewing up the roof tiles like biscuits. It ended just as the sun finally set. I needed to go out for a walk. I couldn't get over what I had experienced in the Colonel's room. When we were done with dinner, I slipped out. She was busy cutting his nails. Auntie Lin had suggested I walk to the east side of the village to see the silk works. They had just installed an assembly line of German machinery. One machine could do the work that had once been done by a hundred craftsmen. I told her I'd have a look, but I wasn't interested in machines. I was thinking about the Colonel, everything he had gone through, all the tears that had been shed for him... I planned to find a place to cry.

In the shade of some damp mulberry bushes on the edge of the village, I cried my eyes out. On the walk back, I tried to pay attention to the village. Unlike my village, trapped by the mountains, this village had spread out across the plains. It felt modern and open. The houses were tidily arranged along wide tree-lined streets. There were even street lights! Everyone in the village kept flowers in their front yard and up on their balconies. Some people I passed even waved to me. They were out for their after-dinner strolls. A few people rode by on bikes. In my village, an outsider would draw attention, but nobody seemed to find my presence there remarkable. Most of the people there were outsiders themselves, having arrived in recent years to work in the factories. When I returned to my own village, there had been stares. I was born and raised there, but twenty-two years away had made me an outsider.

The newspaper said that Reform and Opening had brought a new vitality to China. The country had seen a great transformation that extended from the city to the countryside, and from elementary matters like diet and clothes, all the way to ideology. I could understand that better than most people, since I had experienced both the time before Reform and Opening and its aftermath. I knew what it was like in China and I knew what it was like overseas. The changes I experienced were surprising but welcome.

But in that first year back, the surprises were more painful than heartwarming.

I spent eleven days in my home village on that trip. It was enough to rekindle my memories of the place, and find out what had happened in my absence... The crystal-clear creek had been reduced to a stinking sewer. The paper mills and smelting plants had been using the creek as a natural drainage ditch. The bamboo forests on the hillside had been blasted out to get to the rock underneath. Excavators scooped rock out of the new quarries, and it was used to build roads and factories and apartment blocks. The cobblestones that had paved the lanes of the village were poured over with slick concrete. People had started riding bicycles, and it was hard to ride on cobblestones. A row of machines was installed in the ancestral hall by some clever entrepreneur, and they turned out mountains of white garbage every day. That factory turned out all the disposable chopsticks and plates and napkins that office workers needed in the city.

The stone mason's shop was gone, and his third son, Meathook, had never returned home from Vietnam. He was buried on the Yunnan border.

My cousin got married, then divorced, then had an affair with a woman in a nearby village whose husband was a paralysed from the neck down. The woman gave birth, but I don't know if my cousin was officially named as the father on the child's registration paper.

Wild One followed in his mother's footsteps: she had made a living with a tiny snack bar, but he had bigger things in mind, and moved her operation into the county capital. I'd heard that his business model relied on buying mouldy grain down in the village, then turning it into steamed sponge cake to sell to people in town.

Stumpy Tiger rented the woodshed that the Colonel had been locked up in. He redecorated the woodshed, then bought into a supermarket franchise based in Hangzhou. Most people couldn't afford the things he sold out of his shop.

Mr Seven, the Old Constable, and the village Party secretary were all dead by then. Unlike Grandpa, they had all died a natural, dignified death. Before he died, the Old Constable had chosen a spot for his grave, and planted two cypress trees. A year later, both the Old Constable and one of the trees died, but the other tree had flourished. It was very strange. When I visited, the tall cypress was green with new shoots.

The village changed a lot while I was gone. The change had swept through like a fire, which consumed the village. The village fuelled the flames. It was hard to find things that had been untouched, but there were a few, like Blindboy and his severed tongue and corpse-like hands. He had been rendered useless by the attack, and it had unsettled him in some profound way. When Blindboy's father was still alive, his son had some amount of dignity, and the Blind Man had looked after the basics. But once the Blind Man was dead, Blindboy could only rely on the mercy of the village. Time had worn away all the slogans that the Red Guards had painted on the walls, including Captain Hu's blood-red poem, but it was powerless to erase the deep hatred and resentment that Blindboy had for my family. I didn't go to see him, but on the few occasions when I ran into him in the village, I looked the other way. What I really wanted to do was kick him in the head. My father was so scared of evil spirits, but Blindboy was the only one I ran into. I came across there. If he had never written those lies in the sand with his feet, my family never would have suffered the way they did. My poor father, so scared of the souls of the dead haunting him, when it was the living that were far more cruel...

Many years later, when I had become successful, and matured a good deal, I came to a different conclusion about what had happened during that time. I came to a certain understanding with fate. I began to have a degree of compassion for Blindboy. As the years went by, I realised that I could be the one to help him. But in 1991, the first time I went back, I still hated him. Even when I went back to Madrid, the hatred lingered for a long while after. It was still there that night in Mulberry Village. Auntie Lin made me bed on the floor among the Colonel's toys. The mind's eye mirror of insomnia reflected two faces back at me: first of myself weak and helpless at the sight of the childlike Colonel, and the second of myself with my features twisted by hatred for Blindboy.

I knew I wouldn't sleep much that night. The cold night air slipped in through a crack in the window, and I could smell the mulberry bushes and the mud outside. When the moon rose high enough to enter the room, the Colonel's snoring was reduced to a steady wheezing. I could suddenly hear Auntie Lin's breathing in the next room. Her breathing was ragged and random. It reminded me of the wrinkles on her face. In the morning, the sky in the east was full of dull grey clouds. I couldn't tell how the weather might turn out that day.

LXXXVI

When I had returned from my walk that night, I was exhausted and anxious. Auntie Lin seemed to expect it. She was waiting for me in the Colonel's room, sitting on the stool he had sat on to draw. She had already settled him into bed and laid out the bed for me. There was a cigarette burning between her fingers. There were already two butts in the ashtray. "You want one of these?" she asked.

"No, thanks," I said. I had smoked for many years but I broke the habit to save money to buy plane tickets. The only way I managed to save up enough was by counting every single expense.

"I picked it up when I was at the front line," she said, "working in the hospital." At the time, there were many soldiers with missing limbs, or injuries that made it impossible to hold a cigarette. "I'd feed them their lunch, then feed them their cigarettes." The addiction seemed to be contagious. She picked up the habit. "I quit eventually," she said, "but, the past few years, I guess the fire was still burning in me…"

Auntie Lin had a peculiar way of talking. She'd pause over certain phrases – like when she said she'd "feed them their cigarettes" – and smile. At those times, the wrinkles on her face would deepen.

Smoking is a good way to calm your nerves, and I knew she must have plenty of stress from looking after the Colonel. Have you ever heard the phrase "If a man lingers too long in his sick bed, even his most dutiful son will desert him"? In Auntie Lin's case, the saying seemed to have been reversed: the old woman was looking tirelessly after a child. But Auntie Lin said that it wasn't a burden at all. Even if she was tired, it gave her something to do with her time. It gave her life some meaning. She had something to rely on.

She smoked with a certain mature dignity. She looked calm. It took me by surprise when she stubbed out the cigarette and turned to me to say, "I know you didn't just come here to see him."

Her meaning was unclear to me. I wasn't sure how to answer. I felt like standing up. It was like the weight of the question threatened to crush me.

She saw me stir and motioned for me to stay seated. "I expect you might have been coming to see me," she said.

"I know how they talk about me in Shuangjiacun. They think I'm a very strange person, don't they?"

"Not at all," I said. "They only had nice things to say about you. They call you Little Guanyin."

"Exactly," she said. "They don't understand why I treat him" – the Colonel – "like I do. You must find it a bit strange yourself, right?"

"You were in the war together," I said.

"He joined the army at seventeen. He fought the Red Army, he fought the Japanese, he fought the People's Liberation Army, he fought Chiang Kai-shek, he fought the Americans... He spent half his life on the battlefield. He had plenty of comrades-in-arms. He saved so many people... But why was I the only one that went looking for him? Why am I still taking care of him? There must be a story there, right?"

I realised Auntie Lin wanted to tell me her story. She spent most of her time with a man that had the mind of a child. There weren't many other people to talk to. She must have been lonely. Those memories she kept locked up inside her were begging to come out. Memories age just like the people that carry them, and they know when death is approaching. If memories don't become stories, passed on to the next generation, there will come a time when they cease to exist. Auntie Lin didn't seem as if she was afraid of death, but she was smart enough to know that it would come for her, sooner or later. There were memories – some very painful – that begged inside her to be let out into the light.

I learned later that during all the time she spent in my village, she had never shared her past. Even my father was kept in the dark. Auntie Lin saw the respect everyone had for the Colonel and the gratitude they had for her – and she decided she couldn't share the truth with them. Her life had not been lived without sin, and she knew that nobody in the village would understand what she had been through. People in the village saw only in black and white, but Auntie

Lin's story couldn't be told without shades of grey. She feared she would become like Grandpa, who had lost his life trying to explain the truth. So, she locked her past away and held the venom in her mouth. But my appearance that day was an invitation – or a temptation. I was the right person, she thought: the son of the Colonel's closest friend, and born in the village but sent into exile. I was just close enough and just far enough away. I watched her watching me, her pale lips seeming ready to come to life again. She was begging for the chance to tell her story.

There was no transition, no introduction, and no explanation. She lit a cigarette and began to speak, starting right from the very beginning: "I was born in this room," Auntie Lin said. "It was 1930, the nineteenth year of the Republic. It was right around this time of year, too.

"My family had a plot of mulberry bushes and some silkworms. Papa was lazy, but Mama made up for it by doing some tailoring on the side. We weren't rich, but we didn't suffer. Papa ended up renting out the land and the silkworms to someone from outside the village, and he went into business. He bought silk in our village, then shipped it by the canal to the silk brokers in Nanxun in Huzhou. He made quite a good living that way. He was one of the richest men in the village. I had two older brothers and an older sister. When the Battle of Shanghai started in 1937, my brother was already studying in the city. He was fifteen at the time and I was seven. I had been sent to a school in town, which should give you an idea of how well off my family was.

"My family was wiped out in the war. Papa, Mama, my sister, and one of my brothers all got killed in the same Japanese air strike. My whole family was on a boat, trying to escape to Nanxun. We thought we could hide out there for a while, with Papa's friends. We probably should have just stayed here. Look at this place." She gestured around her. "But that's fate. Papa and my brother were killed instantly, but Mama and my sister drowned. We couldn't swim. My oldest brother was the only one that knew how to swim. I don't know how I survived, but the next thing I knew, I was lying on the bank of the canal. That was fate, too. I was fated to go through all that I went through…"

She paused and looked up at me. I waited patiently for her to start the story again. "My oldest brother and I went back to the village," Auntie Lin said. "My uncle looked after us for a while. He was a good man, but the woman he had married didn't want us there. She'd make a face or say something nasty every time she had to serve us our dinner. My brother couldn't take it. He'd fight with her. Our mulberry bushes were fine, and my brother knew how to raise silkworms, so we could look after ourselves." Just like her story had begun, there were sometimes abrupt changes as she told it. "We had a box of chalk. I don't know where it came from. Every morning my brother would go out to the shed where we kept the silkworms, and draw an X on the wall. He told me: 'You're growing up fast. When you're ready to be left on your own, I'm going to fight the Japs and get revenge for our family.' Pretty soon, the wall was covered in Xs. There were more Xs than we had silkworms. One morning, I found his room empty. He left a note behind, telling me to look after myself, and a bit of money. I wasn't surprised or scared. I had been expecting that day to come.

"Two months later, I got a letter from him. He said he was in Changsha, training to be a machine gunner with General Xue Yue's army. I didn't hear from him after that. Three years or so later, another man that had been fighting in Changsha returned home to a village nearby, and he came to tell me that my brother was dead. He had died defending Changsha. I was only twelve years old at the time, but I was all grown up. I could cook and clean, and I knew how to look after the silkworms and reel silk."

The Xs that her brother had drawn on the side of the

silkworm shed had already faded. There was no sign left of him. She started to draw her own Xs with chalk. She drew one each day she stayed there. When she saw her own marks fading, too, she got a pair of scissors and started carving the Xs into the wall of the shed.

At that time, Auntie Lin knew there were recruiters secretly looking for people to join the cause. She started looking for them, too. She wanted to join up, but she was too young. It was the beginning of summer, 1945, when she finally got an invitation to join the KMT. They sent her to a small village on the edge of Lake Tai and taught her everything she would know to be a battlefield nurse. Even before the training was complete, the Japanese had surrendered. While everyone was celebrating out in the yard, she was despondent.

"All I wanted was revenge," Auntie Lin said. "When I got that news, I knew it was over. My family had died for nothing. I had no purpose left. I was only fifteen and my life was over."

She had spent the previous eight years dreaming of revenge. That night, people sang until dawn, celebrating the end of the war. But she cried herself to sleep.

The night before they graduated, there was another party. Instead of joining in, she went back to her dormitory room. Not long after that, the man that had been training them showed up, looking for her. He wanted to know if she would prefer to go to a hospital on the front lines or get a posting to a big city like Nanjing or Shanghai.

"What do you mean?" she asked the trainer. "How can there be a front line? The war is over."

"We beat the Japs," the trainer said, "and the Communists are next. It's time to fight the New Fourth Army and the Eighth Route Army!"

She had joined the army to fight the Japanese. She didn't hold any grudge against the Communists, so she requested a posting to Shanghai. The trainer agreed, but he wanted something in return. When she refused, he pushed her back against the bed. It was a hot night and she wasn't wearing much, so it wasn't difficult for him to rip off her clothes. She knew how to take care of herself, though. Her life had not been without its own challenges. When the trainer went to undo his pants, she kicked him as hard as she could in the balls.

"He was down on his knees begging for mercy," she told me. "I noticed he'd hung up his holster when he came in, so I grabbed his pistol. I smashed his face in with the butt of it. I didn't stop until he quit moving. After that, I tied him up with some sheets and used a belt to strap him to the end of the bed."

That was her last night there. She escaped.

LXXXVII

I read once in the newspaper that some people can be completely calm while a storm is raging behind their eyes. That kind of serenity was the result of a lifetime of experience.

Auntie Lin could talk about rape and murder without batting an eye. Her voice never cracked and her wrinkled face betrayed no emotion. I guessed she was probably numb. Her heart was as rough and calloused as her big hands. Her face had only one expression: blank. Her voice had only one tone: calm and unconcerned. The Colonel, sleeping in the next room, had more emotion in his snoring than Auntie Lin did in her most harrowing stories.

After Auntie Lin escaped, she knew she couldn't go back to her village. If someone was looking for her, they would search there first. She went to Shanghai, working whatever jobs would keep her fed. Even though there was a demand for nurses, she steered clear of hospitals and clinics, because she knew her training would be another way that somebody could trace her. She had already been through a lot, but her life in Shanghai was even tougher. The city was full of people who had been through hard times, and they were all competing to stay alive and get ahead. Finally, she had no choice but to get a job as a nurse. After that, her life in Shanghai was somewhat stable. She worked there for a few years.

When she had begun her story, I had noticed that she paused over certain words, or she slipped back into her local dialect. I realised it must have been a few years since she had an adult conversation in Mandarin. As she got more comfortable, the narration went by even quicker, but her expression and her tone never changed. She was still completely numb.

"The good days didn't last, though. My life was thrown off the rails again. It was three o'clock in the afternoon on twentieth March, 1949… The head nurse called for me. I was busy giving an IV to a guy that had been hurt in a street fight. But I had to go." Auntie Lin could still recite the time and date, like some women remembered the birth of their children. It made sense, I suppose, since that was the beginning of a new chapter in her life. The Colonel was waiting for her.

"Have you ever heard any stories about the KMT pressganging men into the army? That's exactly what happened to me. It wasn't only men. When I went to see the head nurse, she introduced me to a KMT officer with a Sichuan accent. All the younger nurses in the hospital were lined up in the lobby. He paced in front of us a few times, pointing out who he wanted to take. There were five of us altogether. He picked me last. I knew better than to argue, but one of the girls started complaining, saying she didn't want to go. He took a pistol out and stuck it to her head. She was so scared she peed her pants. He still loaded her into the jeep with the rest of us. We all had to squeeze together in the backseat. The officer was sitting up front. He was a real creep, too. The whole time he was driving, he was humming this sly little tune... I thought we were being taken to work as prostitutes. I knew I'd kill myself before that, though. I wasn't scared of death. My whole family was dead.

"After about an hour, we got taken out of the jeep and put in a big truck with a canvas top on it. It was already full of girls. People started whispering and I realised they were all nurses, too. Some girls still had on their uniforms. Someone said they heard we were going to treat a trainload of injured soldiers. There was a guard with us, though, who had a pistol on his belt and a rifle under his arm. He said he'd shoot anyone that was spreading rumours. We asked him where we were going and he wouldn't answer, but, if we were lucky, we might be able to meet President Li Zongren. He didn't say what would happen if we weren't lucky, but it was pretty clear it wasn't good.

"The truck drove towards Nanjing, stopping off along the way at barracks to drop off nurses. It was usually three or four, sometimes five or six... Three days after we left, I got dropped off with four other girls on the edge of Zhenjiang, near Jinshan Temple. We got marched to a barracks beside the Yangtze River. I learned later it was a naval unit. There weren't many men, but they occupied a huge red brick building. Most of the barracks I had seen along the way looked like they were on the verge of collapse. I was happy that we were at least going to be in a solidly constructed building. It was a strange experience to be suddenly forced back into the army, but I started to relax a bit when I saw the red brick building.

"The five of us were shown to our room and our bunks. All the basic necessities had been prepared for us, and someone had put up movie posters on the wall. There was even make-up for us, and a mirror, and a bunch of bras and panties in the footlockers. It was like going into somebody's house that had just died. I couldn't shake the feeling that the women that had occupied the room before us were dead. I found out later that we were replacing some nurses that had run away. The Communists had been dropping leaflets saying they were about to cross the Yangtze. The KMT was pretty much done. So, those girls had the good sense to run away. I would have run away, too, but the place was locked down tight. When we looked out the window at night, we could see that they had a searchlight up in the guard tower. I was resigned to my fate. When we got given our army uniforms and white coats that night, I realised that I'd probably be buried in them. I wasn't scared, though. To me, death wasn't any worse than falling asleep."

That night, as the girls settled into bed, someone pounded on the door, shouting that there was an emergency surgery. "They only needed two of us," Auntie Lin said. She and another nurse jumped into the sidecar of a waiting motorcycle and roared off. Two minutes later, they were in the operating room. Everything was covered in blood. It looked more like a slaughterhouse than a hospital. The patient was curled up like a wounded animal on the table, barely alive. They watched the doctor working. He was a tall man with a broad back, but his fingers were agile. With one hand, he was holding the patient's intestines in place, and with the other, looking for the bullet wound. "Even though we had plenty of experience," Auntie Lin said, "we'd never seen anything like that. The girl that came with me started throwing up. When the doctor turned around to look at her, I could only see his eyes. He had on a mask and a hood." The doctor's eyes seemed to outshine even the harsh glare of the surgical lamp. "He looked over at me and jerked his head towards the tools he had laid out on the cart beside the operating table. I went right for them, but he shook his head and motioned for me to get on a mask and gloves. I started passing him whatever he asked for and lent him an extra hand whenever it was required. When he found the bullet wound, he said I was his good luck charm."

Finding the wound was only the start of the operation, though. They worked for three hours together. Whenever she handed him the wrong tool, the doctor didn't curse but simply said: "Nope." They worked until dawn. When the operation was complete, she helped him take off his bloody mask and hood.

"He was pale," Auntie Lin said. "He looked exhausted. All he had under his white coat was his underwear. I realised he had probably been dragged out of bed shortly before me." The undershirt the doctor wore had been washed until it was more grey than white. He told her to clean up the room, then left, cigarette dangling from his lips.

"When he was gone, I started packing up his tools. That was when I noticed everything – the scalpels, the lancets, the scissors, the tweezers, the forceps – was made of gold. I had been too focused on the job to notice."

"At nine o'clock the next morning, when he came around to do his rounds, he was in his uniform, and I saw that he was a colonel. I barely recognised him. Unlike the last time I'd seen him, he looked well-rested and healthy. When he noticed me, he asked about the patient, then asked me a few things about myself. When he found out how I had ended up there, I think he figured out that I was thinking about running away. He pointed back to the man we had operated on the night before. 'That's what happens to people that try to run,' he told me. I realised that we had spent hours saving the life of a deserter. Not many people would have cared whether the man died, but the doctor had put all his talent and energy into saving his life.

"The nurses had run away, and the soldiers were deserting. There wasn't much optimism.

"When the PLA finally crossed the river, they took the barracks with barely any shots fired. The PLA took us on board, and we kept working there, but the doctor was never around. There were no wounded to treat because the fight was over. I heard a rumour that the doctor spent most of his time at home, looking after his cats. He was an officer, so everything was taken care of for him: he had someone to bring his paper, someone to make him dinner, someone to wash his clothes... I ran into him one time after that. He saw me coming, and yelled my name. When I turned my head, he smiled at me and said, 'That's your name, right?' I nodded. But that's all he had to say. He just kept going. The sound his boots made on the pavement was like music to my ears. I turned around to look at him. I wanted so bad for him to turn around and look back at me.

"That was the first time in my life that I had ever felt that way. It was the first time I had ever looked back at a man and hoped he would turn around. I was nineteen and he was thirty-one. He was the first and the last man I ever looked back at. He didn't turn around, though. He just kept walking. It felt like he was walking out of my life. I felt empty."

She was telling me a love story. She was telling me how a teenaged nurse had fallen for a thirty-one-year-old war hero. She was remembering the first man to capture her heart.

But in the room next to her, the same man was shrieking. He must have had a nightmare. He snorted in his sleep and his snore became a scream. Auntie Lin got up and went to his room. I assumed she would do what I did when my kids woke up in the night: tuck them in again, stroke their cheeks, and mutter something comforting to them. I knew it probably wasn't even necessary, since my kids would get right back to sleep, but I did it anyways.

Nineteen

LXXXVIII

When she went next door, I stood up, stretched, and walked to the window. It was a dark night and even the street lights seemed to have been shut off. She was about halfway through her story, I guessed. I wondered how she felt, transferring all of her secrets to me. I wasn't sure at that moment if I wanted her to come back and finish the story. I knew she had fallen in love with the Colonel, and I could imagine that she must have grown to hate him, too... But then what? At that moment, I had no idea how she felt about him. Had she regained her love for him? Was looking after him her way of redeeming herself? When love is not met with love, it turns to hate. Hate becomes a wound. A wound becomes infected. The poison spreads throughout the entire body. Was telling me the story her way of expelling the poison? Did she savour its taste? I thought of my first wife. We had never hated together. I had never been wounded by her. Fate had driven us apart. Fate had wounded me. I knew what it was like to have the poison of hate spreading through my body.

When Auntie Lin came back, she was wearing a peach-coloured silk jacket. It hung off her shoulders as if it was a few sizes too big. I realised it probably belonged to the Colonel. A silk jacket like that would have cost a fortune in Madrid, but it was inexpensive here, in a village built by silkworms. It had probably been a gift from a neighbour. If things hadn't turned out how they did, her life might have gone very differently. Before she had left for my village, she had been Mulberry Village's only barefoot doctor, as well as being an expert in spinning and weaving silk. She had made a good living for herself, practising medicine out of her house, and selling her silk. She was the richest woman in the village. The money she saved up back then was mostly gone by the time I met her. She sunk most of it into treatment for the Colonel. For a few years, she lived off her meagre savings, as well as what she made seeing a few patients. Eventually, the government instituted a new policy, and she had a steady pension. She was no longer living hand to mouth. I noticed that she smoked Phoenix-brand cigarettes, which were second in quality only to Peony.

She launched back into the story with no prompting: "As I said, we started working for the PLA. I said they took over with barely any shots fired, but the PLA didn't even open fire. All the shots that night were from KMT officers killing themselves.

"The PLA treated us completely differently than the KMT had. All of the men treated us with absolute courtesy. When we met on the road, they let us pass. It sounds basic, but, the first time they did that, I was shocked. When they stood aside, I just froze, staring at them. I thought they were going to grab me or something. They were good people. Their policy was that anybody that didn't want to join them would be given travel expenses to go back home. When they found out that I didn't have any family left, they said: 'Okay, then you're with us. The PLA is your family now.' I cried tears of joy. It was like I was finally home. When I found out that the Colonel stayed behind, I was even happier. He wasn't there very long, though. He got sent to the front lines. That's where they needed him the most. He never even said goodbye to me before he left. I suppose I expected him to, although he really shouldn't have. As I said, we had only met a few times. We had barely spoken to each other. I was obsessed with him, but, as far as I knew, he hadn't even noticed me. Basically, I had a crush on him. That's what people say now, right? I don't even know if that's what I felt. That doesn't quite cover what I felt for him...

"I stayed at the military hospital and the PLA was as good as their word – they really did treat me like one of their own family. That September, when Shanghai was liberated, they sent me to East China Medical College, which eventually became the PLA Second Military Medical University. I was supposed to spend two years there, studying anaesthesiology, but a war broke out in Korea. China sent the Volunteer Army. The school sent out a call for nurses and doctors to go with them. So many people signed up that I thought I wouldn't get to go. I wrote a letter in blood, begging them to send me to the front lines. I was among the first to get called up. There were seventy-two volunteers in total, sixty men and twelve women. They loaded us into a train carriage and we headed for the front line. We passed the New Year at a train station on the way. Thousands of people came out to feed us dumplings through the windows. Every station we stopped at, the people came... Finally, we couldn't eat anymore. We started stuffing our net bags with the dumplings. We hung them out the window, and once we got past Jinan, it was like a natural refrigerator. I had never been that far north before! I didn't even know it could get that cold. By the time we got to the Korean border, the whole world seemed to have frozen over. Our passion kept us warm. If anyone had seen our car go by, they would have thought we were triumphant fighters returning from battle, rather than volunteers headed to the front line.

"The trip was sort of like when the KMT had drove me out to the barracks. They dropped off groups along the way. The difference was that all along the way, people greeted us warmly, like their own family. They shook off their gloves to shake our hands and hug us." She lit a fresh cigarette, turned to me, and asked, "Do you know the difference between a mulberry silkworm and a camphor silkworm? That's the difference between the People's Liberation Army and the KMT. Both of them look a bit the same, both of them make silk, but you can't do anything with what a camphor silkworm produces – it might look the same, but one is virtually useless!" I didn't know much about silkworms, but I got what she was driving at.

"They dropped me off with twenty-one of my classmates at the east end of the Chosin Reservoir, at a place called Hagaru-ri. We were divided up among three jeeps and a five-tonne truck and sent off to our respective units. I was in the truck along with four male classmates and another girl, headed for the Twenty-Seventh Corps' field hospital. The truck pulled up outside the cave where they had located the hospital, and all of us went inside. That night, we boiled up the dumplings that had frozen along the way.

"Halfway through the meal, four people burst into the cave. Two of them were carrying rifles, one had a medical kit, and the other had blood on his hands. There wasn't much blood, actually. It looked like maybe he had washed them off in the snow. They had just been to the front line. Everyone got quiet when he came in, and I could tell he was important. It took a second before I recognised him: it was my Old Man. I ran over to him and he stepped back, not recognising me. When I told him who I was, he looked me over, and said, 'You look like a pig they decided to fatten up for an extra season!'

"He started laughing, and the whole place joined him.

"I have to tell you, I had put on weight. Before I got sent to school, I'd had a hard life. I finally had enough to eat and not much to do except study. Of course I got fat. And look at me now! Wasted away to nothing. I spend all my time chasing after him..."

She paused as if thoughts of the present had disturbed the flow of her memories. But eventually she launched back into the story: "I blushed. I was looking around for a crack in the cave wall to crawl into and hide. He came over and comforted me, though. He said, 'Two months out here and you'll be as skinny as ever. Maybe I'll recognise you then!' But that made him start laughing again. He loved to laugh. You know how much he loved to laugh. I just wish I could hear it one more time. The only time I can hear it now is when I dream about him. The two years I spent with him in Korea was the happiest time of my life. We were risking death, working ourselves until we collapsed, but I was happy just to be with him. You know, the worse it gets, the more I dream about him now..."

LXXXIX

When the factories in the village shut down for the day, the light bulbs in the house seemed to glow brighter. The stronger the glare of the incandescent bulb above her, the deeper her wrinkles seemed to get. She seemed to grow older before my eyes.

But her mind was still sharp. She remembered everything clearly. Maybe it was because they were such happy memories for her. The stories flowed like a clear stream.

Someone told me once that a taxi driver will forget the faces of everyone that has ever ridden with him – unless they leave behind their wallet. Whether the driver keeps the wallet and spends the money inside, or he turns it in to the police and keeps his conscience clear, it becomes a happy memory. Auntie Lin left something behind at the Chosin Reservoir, too. She discovered something, too. On the bloody soil of Korea, she sacrificed her youth and experienced first love. It was a place more important to her than her homeland, even if she could never truly return there – to that exact place and time. In a way, it was like she carried the time and place within herself, though.

First love is like holding onto a sweet secret. It's the feeling you get when your hand in the darkness finds the hand of another person, and a shiver runs through your body. It's a feeling of nervous anticipation. It's fear and prayer amidst the roar of cannons. It's a warm breeze on a summer afternoon, carrying the faint aroma of wildflowers. It's a sleepless night without a care in the world. It's cracking a secret code and unravelling a mystery. It's delicate and light, it's bizarre, it's exotic, it's uncomfortable… You can't stop trying to explain what it feels like. I knew what first love felt like, and I didn't need her to explain it to me. For the first time that night, I interrupted her: "You're saying you were in love with him."

"Right," she said. "He is the only man I've ever loved. I loved everything about him."

At that point, the story broke down into a rhapsody: she told me exactly how and why and when she loved him, and all the ecstasy and heartbreak along the way. She was lost in the bittersweet memories. Her love of the Colonel was her life's glory. It was the root of all her pain and happiness. It was so beautiful that even her memories of it could take her breath away, and it was so cruel that it was the only thing capable of truly crushing her. Her heart was on fire for him. She was devoted to him. Nobody forgets where they bury their treasure, and nobody ever forgets precisely where the thorn of love has pricked them. I couldn't bear to interrupt her again. I decided to let her get it out.

"I don't know when it happened," Auntie Lin said. "I don't know what made me fall in love with him. I loved his laugh. I loved the way he looked from behind. I loved the way he held his cigarette. I loved the way he'd curse when an operation wasn't going the way he planned. I loved the way he smiled when everything went right. I loved the way he treated his cats. That was his happiest time, walking with his cats, or playing with his cats… I loved his bravery. He was a hero. He went to the front line without hesitation. I loved him when he came back, worn out and relieved. There were seven doctors at the field hospital, and he went to the front lines more than the six others combined."

On the battlefield, there were sometimes men too wounded to be moved to safety. When the Colonel got the call, he always answered. He would say, "I'll go. The gold on my scalpel is getting a bit dull." He charged to the front line and risked his own life. The bullets whizzing by didn't care that he was a doctor. If an enemy plane spotted the Colonel's jeep winding its way towards the wounded, the pilot would drop his bombs assuming that he was taking out a general or an intelligence agent. Auntie Lin had gone with him to the front several times and taken fire. "One time," she said, "a bullet went right between us. I started crying, but he was laughing. 'Bullets have a conscience, too. If that bullet hit us, it would mean that all the men waiting for us would die, too.' Another time, we came under fire and our jeep hit a landmine. We rolled down into a ravine. The driver sacrificed himself trying to get us to safety. I was bleeding and one of my shoulders was dislocated. The pain was so bad I passed out. He was completely fine. He used to say, 'Saving a single life is as great as building a seven-story pagoda.' If you added up all the lives he saved, you would have a pagoda that reached heaven. You could climb all the way up it and live forever.

"That's the only way to explain it. He would run right up to the forward positions and drag men out, even when people were dying around him. The worst injury he ever got was a broken toe. It was like he was invincible. He was blessed. I don't know how he ended up like this."

"You are his blessing," I said.

"You don't know what I am," she said.

I wasn't sure what she meant.

She went back to the story: "That was the time I told him I loved him. When I passed out, he pushed my shoulder back into the socket. Even if I'd been in a coma, I would have come to. That's when I saw I was bleeding. I thought I'd been cut or something, but I couldn't figure out where. He told me to get up and walk around. I felt fine. He realised what was happening before me. When he told me that I'd broken my hymen, I started crying. That's a gift that a woman should save for her wedding night. He laughed and tried to comfort me. He said: 'Don't worry about it! Save the pants. That's better than any medal they'll give you. Anyways, when the time comes, tell your husband to come to me, and I can testify to your virginity!' I fell into his arms and said, 'Just marry me!' He laughed again and said, 'You don't think he'll believe me when I say it was a war wound? I'll sign an affidavit and get the commander to witness it.' I finally confessed everything to him. He didn't seem to take me seriously. He said: 'You're a sweet girl. If I ever need a wife, you'll be first on my list. But right now, my date is with Death.' I said: 'If we fall in love, we can meet Death together.' He said: 'I've seen more dead bodies than you've heard gunshots. Death doesn't care about you.' I said: 'But you said if you decide to get married, you'd choose me.' He said: 'I doubt that day will ever come.' He stepped away from me and pointed at the driver. 'What about him?' he said. 'Did he have a wife? All that means now is someone else suffering for the rest of their life.'"

At that point, the Colonel told her to keep quiet. He said it was inappropriate to talk like that in front of the dead. He said it was bad luck to talk about the future. "All you should hope for now is to return to China safely," he said. He wiped the blood off his face and looked up at the sky: "As for me, I've dodged Death too many times... Every day I'm still alive is a gift that I don't deserve."

After that, the Colonel never took her to the front again. "I assumed it was because he loved me," Auntie Lin said. "I assumed he wanted to protect me. He always left his cats with me. He loved them more than anything in the world. I thought it was a sign of his devotion. Whenever he dropped off the cats, I would always give him a note. I wrote the same thing every time. I told him how much I loved him. I was always worried that he'd get hurt out there, but sometimes I wished for him to get injured – not seriously, but enough so that he would need me to look after him. I wanted to nurse him back to health. He never replied to my notes. It was like shouting into a void. There was just one time, when I handed him a note, he said, 'It's irresponsible to chase after someone that you don't really know.' I repeated a line that he had said once: 'The only way to know somebody is to share the battlefield with them.' It was the type of thing a lot of people said in those days. I told him that I'd spent more than a year with him on the battlefield. I told him that I knew him better than anybody. 'You don't know my past,' he said. I told him: 'I don't care. I'm your future.'"

Auntie Lin pursued the Colonel fanatically, even though he didn't respond. She sacrificed her dignity and her honour, trying to get the Colonel to admit to her that he loved her. "My whole family was dead," Auntie Lin said, "and I was all alone in the world. I wanted somebody to love me. I'd never met a man like him before. He had it all, as far as I was concerned. He was heroic and capable and funny. All I wanted was for him to love me. I would have died to hear him say it." Auntie Lin paused and took a drag of her cigarette. "I know you probably don't understand," she said.

Perhaps I did understand, though. I had experienced loneliness and longing. When I went into exile, I was all alone in the world. I knew that pain like the back of my hand. I knew it as well as I knew the lanes in my village.

XC

When the stool was too hard, I slipped off it and sat on the floor. Auntie Lin tossed me a ragdoll that the Colonel played with and told me to use it as a cushion. She told me the floor was too cold.

"In the summer of 1951," Auntie Lin said, "the enemy was strangling us. They bombed the railways and the highways. Chairman Mao's own son sacrificed himself there. Mao Anying fought alongside Peng Dehuai right until the end. They killed him with napalm. The bombing was fierce. The enemy tried to outflank us, so we would have to constantly change our position. We had to move the field hospital along with them. Sometime in May of 1952, while we were taking shelter in a village, there was a particularly brutal air strike that killed more than a hundred men. They had to have been tipped off by spies in our camp. It was already hot that May, and most of the troops were sleeping out in the open, right along the road. Only the wounded men and the nurses were staying inside with the villagers. The head nurse and I were staying in the same house. It was hit directly. The owner of the house was gone, but his two kids were there, and they were killed immediately, along with the head nurse. I was trapped under a roof beam. I thought I was going to be burned alive."

The Colonel risked his life to save her. He wrapped himself in a wet towel and rushed into the fire, shouting, "Little Shanghai! Where are you?"

"He had been calling me 'Little Shanghai' since we met in Korea," Auntie Lin said. "The fire was already burning my braids when he found me. I could hear my hair sizzling. He snuffed it out, wrapped me in the towel, and carried me out over his shoulder. He snatched me back from Death's grip. The bombers were still circling overhead. The rescue hadn't even started – I mean: he had come just for me. He had risked his life to save me."

Fearing that the planes would return when the sun came up, the troops evacuated that night and fled into the mountains. "We had to get over a stream," Auntie Lin said. "I had a deep cut on my calf and I'd just bandaged it up. But he tossed me on his back and carried me across. He collapsed when he got to the other side. He just sat there, panting. Meanwhile, I was still crying. First, he snapped at me and told me to quit it, but he eventually comforted me, and he told me it was okay to cry. I fell into his arms again. All I wanted was for him to kiss me.

"I told him that if I had died that night, I wouldn't have left anything behind. I want him to say that I'd left my love letters. But he just said, 'War is cruel. Most people that died tonight left nothing behind either.' That's when I asked him to kiss me. I told him that I didn't want to die before he kissed me. He hesitated for a moment, but he eventually bent down and kissed me. It was just a gesture. I could tell there was nothing behind it. I don't blame him. We had been through so much that night, and there was death all around us. But it meant something to me. It was like he had finally answered all those letters I wrote him."

When the troops relocated, they lived in low, log huts. There was only room in each one for two beds, made directly on the ground. At the time, fighting on the front had slowed, and the bulk of the army was preparing to cross the border back into China. There were still many wounded from the air strikes, though. Although Auntie Lin had trained as an anaesthesiologist, she mostly worked as a nurse. That was where she was needed. When the head nurse was killed, Auntie Lin was chosen to replace her. There were five nurses altogether, and she usually worked one of the two night shifts, or both of them. One night, after working the first night shift, she went back to her hut. The nurse that shared the hut with her had gone to work the second night shift, so she was alone. She felt something stroke her cheek and, at first, assumed it was the mosquito net. But someone was there. He put his hand over her mouth.

"I knew it was him," Auntie Lin said. "Who else would it be? He had worked the earlier night shift with me, and we'd got off at the same time. He would have known I was alone in my hut. Nobody else would have just snuck up on me, either. It was my first time, and I was scared. But I gave myself up to him. I wanted to prove to him how much I loved him. The log huts were close together, so we had to make love in complete silence. We had to cover our mouths to muffle even the panting. It was a different time, you know. Back then, the most anyone dared to do was hold hands. You couldn't even kiss someone you weren't married to. He was a bold man, though. He didn't care what everyone else thought. That's why I loved him. I knew he would take responsibility, if anything happened. He was a real man.

"I had kept the pants from that day when we hit the landmine. He had been joking about signing an affidavit, but he went to the head of my work unit and told them what had happened. The head of the work unit had actually written up his testimony and got him to sign it. The day after he came to my hut, I washed the blood stains out of the pants and tore up the paper. I assumed I didn't need them anymore. I didn't need any proof, since he had seen the whole thing himself. I assumed that was part of the reason he came to me, because I wasn't a virgin anymore. He came three more times after that. It was always in the middle of the night. We always did it in complete silence. We didn't want to risk anybody finding out.

"After the war, both got stationed at the 101st Hospital

of the People's Liberation Army in Wuxi, right beside Lake Tai. I went back to being an anaesthesiologist. He returned a hero. They sent him around the country as a model soldier. When he got back, there was a banquet, and the director of the hospital appointed him head of the surgical department. It had been a month since I'd seen him at that point, so I was missing him like crazy. While he was up at the podium giving his speech, I was crying and shaking. He did the rounds at the banquet, then left. I waited for him to come. I could see the light in his room. Finally, I decided to go see him. He lived up on the third floor. It was very private. I knocked at his door, and when he opened it, I fell into his arms. He hugged me and called me Little Shanghai. I waited for him to kiss me, but he just made small talk and told me to take a seat. I refused. I tried to kiss him but he pushed me away. He started trying to reason with me... It was like becoming a model soldier had turned him into some kind of a monk. I felt like he was looking down on me, like I was too low and common to be with a hero like him. I ran out of the room with tears in my eyes.

"I thought he'd come to see how I was, but he never did. I ran into him at the hospital and the canteen, but he treated me like nothing had happened. He'd call me Little Shanghai and joke around with me... I couldn't take it, so I finally went back to see him again. It turned into a big fight. He made me so angry I thought I was going to explode. And if I exploded, I wanted to take him with me. I told him he had to marry me. He reminded me that he'd said he'd only marry me if he needed a wife. But those nights in the huts in Korea made me think he'd changed his mind. Of course, at the time, I didn't say that directly. We couldn't be that direct. It was all hinting at something. But I thought he could figure out what I meant. He had taken my virginity, so I assumed that meant he wanted to marry me. But he said it was all a misunderstanding. 'We were at war,' he said. 'We could have died at any moment.' Then he started laughing. The way he thought about it, none of it had been important. It had happened during the war and the war was over, so any arrangement we'd had was void. I was so angry at him. I cried and said, 'If you don't take me, nobody will ever want me.' He waved me off. He said I was beautiful and young, still, and I had been to university. 'There's going to be men lining up to marry you.' I started to speak but I couldn't tell him exactly what I wanted to say. I wanted to tell him that I had given my virginity to him. He said, 'What about the thing your work unit leader wrote? Don't worry about it. I'll testify to your husband on your behalf.'

"I was shocked! I couldn't understand how he could talk to me like that. I wanted to slap him. I wanted to rip his heart out. But I was shaking too hard to do anything. I couldn't even speak. My whole body was malfunctioning. All I could do was stare at him. I was crying, but I could still see him clearly. He looked like he didn't have a care in the world. I wanted to smash my head against the wall and let him watch me die. I was so furious that I must have looked like my eyes and ears were about to belch smoke. I looked useless, like a piece of trash. I realise now I probably should have gone and smashed my head against the wall, like I wanted to… It would have been better to make a scene. But at the time, I just left."

XCI

A person has two sides, like a coin. There's a good side and a bad side. If you run into someone's good side, good for you. If you get the bad side, that's your own bad luck. But sometimes we get both sides of a person – and that intermingling of love and hate can produce the most heartbreaking result. I read that in the newspaper, too. I don't come up with those kinds of ideas myself. I don't like to say them out loud, either. They remind me of Grandpa. He was full of those sorts of saying. Every time he spoke, they seemed to come out. Grandpa had a good side and a bad side, too. Auntie Lin had seen both sides of the Colonel. That had been hard for her. When she came to those parts in the story, I noticed for the first time, some emotion on her face. Her expressionless face finally melted.

Auntie Lin sighed and said, "I don't know how I got through it. I wanted to die. I was closer to dying then than I had been on the front line. I was an anaesthesiologist, you know. I had everything I needed to do it... All it would take is one shot and I'd be dead. I thought about it many times. One time, I got the shot ready, shut my eyes – and just as I was about to push down the plunger on the needle, I thought about what would happen when I was found. There would be nobody to take my body. I wouldn't have anybody to bury me. I thought about my family, too. If I was dead, there would be nobody to sweep their tombs every year. That was enough of a reason for me to keep living."

Even though she kept living, she couldn't give up on the Colonel. One day, she saw him in the hall and confronted him. She asked him directly. "Do you want to marry me or not?"

The Colonel looked at her and said very sincerely, "Little Shanghai, my comrade, you don't know a thing about me. I'm not going to marry you. I'm going to die a bachelor."

"If you don't marry me," she told him, "then I'll kill myself."

"Are you threatening me?" the Colonel had asked. "I didn't do right by you, but at least I saved your life. You can't go around talking about killing yourself now. I'm doing this for your own good. A pretty girl like you shouldn't be talking about hanging a noose over an old tree like me. I promise there is a man waiting for you out there, and he'll treat you much better than I ever could."

"I already ripped up that letter from the work unit leader," she said. "No man would ever want me."

"It's not that easy," the Colonel said to her. "I'll tell your work unit to make a second version, just in case."

Auntie Lin leaned back on the stool and glanced out the window. "I lost my mind," she told me. "I started cursing him, hoping it would cause some kind of reaction. I wanted him to sympathise with me, or at least get angry at me. I told him that I was going to report him. He was furious. He demanded to know what proof I had that he had done anything wrong. He told me that if I reported him, he'd just show them all the love letters I'd written him. Then he walked away. I watched him go. I'd always liked the way he held his shoulders so square, but that day, I was disgusted by it. It was like there was some horrible smell coming from him. He sickened me. I had to sit down on the floor to stop from throwing up."

That happened on a Saturday. On Monday afternoon, Auntie Lin was summoned by the hospital director. He presented her with a fresh copy of the signed letter from the work unit leader and suggested that it was best that she focus on her career and getting married to a suitable partner. He told her that the testimony of the work unit leader was better than any medal the military could have given her. The director suggested that she take it as an honour, rather than something that could harm her future prospects. She realised that the Colonel had arranged the meeting. There seemed to be no chance that he was going to change his mind. The letter from the work unit leader testified to her purity, but it also testified to the Colonel's innocence. She had to give up on him. All hope was dead.

But even if hope is dead, people go on living, grinding away like soulless machines.

Not long after that, the Colonel was transferred to a cadre training school in Nanjing. It seemed to have been done intentionally, probably at the Colonel's request. The purpose of the cadre training class was to cultivate future political leaders. After graduation, the Colonel would probably return to be assistant director of a hospital. His sudden departure helped Auntie Lin immensely. She did her best to forget all about the Colonel. "It was like those days after my brother left," Auntie Lin said, "when I was carving Xs into the side of the silkworm shed. I counted down the days the same way: I drew Xs in my notebook. After a month, though, I stopped. It was enough. I had X'ed him out my life. I took the notebook and the letters – wait, did I tell you he gave me back all my letters? One day, he showed up and handed them back to me. So, I took the letters and the notebook, and I burned everything. After that, I went to the bathhouse. I wanted to clean any trace of him off me. I wanted to start a new life.

"Back then, there was a set schedule for the bathhouse. We usually had one day a month when we went. It was usually Saturday night. A bunch of people would be there at the same time. So, anyways, after I got out, I ran into the head of internal medicine. He was an older man from Anhui, who had been with us in Korea. We walked back to the dormitory together, talking about this and that. Out of nowhere, he brought up a rumour he'd heard about me. He said my Old Man" – which is what Auntie Lin called the Colonel now – "had been saying he slept with me, and we'd had a bit of a romance, but he'd had to cut it off because he thought I was unfaithful. Hearing that, it was like an old wound that had just healed was suddenly slashed open again.

"I didn't know how many people had heard the rumour. Even if it was only the head of internal medicine, that was still one more person than should have known. I knew I hadn't said anything to anyone about what had happened, so it had to be him" – the Colonel – "spreading the story.

"How do you think I felt? It was like a bolt of lightning hitting me. I told you before, I wasn't a little princess. I wasn't the kind of person that you wanted to back into a corner. Just look at how I handled that KMT man that thought he could rape me. In my mind, the Colonel was just as evil. If he'd still been at the hospital, I would have gone straight to his room and smashed his face into pulp. I might have killed him. But he was all the way in Nanjing, and when he came back, he'd probably be the assistant director of the hospital. I couldn't understand how he could be so ruthless. That night, I wrote to the political affairs department of the army and told them that he had raped me. If he wanted to treat me like that, I could play the same game. I wanted to destroy him! That's what I kept telling myself that night: 'Destroy him!'"

The military sent their men to investigate and the Colonel was called back from Nanjing. He refused to admit anything, but the letter was damning. It was easy enough to confirm all of the details. And with the extra detail of the Colonel requesting a second letter from the work unit leader, attesting to Auntie Lin's virginity, it started to look very bad for him. It seemed to be proof that he was trying to cover up his guilt. In a case like this, the Colonel had no recourse. Evidence aside, it was her word against his. There was no way for him to prove that she was lying.

"He was a hero, though," Auntie Lin said, "and a model soldier. They wanted to protect him. When all the facts came out, the military found out that we'd had some kind of a relationship. I admitted to that. So, they came to me and offered a deal: if I took back all the accusations and dropped the charges, he would marry me. I demurred, but I know deep down that I was ready to go through with it. All I really needed was for him to admit what he'd done. He wouldn't do it. No matter what the military told him, though, he" – the Colonel – "refused. They had set up the deal hoping to make the whole thing go away, and he'd ruined it. He said he'd rather die than marry me. At that point, there was nothing they could do for him. He was discharged and sent back home. All the prestige and honour and rank he'd won – it just disappeared overnight. But it wasn't a real victory for me. I was humiliated and my heart was broken. The next year, I asked for a transfer and my work unit agreed. After what happened, my relationships with the people I worked with were ruined. Nobody was comfortable with me. I wanted to leave and they were happy to see me go. Nobody saw me off. I don't think anyone sympathised with me. I sometimes hated myself for what I had done. I hated myself for ruining his life. But that was only sometimes. I was only human. I had a human response to the situation. It wasn't worth feeling sorry for him or for myself. He had forced me into a corner and I had no choice. People go through things and come out the other side, right?" She tilted her head towards the other room, where the Colonel was sleeping. "We went through things and came out the other side, right?"

XCII

That was where Auntie Lin ended the story. Maybe she was too tired to go on, or maybe she just thought it was the right place to end it. I pressed her for the rest of the story, though. I wanted to know what had happened to her after she transferred out.

Her next assignment turned out to be Changning Hospital in Shanghai. She thought it was the start of a new life, where nobody would know her past. She thought she could start fresh. But somehow her old life caught up with her. She wasn't sure quite how it happened, but within a few months, rumours started circulating. People started embroidering the original story, making it even more salacious. She was branded a slut and a troublemaker. When political campaigns swept through the work unit, and they were looking for people to purge, she was at the top of the list. She was among the first targets of the Anti-Rightist Campaign. She got sent to a reform-through-labour farm on Chongming Island in November of 1957. She stayed there until March of 1959, when they sent her back to her original work unit. Instead of working as an anaesthesiologist, though, she was made a janitor, in charge of cleaning all of the hospital's bathrooms. Even then, she was still the target of various political campaigns. She was dragged onto the stage at rallies and paraded through the street. In October of 1964, when a batch of drugs was stolen from the hospital, the case was pinned on her. She was fired and sentenced to four years at Baimaoling Prison in Anhui.

"I spent four years in prison in Anhui. I couldn't tell you why. Even if I tried to explain, you wouldn't understand. You're too young. You don't know what those times were like. The whole thing was completely absurd." Her story drifted back to the Colonel, like it always did. "I was luckier than him," Auntie Lin said. "I got to sit out the worst of the Cultural Revolution. The Red Guards would have come for me, just like they did for him. At the very least, I would have spent those years with a sign around my neck, paraded through the streets. That's what they did to women like me. They called women like me 'broken shoes'. You know what that means, right? It means we were useless, filthy... They might have shaved their heads and threw excrement on them. Prison was safer than being out on the street. Maybe the Old Man had got me sent there. Maybe that's how I wanted to think about it, like I was redeeming myself for what I had done to him. Maybe he was getting me ready for this." She looked at me and asked, "What do you think? There's no such thing in the world as an impenetrable wall. The wind gets in somehow, right?" I saw then that there were dark circles around her eyes, like the marks left behind when someone wears glasses for too long. She didn't wait for me to answer. "That's what I think, at least," she said. "Word travels, too, doesn't it? It didn't take long for it to travel from

Wuxi to Shanghai. It travelled from your village to mine. It travelled to that prison, too. They knew everything. They knew his name and our history, and everything that had happened between us. They even knew what he had written on his belly." Her voice softened, and she lowered her eyes. "Do you know what's written there?" she asked.

I paused for a second and then shook my head.

She seemed surprised. "That's strange," she said. "You were up here with him so long, I thought he would have shown you."

"He wanted to show me," I said, "but I didn't look."

"You did the right thing," she said. "You know, there was once a time in his life when he would kill a man to hide his shame. Now, it's nothing more to him than a toy. When he meets someone he doesn't know, he wants to show it off. If I try to stop him, he'll cry. Look at what he's become." She paused and studied my face. "I suppose he became what he always wanted to be."

Auntie Lin stood and pulled out a tattered cardboard box from underneath the desk. "These are his masterpieces," she said. "He saved them all. A child knows how to cherish their treasures, I suppose." She rummaged through the many sheets of paper in the box, pulled out one, and handed it to me. "Have a look," she said. "It's the same as what's on his body. The size is almost the same. It's all the same, except for the characters."

I leaned over to take the paper. I was afraid to look at it. It felt shameful.

Rather than the hospital sheets that most of his drawings were done on, it was a sheet of the kind of rough, waxy yellow paper that I was familiar with. In my village, there were many small workshops that made it. We called it spirit paper, because that's what it was normally used for – burning as an offering for ancestors and gods. I turned my attention to the drawing. It was quite good, for a child. The delicate lines sketched out a person's lower body, down to the curve of their legs. There was a black dot for the belly button, and, below it, pubic hair. Everything was in the right place. The proportions were good. I could tell that he must have drawn it many times. My eyes were drawn to a curved row of eight dark-green characters below the belly button: 除奸殺鬼乃我使命 – "my mission is to kill the ghouls and eliminate traitors". The characters were written clearly and cleanly. Between the two characters 乃 and 鬼 there was a red arrow, running down towards the pubic hair. The arrow was blunt and thick. The arrow had characters written on both sides of it, running vertically. On the right side, it said, 軍令 – "military orders" – and on the left side, it said 如山 – "stand like a mountain". Together, the phrase meant "Military orders are unalterable and must be obeyed". The characters on both sides of the arrow were deep blue, a size smaller than the characters above, and slanted and sinister-looking.

Without looking up, Auntie Lin seemed to sense my reaction. "Don't be surprised," she said calmly. "This is what he wanted. He changed the words. He changed it from something bad to something good." As she flipped through the pictures, I thought I saw the Colonel's black cat in one of the drawings. Maybe the white cat was in the picture, too. But she was flipping through too quickly for me to say for sure.

She handed me another picture. It was almost the same, instead of the message about eliminating traitors, it said: 國家興亡匹夫有責 – "the fate of a nation rests on its people" – and, split up on either side of the arrow, 中國必勝 – "victory to China". It was the same number of characters, written in the traditional style, and meant to be read from left to right. She handed me another picture, where each character had been replaced by a black square.

"I can't find the other two," Auntie Lin said. She took the pictures back from me and ran her fingers over the characters, tracing each one. "Sometimes I think it's better this way," she said. I wasn't sure if she was talking to me or to herself. "He can forget about all those filthy things. He can write them however he wants now. I think if he had one wish, it would be to erase those words, change them into something else... This is the only way he can forget about it – amnesia, losing all of his memories..."

"But look at what he wrote," I said. "Look at what he changed the words to. He must remember that time."

"Sometimes," Auntie Lin said. "It comes and goes. That's why the words are different in every picture. It doesn't have any pattern. It's like his memory has been burned. There are just ashes blowing around in there now. His mind was full of those slogans. That's why they keep coming back. They were buried deep inside him. They must be blowing around inside his head, still. They come out sometimes."

Auntie Lin went back to rummaging in the box. It was a sketch of a young woman in an oversized military parka, sitting in front of an ammunition box. There was a pen hanging from her lips. She looked like she was deep in thought.

"Is that you?" I asked.

She nodded and bent to inspect the picture more closely. After a long time, without looking away from the sketch, she said, "He doesn't lie anymore. I guess I made an impression on him."

"He must love you," I said.

"I think he hates me even more," she said. Her finger rested on the pen in the girl's mouth in the sketch, as if she was about to smudge it. "That was the pen I used to write him all those love letters. That was the pen I used to write the letter to the military to report him."

"He just didn't understand," I said, trying to comfort her. "You never got a chance to explain it to him."

"He will never understand."

"You know what he went through," I said. "You know what they did to him in Shanghai. They left those marks on him. If not for that, he probably would have married you."

"That's a fantasy. We live in reality." She was quiet for a long time, then she suddenly asked me, "Do you know what they wrote on him?"

"People have told me," I said. That was the truth.

"What did they tell you?"

"They said a woman put her name there," I said. That wasn't the whole truth. But I didn't want to tell her what the Old Constable had said. It was too dirty to say out loud. On top of that, judging by the Colonel's pictures, 这屌只归日本国 – "this dick is the property of the Empire of Japan" – was one character too short. I was happy not to know, though. I thought it was better to let the Colonel keep some of his secrets.

"That's right," Auntie Lin said. "The name of a traitor. She was an evil woman." She paused and then said, "I had heard her name before, actually. I received a certain amount of political education when I was in the army. When I heard the rumours from your village, I remembered that. I realised why he had refused to marry me. I understood why he had chosen to be discharged from the military instead. How could he marry me? How could he get married at all? That was why he did that to Blindboy. It was a secret that he knew he had to protect with his life. He couldn't let anybody know. He would rather spend his life alone... He would rather nearly kill someone and go on the run... He would rather die than reveal the secret. It was his private shame. When he was finally about to be exposed, he lost his mind. How could he not? He was driven insane. But I helped push him. I hurt him first..."

The way she said it was so soft and sad that it finally broke me. I thought back to everything I had heard about the Colonel. I put the pictures back in the box, got up off the ragdoll, and went back to the stool. I buried my face in my hands and sobbed.

Auntie Lin stood and went to my side. She caressed the side of my head, then went back to her stool. "I hurt him," she said. "I hurt him." I thought she was going to keep repeating herself, but she suddenly raised her voice, and said, "But that son of a bitch hurt me first."

"Who?" I said. I looked up and saw that she was glaring at me, her eyes flashing.

"That liar," she hissed. "The guy from Anhui, the head of internal medicine." She lowered her voice, as if worried that the Colonel would overhear us: "The one I ran into outside the bathhouse. A few months after that, I realised that he'd used me. He wanted to take over as the assistant director, but he knew my Old Man was going to get the job. He was more qualified for the job, but he wasn't a war hero. He waited until my Old Man" – the Colonel – "was in Nanjing, then made his move."

"How did he know about you and him?" I asked.

"I always wondered that, too. I decided there were two possibilities: the Old Man let it slip, maybe while he was drunk, or the guy from Anhui saw the Old Man going to see me one night."

"He was a man that knew how to keep secrets," I said. "I don't think he'd let it slip while he was drunk."

"Right," Auntie Lin said. "But I didn't know that at the time. But..." She shook her head sadly, as if there was something she couldn't bring herself to say. She finally said, "I still hope the Old Man let it slip. I guess I convinced myself that he had. I never thought..."

Tears suddenly ran down her cheeks. "The Old Man never came to see me at all," she said. For a moment, I didn't understand what she meant. She wiped away her tears. "It was never him at all. I falsely accused him."

I finally understood what she meant, but I couldn't believe

it. Even if it had not been the Colonel going to see her on those nights in Korea, and she had falsely accused him, there was no way to place the blame on Auntie Lin for the Colonel's eventual fate.

I thought maybe her memory must have failed her. I stood up and asked, "How do you know it wasn't him?"

She said nothing for a long time. "His body told me," she finally said. "His body. His mind is not the same, but his body is. When we were together..." She tried to find an appropriate way to say it. "I'm a woman," she said. "I could feel it. It wasn't the same person. I'm absolutely certain of that."

She started crying again, and buried her face in her hands. "Don't ask me who it was," she said, ashamed. "I don't know. I don't want to know. There are a lot of evil people in this world." The voice that came out of the old woman sounded like it belonged to a little girl. Her hair looked like a haystack left out in the winter. The wrinkles on her neck looked like a jigsaw puzzle. Every inch of her flesh seemed to stick to her bones. Only her earlobes hung free.

The whole evening, she had been stiff, and her voice emotionless. She was cold. It was like her heart had been completely hollowed out, or completely filled in. I thought she had been made numb by trauma. So, when she finally unleashed her emotion, she was like a dry creek bed soaked by the spring runoff. It was completely unexpected. Her sobs were like a sudden salvo of bullets. I wanted to duck for cover. She stood and left the room as if in a trance. I don't even remember if she said goodnight to me. How useless would that have been? I didn't think either of us were going to have a good night.

The next morning, when I was leaving, Auntie Lin asked, "Will you be back?"

At the time, I was so poor that it had taken years to save up for plane tickets. I didn't know how to answer. But when

I saw the Colonel standing beside her, waving as my own children had when I'd left, I answered, "Of course. I'll be back."

Even if she was not convinced by my promise, I knew the Colonel would be. As I got on the mototaxi and pulled away, I looked back and saw them standing on the stairs, hand in hand. Auntie Lin's face looked as gloomy as the skies darkening overhead, but the Colonel's smile was as brilliant as ever. It was a painful goodbye. The buzzing exhaust of the motorbike seemed to be roaring out to echo my own pain.

Twenty

XCIII

I read in the newspaper once that there is only one true heroism in the world: to see life as it is, and to love it. I don't actually know what the writer meant by the "world as it is", or "heroism", or what it would mean to love your life. The way I see it, life is like a person that's always by your side – sometimes you love the person and sometimes you don't, and sometimes you might even hate them. I don't really know if that's what the writer was getting at, but I always remembered the phrase. It was something I learned from my first wife shortly after we met. It was one of the last words she said to me on her deathbed.

Like I said, the first place I worked after I left China was in a shoe factory. After six years there, I could have done the job with my eyes closed. I knew my own small part of the job, but I didn't actually understand how shoes were made. That's how most people are at work. That's how most industries operate. If you teach a worker the entire process, they'll come up with their own ideas about how it could be done differently, or, at worst, they'll take what they've learned and set up their own workshop. That might strike you as selfish, but it's one of the basics of being a boss. When I first got to the factory, I had a supervisor: she was two years older than me, and her parents had been professors at Zhejiang University. She grew up with her maternal grandmother in Quanzhou in Fujian, so she spoke Hokkien. She'd sometimes drop Hokkien phrases in when we spoke Mandarin. There was one that she pronounced like *tin-oo-oo*, which meant that the sky was dark and it was going to rain, but had more metaphorical meaning, too... She had another phrase she used a lot, too, which she pronounced like *lin-sing-hai-hai*. I couldn't understand any of those Hokkien phrases.

We worked together twelve hours a day. After a month, my hands were permanently marked with the imprint of shoe buckles. I laboured like a beast of burden. I hated everything about my life. Not only was there no love in my life, but I hated the very idea of love. I buried any thought of love at the bottom of the ocean.

One day, the foreman came around and gave me a command in Spanish. I only half understood him. I ended up screwing it up and he slapped me. The foreman could speak Chinese just fine, and he knew that I didn't speak Spanish. I didn't know what he was trying to do, pretending to be a foreigner, swaggering around, beating people up... I decided I'd had enough. I decided I would just sit on the line, doing nothing, until they fired me. I refused to eat or drink. I figured dying on a street corner would be better than working for people like that.

She brought me food. She tried to cheer me up with a newspaper. There were no Chinese newspapers at the time, but she had gone through and translated the articles line by line. She wrote her Chinese translation above each line of Spanish. That was where I had first learned the thing about heroism and seeing life as it is.

I wasn't surprised to learn that she was the daughter of professors. She had a talent for learning. I'd even seen her cursing people out in Spanish. She taught me all the Spanish

I knew. Each day at work was like a tutoring session. I got the habit of reading the newspaper from her, too. At the time, I could barely read Chinese, let alone foreign languages. I hadn't even graduated from junior middle school. All those fancy phrases I learned, I either picked them up from her or the newspaper. I would go through the newspaper with her and ask her what things meant.

Like that line about heroism and loving life... I went through the sentence word by word, asking what each one meant. She said it was impossible to understand that way, since it was sort of a colloquial phrase. She struggled to explain it to me. "It's like... *lin-sing-hai-hai*. You know what I mean?"

I was an uneducated seventeen-year-old kid from the country. I had only left the village because I had to run for my life.

I had no idea what *lin-sing-hai-hai* meant.

She laughed and told me it wasn't Mandarin, but Hokkien. She wrote it out for me: 人生海海 – literally, it meant something like "life is an ocean", but she explained, "It means life is complicated. It's always changing. But it's more than that... The ocean is big, right? It has that meaning, too. A lifetime is like an ocean – it's massive and it's always changing. But, basically, you say it to someone to encourage them. It's like, 'keep living, because you don't know what's coming next.'"

She told me: "Just because life is hard, you can't decide to go off somewhere and die. If that was the case, I wouldn't be standing here right now."

I found later that she'd had a hard life. Her father had been beaten to death by Red Guards and her brother had gone to get revenge. He ended up murdering a Red Guard before they beat him to death, too. At the time, the local Red Guards were split into two factions. One faction planned to go to her house and murder the entire family, and the other faction went to warn them. She escaped, but her mother stayed behind to be tormented, because she couldn't bear the thought of them desecrating her husband's and son's bodies. She ran back to her grandmother's place in Fujian and hid out. But finally there was nowhere to go. She sold her body for the money to escape overseas.

In the sea of life, we were like two grains of sand. In the sea of life, we ate and worked side by side, for three years. After that, she left. She used the money she had saved up to open a shop. She decided to sell *youtiao*. It was a risky idea, since there were very few Chinese there, and even fewer with disposable income. But she figured out how to sell them. She knew that youtiao were pretty close to churros, so she shrunk them down to about the size of French fries and sold them with a chocolate sauce for dipping. The shop was a success.

The shop was close to the factory, and I had to walk by it to get to my dormitory. I was happy to see her thriving. She knew I was broke, so she would always give me some youtiao for free. I tried to turn her down, but she would press a bag into my hand as I passed, saying they were leftovers from the day before. Our friendship deepened and her business improved. Finally, she offered to hire me on as her assistant. I had already paid off the loan to the snakehead, and she was offering the same wages as the factory and a place to stay, so I agreed without hesitation. A few months after that, I asked her to be my girlfriend. She was shocked.

"You don't know my situation?" she asked.

"I know about it," I said. What she called her "situation" was her ongoing relationship with the snakehead. He came around three or four times a year and had his way with her. Everyone at the factory knew about it. They said she was the snakehead's whore. But I knew whatever agreement they might have come to in the past must have long since expired. I told her: "I want you to put a stop to it."

"You're scared people are going to make fun of you?" she asked.

"I'm not worried about that," I said. I had other things to worry about.

"It's not fair to you," she said.

"Is your arrangement with the snakehead fair to you?"

"I could put a stop to it, but not for you, not for this place... I want to leave. I want to save up enough money to start a new life."

"Let's leave together," I said. I finally convinced her with that line from the newspaper. I changed it a bit, though. I said: "There is only one true heroism in the world: to see you as you are, and to love you."

When she heard that, she started crying. She told me that she'd never leave me and that she'd be good to me for the rest of her life.

"You've always treated me well," I said.

"Then I'll treat you even better," she said.

She was as good as her word. She was always a decent person, but her life was hard. We were only married seven months before she passed away. We had moved to Madrid by then and opened up the same sort of shop. She had spent all of her savings to relocate, but for various reasons, the business was a failure. To save money, we drove seventy miles out into the countryside to buy flour. We had to rent a truck each time, and it was cutting into our profits, so she pawned the gold ring that she had pulled from her father's dead finger. We bought a beat-up old pickup truck. The brakes were shot on it but we couldn't afford to fix them, so we just drove everywhere as slowly as possible. We had plenty of time to get places, since the shop was closed most of the time. The old shop had been such a success that it was even humiliating to watch the shop in Madrid slowly fail. She had only relocated in the first place so that I wouldn't be made fun of. She was trying to save my masculine dignity. Nobody knew me there. They didn't know about her situation. I never expected that preserving my dignity would lead to her death.

One day, on a trip out to pick up flour, we loaded up the truck, and got about a half mile down the road when the brakes failed completely. She was driving at the time, even though she was six months pregnant and she had to reach over her belly to touch the wheel. I used to say that she was the best driver in the world, since she didn't even have to use her hands to drive. Most of the time, she just steered into the ditch, but it was too late. We were headed down a hill, and the truck was completely unstoppable. She pulled off the road and into a field, but the truck kept going. She screamed for me to jump. I screamed back, telling her to go first. With her stomach swollen, she could barely move from behind the steering wheel. She kept screaming for me to jump, and I kept screaming back at her.

"Just jump," she said. "You're going to die!"

"That's fine," I shouted back at her. "You're carrying my son. You need to jump now."

"Then we'll die together." she said.

"Let's die together," I said.

But in the end, she died and I survived with a few cuts and bruises. She bled out of her vagina and mouth. Her liver had been pulverised by the steering wheel. We were so far out of town that even an air ambulance wouldn't have been quick enough. She only had enough time to say goodbye to me. We cried, but we didn't actually know what to say to each other.

"I deserve to die," she said. "I didn't save the child."

"You can't die. I want us to die together."

"You can't die. I need somebody to sweep my tomb. My family is all gone."

I couldn't speak. I could only sob. I held her in my arms and felt her body grow light in my arms. Within moments, she was as light as an armful of hay. She seemed about to slip away, to melt back into the earth. All I could do was cry.

Life is fucking painful.

She had a painful life, but she never let on. She always treated other people well. If she hadn't told me to apologise to that foreman, I might have starved to death on the streets of Barcelona. If she hadn't told me to go on living, I might have dug a pit for both of us on that hillside. My wife and my child were both gone. I had nothing to live for. But she used her last breath to tell me this: "Remember, *lin-sing-hai-hai*, life is an ocean. You don't need courage to die. You need courage to live. If you come looking for me in Hell, I'll pretend I don't know you. Remember what you said to me that day? The only true heroism in the world is to see life as it is, and to love it."

When I'd told her that the first time, I had changed "life" to "you" in that sentence, but she changed it back. She told me that it had been written by a famous writer named Romain Rolland. "Remember it," she said. "If I didn't read that line, I probably would never have met you."

I knew that the quote must have seen her through some dark times. It had given her the will to live. Even when she had been humiliated and insulted, she had kept going. She had turned her life around. She had regained the will to live. She did it all by herself. She told me once that she knew she would never be rid of the snakehead, even after she left the factory. That was why she was trying to save money. She wanted to fly away from that place. I knew all of those things. But I couldn't understand why her life had to be so painful.

That night, trying to sleep in the Colonel's play room, I thought about everything Auntie Lin had told me and everything I had been through, and I thought about that quote. I found out later that the sentence hadn't even been in the newspaper. I thought it was a translation, but it was just something that she had added. She knew I didn't understand Spanish, anyways.

She was a good person.
So was the Colonel.

XCIV

I only ever had a handful of long conversations with my father. The most he ever spoke to me was that time in 1991, when I went home for the first time, and I found him cleaning up the Colonel's house. We had talked mostly about the Colonel that day. That had been what I wanted to talk about. When we were done talking about the Colonel, he asked me a bit about myself and what I'd been up to for the previous two decades. I told him about my wife and the car accident.

When he heard that story, his eyes suddenly brightened. "Now I understand," he said joyfully. "She died so that you could come back here."

I wanted to tell him that he had it wrong, that I was living for her, but I bit my tongue. My father's selfish detachment made me ashamed. I could take him insulting me, but I couldn't take him insulting her. The memory of her passing was like a deep wound in my heart. I still loved her, though. I didn't bring her up again around him.

Many years later, I saved up enough money to bring her remains from Spain to China. I wanted to bury her beside Grandpa and my mother, so that I could keep all of their graves clean. I wanted her there so that I could one day rest beside her. It broke my heart to bury her in a foreign country. I wanted her to return to her homeland. That was in the year 2000. I picked the hottest day of the summer to bury her. After so many years in cold foreign soil, I wanted her to finally feel warm. When my father found out, he risked his life walking into the hills to stop me. He was already an old man by then, and one slip would have ended his life. Nothing I said would convince him to let her be buried alongside my family. My father's reasoning was simple: she had died when I should have, and all of my success afterwards had been because she had been looking out for me from Hell.

"So, why can't we let her finally rest?" I said to him. "She should be with our family."

"Don't do that to her," my father said. "Our family has committed grave sins. All the spirits on this hillside are cursing them. If you bury her here, she'll be cursed, too. If you do that to her, she won't protect you anymore. You'd be bringing a lifetime of curses down on her head – and on yourself."

My father was haunted by the disasters that his family had endured. There was finally no way to convince him to bury my wife with our family. When he threatened suicide, I finally relented. In the end, I went to Hangzhou and found where her parents had been buried. I thought I could bury her alongside them, but in the thirtysomething years since they had passed, many other people had been buried around them. There was no room to lay her to rest near them. At the end, I picked out a plot up on a hill, where she could look down on her parents. I thought that was a nice solution. At the same time, I bought the two plots beside hers, so that I could be buried there, along with my current wife. I thought it would be fun to whisper to her in Spanish. I thought it was a good arrangement, but I realised some people might think it was strange... A wife should be buried with her husband's family, not the other way around. The only time a husband was buried with his wife's family was when, like my eldest brother, the husband took the wife's surname. My brother and I might share the same fate in the end, I supposed. Maybe that was the only way to really escape the village. Perhaps my father was right that it was a cursed place...

I said "remains" but there wasn't much remaining of my wife. There was nothing but ashes and some bone fragments. Nowadays, the cremation technology is so good that a body is reduced to clean white ash, but it wasn't as good back then.

Out in the graveyard, it was so quiet that I felt like I could hear the sun sizzling down on me. At that moment, I was surrounded by countless dead people. I was the only living human for miles. It took me a few hours but I did it all by myself: I dug the grave, placed her remains, spread gravel on top, put up the headstone, and burned incense. After twenty years in the ground, her remains were indistinguishable from the dirt that I laid them into, but when I touched them, they seemed to be warm. All of the pain of the past bubbled up again. I had been carrying her remains with me for three years at that point. Chinese people are always worried about laying the dead to rest, so why did I carry her around with me for so long? Simple: I was broke. I wanted to wait until I had enough money to give her a proper burial.

When we had moved the shop from Barcelona to Madrid, we had used up most of our savings. The shop in Madrid never really turned a profit. It earned us enough to scrape by, but my wife was keeping it afloat. When she died, there was no way I could run the shop myself. I had to shut it down. After that, I had no money to rent a room, so I slept on the street. I fed myself from the garbage. I learned how to survive off garbage, and I eventually found a way to make money from it, too. Foreign garbage cans are full of treasure, especially in rich neighbourhoods. People would throw away clothes that other people could still wear. There were sometimes pots and pans, too, sometimes records, and even record players...

If there is a rich neighbourhood, there has to be a poor neighbourhood. And there are always more poor people than there are rich people.

I read in the newspaper that the poor occupy a massive gulf that would take hours to sail across, while the rich live in a tiny lake that you could row around twice in an hour. After years of experience travelling between rich and poor neighbourhoods, I can tell you that this is not an exaggeration.

I carried my wife's ashes with me day and night. She comforted me more than any living person could. She gave me the strength to keep going. When I was rooting around in the garbage, I was doing it so that I could someday give her a proper burial. Today, I could buy a mountain of granite and have headstones carved for every member of my family. Back then, scraping together enough money for a simple stone seemed as impossible as buying Puerta del Sol. After three years, I still didn't have enough money, but I found somebody to help me get it.

One day, as I was walking down the street, minding my own business, scoping out garbage cans, I heard someone calling me. The voice seemed to be coming from a great distance. I thought for a moment it was coming all the way from China. The voice seemed to carry with it an aroma as sweet as honey. I had spent the last three years in the company of a woman that could not talk back to me, so I didn't expect to hear a woman's voice, let alone one calling me by name. I knew it couldn't be my wife: she was safely stowed in my bag with a sheet of canvas over it to keep out the rain. I thought it might be a hallucination, but the voice called again, even closer.

I looked around for the sound and saw that it was a little girl calling me. It was a drizzly summer day and she was holding an umbrella. The way she skipped up the street made her look even more girlish. I guessed she might be a middle-school student. I didn't recognise her, but she knew my name. I had spent the three years before that concerned only with garbage. I had forgotten many people and many things. She knew my wife's name and said she had been to our shop. She was from Qingtian, near Wenzhou, which wasn't very close to my village, but we were at least from the same province. She used to come by the shop when it was still open. My wife and I didn't know much about her, back then. We recognised her by her slight limp.

I learned later that her parents were from the first generation of Chinese people to arrive in Spain, and she'd been born in the country. She suffered from polio as a child and her family was too poor to afford proper treatment. As she put it: God borrowed an inch of my leg but didn't pay me back. We talked for a while and she told me how much she missed our *youtiao*. And at that moment, God threw me a life raft. The rain started coming down heavily, and she let me stand under her umbrella. At the same time the sky opened up, I opened up to her, pouring out everything that I had been bottling up for years. She promised to find me a job. There were more Chinese in Madrid than Barcelona, and there was a sort of Chinatown in the Usera district to the south. She knew the area well and had no doubt that she could find work for me. When I asked what kind of job she might be able to get me, she told me not to worry about it: "Whatever it is, it'll be better than rooting through trash cans, right?"

"I don't know," I said, patting the bag that held my wife's ashes, "who would hire an old bum dragging his wife's bones around with him." Chinese people are superstitious. Carrying around someone's remains was bad luck. "I just want to get together the money to bury her," I said.

"How much do you need?" she asked.

I told her roughly how much I needed, and she immediately agreed to lend it to me. "Forget about it," I said. "You don't know how long it would take me to pay you back."

"Once you get a job, it won't be a problem."

In the end, I never paid her back. I married her instead. She's still my wife. I asked her one time why she wanted to marry a garbage picker, and she said that any man willing to carry his wife's ashes around for three years had to be a good husband. In a way, it was almost like my first wife brought me a replacement. She had paved the road for me, you could say. That road took me through a garbage dump, but that was on purpose, too. Garbage is what made my dreams come true. Garbage is what made me a fortune. I started three companies from garbage.

I read in the paper once that China today is the easiest place to get rich. Anybody can get rich in China these days, it said. You can turn anything into money – even trash. When I read that, I smiled to myself and wondered if the writer had me in mind.

XCV

As I write this, on a December day in 2014, my village is taking a new path, one that is virtually paved with gold. You can't look anywhere without seeing money. Even the pale yellow leaves on the gingko trees might as well be sheafs of copper coins. One day a few years back, an entrepreneur passionate about equestrianism happened to come through on a horseback tour, and decided to restore the village back to what he called the Age of Horses. He invested tens of millions of yuan in the project, which included a renovation of the ancestral hall, stripping the cement off the roads to bring back the cobblestones, and restoring all of the old houses – including my family's home – in a consistent style. What had once been pigsties and cowsheds were converted into stables for horses. He raised dozens of American Shetland ponies, a breed known for being docile and ideal for children horseback riding. That was the beginning of the village's exploitation as a tourist site. Buses of tourists come on the weekend to experience it, and to taste the local delicacies. In the spring, they come to see the bamboo shoots poking out of the soil. In the summer, they hunt wild boar on a farm that someone in the village set up. In the winter, they pick wild persimmons and dates, but unlike when we were kids, they have to pay for the privilege. The village only gets quiet in the wintertime. I haven't seen all the statistics, but the number of visitors surely exceeds the number of leaves shed each year by the ancient gingko tree in the yard of the ancestral hall.

The village has become a tourist site. Most people moved out of the village and built houses on the other side of the stream, down at the bottom of Front Mountain. Wild One built the biggest house in the village. He opened a snack stall in Hangzhou that he expanded into a restaurant. As he told it, he was making money hand over fist. I don't know how true that is, but it seems clear that he's done okay for himself. You just had to look at the house to know. Many years before, he bought up the land formerly occupied by the school. He knocked down the whole thing, including the woodshed where the Colonel had been locked up, and put up a mansion on it. The plans had come from an American architect, and it was done up in a completely Western style. It even has a sauna in it. I've tried it out, and so has every county head and Party secretary in the area. Whenever I go back to the village, I always stop off there. Seeing that house, the free and easy life he leads, and the way he tosses money around like splashing water – it always encourages me to keep making money.

When I tell people my business is garbage, they sometimes turn up their nose. That's how I made my money, though. I got my start picking out anything I thought I could sell to poor people. Nowadays, I make my money selling garbage to rich people. I sell mostly to paper factories and smelting plants, but it all ends up in the manufacturing industry, basically. Even though I buy low and I sell high, a lot of profit is eaten up in between by shipping, labour, and rent. At the end of the day, only a small amount goes in my own pocket. I never aimed for a windfall. I was always about the long game. Life is never simply a tragedy or a farce or a romance – it has all of those, one after another. If I hadn't spent three years eating out of the garbage, I wouldn't be running a recycling business. I humiliated myself digging in trash cans, and now I have wealth and prestige because of it.

A reporter from my hometown interviewed me once and wrote an article. It was a very beautiful piece that included a line about garbage being a metaphor for our age. I didn't really understand it, but it sounded good. Trash was a metaphor for my life, at the very least. The article said that the inspiration for my recycling business had come from something that my cousin said. That was true. When I went back to the village for the first time in 1991, I went to see my cousin at the paper plant where he worked. He was unloading a truck when I got there. It was early spring and still chilly, but had worked up a sweat. He was unloading square packages wrapped in what looked like snake skin. I asked him what it was. He told me it was garbage, shipped over from the United States.

"What does a paper plant do with garbage?" I asked him.

"It's not garbage to us," he said. "If you can bring us some from Spain, you can make a fortune." He told me that all the factories around there used recycled materials. His job was sorting through it. He separated out the paper, the metal, the plastic, and anything that looked like it was in one piece. If something was salvageable, they sent it to a middle man that could have it refurbished. The metal went to the smelting plants, the plastic went to a chemical plant. My cousin's plant used the wastepaper directly, feeding it into a pulper, bleaching it, and making their own new paper. That was how I found out that garbage is a commodity. It's worth money. You can make a fortune digging in the trash.

Of course, it's easier said than done. I spent three years digging in the trash, but it took more than that experience to build a business. It wasn't an immediate success. It took five years before I landed my first shipment at Beilun in Ningbo. I sold those first eight containers to a middleman for about eleven thousand American dollars. It was the most money I'd ever made in my life, but I made even more the next time, and the time after that, and the time after that... Business was going smoothly and I was slowly figuring out how to maximise my profits. In 2001, I formally established my own company, cut out the middleman and started running my own trucks to deliver the product. I used my cousin to connect directly with the paper plants and smelters near the village. In 2003, I set up a second company and rented a space at Beilun's container port. I used that space to sort the garbage before selling it. That meant I could charge even more for what I was delivering. I realised that I had a talent for business. I was cautious and shrewd. I also had a certain ability to size people up and find a way to use them.

In 1991, the first time I returned, my father thought you could get to Madrid on horseback. He wanted me to take my nephew back with me when I went.

"You better take him now," my father said. "He won't last long here. This house is haunted."

"Next time," I told him.

"When is that?" he asked.

I had no idea. It had taken me years of hard work and saving to buy the first tickets. But five years later, when I started making real money, I took my nephew with me. I felt like a debt to my father had been settled. My nephew ended up to be quite competent. I spent a lot of time training him. He ended up running my Spanish operations. But he missed his grandfather – my father – and returned to China six years ago with his wife and kids. He handed the reins over to my own son. He wanted to look after his grandfather in his old age. My father still refused to let him live in the house, though. He still thought the place was cursed. My nephew built a new house on the other side of the creek and went down to see his grandfather every few days. My father was so convinced that the place was cursed, but he never moved out. His idea was that the ghosts would stay with him, instead of going out to look for me. He was willing to suffer to keep us safe. He thought that all of his family's later good luck had been because he had kept the ghosts at bay.

My father whispered to me once that our house was haunted by four ghosts. He could describe each of them. One ghost had three eyes, another had horns, one was covered in white hair, and another had long hair and no face. A few days later, he told me that there were three ghosts and they were all men. He started describing them, but I cut him off. "I thought you said there were four."

"I killed one of them," he told me.

The number of ghosts changed each time. Sometimes it was as many as five or six. Only the ghosts haunting the place really knew for sure. My father had no idea. Apart from that, though, his mind was sharp. His memory was good, too. He would sometimes tell me stories from my childhood that I had forgotten completely. He remembered everything that had ever happened with the Colonel. But when it came to ghosts, he was as childish as the Colonel. The Colonel was driven mad by the living and my father was driven mad by the dead. My father was petrified of ghosts, but he stayed in the haunted house. Even though my father had never shown me much affection, I came to understand this as a powerful expression of his love.

I read in the newspaper once that love is the same as physical fitness. Some people are genetically gifted, others build it over time, and others are destined never to have it. It made think of my father and the Colonel. The Colonel was the opposite of my father. When it came to love, he was the strongest man in the world, and my father was a weakling. That's why they were so good for each other. Opposites attract. I never had a man in my life like the Colonel, but both of my wives were of a similar type. That was enough for me.

I read in the paper once that money is the best friend you'll ever have. I'm never lacking for friends.

XCVI

After my business took off, I went back to China often. I always took time off to stop by the village. Blindboy had become the first "tourist". He had nothing to do, so he spent all his time wandering around, taking in the sights. When he was tired of strolling, he parked himself in front of the ancestral hall and watched people go by, waiting for someone to tease him or take pity on him. The people that teased him did not pity him, and the people that pitied him did not tease him.

When I went back to the village the first time, I had two hopes: the first was that my family would be safe, and the second was that Blindboy would be the same as ever. I was worried that he would find a doctor to fix his tongue or his hands. He was a mess: he had wasted away to nothing, he was filthy, and his face was covered in scars. I had no sympathy for him. It was like drooling over a stinky, brown hunk of fermented tofu. I wanted to say to him: "You got everything you deserved. I had to run for my life because of you. I spent more than twenty years in exile. This is the price you paid. I am home safe now, and you are still suffering. The Heavens have passed judgement on you." I didn't say anything to him, though. I wasn't afraid of him, but it seemed undignified. I had been thinking for years about what I would say to him. I thought maybe I owed it to myself, to expose myself for a moment. Everyone else had a chance to say what they wanted to say, but I never got the chance. I wanted to do it just once, as a reward to myself for so many years of exile and pain. But I realised I was the only one that felt that way. I was all alone in the world again. In the twenty-two years that I had been away, everyone, including my father, had forgiven him. My time in exile had made me timid, too. I held my tongue. Even after returning to Madrid, I still cursed him. I hoped he would be dead before I returned again.

Blindboy just kept living, though. He had his father to rely on. Without him, he would have starved or froze to death. Even if the Blind Man hadn't been a fortune teller, he could have guessed that his son would suffer after he was gone. He knew his son would have to rely on the benevolence of the village. It would take more than just pity. Pity is not something that you can live on. It's usually only a glance or a sigh. Benevolence is a sense of responsibility. It comes from the bottom of your heart. But it needs to be aroused in people. That's what the Blind Man wanted to do. He went to the ancestral hall, knelt down, and repeated over and over again: "I know that I deserve to die. I did horrible things to the Colonel. My crimes deserve ten thousand deaths. When I die, I will go to heaven and watch over you. I will ensure that all of you live in peace, happiness, and contentment. The only thing I ask of you is that you take care of my son." He stayed there for three days and three nights, repeating his pledge. The plaques in the ancestral hall's shrine began to quake, and the guardian lions out front seemed to silently echo his chant. Finally, a group of people – retired cadres, teachers, elders – finally showed up and tried to pull him up. They told him that they would see to it that his son was taken care of. The Blind Man refused to stand up, though. He said that he would kneel there until he died. He wanted to die on his knees, begging for benevolence.

That was how the Blind Man aroused a sense of benevolence in the village. He was wrapped in mercy, safe from the long, cold night. He was saved from certain death. But there was no way to save him a fate worse than death, which is to suffer through life, hanging on by a thread, being tortured, and always waiting for the final moment. Every time I left the village, I assumed that I would never see him again. But his life-force was strong. Maybe the Blind Man had saved his son, maybe he had doomed him to suffer, and maybe the King of Hell simply didn't want him. But whatever it was, each time I saw him, he seemed renewed by some force that was just strong enough to keep him on the side of the living.

I read in the newspaper once that time waits for no man. You can't look back. But time does wait for some people... In 2001, when I went back to the village, I had finally had enough of Blindboy's suffering. I had hated him long enough. On that trip, I ran into him outside of Stumpy Tiger's supermarket. He moaned at me like he always did. He was begging for money. For some reason, I tossed him two hundred yuan. I went into the store and when I came back, he was still standing there. He pointed at the ground with his corpse-like hands. He had written something in the mud with his toe: "A powerful man does not harbour grudges towards the weak. Thank you."

It was a common idiom, which we'd all learned in school. I didn't think much about it. I didn't think of myself as a powerful man. There was no need to thank me. But for some reason, that small act – tossing him the money – and the gratitude he showed me left a lasting impression. In a way, it felt like claiming victory to finally forgive him and to forgive myself. At that moment, I realised again that I was alone. I was a soldier fighting a war that had ended years before. The battlefield became my garden. Even if I was alone, I should enjoy it. I could walk there whenever I wanted. I could finally be at peace.

Before I left that time in 2001, I told Stumpy Tiger that from then on, whatever Blindboy wanted was on my tab. I asked him to keep a running tally, then give me the bill. Stumpy Tiger joked that he wanted me to run a tab for him, too, just like Blindboy. I told him to go ahead. "Fuck," Stumpy Tiger said, "I knew you were making money, but I didn't think you'd made it big already." I asked him what he considered making it big, and he told me that Wild One was already earning at least a million a year. I told him that I wasn't making as much as Wild One, and I didn't plan on it.

I was telling the truth. At the time, I was making maybe half of what Wild One was, but it felt like enough. Comparing yourself to others is a good way to drive yourself crazy.

I never compare myself to others. I measure myself against my own accomplishments. I read in the paper once that "happiness gets reflected in your own eyes, not in others".

XCVII

Telling Stumpy Tiger anything was as good as broadcasting it to the entire village. When I returned, everyone in the village knew that I was covering Blindboy's expenses. I expected my father would be upset. I assumed he would be offended by it. I thought he would say something like: "You can bury me, but I'll crawl out of my coffin to bite you." Even before I got to the house, I felt like I could hear his voice.

That was the last time I was ever scared of my father. That was thirteen years ago. He was eighty-three that year.

My father was like a rotten tree stump. He was sitting where I left him: right in front of the eastern addition, where Grandpa and I had once slept. He was almost unrecognisable. He had no hair left on his head and his wrinkles went from his forehead all the way to the peak of his skull. When I saw him that time, it was three years on from his stroke. The wrinkles on the right side of his face were deep. He had not scrubbed himself clean since then. His right hand was paralysed, and he had only learned to do the basics with his left hand. He could feed himself, but that was it. He was almost blind. I'm sure he could have seen Death approaching, but it seemed never to come. Death was like one of the cobwebs in the pigsty, swaying in the breeze, threatening to drop on him at any moment, but never actually falling...

Whenever I went back, he would always say the same

thing: "I keep telling you not to come back here, but you keep showing up here."

One time I told him: "I keep coming back because you just won't die."

"Just pretend I'm dead," he said.

After dealing with my father, I reached the conclusion that the most ruthless people in the world are old people and rich people. Old people are not scared of anything because they're already waiting for death. Rich people are not scared of anything because they think they can buy their way out of trouble.

I waited for him to scold me for looking after Blindboy, but he had the opposite reaction. He praised me for my kindness. "Stop wasting your money on me," he said. "I told you, just pretend I'm already dead. You might as well feed him. At the very least, he won't haunt you when he's dead."

It seemed to be the conversation he had been waiting for. He shifted from that to telling me that Auntie Lin had visited him. She had told him about a Great Master in Xi'an, specialised in paralysis. She had supposedly seen the Master at work, many years before, waving his hands over a man, then dragging him out of bed, despite the fact that he had supposedly been paralysed for years. She had wondered if the Master might be able to help Blindboy.

"Why do you still want to help him?" I asked.

"I don't want him to haunt you after he dies," my father said.

"Aren't you afraid that if somebody fixes his hands, he'll come and slap you?"

"I'm not afraid of anything," my father said. "If he wants, he can beat me to death. I'm more worried about him haunting you."

I couldn't understand how my father, so cold and distant his whole life, could suddenly care about Blindboy. I couldn't understand how he could suddenly show mercy to him. It went much deeper than hoping Blindboy would survive. It was more than hoping I would give Blindboy enough money to survive the winter. He wanted me to go to great effort to bring in the Master from Xi'an. Was it because so many years had passed? I finally guessed that he wanted Blindboy's fingers healed so that he could write again. He wanted to read what he had to say. He wanted to know why Blindboy had started the rumour about the Colonel being a sodomite, which had led to the ruin of our family.

I had thought about that before, too. In 1996, when I made my first money from garbage, I bought my family a computer. My kids needed it for school, at the very least. It had no brand names on it, just three lumps of plastic and metal. I was deeply impressed by what was called the "memory". It was the heaviest piece of the computer, but it was the smallest. It was like lifting an ammunition box. It was even painted army green. At the time, we hadn't rented a place for ourselves yet, but we had a couple rooms for ourselves at my father-in-law's house. There was no space in the kid's room to put it, so it went out on our terrace. The terrace had a canopy over it, so nothing could get wet.

Computers were attractive and novel things at the time. When the kids were at school, I had time to screw around on it. I couldn't really type on it, but I mastered pecking away at the keys with two fingers. There was no system yet for inputting romanised Chinese, or we didn't have it on our computer. When I was trying to get another Chinese character input to work, poking at it with my two stiff fingers, I immediately thought of Blindboy. He couldn't even hold chopsticks, but I figured he could master typing on a keyboard. I thought maybe the computer could speak for him.

I thought about it at the time, but I didn't actually go through with it.

As my business developed, I had to start using email, so

I bought myself a laptop computer. It was the weight and size of a magazine, small to carry around in a bag. It was a convenient and fashionable item at the time. When my father brought up the idea of contacting the Great Master from Xi'an, the idea of Blindboy using the computer popped into my head again. "If you just want to know what he has to say," I told my father, holding up the laptop, "you can use this." Blindboy had been through middle school, so he knew enough characters to compose the basics. I thought it would probably take him a couple nights to get through his story.

My father asked me what exactly I was planning, and I gave him a simple explanation. But he shook his head and said, "I want him to speak. I want you to do something good for him. I want him to be able to live like a normal person. If you don't do that, at least, he'll haunt you when he's dead. The poor kid doesn't even have hands! If you don't have two hands, you aren't fully human." A year went by. My father brought it up again, right as he was approaching the end: "Did you ever talk to that Great Master in Xi'an?" When he saw me shake my head – or guessed that I was shaking my head, since he was blind already – he repeated what he had said: "If you don't have two hands, you aren't fully human." His meaning was clear: he wanted me to give Blindboy back his hands. My father only had two deathbed wishes: the first was that I restore Blindboy's hands, and the second was that I deal with the old house. He told me to sell it, but if I wasn't able to sell it, he wanted me to tear it down. The two wishes had the same root, which was to avoid being haunted by any evil spirits.

I read in the newspaper once that people spend their whole lives talking, but people only really listen to them when they're on their deathbed. If nobody listens to those deathbed words, it's as if they have spent their whole lives yelling into an abyss. My father was a man of few words. Even on his deathbed, he didn't have much to say. I thought I should try my best to honour his final requests. I didn't know whether I could find the Great Master, but I owed it to my father to at least look. It might give him some comfort in the afterlife. When my father's funeral was over, I went to see Auntie Lin to ask her about the Great Master. At the time, I was in China quite frequently, and I had gone to see Auntie Lin and the Colonel many times. I tried to go down there at least once a year. I learned that May and June were the best times to go. That was when all the work of raising silkworms was done, and the Colonel was always at his best in summer. If you visited at the right time, he was almost normal. Auntie Lin said that when he went into the silk shed, his intellect seemed to become like a normal person again. If I hadn't seen it myself, I never would have believed that the Colonel was a master at raising silkworms.

XCVIII

The second time I visited Auntie Lin and the Colonel had been in the middle of May. The first time I had been there, the mulberry bushes had been bare, but that time, they were lush and green. The leaves were so thick on the bushes that you couldn't see the branches. The mulberry bushes stretched all the way up to the foothills. That had been the trip when I had landed eight containers of trash at Ningbo. I took some of the money and bought a box of coloured pencils and some paper for the Colonel. When Auntie Lin saw the gift, she was surprised. "He doesn't draw much at the moment," she said. "You should have brought him a box of snacks. He's up at all hours of the night, and they keep him going..."

Auntie Lin led me out through the backdoor of their house, where they had a simple wooden silkworm shed. Inside were two rows of racks made from bamboo poles. The racks held small sheets woven from thin bamboo strips. Each sheet was covered in tiny green silkworm pupae. They really were like babies – fragile and defenceless, requiring careful climate control and hourly feeding. If the mulberry leaves offered to them were not fresh, tender, and clean, they would refuse them. Unlike babies, though, if they refused to eat or got sick, they'd end up being fed to the chickens. Raising silkworms was not easy work. You had to pick mulberry leaves once before the sun came up and once after the sun went down. Since the silkworms required hourly feeding, you had to bring them fresh mulberry leaves in the middle of the night. Raising silkworms usually requires at least two people, but the Colonel did all the work himself.

"Most of the people in the village raise silkworms," Auntie Lin told me, "and they all say that my Old Man is the best there is. His silkworms are big and healthy. Their silk production is excellent, too. He sells them for big money."

"What's his secret?" I asked.

"He takes it seriously. He's like a child in that way. I taught him how to look after them, and he follows my instructions to the letter."

Perhaps, compared to most people, the Colonel's greatest strength – and perhaps his greatest weakness – was that he refused to compromise. If he was given a task, he would complete it exactly as it had been laid out for him. He would not try to find a workaround or some way to make the job go faster. He would also never tire of doing a task. When I watched him work, he had complete focus and dedication. He looked more like a robot than a human. For example, most people picked mulberry leaves by ripping down whole stalks, but the Colonel picked the leaves one by one, leaving behind any that didn't pass his careful inspection. He washed and dried each leaf individually. He set an alarm for each feeding, and as soon as it sounded, he was on his feet and ready to work, even in the middle of the night. When it was hot outside, he would fan the silkworms to keep them cool. When it got cool, he put newspaper in all the cracks in the shed and put rice straw over the silkworms to keep them warm. He could spend an hour just watching over his silkworms, and he would weep when they died.

Auntie Lin told me that she had trained him in a number of tasks around the house, like growing vegetables, cooking, feeding the chickens and ducks, and looking after his cats. But his real talent was raising silkworms. He picked it up immediately, and his understanding seemed to grow each year. It was like fate had delivered him to Mulberry Village to become a master sericulturalist. In a way, it seemed like he was trying to prove himself to the silkworms. Perhaps he had given up on trying to impress the people around him, but he thought he owed it to the silkworms.

After that second visit, when I found him at work, I tried to visit in the silkworm rearing season. I liked watching him at work. There were times in the silkworm shed when he seemed to have fallen into a trance. It looked like he was at peace, I thought. It comforted me, sometimes, but there were other times when it made me feel sad. It reminded me of how my daughter would focus even harder on her homework after being scolded. I was happy to see her working, but it hurt me to have to yell at her. He had the mind of a child, Auntie Lin said, but I thought his dedication to the silkworms was that of an adult. I couldn't help but feel a deep tenderness towards him at those moments. One time, I found him in the shed on a hot afternoon, fanning his silkworms... There was sweat pouring down his face, but he wouldn't stop working. I couldn't hold back my emotions, and I went to hug him. He shushed me and said, "Keep it down. They're sleeping."

I read in the newspaper once that life is hard, but it's the only thing worth living for. Maybe that's one way to explain the Colonel's later life. In those years, I treated him like a father figure. I visited him as often as I could. I felt as if I had a certain filial responsibility to check in on him.

That time, when I went to visit after my father's death, I was taking care of his deathbed wish. I saw the Colonel on the edge of the village, hunched over, carrying a basket full of mulberry leaves that he had just picked. In those years, he had seemed to age quite quickly. He had liver spots on his hands and face, and he could no longer manage the carrying pole that he had once used to bring back loads of leaves. He had been forced to reduce the number of silkworms he reared each time. The quality of the silkworms had gone down, too, since he was so deaf that he sometimes slept through the midnight alarms. But he insisted on sticking with it. The silkworms he raised might not have been quite as robust as before, but the fact that he continued raising them into his eighties was impressive. Auntie Lin told me that his memory and intelligence were in decline, too. At the time, he had the intellect of a four-year-old. He was incapable of speaking in long sentences and his mind would often wander. Sometimes he even forgot who I was. On some visits, he would spend the whole day avoiding me, thinking I was a stranger. Auntie Lin always stayed about the same, though. She was still a bag of bones, but she was as sharp as the first time I had met her.

When I mentioned the Great Master to her, Auntie Lin didn't remember much. She said it had been more than thirty years since she had seen him perform his miracle.

"He was already in his seventies or eighties at the time," Auntie Lin said. "Unless he discovered the secret to immortality, he's long since dead."

Even if the Great Master was still alive, there was no telling where we might find him. Without an address, it would be next to impossible to track him down. Instead of wasting my time on that, I could have used the time to find a specialist doctor in the field – and there was still only the slimmest chance that Blindboy could be rehabilitated. If there was ever a chance to give him back the use of his hands, it would have happened a long time before. Common sense told me that my father's wish would never come true.

Auntie Lin had medical training, so she was even more clear on the matter than I was. "If anybody ever tells you they can rehabilitate him," she said, "you're either talking to a liar or the Buddha himself. If your father really thought you were going to find some Great Master to heal Blindboy, his mind must have been going already. Mentally, he probably wasn't far off from where my Old Man is now."

At that point, I knew I probably couldn't honour my father's final wish, but I had made an effort to, at least.

That time when I left, the Colonel was still eating his lunch. His appetite had not faded with age. He could put away more food than I could. "Just look at him," Auntie Lin said, forcing a smile. "I sometimes worry he's going to outlive me. I don't know what would happen if I went first."

Those words haunted me. I heard her say them again, on other visits. I always thought of how painful her life had been, how dark clouds always seemed to be hovering over her. Sometimes when I thought about it, tears would come to my eyes – just two, two tears sliding down my cheek and clinging to my jaw, two tears like two droplets of blood, two tears as if they stood in for Auntie Lin and the Colonel, muddling their way through their miserable, lonely lives, just barely hanging on...

XCIX

When my father passed away, my nephew moved out of the village and into the county capital. He went back quite often, but I would only visit for Tomb-Sweeping Day. That had been the second of my father's deathbed requests. He had told me to get rid of the old house and stay away from the village. I never healed Blindboy's hands, but I honoured that request, at least. In fact, I never really put much effort into the first request, other than asking about the Great Master. I felt a bit guilty sometimes that I didn't put more effort into that. That was one reason I didn't go back to the village very often: I didn't want to see Blindboy. He brought up complicated feelings that I didn't want to address. There were more pragmatic reasons for not visiting the village, too, though. At first, much of my business had been serving the paper factoring and smelting plants there, but cost-cutting measures had meant that they had mostly relocated further west, towards Anhui and Jiangxi. When they moved, my focus shifted, too. The small amount of work left around my own village could be left to my nephew. I didn't have much to do with it.

Not long after my father died, probably around the summer of 2008, I was talking to a friend on QQ, when I suddenly got a friend request from someone using the screen name Pitiful Worm. Whoever it was said they knew my name and wanted to talk to me about something important, so I added them. I just ignored them after that, though. It wasn't particularly unusual. Plenty of people knew my name. But I didn't like people going under silly nicknames like that. As I saw it, you shouldn't try to hide behind a fake identity.

Pitiful Worm seemed to be reading my mind. A message popped up: "Your grandpa used to say, the world is full, so don't be full of yourself." That was definitely something Grandpa had said to me. I guessed that Pitiful Worm was probably from my village. With his next line I was sure: "Don't leave the village and act like a king. If you go to the moon, we're still tending your ancestors' graves." The tone and the sentiment came straight from Grandpa. He was always tossing out lines like that.

"Who is this?" I typed.

"Guess!"

"Cousin?"

"Now I know what you really think about your cousin! You saw 'Pitiful Worm' and that was the first person that came to mind." Whoever it was, they could type far faster than I could. New lines kept appearing on the screen. "He's too busy with your garbage to get on the Internet. Guess again! I want to know if you can guess!"

I took four or five more guesses, but they were all wrong.

Pitiful Worm: "I could let you guess all day and you'd never get it."

He was right. I could have spent a month guessing and I never would have hit the right name – Blindboy! How could I have ever guessed that the person on the other side of the screen, firing lines faster than I could type, was a man that could barely lift food to his face? It was simply unimaginable.

Times had changed. Even the lives of the poorest and the most isolated had been improved. Computers and the Internet had made it even to rural China. It was true what they said, that the whole world had gone online. Blindboy's computer had been given to him by Wild One. To Wild One it had been just another outmoded gadget that he would replace with whatever had come on the market, but for Blindboy, it was worth its weight in gold. He spent all of his waking hours on it, sometimes becoming so absorbed that he would forget to eat. His hands had been useless for decades, so to finally come across a mysterious machine that allowed him to speak to the world was like magic. He felt as if he had regained his voice. And he could use that voice to talk to the entire world. I saw later that his QQ friends list was full of all sorts of people, most of them hidden behind bizarre screen names, with profile pictures that identified them as Leonardo da Vinci or Qin Shi Huang or Queen Elizabeth... Blindboy's own QQ profile picture was a sad penguin with a broken wing. It fit his real life situation, at least.

Even if he was a "Pitiful Worm", he finally had a fantasy world to escape into. The people he met online had no idea who he really was. He claimed to be a great fortune teller, descended from a long line of soothsayers, capable of speaking to the dead. There were always people online willing to entertain his flights of fancy. He was online almost all the time and always ready to talk. Perhaps he had found some kind of enlightenment while he had spent so many years balanced between life and death. The real world had destroyed Blindboy and reduced him to a wandering ghost, but in the fantasy world of the Internet, he fit right in. He had found a large group of friends and followers. I knew him as a decrepit man begging for food, but on the Internet, he was something of a folk hero. He eventually changed his screen name from Pitiful Worm to "Web Worm". The new name fit better with his online persona. On the Internet, there was nothing pitiful about him. My nephew told me that Blindboy made a decent living off donations he got from people online. He had even found love. At least two of his Internet girlfriends were brave enough to take the trip to the village to see him in person. In the end, neither relationship had amounted to anything long term, but Blindboy wasn't discouraged. He was an eternal optimist. He told me that the next one would work out for sure. It was just like I read in the newspaper: the Internet broke the hearts of plenty of dreamers, but it also gave hope to the hopeless.

I chatted with Web Worm every now and then, but I was too busy to spend much of my free time on the Internet. One snowy night, while I was staying at a hotel in Jiangxi, I got online to read the news. Web Worm was online, as he always was. We talked about this and that, but a thought suddenly came to my mind... I typed without thinking: "If you don't want to talk about it, that's fine, but I always wanted to ask you how you saw the tattoo on the Colonel's belly. What actually happened that night?"

The thought came to my mind by chance that evening, but it had never really gone away. The central question I had about that strange, inexplicable night was planted in my mind like a statue in a city square. By that I mean, as powerful and monumental as the question was, it had become like the type of statue that I drove by every day without noticing.

"Lucky for me he's crazy now," Web Worm typed. "I'm the only one that can answer that question now."

"There was nothing lucky about it, especially for you," I typed.

"True. I spent a lifetime in pain because of that night. But I came out on top, didn't I? At least I still have my mind. I must have some good luck on my side."

"He's an old man now. Would a bit of sympathy kill you?"

"I appreciate your sympathy, but I don't have much for anybody else."

"Fine, fine."

Blindboy wouldn't answer the question, though. It was just more cryptic cursing, dirty jokes, and sarcasm... He only told me because I threatened to go offline.

"Fine. I'll tell you. You know the basics already. He drank all our liquor and passed out. He hadn't really slept for a few days. He was snoring something fierce, too. We had seen the words on his belly when he took a bath, but we couldn't actually read what they said. When I saw that he was completely out, I went over to peek inside the woodshed. He was still tied up, anyways. He was only wearing his long underwear. I was curious. I found a long stick, then went into the woodshed. I poked him a few times to see if he was really asleep. I eventually got his pants down, but he had a pair of underwear on underneath them. He was wearing a pair of briefs that came all the way up to his belly button. There was no easy way to get them off, but I tried anyway. He didn't wake up, at least."

That's not exactly as Blindboy typed it, of course. I'm editing out the typos and some other unnecessary stuff. I ended up taking out a section where Blindboy explained that he also had a flashlight. I thought I should make a note of that, since it's necessary to explain the rest of the chat log: "At some point, I happened to shine the light in his eyes. I guess he was sensitive to light, because he reared up and kicked me to the ground. I thought he was going to bring the whole place down on top of him. He managed to break the ropes we'd tied him with, too. He beat the shit out of me for a long time. He got me down on the ground and put his foot on my neck and asked me what I'd seen. I told him I hadn't seen anything.

"Actually, I could swear I saw that one sentence... I mean the one that my uncle wrote on the sign that day. But I didn't have time to actually read anything. It was in traditional characters, and written the opposite way, and a bunch of the characters had scars on them. I didn't really see that one sentence clearly. I saw the big red arrow and I knew there was something written on both sides of it, but I didn't have time to read it. He didn't believe me, though. He kept kicking me. I didn't have anything to say, though. My mind was blank.

"But he still wouldn't believe me. He thought I knew. He was scared that I might know. That's what upset him. I thought he was going to kill me. But I really didn't know. He would have been killing me for nothing. There was nothing I could have done. He thought he was so clever, though, like he'd figured it all out, even though he was completely clueless. That's it. He was hurting me. But he was also hurting himself."

I had spent so many waking hours trying to figure out what had happened that night, even seeing it in my nightmares. But the truth – that the Colonel had made a horrible mistake that night, attacking Blindboy thinking he knew something he didn't – was something I had never imagined. I was fairly certain he was telling the truth. First, I had a pretty good idea of how the Colonel's mind worked. Carrying such a disgusting slogan on his stomach, along with the name of a traitor, in such a private spot – in a time when everyone had been turned into political bloodhounds, it was like having a bomb strapped to him. In the Colonel's mind, Blindboy held the detonator, and he had to snip the lead. It was better to make a mistake than take the risk of letting him run free! Second, if he really had seen what was tattooed on the Colonel, he wouldn't have had to make up the lie about the sodomy. If he saw the slogan or the name, he could have used either one to crucify the Colonel. So, I had to ask: "If you knew that the Colonel's tattoos had nothing to do with sodomy, why did you accuse him?"

Blindboy answered: "Because your father was a sodomite!"

"Bullshit."

"You still don't believe me, do you? It's the truth. If I'm lying, may I be struck dead right now."

That's exactly what I was wishing for – for a bolt of lightning to come down and fry him and his computer. But when I looked back at the screen, I saw another wall of text from him. Once again, I've filtered out the typos and long-winded sections, but this is what he said: "You know what they say about barking dogs never biting people? Your father was like that. He wasn't one to bark.

"When I went back to the village, he was the one I was afraid of. I knew he wanted to get revenge for what I had done. I knew he would do something, but he went further than I could ever have imagined. The first time was three days after I got out of hospital. It was the first time I'd left the house since coming back. I was going out to buy a pack of cigarettes. Right as I went around the ancestral hall, he appeared out of nowhere. He grabbed me and threw me down. He pushed my face into a pile of dog shit and told me to eat it. The next time he caught me, he made me eat cow shit. He said he was going to make me eat every piece of shit in the village. He said it was revenge for what I had done to the Lunatic" – that was how he referred to the Colonel.

"For a long time after that, I never went out alone. But I eventually started to slip. One day, he was hiding behind the Lunatic's gate. When I went by, he dragged me inside. I was shaking my head, trying to say I wouldn't eat shit again. You know what he did instead? He jerked down my pants and fucked me in the ass. That was only the first time."

After that day, Blindboy was always on guard, but he was defenceless against my father. He was raped over and over again. What Blindboy was saying was revolting, but it had enough of a ring of truth to it that I couldn't reject it completely. "At the time," he continued, "I had no idea what was written on the Lunatic. I made up the sentence about him being a sodomite because I thought suspicion would eventually land on your father. At the time, nobody could say for sure what was written on the Lunatic. I couldn't talk and I couldn't use my hands, but I wanted to ruin your father's life for raping me. My plan worked because everyone started saying your father was a sodomite, too. Your father assumed I couldn't rat on him. But I was smarter than him. I managed to kill two birds with one stone." Following the wall of a text was a line of emojis crying with laughter.

Outside the window, it was snowy and cold, but a fire was raging in my heart. I cursed Blindboy and told him about my father's last wish that I help him locate a Great Master to heal his hands. If what Blindboy was saying was true, why would my father have made a deathbed request to help him? My father was not completely mentally sound at the end, but he wouldn't have made a mistake like that. It fucking pissed me off, the way he was talking. My father was dead and Blindboy was still spreading lies about him. At that moment, I didn't feel guilty anymore about not trying harder to help Blindboy.

I didn't expect Blindboy to suddenly develop a conscience, but if he wanted to occupy the moral high ground, he needed more proof of what had happened. He could say whatever he wanted, but I needed real proof. If he wanted to prove his case, he needed more than his own testimony. His own testimony was as useless as he was!

But he went on the same way as before, adding even more obvious falsehoods: "I believe he said that. He talked to me about it, too. He knew I wouldn't expose his secret. Your father and I were close. We were more than close, you might say. We were a couple. He infected me with his disease. You wouldn't understand. Until you've experienced it for yourself, you'll never understand. I hated him at the beginning. But things changed. When I had been completely abandoned by everyone else, he was there. When I was tossed out to suffer like a stray dog in the street, he took me in. He treated me well most of the time. Finally, I got used to it. In the end, I was addicted. He showed me how to become the person that he desired the most. To be honest, I don't hate him at all. If it hadn't been for him, I would have starved or froze to death. He saved my life. He's the only reason I'm still alive. He ransacked the Lunatic's house to support me. You know what the Lunatic treasured more than anything else? It was his gold surgical tools. Your father pawned those for me."

I knew it had to be bullshit.

"You're full of shit!" I typed. "You're not worth dogshit, let alone gold. I saw what you looked like. You stunk. You were crawling around the streets like an animal. Who was supporting you then? The only reason my father ever treated you well is because he was scared you'd come back and haunt us all when you were dead. That's why he asked me to find that Great Master. When you get to Hell, ask the Old Constable if the Colonel ever fucked a man in the ass. You think he could spend all those years with my father and not know the truth? Is a single word you said even true, you son of a bitch? You've spent so long lying to people that you can't even remember the truth. You think because you can cheat the people you meet on the Internet that you can blackmail me now? Go to hell."

I was furious. I wanted to scream in his face. I wanted to curse myself. I wanted to curse my father for treating Blindboy so well, when it had all been for nothing! But I controlled myself. I angrily slammed the laptop shut. It was a wise choice. It was also the only choice.

I opened the laptop again and deleted him from my friends list. When I had done that, my anger subsided. In a way, it felt like I had killed him. I had satisfied my craving.

I knew I couldn't kill him, and it would take more than simply deleting him from my QQ friends list to shake that shadow. My father worried that after Blindboy died, he would come back to haunt me, but I didn't have to wait for him to die. Blindboy always found a way to slip into my mind, gnawing at my nerves, trying to shame me.

I flipped through the newspaper, looking for profound words to comfort myself. I couldn't find any.

C

The Colonel died at 9:43 on second December, 2014.

He took his last breath without any pain or anxiety. He was wrapped in a navy blue cashmere blanket, with Auntie Lin and me by his side. The room was filled with the thick smell of soybean oil and burning candles. Auntie Lin coughed while positioning the eartips of the stethoscope. She put the diaphragm of it on his neck. Very softly, she said: "Time of death, 9:43 p.m."

The Colonel was born on the seventh year of the Republic, 1918. He lived for almost a century. He outlived most people that knew him in his prime. Just think how many of his comrades-in-arms, his friends, his lover, his friends, and his enemies must have been waiting for him down below!

In those years, whenever I visited, Auntie Lin would say, "I think he's going to live forever." Four days before he died, sprinting towards his hundredth birthday, the Colonel had tripped on the stairs. He went down in a heap and never regained consciousness. Auntie Lin knew that it was the end. She cleaned his body, prepared his graveclothes, and waited for him to die. She never expected him to hang on for four days. I happened to be in China at the time, and I arrived the day after he fell. I never thought he would still be alive when I arrived. During those three days, she repeated many times, "I think he's going to live forever." But she also said: "I guess I outlived him." When she said that, the joy on her face was unmistakable.

During those three days, I wanted to do something to help her, but there wasn't much I could do. Auntie Lin had already prepared everything. She had even trimmed his nails and his nose hair. The place where he would be buried had been chosen years before: a sunny hillside on Tail Mountain. By the time he died, the tomb had already been built and the headstones carved, including one for Auntie Lin. It made sense that she would be buried beside him. She was his wife, after all. Some of the older people in the village still remembered how she had wailed and sobbed at the Colonel's mother's funeral. They thought it would be an honour to be buried beside such a dedicated woman.

My only task in those three days of waiting was to stay by Auntie Lin's side while she waited for the Colonel to take his last breath. He had a long, hard birth, and his death took even longer. Auntie Lin would occasionally touch his forehead or put the stethoscope to his neck. The first day, we sat in silence, waiting for the moment. We lit a soybean oil lamp and a pair of red candles. It was our idea of sending him off with ceremony. All the windows were shut against the damp, gloomy early December chill, and the smell of soybean oil and burning candles was suffocating, but it didn't seem to bother the Colonel.

The first night, I went to sleep in the Colonel's play room. Auntie Lin slept beside him, holding him the entire night. If anyone had seen them lying together, they would never have guessed that she was waiting for him to die. The next morning, when I went into the Colonel's room, Auntie Lin was already sitting beside him on the bed. "His pulse seems to be getting stronger," she said. "I think he's going to live forever." That old line seemed to break the solemnity. We could finally talk openly. There wasn't much to say, though. I had visited many times, and we had discussed everything that there was to discuss. It wasn't until the afternoon of the next day that we managed to scrape up a topic that had been left undisturbed until then.

That afternoon was when Auntie Lin noticed that the Colonel's pulse was weakening. She sat on the chair beside his bed and took his hand. "He won't make it through the night," she said professionally. When she attended to the Colonel as his physician, she was always cold. When she tried to stand up, it seemed like she was stuck to the chair. She reached for my hand. I helped her to her feet and felt how cold her hands were. It was like the Colonel had sucked all her body heat into himself. She led me to the Colonel's play room. I had spent many hours in that room, but it seemed to have been transformed since my previous visit. It felt empty. All of the Colonel's toys and other things had been packed up and placed downstairs. When the time came, they would be burned along with his body. The only thing that remained from before was the desk that he used to draw at. The paper and coloured pencils were gone, but there was a screwdriver and a hammer in their place.

"Grab those," Auntie Lin said casually. She tore the tablecloth off the desk. The desk had been made from an old door, stuck on a wooden base. She motioned to a few nails that held the door plank to the base. It was easy to pry them out. I lifted the plank and looked into the base. Inside of it was the Colonel's black leather satchel. There was a time when he had carried it almost everywhere he went.

Auntie Lin motioned for me to open it.

I gingerly unzipped it, like I was dealing with a sack of dynamite. There was a burst of golden light. I was looking down on the Colonel's golden surgical tools: the scalpels, the lancets, the scissors, the tweezers, the forceps... They all looked brand new. It was like the years in storage and the darkness had made them shine even brighter than the day they were forged. I began to weep when I saw them.

"These tools saved more lives than you can imagine," Auntie Lin said. "They witnessed their fair share of death, too. They don't share any of the blame for that, though. Nobody would blame these tools." She lifted a lancet out of the bag and held it in her hand, gently caressing its handle. "If my Old Man couldn't save someone," she said, looking up from the tool, "there's nobody on earth that could. These tools are far more valuable than whatever it is they're made out of." She put the lancet back into the bag, zipped it up, and handed it to me. She patted my arm and said, "You keep them. They'll bring you good luck." I was going to decline, but she seemed to read my mind. "You were always there for us," she said. "You deserve to have them. I'm entrusting these to you. But I'm doing it with a final request: I want you to take care of our funerals." She nodded back towards the Colonel's room. "He won't make it through the night. I won't be around much longer, either. Take these. Look after us when we're gone."

I had no reason to refuse. I promised her that I would look after everything. "When he's gone," I said, "I can take you back to the village. That way, you can go see him whenever you want. There's a road that goes run up to the cemetery."

"Great," she said immediately. "I'll leave it up to you."

We went back to the Colonel's bedside. Auntie Lin seemed to have a sense that the time was approaching. She took his hand and held onto it for the next five hours. When she let his hand go, she put the eartips of the stethoscope in her ears and put the diaphragm on his neck. She performed her final duties as his wife and his physician. In a low voice, she announced the time of his death. She gestured for me to help her remove the Colonel's blanket. When we were done, she sent me downstairs to get a basin of warm water to wash his body before putting his graveclothes on. When I returned with the basin, I saw that the Colonel had been stripped to his pyjamas. She was about to take off his underwear. I didn't think either she or the Colonel would want me to be there, so I quietly set down the basin and went out into the hall.

"Come back," Auntie Lin said. When I went back in, I saw that she was holding his underwear. The Colonel was completely naked. His body seemed to glow with an internal light. Without thinking, I shut my eyes. "Open your eyes," Auntie Lin said to me. "The Old Man would want you to see." When I opened my eyes again, Auntie Lin was sitting on the bed beside him. Her left hand was on the bed, holding herself up, and her right hand was on Colonel's belly. Her head was down. Her eyes were fixed on her right hand. "Come here," she said. Her voice was soft but I knew that I could not refuse. "I did this for him a few years ago. It took me months." I tried to walk forward but I couldn't move. "I learned how to do it at the tattoo shop in the village. It's not as difficult as it seems." Through my tears, I could faintly make out a row of dark-green letters. When my eyes focused again, I couldn't believe what I saw. My head swam. I thought I was hallucinating. It wasn't letters at all... It was a drawing. There was a tree with a thick brown trunk and an umbrella shaped crown, shaded dark green. Two vines stretched from the tree, and two red lanterns hung on each one. The lanterns seemed to glow, reflecting the light in the room.

In that drawing, I could see everything.

I could see his past and his present.

The trunk of the tree had once been part of a blunt red arrow. The crown of the tree seemed to stretch out to cover up the place where there had once been a row of characters.

The vines and the lanterns dangled down beside the trunk, blotting out any names that might have been written on him.

Anything that had been carved into his lower abdomen in years past was blotted out. Even if somebody had seen the original tattoo, its memory would be burned from their minds.

I felt as if I was paralysed. I looked down on the Colonel. Tears ran down my cheeks.

"I know he wanted to write something different there," Auntie Lin said in a low voice, "but this is the best I could do. I knew he would like this. Look at this…" She pointed to two places where scars were still visible. "He tried to carve it out of his skin, but he couldn't do it. It's hard to do something like that to yourself. I knew what these tattoos meant for him. I knew what he had gone through because of them. He refused to marry me because of those tattoos. But everything's okay now." She took the Colonel's hand. "Old Man," she called to him softly, "everything's okay now. Wait for me on the other side. You can marry me in our next life."

She let his hand go, picked up the basin, and began to clean his body. Finally, she covered him with a white cloth. She smoothed the shroud and looked up at me with tears in her eyes. "The dead don't mind the cold. All they want is to be clean." The white shroud glowed, as if the Colonel's body was giving off some warm light. I thought at first she was smoothing the shroud, but I realised finally that she was caressing his body. Her tears fell soundlessly down onto the pure, white cloth.

Watching her weep for him, I couldn't hold back my sobs. It seemed to surprise her. She looked up at me, as if waking up from a deep slumber. She motioned for me to come close, wiped the tears from my cheeks, and said, "You should sleep now." She held my hand tightly, as if she was hesitant to let me go. "You should sleep. Hold onto those tears. There are not many people left in the world to cry for him, except us. Give me tonight. You can have tomorrow."

I walked back to my room as if in a trance. I sat down on the floor. The door was still open. I knew there was no way I could sleep that night. According to custom, people in mourning should cry for the dead and the door to their room should be left open. In that way, mourners from the world of the living and the world of the dead could both come and go as they pleased, offering their condolences.

Auntie Lin did not sob or wail. She cried softly. I don't know if it was because she was worried that I would hear or because she only needed him to hear her. I could barely hear it.

I was prepared to stay up all night listening. But sleep overtook me. I woke up again around four o'clock in the morning. I could no longer hear her crying. I thought maybe she had given in to exhaustion, too.

I thought about going to see her, but my gaze fell on the Colonel's black leather satchel. I had fallen asleep with it beside my pillow. The sky right before dawn was pitch black and the lights in the room seemed to blaze. The black of the leather gleamed. I picked it up without knowing what I was doing. I couldn't stop my hand from opening it. That afternoon, when I had seen the gold tools inside, I had been moved to tears, but, at that moment, I finally knew why. I had wept because I had realised that Blindboy was lying to me. My father had not sold the tools to support him. Auntie Lin had said that the tools might bring me luck, and I noticed that they already had. The words of Blindboy had haunted me for years, but they had finally been extinguished. As I caressed the bag, I felt a warm hand on my shoulder.

Maybe it was the hand of the Colonel.

I knew she must be sleeping in the other room. I waited until eight o'clock before I went to see her. I found her beside him on the bed. She had changed her clothes and brushed her hair. She wore a brand new black suit that matched the Colonel's graveclothes. On the table beside the bed was a note. She had placed their wedding bands at the bottom of the note. I noticed the IV stand from the clinic downstairs was standing beside the bed. The medicine had long since drained into her veins.

She had planned everything long in advance. She knew that when her husband died that she would follow him. Her skills as an anaesthesiologist made the passage painless. In this life, fate had driven them apart, but in death, they would be together forever.

I know why you did it, Auntie Lin. You wanted to spend the rest of your life with him.

Go in peace.

I broke down and sobbed, like I had when my wife had died thirty-eight years before.

I cried until my voice gave out.

It wasn't long: I am already sixty-two years old.

I read in the newspaper once that there is no such thing as a perfect life, but it's a life, all the same. I wondered who would hear me crying. I wondered who would come – from the world of the living and the world of the dead – to see them off.

About the Author

MAI JIA was born in 1964 and spent many years in the Chinese intelligence services. His first novel in English, *Decoded*, was published by Penguin Classics in 2002 and has been translated into over twenty languages. Jia's novels have sold over 10 million copies and he is a winner of the Mao Dun Literature Prize, the highest literary honour in China.

About the Translator

DYLAN LEVI KING is a writer and Chinese translator based in Tokyo.